GRAY MAGIC

A STONER McTAVISH MYSTERY
BY
SARAH DREHER

Published by New Victoria Publishers, Inc. PO Box 27 Norwich, Vt. 05055, a non-profit feminist literary and cultural organization.

Cover design by Ginger Brown
Author photo by Susan Wilson

Printed on recycled paper
Second Edition, third printing, 1993

Authors note
The mysticism portrayed in this book was inspired by my readings of Hopi legends and myths. It is not intended to be an accurate description of Hopi beliefs, but to express my deep respect for a way of life from which we have much to learn. If I have given offense, it is out of ignorance, not intent. May we all, one day, cross the rainbow together.

ISBN 0-934678-11-1

Library of Congress Cataloging-in-Publication Data

Dreher, Sarah.
    Gray magic / by Sarah Dreher. -- 2nd ed.
       p.   cm.
    ISBN 0-934678-11-1 : $9.95
    1. McTavish, Stoner (Fictitious character)--Fiction. 2. Women
detectives--United States--Fiction. 3. Indians of North America-
-Fiction. 4. Lesbians--United States--Fiction.   I. Title.
PS3554.R36G7   1993
813'.54--dc20   93-33332
                                                         CIP

for Kaye Alleman

ONE

Talavai, Dawn Spirit, spilled mercury across the sleeping desert. It eddied around mesas, lapped the humped crests of bread-loaf buttes, flowed like the tide down shallow, parched arroyos, caressed the base of the Sacred Mountains. The air was cool, silent. One by one, the Star People withdrew into the morning twilight.

The ruined pueblo lay in silhouette against purple velvet, a clutter of sandstone and adobe walls, fashioned of earth, returning to earth. Birds nested on naked spruce beams. Deer mice hid grain and pinyon seeds among ancient pottery shards. Door and window holes gazed unseeing into the plaza, and snakes made nests in the abandoned kiva.

The old woman who now called herself Siyamtiwa rubbed the chill from her aching fingers and squinted toward the south. Long Mesa, below and in the distance, caught the first rays of sun that arrowed between the twin peaks of Tewa Mountain. Smoke from the breakfast fire at Spirit Wells Trading Post rose in a feathery column. A battered and rusted pick-up truck chugged along the dirt road that rambled through the Navajo Reservation, bringing the mail to the Hopi Cultural Center.

An ordinary August morning.

Except that the air stirred with tiny winds that eddied back upon themselves and whispered uneasily of Something out of Harmony. Of forces gathering, building strength as they had been building all this long summer.

Forces that would come together very soon now...

To fight once more the battle fought so many times.

So many times.

Siyamtiwa sighed, took a sip of water, and chewed on a shred of *piki* to chase away the copper taste of sleep.

One comes from the south, she knew, and one from the east. The south-walker is *ka-Hopi*, this much the Spirits had told her. No peace, no beauty, no harmony in that one. And the other—the other a stranger, with much to learn. Too much, maybe, and not enough time.

1

Two strangers, from beyond the walls.

Siyamtiwa pursed her lips with disapproval.The Spirits chose some fine warriors for their battles these days. Or perhaps all the warriors were gone. Perhaps it was time to listen for the song of the Hump-Backed Flute Player, whistling up the Fifth Emergence.

Or perhaps this tired old world had to grow worse before the Giant Mushrooms bloomed and it was over.

Meanwhile, she would do what must be done.

From the folds of her blanket, she drew out the whittling knife and the unfinished cottonwood doll, the image of the green-eyed *pahana*.

* * *

"I'm going to tell her," Gwen said.

Stoner looked up from the pot of African violets she had been inspecting for white-fly infestation. "Tell who what?"

"My grandmother. About us."

She swallowed hard, put the pot down, and rummaged furiously in the undersink cupboard. "Where's your plant sprayer?"

Gwen handed it to her. "You think it's a mistake."

"I didn't say that." She filled the sprayer with warm water and added a few drops of detergent. "You have white-flies, by the way."

"Any time you pretend not to hear me, it's because you don't approve."

"I don't disapprove, exactly…" She attacked the plant like a redneck cop with a water cannon at an anti-nuke rally. "I just think it might not be the right time."

"Why?"

"Because it's the hottest night of the summer, your air conditioner's broken, and Aunt Hermione and I have just beaten the two of you in three straight rubbers of bridge."

Gwen shrugged. "That doesn't bother me."

"Well, it bothers her. Boy, does it bother her." She placed the violets on the windowsill and glared out over the haze-choked Boston skyline.

Gwen ran her finger around the top of her glass of bourbon and ginger ale. "I have to do it, Stoner. Living here, with her not knowing …I feel like such a sneak."

She couldn't look at Gwen. She knew what she would look like, her eyes dark and soft and frightened. She knew, if she saw that, all sense and reason would fly out the window. She turned her back and took aim at the philodendron—and sprayed the plant, the window-

2

sill, the screen, and the back porch of the downstairs apartment. "If I had your grandmother's way with plants," she said, "I wouldn't waste it on philodendron."

"I can wait until you leave..."

She felt trapped. She lifted the Swedish ivy and drenched the undersides of its leaves. "No, you're not going through that alone."

"Maybe she'll take it all right."

Stoner laughed without humor. "I know Eleanor Burton. It'll be awful." She picked off a yellowed leaf. "Aunt Hermione read the Tarot about it. The outcome card was the Hanged Man."

"That's good, isn't it? Change of consciousness...?"

"Reversed. Arrogance, ego dominance, wasted effort..."

"Your aunt doesn't believe in reversals," Gwen said.

"I do."

"You don't believe in the Tarot."

"If I did, I would believe in reversals." She settled the ivy back onto its saucer.

"If you were me," Gwen persisted, "you'd want to tell her, wouldn't you?"

"She says she's moving to Florida," Stoner suggested hopefully. "You could wait, and then write her a letter or something."

"She's not moving to Florida," Gwen said. "She talks about it every year, but she'll never do it."

"Maybe she meant it this time."

Gwen sighed. "She didn't mean it. She hates the South. She couldn't bear Georgia. After my parents' funeral, she got me out of Jefferson so fast, you'd have thought the Seven Plagues of Egypt were arriving on the two-forty- nine train."

"Yeah." Stoner reached for her Manhattan. "The trouble is, in *her* eyes, *lesbians* are one of the Seven Plagues of Egypt."

"She doesn't hate you."

"She tolerates me. She has to. I saved your life."

Gwen frowned down into her glass. "I thought you always said hiding eats your soul."

"This is different."

"Why is it different?"

Because it's *you*, Gwen. Because I love you, and you're going to be hurt, and I can't bear... "I have a funny feeling, that's all."

"Stoner..."

She jerked the water on and scrubbed her hands frantically. "Do you have any idea how nasty this can get?"

"Well, what am I supposed to do?" Gwen demanded. "Lie? Pretend to flirt with every man who looks my way? Skulk around as if we're doing something *dirty?* I love you, Stoner. I want the whole world to know it."

She looked around for a dish towel, couldn't find one, and wiped her hands on her jeans. "I've seen more than one coming-out. It isn't always awful, but it's seldom fun." She scowled at the African violet. "I think you have spider mites."

Gwen put her drink down with a bang, marched to the refrigerator, and yanked on the ice trays.

"You should defrost that thing," Stoner said.

"I can't. My blow-dryer's broken."

"For God's sake. You have white-fly and spider mites, all your appliances are falling apart, and you think this is the appropriate time to come out to your grandmother?"

"Okay," Gwen said angrily, "forget it. I'll do it when you're not here. But I'm going to do it, Stoner, whether you like it or not."

Stoner held out her hands. "Please Gwen, let's not argue."

"I'm not arguing. You are."

She raked her hand through her hair. "Look, I'm sorry. I know you're right, but—"

"You're afraid," Gwen said in soft amazement.

"You bet I am."

"I don't believe it. *You're* afraid."

"I'm afraid."

Gwen shook her head. "Stoner, you killed my husband. You single-handedly took on a nest of extortionists in a haunted mental hospital. And you're afraid of my grandmother?"

"Your grandmother," said Stoner, "is in a class by herself."

"She's always very polite to you."

"Sure. Polite. Do you know how that kind of polite makes me feel? Like Bill Cosby giving the after-dinner speech at a Ku Klux Klan convention."

Gwen laughed. "All right, I see your point." She managed to separate one ice tray from the freezer wall and carried it to the sink. "So what would you do in my place?"

Stoner gave it serious thought. "Tell her. But pack first."

Gwen turned, rested her arms on Stoner's shoulders, and looked solemnly into her eyes. "I love you, Stoner McTavish."

Her stomach turned to butterflies and her knees turned to jelly. This woman loves me, she thought, and felt the Earth wobble on its axis. She shook her head in helpless resignation. "Okay, if you can't make it through the hottest night of the year without turning your

4

grandmother into a raving maniac…well, let's get on with it."

"Make a novena." As she pulled away, Gwen slipped an ice cube down the back of Stoner's shirt.

*   *   *

Aunt Hermione and Eleanor Burton sat side-by-side on the overstuffed, chintz-covered sofa, a large Florentine leather photograph album spread across their knees.

Wonderful, Stoner thought wryly. The perfect time to pig out on nostalgia.

Mrs. Burton glanced up. "Stoner, have you seen this perfectly adorable picture of Gwyneth and her brother?" She squinted near-sightedly at the page. "It was at Kentucky Lake. The TVA project?"

"She's seen it, Grandmother. We…"

"Wasn't this the trip to Kentucky Lake?" Mrs. Burton prattled on. "The time Donnie fell out of the boat and you jumped in after him?" She leaned over to Aunt Hermione. "He wanted to touch the rocks at the bottom, don't you know, and it was way over his head."

Aunt Hermione, who detested family photograph albums, smiled and stifled a yawn.

Stoner wondered if the ice cube, which had caught at her waist, would evaporate before it ran down her leg and disgraced her. She doubted it.

"Little Gwyneth went flying out of the boat after him," Mrs. Burton burbled. "She didn't even stop to think that *he* knew how to swim and she didn't. Isn't that precious?"

Stoner couldn't recall that particular picture. Curious, she went behind the couch and looked over Aunt Hermione's shoulder.

It was a typical, out-of-focus pre-Instamatic family photo. Gwen all legs and arms and forced, painful smile. Her brother making a face and acting goofy.

"They had *such* a good time on that trip," Mrs. Burton cooed.

Stoner winced. She had heard all about that vacation, and the terror of being in a moving car, far from home, with a father whose response to frustration was to slap a few faces, and a brother whose response to tension was to provoke. Just your average, fun-filled, all-American nuclear family vacation.

"Grandmother," Gwen said, "you shouldn't try to look at that without your glasses."

"Oh, dear." Mrs. Burton gave a little jump, her eyes darting about the room as if someone had just told her a Bengal tiger had slipped through the kitchen door. "I know I had them while we were playing

5

cards. See if you can find them, would you, Gwyneth dear?"

Stoner retrieved the glasses from the card table and handed them to Mrs. Burton.

"My goodness," Mrs. Burton said. "They were right there all the time! What a silly thing. I'm so forgetful."

"A simple 'thank-you' would suffice, Eleanor," said Aunt Hermione.

Mrs. Burton slipped her glasses over her ears and peered back at the album. "Why, that isn't Kentucky Lake at all. It looks like . . . why, it looks like that trip you took to North Carolina, the summer before your parents died. Or was it two summers?"

"It doesn't matter," Gwen said. "They were all the same."

Stoner looked at Mrs. Burton and realized she didn't like her very much any more. The thought surprised her. Last year, when she had met her, she had liked her—or at least felt some sympathy for her. But being around her now made her feel like a cat in a room charged with electricity. Vague anxieties buzzed like gnats. The slightest unexpected noise sent her into little yelps of apprehension. Her ears picked up sounds no one else could hear. If a match smoldered in the ash tray, she was convinced all of Cambridge—or at least their apartment house—was about to become a raging inferno. If she felt a draft, someone was climbing in the bedroom window intent on evil. She couldn't take public transportation, you never knew *what* might happen while the T was underground. In cars, she clutched the door handle and slammed her foot against the floor every time the driver touched the brake. She refused to leave the house after sundown or during rainstorms. If Gwen stayed out after eleven, light burned in her grandmother's bedroom until she got in. If she stayed at Stoner's over-night, she had to call in before she went to bed. And the way Mrs. Burton carried on, it was often easier to go home.

It could be her age, of course, as she claimed. But Aunt Hermione, who was two years her senior, said it wasn't age, it was frame of mind.

Gwen said it was only dependency, and once she went back to teaching and Mrs. Burton had to fend for herself, she'd straighten out.

Maybe.

It had crossed Stoner's mind at times—once when they were taking a weekend trip to Hampton Beach to wallow in tackiness and had to cancel their plans because Mrs. Burton came down with an undiagnosable summer malady—and once when she had turned suddenly as she and Gwen were leaving the apartment for dinner, and had caught a glimpse of what sure looked to her like jealousy on Mrs. Burton's face...

It had crossed her mind that Mrs. Burton wasn't all that ignorant of, or all that pleased by, what was *really* going on beneath that "just good friends" façade they had put up.

It had also crossed her mind that there was a little unfriendly competition going on here, and that Mrs. Burton had figured out that there could be strength in weakness. And she might very well be right.

Whatever the truth of it, it looked to Stoner as if they were headed for a serious spell of rough weather.

"Grandmother," Gwen said tentatively.

Mrs. Burton marked the page with her finger and closed the album. "Yes, dear?"

"There's something we...I have to tell you."

"It *is* white-fly, isn't it?" Eleanor Burton said with a sigh. "I *told* the florist that violet didn't look right, but you know how they are, no one can tell them anything. Just like the hardware store. If they don't have what you need, they claim it doesn't exist or you don't know what you're talking about. Really, it's an outrage."

Gwen cleared her throat. "That isn't important. I have to..."

"Of course it's important," Mrs. Burton interrupted. "When you get to be my age, you'll realize what it means to be treated with a modicum of respect."

"That's the point," Gwen said. "I...we *do* respect you, and that's why we want you to know—"

"Can't it wait, dear?" Mrs. Burton fanned herself rapidly with her handkerchief. "It's a terribly hot night, and you look so serious."

"It *is* serious," Gwen said. She glanced at Stoner helplessly.

Stoner crossed the room and took Gwen's hand. Gwen squeezed her fingers. In the window opposite, their reflections looked like figures on top of a wedding cake.

Gwen took a deep breath and started over. "I don't know how you'll take this, but it's made me very happy."

"That's all I want, dear," her grandmother said. "Your happiness." Her eyes slid to their locked fingers.

"Stoner and I..." Gwen tightened her grip on Stoner's fingers. "We...uh...we..."

"What she's trying to say," Aunt Hermione broke in, rummaging through her huge, multicolored tote bag and drawing out a ball of yarn and a crochet hook, "is that your granddaughter and my niece are lovers."

7

Mrs. Burton looked at Gwen.

Gwen looked at the floor.

Mrs. Burton looked at Stoner.

Stoner looked back at her.

Mrs. Burton looked again at their locked hands. She took off her glasses, folded back the hem of her dress, and polished the lenses on her slip.

"I see," she said. "Would anyone care for one last rubber of bridge?"

"Grandmother," Gwen began.

"Why don't you make us some iced tea, Gwyneth? I do believe we might all perish from the heat."

"Mrs. Burton..." Stoner said.

Mrs. Burton laughed. "But, of course, this is nothing compared to summers in Georgia."

Aunt Hermione put her crocheting down. "I know Gwen has missed more than one night's sleep over this, Eleanor. At least have the decency to acknowledge you heard it."

Eleanor Burton turned to her. "Perhaps you can explain to me, Hermione," she said in a perfectly conversational voice, "why my granddaughter is trying to kill me."

"Oh, shit," Gwen said under her breath.

"I know I'm not perfect," Mrs. Burton went on, "but God knows I've tried to treat her well, to the best of my ability, limited though that may be. I certainly can't imagine what I've done to cause her to want to play such a cruel, cruel joke on me."

"It's not a joke," Gwen said.

Mrs. Burton folded her hands in her lap. "In *my* day," she said to Aunt Hermione, "ladies didn't speak of such things."

"Maybe not," Aunt Hermione said, "but they did them."

Mrs. Burton's back stiffened. The skin on her neck took on a stretched appearance. She opened the photograph album and began turning pages rapidly and at random. "Look at this," she said to no one in particular. "Look what a beautiful child she was. Everyone said she was a beautiful child."

"Lovely," Aunt Hermione said. "Though what *that* has to do with anything is beyond me."

"Would you ever think, to look at that *sweet* child's face..."

Aunt Hermione picked up her crocheting. "Eleanor, don't be an ass."

"Grandmother..." Gwen began. She seemed to have forgotten she was holding Stoner's hand. Her skin felt cold and waxy, as if all

8

the life in her had shrunk to a small, hard lump somewhere deep inside.

"I admit she hasn't been treated well by men," Mrs. Burton went on earnestly. "My goodness, who has? First her father, then that dreadful Bryan Oxnard creature she insisted on marrying. But that's no reason to give up on them completely."

"Sounds like a good reason to me," said Aunt Hermione, and consulted her pattern.

"It doesn't have anything to do with men," Gwen said. "I love Stoner." Her voice was clear and strong. Her hand trembled.

Mrs. Burton looked in their general direction. "You're indebted to her, of course. We both are. But this silly infatuation will pass."

"*Grandmother.*"

"Your granddaughter's a lesbian," Aunt Hermione said placidly. "Might as well get used to it."

Mrs. Burton snorted. "We would *never*," she said, her voice rising a little, "have one of...of *those* people in *my* family."

"Why not?"Aunt Hermione squinted at her crocheting. "You already have child abusers."

"And given a choice, I would *prefer* child abusers."

Aunt Hermione sighed. "Eleanor, don't make a bigger fool of yourself than you already have."

"Well," said Mrs. Burton, getting to her feet a little unsteadily, "I won't have this in *my* house."

"Fine," Gwen said. "I can be packed in half an hour."

Stoner looked at her. Gwen's face was gray, her eyes burning. She's going to crack, she thought, and slipped a steadying arm around her shoulders.

"Will you kindly," said Mrs. Burton in a voice shaky with indignation, "take your filthy hands off her?"

Startled, Stoner unconsciously took a step back. "What?"

"What you do in your own home is your business. I don't want to know about it. But as long as you're in this house..."

"Wait a minute," Gwen said. "I pay half the rent."

Mrs. Burton turned on her. "That doesn't give you the right to bring your trash in here."

"Damn it," Gwen snapped. "Stoner *saved my life.* If it hadn't been for her, Bryan would have *killed* me."

The older woman's face was hard as stone. "I wish he had."

"Honest to God," Aunt Hermione said in the shocked silence. "I've heard enough silliness in the last five minutes to last me a lifetime."

Mrs. Burton turned on her. "We don't need your opinion, Hermione. You and your house full of perverts."

"House full of perverts?" Aunt Hermione raised an eyebrow. "Stoner, are you up to something you haven't told me about?"

She forced herself to shake her head.

"Too bad," Aunt Hermione said, and returned to her crocheting. "Might have been profitable."

"I suppose," Mrs. Burton said to Aunt Hermione, "you *like* thinking about your niece putting her hands all over other women."

"I have other things to think about, Eleanor, and so should you. If you can't control your imagination..."

Mrs. Burton turned on Gwen. "Promise me you won't see her again, and we'll forget all about this."

"I intend to see her again," Gwen said, her voice deadly, "and I won't forget *any* of this."

We're doing this all wrong, Stoner thought. We should sit down and discuss it calmly. Everyone gets five minutes to speak, to tell how they feel, no name calling, stick to the subject, no threats, and if we can't make progress we call for a cooling-off period. Not the easiest thing in the world, but not a mess. *This* is a mess.

"Look," she said, "maybe if we all...I mean, let's look at it...well, what does everyone *want* from this?"

"I'll tell you what I want," Mrs. Burton shrieked. "I want you out of my granddaughter's life."

"That's the *last* thing you'll get," Gwen said coldly. "Where I go, Stoner goes."

"It seems to me, Eleanor," Aunt Hermione put in, "you have the most to lose here."

It seemed to slow Mrs. Burton's momentum. She sat back and plucked at her sleeves. She looked old, and tired.

"You must understand," she said at last. "The way I was brought up...we would never... " She looked up at Gwen helplessly.

"The way *I* was brought up," Aunt Hermione cut in, "we would never treat another person cruelly. You should thank your lucky stars Gwen's fallen for Stoner. At least she has better taste in women than she does in men."

Mrs. Burton turned on her. "I've given her a decent life. The least she can do is be a decent person."

"She *is* a decent person," Aunt Hermione said. "Head and shoulders above what Stoner *used* to bring home."

"Aunt Hermione..."

10

"It's all right, dear. Like all of us, you're evolving."

"Well," Mrs. Burton said, "you can evolve yourself right out of this house." She turned to Gwen. "As for you, I'd rather see you dead."

"Gwen," Stoner said softly, "would you like me to leave now?"

Gwen shook her head. "Grandmother, I want to explain—"

"Explain?" Mrs. Burton gave a harsh laugh. "Explain this...this sickness?"

It's always the same, Stoner thought wearily as she went to the window and leaned against the sill. Recriminations, anger, blame, guilt, rejection—all because we love the wrong people. *Love* the wrong people. In a world where school lunches are traded for nuclear warheads, and the air gives you emphysema, and the water gives you cancer. Where the FDA sets the "maximum allowable rat feces" per can of tuna. Where rapists walk the streets, free on probation, and you can drop a few coins in a slot and watch a movie of a Real Life woman being Real Life beaten to Real Life death for kicks and profit. Where we finally got a woman nominated for vicepresident, the most innocuous office in the country, and all the woman-haters came screeching out from under their rocks to tapdance on her coffin, and some of the woman-haters were women, and what does that say about how we're taught to see ourselves? It should have been the signal to start the Revolution, but we'd forgotten about the Revolution, and now we have Yuppie Dykes in designer clothes getting their M.B.A.s from Closet University, and before we know it, it'll be 1950 again and all we'll have left will be *The Well of Loneliness* and *The Children's Hour*, and we'll wake up some morning believing the best thing to do if you're a lesbian is kill yourself.

"What are we doing?" She heard herself say into the stretchedrubberband silence. "We should be out in the streets screaming our heads off."

Everyone looked at her.

"Stoner's been on a rampage since the '84 election," Aunt Hermione explained. "She thinks it would have turned out differently if only she'd done something, but she hasn't figured out what the something is."

"I only mean," Stoner said, "there are more vital things to be upset about."

Mrs. Burton sniffed. "Of course *you'd* say that."

"Grandmother," Gwen said softly.

Mrs. Burton turned her head away.

11

Aunt Hermione met Stoner's eyes, and shrugged. "Go figure."

Gwen stood in front of her grandmother, fists clenched, her face about to crumble. "Please," she said, "I love her, and I love you. Please try to…"

Mrs. Burton's eyes were burning coals. "Love? You call this love? This disgusting…revolting…obsession?"

Stoner felt something break. "God damn it," she barked. "That's enough!"

Mrs. Burton turned her back. "I'm not interested in anything you have to say."

"I don't give a damn!" The words exploded from her. "You're an ignorant, self-righteous woman. Do you have any idea what it means to be a lesbian?"

"I do not," said Mrs. Burton. "And I don't want to."

Stoner strode across the room. "We do the dirty work in this world. We set up Crisis Centers to protect you upright, uptight 'normal' women from battering husbands. We fight for your Medicare and Social Security. We push your wheelchairs and wipe up your urine when you're too old and feeble to do it yourself. We do all the work you're too 'lady-like' to touch. And for that we're called names, and fired from the jobs nobody wants. When we go in public restrooms, we see hate written on the walls by people who are too ignorant to spell but claim the right to judge us. When we pick up a newspaper, we see letters from Bible-quoting cretins telling us our gay brothers are dying of AIDS because God despises what we are. But we go on living, Mrs. Burton, because we earn the right. We live in a world of hate, and still we manage to love. You live in a world of love, but you hate. I don't understand that. I don't understand it at all."

Mrs. Burton glared at her. "How dare you talk to me like this?"

"I love Gwen. I'd give my life for her. If she left me for one of those 'nice young men' you think so highly of, I'd still love her. If he was cruel to her, I'd take her in and comfort her, and try to keep her safe. If she went back to him, I'd go on loving her. And I'd never, ever say the things you've said to her tonight. If this is your idea of love, I don't want any part of it."

She forced herself to break away and went to the window. The street was gray and empty. Old newspapers lay limp in the gutter. The air above the city was an oily yellow. She felt sick.

The silence was heavy behind her. She tried to imagine what they were thinking, but couldn't.

I hope Gwen understands. I hope I haven't ruined it for her.

12

She felt a hand against the side of her face.

"Hey," Gwen said.

"I'm sorry, Gwen. I couldn't help…"

"It's fine. I love you."

"Well," said Aunt Hermione as she gathered up her yarn, "I think we've about covered it. It's been an entertaining and enlightening evening, but I have an early reading with a Virgo, and you know how they are. Coming, Stoner?"

"I won't leave Gwen," she said.

Mrs. Burton's face was white with fury.

Stoner held her ground.

"I'm going with you," Gwen said. "I don't feel welcome here."

"If you leave this house tonight," Mrs. Burton snapped, "don't come back."

Gwen turned to her. "I'm thirty-one years old, Grandmother. I'd like you to understand what Stoner means to me, but I don't intend to beg."

Eleanor Burton was stiff with righteous indignation. "You'll regret this, Gwyneth."

"I probably will. But if I stay, I'll regret that, too. So I might as well go where I'm wanted. I'm sorry it has to be like this, but I will love whom I love, and I don't intend to feel guilty for it."

"Well, don't expect me to…"

"I don't expect anything," Gwen said. "When I find a place, I'll let you know where I am. If you need to get in touch with me, you can do it through Marylou at the travel agency."

"I wouldn't hold my breath if I were you," said Mrs. Burton.

Gwen left the apartment without speaking.

"Eleanor, Eleanor," Aunt Hermione clucked as she slung her tote bag over her arm, "you have some serious thinking to do." She jiggled Mrs. Burton's wrist affectionately. "I know you're a Leo, but try not to be a jackass."

The door slammed behind them.

"The trouble with bigots," Aunt Hermione muttered as they went down the stairs, "is they're so unoriginal. I wonder if Freud had anything to say on the subject."

Stoner couldn't answer.

"I've always suspected," Aunt Hermione went on, "that you were wise to slip away from your family in the dead of night instead of going through this. Tonight has convinced me I'm right."

The ground felt littered with broken things. Broken trust, broken love, broken…

Gwen was huddled at the bottom of the stairs, arms around her knees. A white line rimmed her lips. Her mahogany eyes were gray. Her hair had a powdery dullness.

She looked, Stoner thought irrelevantly, as if she'd been bleached. She knelt beside her. "Are you okay?"

Gwen looked up. "Oh, God, Stoner. What am I going to do?"

TWO

At last count, eight-hundred and fifty-nine travelers had stepped off Trans-Continental Airlines at Sky Harbor International Airport, Phoenix, Arizona, at high noon in Mid-August without sunglasses. No one has ever done it twice.

The desert sun, at high noon in Mid-August, rains down a torrent of silver needles. The sky burns white. The mountains that ring the city—Maricopas, White Tanks, Superstitions—flatten into dusty, two-dimensional mounds. Desert plants turn pale. Crawling, slithering, running creatures surrender to the heat and hide. The air shimmers on the horizon and flows in sluggish currents along the airport tarmac. Tires go soft. The odor of melting tar lies heavy along the ground. Light explodes in tinsel stars from moving glass and chrome. Phoenicians huddle indoors around their air conditioners and wait for the time of long shadows.

Sky Harbor International Airport, Phoenix, Arizona, at high noon in mid-August is a white-hot Hell.

Stoner winced. The muscles around her eyes were tight. Her pupils ached. She fumbled and stumbled her way to a seat in the waiting area and sat down. Dark shapes moved around her in a steady stream. I've gone blind, she thought. Blinded by the Light, Hallelujah.

Well, even if she couldn't see, Stell could see her. But nobody came forward out of the shadows. Stoner chewed her lip nervously.

Maybe she doesn't want us here.

Maybe we got the wrong day.

Or the wrong airport.

What if she doesn't show up?

What if we were supposed to meet her outside?

No, she said inside. Inside, in the TCA lounge. I'm sure she said that.

Maybe TCA has two lounges.

Nonsense, airlines don't have two lounges.

Airlines have *dozens* of lounges.

Did I give her the right flight number?

15

Come on, if she misses me, she'll have me paged.

Maybe I should have *her* paged.

She started to get up.

But I'd have to find a phone to have her paged, and she might show up and think she'd made a mistake and leave.

She sat back down.

I should have made the arrangements myself. I shouldn't have left it up to Marylou. I *hate* other people to make my travel arrangements. I mean, how do you know they haven't screwed up? If *I* screw up, at least I have some general idea where the screw-up lies. I screw up dates and times. I don't screw up transportation and destinations. So, if I'd made my own reservations and Stell didn't show up, I'd know I got the wrong date or the wrong time, but I'm in the right place. Which is more than I know now.

Marylou says travel agents who make their own reservations are like psychotherapists who treat family members and close friends. Or lawyers who represent themselves in malpractice suits. Marylou says...

Marylou never travels. Marylou hates to travel.

Marylou probably knows something I don't know but am bound to learn the hard way.

"I'll be darned," said a familiar voice. "You looked worried last time I saw you, and you *still* look worried."

She squinted into the glare. "Stell?"

"It ain't Dale Evans." A tall, thin shadow planted itself in front of her, hands on hips, and laughed. "I'll just bet you thought you could get away without sunglasses."

"Yeah," Stoner said with an awkward grin. "I did."

"Well, are you going to let me hug you? Or are you going to sit there and break my heart?"

To her great embarrassment, she felt tears spring to her eyes. "Oh, God, I've missed you,"she said, and threw her arms around the older woman.

"Missed you, too, kid." Stell squeezed her tight. "Thought you'd never get here."

Stoner rested on her shoulder. "You still smell like fresh bread."

"Well, I should. I'm still baking it." She held Stoner at arm's length and looked her up and down. "You're about the same. Where's your lady love?"

"Picking up the suitcases. She'll meet us outside."

Stell reached for Stoner's carry-on. "Might as well take our time. What you gain in travel time, you lose waiting for your doggone

16

luggage." She led the way to the entrance. "Hope you didn't have your heart set on Timberline. It's been a topsy-turvy summer."

"I don't mind. I've never been to the desert before."

"I'll have to admit," Stell said as she strode ahead, "there have been moments the last month when I'd give my good right arm for a breath of Wyoming air. But family's family, and you gotta do what you gotta do." She stood back to let Stoner pass through the door first. "Watch yourself, kiddo. That sun's a killer."

A blast of searing air knocked her back on her heels. "Good God!"

"Hot enough to blister paint," Stell said. "Stick close until I find the pick-up. If you get lost in the parking lot, you can go critical in ten minutes."

Heat from the pavement burned through the soles of her boots. She squinted against the sun and gasped for breath. "This is unbelievable!"

"It does get better." Stell picked her way between and around parked cars. "We have the altitude on our side in Spirit Wells. You might bake your brain by day, but you can count on freezing your tail off at night."

"Spirit Wells? I thought the trading post was in Beale."

"Beale's the nearest Post Office. Spirit Wells was a settlement of some kind about a hundred years ago. Or that might be a rumor. Anyway, I haven't seen any towns, Spirits, or wells." She stopped beside a light tan, rust-pocked, dust-coated Chevy Luv that had seen better days, but not in a long time.

Stoner reached for the door handle.

"Hold it!" Stell knocked her hand away. She took a bandana from her hip pocket. "Use this. Metal gets wicked hot out here."

"Everything's hot out here." She yanked the door open and let the dead air fall out.

Stell swung up into the driver's seat and scrounged through the glove compartment. "Use these," she said, handing over a pair of scratched and battered sunglasses. "They're not pretty, but they'll save your retinas."

Stoner put the glasses on and sighed with relief. "How's your cousin?"

"Seems to be doing a little better," Stell said as she started the motor. "They still don't know what's wrong with her. Darndest thing, she just seemed to wither up overnight. Wouldn't be surprising, considering the climate. Except Claudine and Gil have been running that trading post for over thirty years, and Claudine's folks

17

before that. She's not exactly a stranger to Arizona summers."

She rammed the truck into reverse and backed up, narrowly avoiding a collision with a yellow Mercedes, and eased toward the ramp.

"There's been rumors of the same kind of illness farther north on the reservation, which makes you think about radiation. Especially since Anaconda and Kerr-McGee pile the uranium slag from the mines out in the open. But they tested Claudine for that and she's come out clean. Matter of fact, they've tested for everything from leukemia to ectopic pregnancy—which would be a small miracle at her age."

"Maybe it's the water," Stoner suggested. "Or even the fresh vegetables. If the soil out here's deficient in something…"

"Not likely. Gil doesn't show any signs. Anyway, they're keeping her under observation. Which is a fancy way of saying the doctors don't know what they're doing and they want her to pay the bills while they find out."

She cut in front of an airport limousine and came to rest in a No Parking Zone.

"Who's looking after Timberline?" Stoner asked.

"Ted Jr. and his lover." Stell laughed. "Can't wait to hear how that goes down with some of the regulars. Well, it should separate the wheat from the chaff."

"Uh…do you like his lover?"

"So far. Rick seems like a nice young man." She shot Stoner a knowing look. "Quit trying to test the water. You know it's okay by me."

"I'm sorry. We've had our problems lately."

"Yeah." Stell dug a cowboy hat from the floor behind the seat and crammed it on her head. "How are things going?"

Stoner shrugged. "So-so. Gwen doesn't seem to know what her next move should be. I think she's hoping for a reconciliation, but so far she hasn't heard anything from her grandmother. It must be getting her down, sometimes it's hard to tell with her. She's better than I am at pushing things into the back of her mind."

"Probably a good thing to get away, then. Might give her a new perspective." She tapped the steering wheel with her fingers. "How much am I supposed to know about this? I wouldn't want to put my foot in my mouth."

"She knows I told you. It's fine."

"I might feel compelled to express my opinion."

Stoner smiled. "Your opinion's always welcome."

18

"Tell that to my ever-loving husband. He's had thirty-five years of my opinions."

If Gwen doesn't show up soon, she thought, there won't be anything left of us but grease and bones. The truck cab felt like a kiln.

"Do you like running the trading post?" she asked.

"It's a challenge." Stell pushed open her door and stretched one leg onto the running board. It made her look a little like an aging rodeo queen. "Most of the Indians trust us enough to keep shopping there, on account of we're related to Gil and Claudine, and being related counts for a lot with them. But it's hard to forget we're visible representatives of a race that's been screwing them for four hundred years. Makes you kind of overly cautious and overly sensitive." She glanced over at Stoner. "Shoot, why am I explaining this to you? You know what it's like being hated for nothing you did yourself."

"I'm glad we decided to come here, Stell. It'll be good for Gwen to be around you."

Stell hooted. "First time anyone ever called me a good influence on the young." She peeked up from under her hat brim and jabbed her thumb in the direction of the terminal. "Don't look now, but this vacation's about to get under way officially."

Gwen backed through the door, lurching under the weight of their luggage.

Stoner leapt from the truck.

"Jesus!" Stell exclaimed loudly. "Must be love."

Gwen dropped a suitcase and shielded her eyes. "They're trying to kill us!" she gasped. "Hey, Stell."

"Hey, yourself. Scooch in next to me. It's tight, but it beats riding sternside in the sun."

Stoner tossed the suitcases into the truck bed. "Should I tie these down?"

"You better. There's a lot of bounce between here and Spirit Wells."

Stoner secured the suitcases and climbed in next to Gwen. Gwen reached over and jiggled her sunglasses. "Very butch."

"Stop that," Stoner said, and slapped at her hand.

Stell slammed her door, turned the air conditioner up full, and revved the motor. "Hang onto your bra straps, kids. We're making tracks."

"How far is it?" Gwen asked as Stell pounced on the exit ramp.

"About two-hundred miles, as the crow flies. We'll be home late afternoon."

Stoner made a quick calculation. "Two hundred miles—that's

19

close to four hours."

"More or less. Out here, we have a healthy disrespect for speed limits. I have to stop at the IGA in Beale. Won't take a minute."

"Great," Gwen said. "I can pick up a trashy book. I don't imagine you'd have anything like that at your place."

"Absolutely not. Out here, we never read anything but the Great Books of the Western World."

High-rise buildings, monoliths of concrete and glass, lined the streets in their ugly functional way. Family cars and taxis inched forward against the lights, motors snarling menace, drivers casting dark and hostile looks. Pedestrians jay-walked. Teenagers skate-boarded with wild and life-threatening abandon. Buses fouled the air. Only an occasional patch of grass, a Victorian or Mission-style touch of architecture broke the monotony and provided a glimpse of Character.

"What's your first impression?" Stell asked.

"It's very clean," Stoner said politely.

Stell laughed. "Let me tell you about Phoenix. Of the six tallest buildings in the city, five are banks. The sixth is the Hyatt Regency."

"That's all you know?" Gwen asked.

"That's all I *need* to know." She braked for a red light and rolled down the window to release the heat that built up immediately in spite of the air conditioning.

So this is Arizona. Pueblo Country. Cattle Country. Gold Country. Indian Country. Cactus Country.

The only pueblos she could see were fifteen-story apartment buildings. There were no cattle being driven to market, only expensive cars with vanity plates. The only Indians were two little kids playing dress-up. And instead of cactus, there were palm trees, as artificial-looking as set pieces for a 1920s musical.

She watched the people crossing the street in front of the pick-up. They were just like people in cities everywhere—a little dulled out, as if they didn't want to see too much, or hear too much, or think too much. As if they had somehow managed to cancel themselves out. On a Citiness scale of one to ten, she'd give Phoenix a seven.

Provincial, she scolded herself. There are thousands, maybe millions of people who genuinely like cities. Who enjoy, or at least tolerate, standing in lines. Who thrive on noise and motion. Whose idea of Hell is a small town with no all-night deli.

"Stoner," Gwen said, "you're grinding your teeth."

"Sorry."

"Are you going to be sick?"

"I hope not."

"Want another dramamine?"

She shook her head. Too little sleep, she was barely coherent as it was. Darn Marylou. Nobody in their right mind would choose to crawl out of bed at four a.m., tackle Logan Airport at five, cross most of the country and three time zones, to be assaulted by airline food and High Noon in Phoenix—and then try to appreciate the scenery. "Get a jump on the day," indeed. The next time a day needed to be jumped on, Marylou Kesselbaum could jolly well do the jumping.

"What's new in Boston?" Stell asked as she turned north through a suburb of Spanish adobe houses with tiled roofs, sprinkler-lush lawns, waiting barbecue pits, and white wine chilling in the refrigerators.

"Aunt Hermione was initiated into the coven. They finally waived the herbal healing requirement. I don't know why, but she can't seem to keep the herbs straight."

"Hasn't poisoned anyone, has she?"

"Not yet," Gwen said.

"Well, that's a blessing."

"We're in our seasonal slowdown at the travel agency. Marylou's joined a Fat Oppression Support Group."

"Marylou's an inspiration to us all," Stell said.

"Now we keep lists of Fat Oppressive resorts, and won't book into them." She laughed. "Between my politics and Marylou's, one of these days we're going to put ourselves out of business."

"Well," Stell said, "if you find me doing something wrong at Timberline, I'd appreciate a chance to rectify the situation."

"Believe me," Stoner said, "there's nothing oppressive about your cooking."

"Except the lettuce," Gwen said. "I think you must serve the world's most pitiful lettuce."

Stell grunted. "Tell that to our supplier. I've been trying to get his attention for years. I figure they shunt the stuff onto a siding in Laramie and let it sit a week or two. Even thought about growing my own, but I'm not the farming type."

They crossed over a dry river bed and were suddenly in the desert. A few paloverdes and creosote bushes clung to pebbly soil. Saguaro cactus jutted from the ground like thorny telephone poles. Tan boulders, pitted by wind and scraped clean of vegetation, tilted into an immense sky.

"This is the Salt River Indian Reservation," Stell said. "Pima and

21

Maricopa. Pimas used to be a fierce people. Now they live cheek-by-jowl with the rich white trash, and there's not a bit of trouble. Which tells you how the fight's been taken out of them." She gestured at the dried-up river bed. "That dry wash used to be the Salt River, before the Anglos dammed it. If they ever revolt, they'd do well to blow up the dams first. The water around here's in serious need of liberating."

She glanced over. "Listen to me, on about it again. Every time I come to Phoenix it sets me off. Get so darned mad and ashamed. But I shouldn't be mad, not when I have my gals back with me."

"Thank you, Stell," Gwen said sincerely. "That makes me feel warm all over."

"Last time *I* felt warm all over," Stell said, "it was a hot flash." She pushed her hat up with her forefinger. "Hell, don't know why it's so hard for me to say what I want to say. I've missed you two, and that's a fact. Even if you *did* worry me half to death last summer."

"I'm really sorry about that," Gwen said. "I—"

Stell cut her off. "I'm not looking for apologies. Just hope you aren't planning to give me a scare like that this year."

"I'll try to stay out of trouble," Gwen said.

"It's not you I'm worried about."

Stoner looked at her. "Me?"

"Yes, you."

"What kind of trouble could I get in out here?"

Stell shook her head. "You'll find something. I have great faith in you."

The land rose gently. In the distance, a range of mountains lay low against the earth. Small gray-green bushes were scattered about like grazing sheep. The sky had washed out to the palest blue.

It's beautiful, Stoner thought.

Beautiful and cruel.

*   *   *

Grandmother Eagle soared high over the Colorado Plateau and rested on the wind. Her time was coming. For days now she had heard Masau's gentle voice calling her home to her ancestors. The sun was soothing to her tired bones, bones that carried the chill of winter even through sun-baked summer days. She had seen her final Niman Kachina, the dances, the ceremonies, the Going Home of the Hopi Spirits to the Sacred Mountains. Soon she, too, would go to rest, and embrace the Spirits of her slaughtered young. Her bones would become whistles for a Dineh child to play on. Her feathers, her long, beautiful feathers that sang the Wind-Song, would be gathered for

22

prayer sticks, to carry the pleas of the People over the rainbow bridge to the ears of the Spirits. The thought gave her pleasure.

Now she was saying good-bye. Good-bye to the vast canyons and buttes and mesas of her earth home. Good-bye to the broad arroyos that churned with chocolate waters in the spring rains. Good-bye to the tall sandstone pinnacles, the windswept mountains where she had built her nests and raised her young and squabbled with her lazy, ill-tempered mate.

She smiled to herself, thinking of Old Man Eagle, their fights and matings, their hunting flights, the glint of sunlight through his wingtips, his strong presence through the hours of darkness. But she remembered, too, the blue-white flash from the poacher's gun, the handsome body shattered, the feathers drifting earthward through the still air, the echo of the shot cracking her heart, the long and silent years that followed.

She would see him soon, her Old Man, and once again they would soar upward to the sun, lifted by the Wind Spirits, to play among the Cloud People. Once again they would mate and argue. She had missed their mating, but she had missed their arguments even more.

The wind-river took her over Indian land, with its cluster of adobe homes and two-room ranch houses, its trailer parks and solitary *hogans*, the ancient ruins. Over peach orchards and dark green rows of Hopi corn. Over the tortured, twisting San Juan River, the sharp turns and gouged canyons of the Colorado. Over the mounds of tailings from the uranium mines that brought the terrible Gray Sickness. Over the black-plumed power plants that defiled the sacred Four Corners.

She felt a pull at her heart and turned her attention southward. Curious, she drifted slowly over the old Town That Has Forgotten Its Name, past the rough shale of Long Mesa, past Dineh Wash and Tewa Mountain where the sun rises. Spirit Wells Trading Post lay still beneath the mid-afternoon heat. Her sensitive ears picked up the blare of a television set from Larch Begay's Texaco Service.

Everything seemed as usual.

She circled west over the Painted Desert, searching for...she wasn't sure what. Her eyes caught a faint movement in the shadow of a rock. Rattlesnake. A delicacy, but she wasn't hungry very often these days. Lucky for you, Brother Snake, grown careless with the heat. She shrieked once, to put him in his place, and circled wider.

As she swept again over the old town, she spotted something she had missed before. A Two-leg, an old Indian woman. She had never

23

seen such an old woman. Older than the cedars. Older than the ruined town, it seemed. Maybe older than Long Mesa.

Two-leg faced south, waiting.

The eagle slipped closer. Careful, it could be a trap, experience warned her. Maybe old Two-leg is hunting nice, fresh feathers for her prayer sticks.

A little shudder swept through her. To be sacrificed in a ceremony may be an honor, but it's no pleasure.

Curiosity nibbled at her caution. She circled again.

Two-leg looked up. Their eyes locked.

Ya-ta-hey, Grandmother Kwahu. Two-legs sent thoughts to her.

Ya-ta-hey, Grandmother. Eagle returned the Navajo greeting, but kept a safe distance.

Something is going to happen here, sent Two-leg. Do you feel it?

All I feel these days is winter in my bones. I've been singing a duet with Masau since the time of the Planting Moon.

Two-leg grunted in agreement. This will be my last battle, then my Going Home.

Battle? Grandmother Kwahu soared upward and slid down a windfall. Old woman, your mind has already Gone Home. A bag of hollow bones like yourself is a poor spear for battle.

Nevertheless, Two-leg said. Maybe this old world has one more surprise for you.

Or one more disappointment for you. Eagle circled to leave.

The old woman raised a hand in farewell. When you see your friend Masau, tell him Siyamtiwa will come to him when this is over.

She gave an indignant snort. The Guardian of the Underworld doesn't take orders from broken-down Indians.

The Guardian of the Underworld hasn't met Siyamtiwa.

Grandmother Eagle flapped her arthritic wings and made a great display of climbing a sunbeam. The exchange of insults had rejuvenated her. Maybe Masau will let me stay a while longer, she thought as she turned a somersault. I'd like to see one last battle.

In her excitement, she nearly overlooked the pick-up truck as it crossed the reservation boundary, trailing its ribbon of dust.

* * *

She started to feel it about the time they passed the bullet-riddled sign that marked the edge of the Navajo Reservation:

NO LIQUOR   **NO FIREARMS**

24

OBSERVE TRIBAL LAWS   OBEY TRIBAL POLICE

A strange sort of concentrated restlessness, as if all her neural impulses were gathered in the pit of her stomach.

It was probably a delayed reaction to the plane ride, seven hours on the Sardine Special, crammed in a seat designed for Munchkins.

Or the air, arid as the inside of a clothes dryer.

Or the light, angled with evening and violently gold.

Or the way the wind picked up whorls of dust and set them dancing.

Or maybe the scenery, the vast emptiness, the ground falling away from the roadbed, as bare as if a tidal wave had swept through and scoured the land clean of sagebrush and trees and rabbitbrush, and all other forms of life foolish enough to try to live there.

To the west stretched low hills of packed clay and shale, purple with shadows, folding back on themselves, ridged with gullies, soft as whipped cream. To the east, mountains. To the north, mesas rising in silhouette against the sky.

A little house of logs, octagonal, its doorway facing east, stood in the shadow of a butte. A tin stovepipe protruded from its mud roof. A ragged blanket covered the door. Nearby, a raven picked at something unseen.

"*Hogan* ," Stell explained. "Navajo house. Probably empty. They take the sheep back into the canyons in the summer. Navajos are great rug-makers, you know. Spin and dye the wool themselves. North and west of here, along the Grand Canyon Road, you'll see them sitting beside the highway, weaving. Just set the looms right out there in the blazing sun, trees being at a premium. Every now and then one of the men'll build his wife a shelter to keep the sun off, but men like that are rare. Which just goes to prove the races are more alike than we think."

They were deep in desert now, past the hard-top road, off Navajo Route 15, onto packed sand and dirt. The sky stretched above and around, going on forever. Far in the distance, a windmill stood motionless. A shred of cloud hung in the blue air like a smudged fingerprint. There was no sign of life anywhere.

"We've set you up in the bunkhouse," Stell said. "It's small and not very fancy, but I figured you'd prefer privacy over amenities. If it doesn't suit you, you're welcome to move into the spare room."

"I'm sure it'll be fine," Gwen said.

Stell glanced at her. "There's one thing I want understood before it becomes a problem. Stoner's like family to me, and that makes you family, too. So let's not have any unnecessary politeness."

25

"She can't help it," Stoner said. "She was brought up in Georgia."

Gwen was silent, looking down at her hands.

"I say something wrong?" Stell asked.

Gwen shook her head. "I was thinking about my grandmother. *She'd* have me in the bunkhouse and Stoner in the spare room. Or vice versa."

"One thing I'll never understand," Stell said, giving Gwen's wrist a squeeze, "is how some folks have to take an attitude toward things. Shoot, I have enough to do just getting through the day."

"Well," Gwen said, "you're one in a million."

A broken-down jumble of buildings appeared on their left. A cabin of pine slats, with an attached two-bay garage and a tin roof that jutted out toward the road and provided about a foot and half of shade. Antlers and cow skulls and other souvenirs of killing hung beneath the eaves. A fox skin was nailed to the garage wall. Two Texaco pumps were rusting to death out front. A hand-lettered sign propped against the cabin wall announced 'Begay's Texaco, Flats fixed'. A scattering of tires and rims provided evidence that something, at least, was done to old tires at Begay's.

Stell sped by in a cloud of dust and a friendly honk. "Mr. Begay's kind of disgraceful, but we try to keep on good terms, since this dump and the trading post constitute the entire village of Spirit Wells. And he has the only gasoline between here and Beale." She laughed. "Speaking of taking an attitude…"

"We all have our limits," Stoner said. The torn screen door that led to the cabin had been thick with flies.

A long, low building appeared in the distance, tucked up against the foot of a mesa. Sun glinted copper from the windows. A long porch ran the length of the west side. As they drew closer, she could make out benches and rockers on the porch, a door standing open to the inside, and a weather-beaten sign that spelled out 'Spirit Wells Trading Post. Est. 1873. Gil and Claudine Robinson, props.' A wisp of smoke rose straight as a pillar from a stone chimney.

"There she is," Stell said. She wrinkled her nose. "Don't like the look of that smoke."

Gwen squinted through the dusty windshield. "Do you think something's wrong?"

"Worse. The only time Ted lights that fire before dark is when he's roasting something the Indians gave him in trade. Could be anything."

"Deer?" Stoner asked, hoping for the more edible of a multitude of possibilities.

"Deer, jackrabbit, rattlesnake. Hard telling."

"I've eaten *sushi* ," Gwen said weakly, "but only once."

They pulled off the packed-dirt road into the packed-dirt drive-way, which was barely distinguishable from the packed-dirt yard. Salvia flamed in window boxes. A string of red peppers hung drying against the wall. The temperature in the shade dropped twenty degrees.

The restlessness Stoner had felt in her stomach gathered itself into a soft ball that radiated warmth upward to her shoulders and down her arms. She hoped she hadn't picked up a bug.

Stell stopped the car in front of a rough barn that doubled as a garage. The barn was attached to a corral. The corral contained horses.

Very large horses.

Large, brown, energetic-looking horses.

Stell caught the look of horror on her face, and laughed. "That's Maude and Bill. You don't have to ride them. Think of them as part of the scenery."

"They can't be ridden?" Gwen asked.

"You can ride them," Stell said. "And I can ride them. *She* can't ride them."

"Don't worry about me," Stoner said. "I do real well on the ground."

"However," said Stell as she got down from the truck, "we have something here I'll bet you'll like." She put two fingers in her mouth and let out an ear-splitting whistle.

The world's tallest dog, with the world's largest, squarest head elbowed itself out from under the barn and threw itself in Stell's general direction. Its hair was short and brindle-colored. One ear stood up to a point, the other lay limply on its forehead.

"This," Stell said as the dog rested its front paws on her shoulders and licked her ear, "is my good friend, Tom Drooley. Half Great Dane, half St. Bernard, and all lap-dog."

"I'm afraid to ask," Gwen said, "but why is his name Tom *Drooley?*"

Stell kneed the dog to the ground and wiped her ear on her shirt sleeve. "Three guesses."

Tom Drooley loped around the truck and began a minute, sniffing examination of Stoner's pants legs. Satisfied, he sat down, scraped the ground twice with his tail, looked her in the eye, and said, "Woof."

27

"He likes you," Stell said.

Stoner put her hands on either side of the big dog's head and shook it back and forth. "I love him."

Tom Drooley made low, throaty, sensual noises.

Gwen looked mildly astonished. "I like dogs as much as the next person. But tell me he's not allowed to sleep in the bunkhouse."

"He sleeps in our bedroom," Stell said. "To tell you the truth, I think he's afraid of the dark." She hauled bags of groceries from the back of the truck and handed them over. "Now, you're about to meet my dearly beloved. Hope you're not disappointed. Gary Cooper he ain't."

The kitchen was large and smelled of linoleum and fireplace ash. Sunlight poured through the western windows. Over the sink, checkered curtains framed a view of sagebrush, the mesa, the little bunkhouse, and a path lined with whitewashed rocks. Herbs grew in terra cotta pots on the sills. Against the back wall a fire crackled in an ancient wood-burning stove. A cast iron cooking pot rested on top, steam escaping around its lid. In the center of the room, a long plank table was set for dinner.

Beyond the table and through an arch, the room became a sitting room. It was dark and looked cool, furnished with overstuffed chairs, bookcases, and table lamps. A magnificent Navajo rug in grays and blues lay on the rough floor. The pine walls were covered with sepia photographs in hand-made frames. A break-front held a pile of books, playing cards, a basket of mending, and—looking like an afterthought—a minuscule television set.

A curtained doorway led to the trading post itself.

From behind one of the three doors in the east kitchen wall came the sound of hammering.

"Ted!" Stell hollered through the pounding. "The gals are here."

He might not be Gary Cooper, but he'd do in a pinch. Ted Perkins ambled into the room, tall, muscular, graying, with the rugged grace and blue-eyed squint of a man who works in the sun, and works hard. He carried a hammer in one hand, a tin cup of water in the other.

"Hah," Stell said as she dropped her shopping bag onto the table. "The minute I turn my back, you start goofing off."

Ted grunted, and nodded a greeting in Gwen and Stoner's direction.

Stell introduced them. He put down his cup and shook hands. "Heard a lot about you," he said. "Is it true?"

"Probably."

28

He turned to Gwen. "Sorry about your husband, the son-of-a-bitch."

"Yes," Gwen said, "he was."

"What horror do you have in that pot?" Stell asked.

"Pot roast. It's a pot, ain't it?"

"This outfit comes with a gas stove, you know. Or are you trying to impress the greenhorns?"

"It's you I'm trying to impress, Stell."

She kissed him on the cheek. "Old man, you've been impressing me for thirty-five years."

Gwen edged over to Stoner. "Do you think this is our signal to slip discreetly away?"

"Not yet," Stell said, "but if we get to talking dirty..."

Ted turned his attention to the grocery bag, found an orange, and began to peel it. "You get to see Claudine this morning?"

"She's about the same." Stell said. "I wish Gil'd step in. He just sits there like a rock."

"Hell, Gil gave up trying to get a word in edgewise years ago. Just like I might do any day now."

Stell glowered at him. "I could have done a lot better than you, Perkins. Why didn't I?"

He ran his hand down her hip. Stell slapped it away.

"Well, she might've been the same this morning, but she up and walked out of the hospital this afternoon."

"She what?"

"Walked out," Ted said. "Claimed she felt fine all of a sudden, and they weren't doing her any damn good, anyway."

Stell leaned against the sink. "I don't believe it. You know how she looked last week. She was almost that bad this morning."

Ted shrugged heavily. "Whatever she had just let go of her. Same way it came on her." He tossed the orange peels into the garbage and passed the fruit around. "They want to run over to Taos and see their kids for a while if we don't mind staying on. That suit you?"

"Sure. Everything's under control back home." She shook her head. "I still can't believe it."

"Well, that's no surprise, considering your stubborn temperament. She'll give you a call this evening."

She caught him reaching for a bunch of grapes. "Leave that stuff alone."

Ted heaved a gigantic sigh. "You're a hard woman, Stell. Remember to get those flat-head screws I've been begging you for at least three weeks?"

29

"I got them."

He lounged against the wall. "'Bout time to put the potatoes in, or do I have to do that, too?"

Stell glanced at the sink. "You haven't even peeled them."

"Didn't want to scrape away the vitamins."

"How've you been spending your time, Mister?"

He sneaked a grape while Stell's back was turned. "The Lomahongva kids came by for a pound of coffee and white thread. Said the grandmother's failing. Tomás is of the opinion she's suffering the same affliction as Claudine."

"Which is?"

"Sorcery."

Stell shot him an impatient look.

"They're traditionals," Ted pointed out. "Might be something to it."

"Maybe for the Lomahongva woman, but Claudine's white as snow." She turned back to the sink.

Ted filched another grape. "Mr. Larch Begay did me the honor of a visit."

"Was he sober?"

"Not so you'd notice."

Gwen reached for the potato peeler. "Let me do that, Stell."

"Careful," Ted said. "You don't want to peel off the vitamins."

Stell turned in time to catch him reaching for another grape. "You know I hate that, Perkins. If you're so darned restless, take the gals' luggage out to the bunkhouse."

He slouched toward the door. "Incidentally, I fixed that squeak in the bedsprings. Maybe tonight we can have a little fun without informing the entire Navajo Nation." He let the screen door slam behind him.

"Men!" Stell exclaimed. "Don't know why I stay with him, except he has such a cute ass."

Stoner reached into the bag and handed Stell a box of pepper. "I'll say one thing for you, Stell. You attract good men."

"Well, I learned it the hard way, just like anyone. Kissed a lot of frogs in my time." She shook her head. "Sorcery , for the love of Mike."

"What was that about?" Stoner asked.

"It's one of those rumors that starts up from time to time. Most of the folks around here don't believe in it any more. When I used to visit as a kid, there was always a lot of talk. Wonder what started it up again."

30

Gwen tossed the potatoes in the cooking pot. "There you go, vitamin-less." She took a bag of groceries to the refrigerator and started putting them away.

Hands on hips, Stell marched over to her. "What are you doing, Owens?"

Gwen looked up. "Helping."

"Well, don't." Stell took the bag from her. "You'll do it all wrong."

Stoner palmed the bottle of oregano she was about to put on a shelf and slipped it back onto the table.

Stell caught her. "My God, if I had this kind of anarchy back at Timberline, I'd be out of business."

"You're pretty testy," Gwen said.

"I'm sorry." Stell handed the bag back to her. "That sorcery talk gives me the heebie-jeebies. Offends my sense of order."

Gwen rearranged the contents of the refrigerator. "I don't know how you can talk about order. This ice box is in complete chaos."

"That does it!"Stell shouted. "Out. Both of you." She waved her arms. "Out, out, out!"

"Just let me straighten this," Gwen said. "It won't take a minute to..."

Stell grabbed her by the collar and pulled her away from the refrigerator. "Out! Before I lose my temper."

"Come on," Stoner said, and tugged at her sleeve. "She means it."

Stell shooed them out the door. "And don't come back until I call you, you hear?"

"Yes, ma'm," Gwen said, saluting.

Tom Drooley came out from under the barn, followed them to the bunkhouse, and went back under the barn.

"Hey," Gwen said. She looked around the bunkhouse. "This is cute."

It was a single large room, with pot-bellied stove and closets curtained with grain sacking. One window looked west, and one east. The floor was worn linoleum over rough planking. The bunk beds had been removed and replaced with one double and one single. The double was made up.

Gwen pulled back the spread. "Very subtle. She obviously expects us to sleep in the double."

"Of course she does."

Gwen sighed. "Do you think we could stay here forever?"

Stoner looked around at her. "Are you having a bad time?"

31

"Moments." She tossed her suitcase on the bed. "At least, out here, I don't have to think about *doing* something about it."

Light from the setting sun highlighted her suntanned arms and gentle hands, and tipped her eyelashes with gold. Stoner fell in love all over again. She took her in her arms. Gwen's skin had the salty, burnt smell of summer. "Oh, God", she said hoarsely, "I love you."

Gwen held onto her hard. "I don't care what happens, the only way you'll ever lose me is to send me away."

"Fat chance."

Gwen ran her hands under Stoner's shirt and up her bare back. "You're tense. Is anything wrong?"

"I feel a little funny. Maybe it's the altitude."

The touch of Gwen's hands, the feel of her arms brought several dormant urges back to life. She reached to stroked Gwen's face with the backs of her fingers.

A surge of energy passed between them.

"Hey!" Gwen said. "What was that?"

"Probably static electricity."

Gwen shook her head. "Not like any static electricity I ever felt."

"Actually, what it reminds me of is the feeling I get when I look up suddenly and see you."

Gwen's eyes went dark and deep. "That's one of the nicest things anyone's ever said to me."

Stoner toyed with the buckle on Gwen's belt. "Well," she said self-consciously, "that's how it is."

She felt Gwen touch her hair. "Let's chow down and get back here pronto."

"Honest to God," Stoner laughed. "You're shameless."

Gwen began pulling shirts from her suitcase and ramming them into the bureau drawers. "I only hope," she said, "we can have a little fun without informing the entire Navajo Nation."

THREE

Something had called her awake. She stared into the darkness and listened. She had never heard such silence, such velvet, absolute silence. There ought to be little noises—the scurrying of night creatures, tiny pops of wood as the cabin cooled, the fluttering gasps of a dying ember in the stove.

But there was nothing. Only Gwen's deep, slow sleep-breaths.

Gradually she separated the darknesses. Obsidian where the roof peaked, indigo beyond the window. The darkness of things, and the darkness of spaces.

The call came again. Not a voice, but a sense of urgency.

Carefully, she sat up and eased out of bed.

Gwen murmured, floating below wakefulness.

"I'll be right outside," Stoner whispered. "Don't worry."

She slipped from the bunkhouse and closed the door noiselessly behind her.

The sky was thick with stars, cold pinholes of light in endless blackness. In the west, Virgo reclined over the San Francisco Mountains. A thumbnail sliver of moon, pale as honeydew melon, hung between the Tewa Peaks. The ground beneath her feet had lost the day's heat. The sun was hours from rising.

The knot of energy in her stomach seemed to throb, to grow, to pulsate in rhythm to her heartbeat.

Silence vibrated like a plucked guitar string.

She caught a movement among the rocks at the base of Long Mesa. A shadow, or the shadow of a shadow. Moving, pausing, edging toward her.

The creature caught moonlight and glowed silver.

Unconsciously, she made a sound, a sharp intake of breath. The creature froze. Its eyes were flat and round as dimes.

They stared at each other for a long time.

Something passed between them. A knowing of something. She couldn't make it out.

The animal broke first. A coyote, silhouetted against the gray earth. It loped along, unhurried. Its silver fur flowed like water. It

33

paused once, looked back, and faded into the night.

The screen door creaked behind her. "Stoner?" Gwen peered around the door frame.

"I saw something," Stoner said. "A coyote, I think."

"I don't see it."

"It's gone. It looked at me."

"Wonderful," Gwen said, and shivered a little. "It's forty degrees and you go out to commune with the wildlife."

"I don't feel cold."

"Trust me. It's cold." She touched Stoner's shoulder. "Come back to bed."

"It looked at me, Gwen. As if it knew me."

"I don't care if you sat down over beer and pretzels. Come back to bed." She looked down. "Where are your shoes? Do you have any idea what might be crawling around out here?"

"No. Do You?"

"I'd rather not know. Come on, Stoner. At this very moment, anything could be climbing up your leg."

Stoner laughed. "There's nothing out here."

"Then what was that coyote hunting?"

"I think," she said slowly, "it was hunting me."

"Stoner McTavish, if you're going to turn *weird* on me, I'm taking the next plane back to Boston."

She followed Gwen into the bunkhouse and sat on the edge of the bed. "Have you ever gone somewhere and had the feeling you'd been there before, but you hadn't?"

"Yes," Gwen said, tossing a few sticks of wood into the stove and sprinkling them with kerosene-soaked sawdust from a Maxwell House Coffee can. "It's called *deja vu,* and considered a perfectly normal phenomenon, or a symptom of incipient psychosis, depending on your point of view."

"I felt it just now, out there. But it was more than that. It was as if something was trying to remind me of something."

"It's a common occurrence, Stoner," Gwen insisted. She struck a match and tossed it into the fire. A billow of orange light illuminated her face. "So common it's in the dictionary."

"I don't know..."

"Look, this is a strange place. We might as well be on the moon. You're disoriented, that's all." She got into bed and pulled Stoner down beside her. "Get some sleep. It'll be dawn before we know it, and something tells me the dawn comes up like thunder out here."

Stoner curled around her. "I just have a funny feeling."

34

"You're a Capricorn," Gwen murmured. "Everything feels funny to a Capricorn."

High on Long Mesa, the coyote watched the bunkhouse windows and waited for the day.

*　　*　　*

She left Stell and Gwen to gossip over the breakfast dishes and strolled out toward the mesa. The ground was still cool where night had eaten the last of yesterday's heat and morning shadows lay in slate-like pools. The low rolling desert hills, their layers of yellow and lavender and brown vibrant in the clear light, were stacked like unglazed pottery bowls turned upside down to dry. Distant mountains stood out in sharp relief, a few lace wisps of cloud flying from their peaks. At the horizon, earth melted into sky in a watery smear. A hint of gray-dawn dew had settled the dust. The air was clear, and crisp as celery.

At the foot of the mesa, she searched among fallen rocks for signs of last night's visitor. "Coyotes!" Stell had scoffed. "They'll lose their charm in a hurry once they've kept you up three nights in a row with their infernal howling and yipping."

But this was no ordinary coyote. This coyote had looked into her eyes. This coyote knew something.

And what will you do if you find it? Hunker down for a chat about its Eastern cousins, who are—even as we speak—being hunted, poisoned, and blasted into oblivion, sorry about that, but you know how it is, boys will be boys?

Suppose it asks you to lunch? Are you prepared to share a desert rat in the interest of cross-species good will? Would refusal be perceived as an insult? How far are you willing to go for Peace on Earth?

She knelt to examine a minute disturbance in the sand. Tracks of insects and small rodents. Broken lines where a clump of uprooted brush had raced ahead of the wind. A row of delicate, dog-like prints.

It had crossed the road. She followed, slid down a packed-clay hillock, followed a dry gully for a while, picked her way across a valley floor. The tracks led her around a butte and into the desert.

This is absurd, she told herself. It's miles away by now.

But the tracks drew her on. Across another dry wash. Around the next hill, and the next, and the...

I shouldn't do this, she told herself. I'll get lost.

Lost? Out here? With the air so clear you could see Los Angeles with a cheap pair of seven by thirty-five binoculars?

35

Overconfidence, she told herself, is the hiker's greatest enemy. She kept walking.

Something caught her eye. Something pinkish lying in a heap in the shadow of a rock. An old knee-sock, maybe, or a cast-off belt. A dead sneaker? Litter, even out here. Narrowing her eyes against the glare, she reached for it.

The snake raised its head. Its body was tightly coiled, and still as stone. The tongue flicked in and out, tasting her scent. At the tip of the tail, a pyramid of rattles trembled.

Damn.

She tried to estimate its length. Also the distance to her right ankle. They came out just about the same, with the advantage going to the snake.

Well. Now what?

She felt the prickle of her own sweat, tasted the rusty taste of fear. Pictured the emergency snake-bite kit Stell had given her, lying new and useless on the bureau back at the bunkhouse.

Ten minutes from civilization, and already I'm in trouble. No boots, no snake-bite kit, no means of defense. And nobody's going to come looking for me because I didn't tell anyone where I was going.

Welcome to the desert, McTavish.

She blinked at the snake. The snake didn't blink back.

Be casual. No threatening moves.

She forced the tension from her arms, twisted her body into a pose of nonchalance, and hoped Brother Snake could read her intentions better than she could read his. Because, if he couldn't, Gwen's homophobic grandmother was going to be the least of their problems.

Nice morning, she said silently. Perfect for a walk.

The snake lowered its head a fraction of an inch.

Looks like it's going go be a scorcher. If I were you, I'd hang right in there in that patch of shade and not exert myself too much. If you know what I mean.

She fought against a compulsion to clear her throat, knowing it would sound like dried beans in a tin can and be construed as a sign of hostility.

Listen, I'm new around here. What you locals call a 'green-horn'. Don't know the customs, and I certainly didn't mean to intrude. . . .

She took a tentative step backward.

The snake didn't move.

Haven't learned the rules yet, don't you know? But willing to learn, oh yes.

She took another step.

We don't have many snakes back east. At least, no fine, handsome creatures like yourself. We used to, but they were all extermin... Excuse me, I didn't mean that, I...

The snake appeared to inhale deeply. About to speak? Or strike?

What I'm trying to say is, I've never in my life seen such an elegant reptile.

The snake's tail twitched.

I know, I know, 'reptile's' an ugly word. But it's only a word, no judgment intended. We human beings have an obsession with naming things. Even though our language isn't always aesthetically pleasing. Now, my lover—Gwen—she was married to a man named Oxnard. How would you like to be called an Oxnard? Next to Oxnard, 'reptile's' sheer poetry. But she married him, which just shows you we don't put much stock in names.

She risked another step.

Of course, he tried to kill her. But I don't think it had anything to do with his name. I mean, who would kill over a name? Did you ever hear such foolishness in your life? Ha Ha?

The snake gave her a look that resembled disgust and slithered down a crack in the ground.

At which point she looked around and realized she was lost.

The scenery was completely unfamiliar, landmarks gone, the trading post out of sight behind a hill.

Which hill?

No sweat. Turn around and follow those old coyote tracks back the way you came.

Except that the coyote tracks were gone. So were her own.

She searched the ground, got down on her knees and looked from a dozen different angles. Nothing.

It must have been the wind, blowing the sand, covering. . . .

There hadn't been any wind.

All right, all right, let's not fly into a panic here. Tewa Mountain lies east of the road. Tewa Mountain was behind me when I started out. It's morning, the sun in the east.

Basic stuff, orienteering for beginners and idiots.

She kept her eyes fixed on the ground and walked away from her shadow. The sun was hotter now, and seemed to burn from everywhere at once. Her lips felt dry. A soft white powder sparkled on the backs of her hands. She tasted it. Salt.

37

A feeling like claustrophobia swept over her.

Claustrophobia? In the middle of nowhere?

In the middle of the greatest amount of Nowhere she'd ever seen in her life?

She was paralyzed. Everywhere she looked there was nothing but sand and sky and scrubby bushes and...

"*Pahana.*"

She whirled around. On a little rise of ground a few yards away sat an old woman. A very old woman.

A very old Indian woman who hadn't been there fifteen seconds before.

She was painfully thin, her skin dark and creased as cedar bark, her nearly white hair falling across her shoulders. Her hands, knobby with age, lay quietly in her lap. She wore an age-worn purple velvet dress that reached to the tops of ragged blue sneakers.

She raised an arm and gestured Stoner forward. "*Pahana,*" she repeated.

"Oh, hi," Stoner said. "My name's Stoner McTavish, and I'm lost."

The woman gazed at her.

"I mean, I'm staying with Stell and Ted Perkins at the Spirit Wells Trading Post, and I went for a walk and I can't find my way back..."

She felt foolish and let the sentence die.

The old woman's eyes were black, and hard as coal.

She probably doesn't speak English. "I'm sorry I disturbed you. I'll go right along as soon as I figure out which way..."

The woman was silent, her face expressionless.

Stoner hesitated for a moment, shifting from foot to foot. "I'm sorry," she muttered, and turned away.

"*PAHANA!*" The word resonated like thunder.

Stoner turned back. "I don't understand..."

"Means White person."

"Oh." She brushed her hair aside nervously. "I see."

The old woman gestured again. "Come. Sit."

Stoner climbed the little hill and sat. The woman stared at her.

"My name's Stoner McTavish," she repeated.

"That's okay." The woman went on staring.

"What's...I mean...do you have a name?"

"Plenty."

"That's nice. Plenty. That's a nice name..."

The old woman grunted. "I have plenty of names."

38

"Oh. Well...uh...what should I call you?"

"Why you want to call me? I'm here."

"I mean..."

"If you say what you mean the first time, you don't have to explain so much."

"I..."

"Maybe you enjoy explaining, eh?"

Stoner clenched her fists. "Can you just tell me your name? Okay?"

"Okay." The old woman bent over and wrote something in the dust with her fingertip.

"Siyamtiwa?" Stoner read.

"Siyamtiwa."

"And that's your name?"

"It's how I'm called."

"It's pretty," Stoner said, feeling as if she had cleared a tremendous hurdle. "Is it Navajo?"

"Hopi." The woman offered her hand. Stoner took it. Siyamtiwa held her hand firmly, no pumping or shaking, for a long moment. Stoner had the feeling she was being read.

"What does your name mean in English?" she asked.

"Something Disappearing Over Flowers. What does *your* name mean?"

"Nothing. I mean, I was named for Lucy B. Stone, but it doesn't mean anything."

"Grandmother Stone was a great woman," Siyamtiwa said disapprovingly. "If her name means nothing to you, you dishonor her memory."

"I'm sorry. I didn't think you'd..." She caught herself. "I'm sorry."

The wrinkles at the corners of the old woman's eyes deepened. "You say 'sorry' a lot. Maybe you did something pretty bad, to be so sorry. Maybe Grandmother Stone should come get her name back."

"I didn't take it," Stoner said. She felt like a fool. "My Aunt Hermione gave it to me." A pebble was cutting into her ankle. She shifted her foot. "She reads palms. In Boston. That's in Massachusetts."

"I know Boston," Siyamtiwa said.

"Right." She wondered what asininity would pop out of her mouth next. "Look, I'm a little nervous. I've never met a Native American before."

"Is that how they call us now? Kinda hard to keep up."

39

"I'll call you anything you prefer," Stoner said eagerly.

"We call ourselves The People."

"Okay."

The old woman chuckled. "Okay. If we're the People, what does that make you?"

Stoner realized she'd been had. She sighed. "You know, this is a little frustrating."

"So now you will take out a gun and make me walk a thousand miles to die in a strange place."

"What?"

"That's what *pahana* do to Indians who annoy them."

"I know," Stoner said. "It was a terrible thing. I'm sorry."

The old woman covered her head with her arms. "You gonna shoot me now?"

"I'm not going to shoot you."

Siyamtiwa shrugged. "My great uncle was shot by a white man who stepped on his foot. It's your way of apologizing."

Stoner was silent.

"Of course," the old woman went on, "I wasn't there so I don't know if it's true. But my grandfather told me, so it's probably true." She glanced at Stoner. "You look like a raincloud."

"You're not being fair," Stoner said. "I don't even know what's happening here."

Siyamtiwa patted her arm. "I test you. See if you have a sense of humor."

"Not much."

"Well, that's okay." The old woman sat in silence for a while. "Got anything to eat?"

Stoner felt her pockets. "I'm afraid not, but I can get something. If I can ever get unlost."

"Look out there," the old woman said, and gestured with her chin toward the endless desert. "Think you can walk across that?"

Stoner laughed. "No"

"Humph." Siyamtiwa glanced at her sideways. "I did. But it was a long time ago. Lots of people did that, back then."

"It must have been frightening."

"Not frightening. Hot. Lots of sand. Some animals. Nothing bad." She contemplated the desert. "So now you met a real, honest-to-God Indian. What are you gonna do about that?"

Stoner looked at her. "I don't know what you mean."

"Want me to sneak you into a ceremony Whites aren't supposed to see?"

40

"Of course not. It wouldn't be right."

"Want to buy some rugs and jewelry cheap? Want to take my picture for a quarter?"

Stoner shook her head.

"Well," said Siyamtiwa. She folded her arms and stared toward the horizon. "I got to think about this."

Stoner waited. She tried to project herself out onto the desert and back in time, to when the wagon trains had crossed. She could feel the sun, and the baked earth beneath her feet. Could see the scorched land all around, the unbroken, waterless distances. Could taste the mineral salts that whiskered the rocks with white. Could hear Death as it crept along behind her...

She shook her head to get rid of the image, and saw Siyamtiwa looking intently at her.

"So," the old woman said.

"So?"

"You feel Masau's breath on your neck."

"Masau?"

"What you call death."

Stoner felt her skin crawl. "How did you know...?"

"A trick," Siyamtiwa said. "I bet this Hermione of yours that reads palms in Boston, Massachusetts, can do it."

"Yes," Stoner admitted, "she can. It's pretty disconcerting."

"Maybe sometime I can meet this Hermione. Maybe we have a contest, find out who has the most *kataimatoqve*." She held up her hand before Stoner could ask. "*Kataimatoqve* means spirit eye. What you call psychic."

"She'd love that," Stoner said eagerly.

"Maybe I can help her with the medicine plants, eh?"

I didn't tell her about that, she thought uneasily. I know I didn't.

"Maybe she has things to learn from me," Siyamtiwa went on. "Maybe I have things to learn from her. Put us together, makes a lot of Power, eh?" She sat for a long, silent moment, rocking and chewing a thought. "This coyote you look for, you won't find him. Hosteen Coyote will find you if he wishes. That's how it is with him."

"How did you...?"

Siyamtiwa cut her off with an impatient gesture. "Too many questions. How can you hear answers with your head stuffed with questions?"

"I'm sorry," Stoner said.

41

"What terrible thing have you done?" Siyamtiwa asked sharply.

"Nothing. I think."

"Then why do your Spirits order you to beg forgiveness of everyone you meet?"

"It's...a habit."

"Maybe something not so good happens to me if I talk to someone with all this sorry." The old woman looked closely at her, her black eyes bright and deep. "This Hosteen Coyote is dangerous. I think you better stay away from him until you know more." She glanced away. "I think he may be *istaqa*, Coyote-man. Sometimes man, sometimes coyote." She frowned. "It has been a long time since I saw Coyote-man. I thought they had all gone away. I don't like this thing." Siyamtiwa's mouth turned down in a thoughtful pout. "If this is true, if this is a sorcery thing...you know what a sorcerer is?"

Stoner nodded. "I know what a sorcerer is."

"Your Hermione is a sorcerer?"

"Well, yes and no." She hesitated, wondering how to explain. "She does magic. I mean, she might do a spell, but only to make something good happen...like if someone needs a job or something. But she says black magic comes back at you threefold. She believes in *karma*."

"I know *karma*," Siyamtiwa said.

"Sometimes she talks to Spirits."

"Everyone talks to Spirits. Lotta time they don't know it." She looked hard at Stoner. "Is she your mother's clan, or your father's clan?"

"My mother's."

"Good." She drew an object from deep in the folds of her skirt. "I think this is for you."

It was a doll, crudely carved from cottonwood. The hair, an animal's fur, was chestnut brown. The eyes were green.

It gave her an odd feeling.

"It looks a little like me."

Siyamtiwa shrugged. "All Whites look alike."

"With green eyes?"

"Maybe all Whites look like Shirley MacLaine."

Stoner laughed. "Thank you for the compliment." She held up the doll. "And for this. I'll cherish it."

"It brings luck. Maybe you will need that." The old woman made a low noise deep in her throat, the kind of noise a dog makes when it thinks it hears something but doesn't want to make a fool of itself by barking at nothing. She glanced at Stoner. "This sound makes bad things go away. Don't want bad things on your doll. You visit the new trader?"

"Yes."

"The old one, how does it go with her?"

"Much better. She left the hospital."

"Good. That's a bad place. Take stuff from you. No harmony in that place."

"She's better," Stoner pointed out. "They must have helped her."

"Maybe something else helped her. Maybe something came along."

"Something?"

Siyamtiwa ignored her question. "You have Power?"

"Psychic power? I'm afraid not."

"Hosteen Coyote thinks you have Power. That's why he watches you in the night."

Stoner had to laugh. "Then I'm afraid he has his signals crossed. Whatever he's involved in, it doesn't have anything to do with me."

"So," said Siyamtiwa.

She scraped up a handful of pebbles and toyed with them. "I have to ask another question."

"Well," said Siyamtiwa, "that's how it is with you."

"How did you know that? About the coyote watching me?"

"I know how he thinks." Suddenly she grabbed Stoner's wrist. "You are too innocent, Green-eyes," she hissed. "There are things here you should fear."

"But I'm only..."

"Already you have been lost on the desert."

"I was following tracks..."

"Left by this coyote," Siyamtiwa finished for her. "Is this how you do in strange places? To wander off? To tell no one where you are going?"

"How did you...?"

Siyamtiwa shook her arm roughly. "Is this your way?"

"Of course not. I'm usually very careful."

The old woman took her by the shoulders and looked deep into her eyes. "You listen to me, *pahana*. Something is going to happen here. You got to be ready."

"Sure," Stoner said.

Siyamtiwa let her go. "Now I would like water."

"I'll get you some," Stoner said, and scrambled to her feet. "If you can help me find the trading post."

"You have eyes. Use them."

43

She looked over the old woman's head. The road was only a few steps away. She could read the lettering on the trading post sign.

She knew it hadn't been there when she sat down.

Siyamtiwa gave her a push. "Go."

"I'll be back," she said, and trotted toward the road.

At the kitchen door, Stoner glanced back. Siyamtiwa stood watching her, solid as a tree trunk and still as stone.

Either cross-cultural differences are greater than I realized, she thought, or something very strange is going on here.

The hair at the back of her neck rose like a dog's.

* * *

Grandmother Eagle slid down a sunbeam and came to rest on the ground beside the old woman. "What are you up to, Ancient?"

"Medicine."

Eagle spread her wings and fluttered them in annoyance. "You make medicine with a white girl? Age has stolen your senses."

Siyamtiwa shrugged. "I think she will be okay."

"Whites bring nothing but trouble," Kwahu said. "That's how it's always been."

Siyamtiwa glanced at her. "Your Navajos bring trouble too. It's always been like *that*."

"Hopis are fools," Eagle grumped.

"Navajos are thieves."

"You think you make the sun rise with your dances."

"Steal our horses, steal our land, steal our water—"

"The Anglos steal your land," Eagle interrupted. "Steal your traditions, steal the minds of your children. All the time you sit on your mesas and wait for the Lost White Brother to come and save you."

Siyamtiwa shrugged. "You think like a Navajo, old Kwahu. You don't understand symbolism."

"Dreamer,"Eagle said, and scratched the dust."Mask-painter."

"Silver-pounder, rug weaver."

Eagle kicked pebbles.

"Is good to fight," Siyamtiwa said. " It warms the bones."

"Listen to me, Grandmother. That girl…" She gestured with her beak…"that Green-eyes is not the Lost White Brother. That Green-eyes will not bring Harmony."

"Harmony!" Siyamtiwa threw back her head and laughed. "I have looked for Harmony for more years than the grains of pollen on the Corn Mother. This is another matter. I think maybe a Ya Ya matter."

Eagle paced in a circle. "This is how you spend your last days, talking Ya Ya foolishness? The Ya Ya are gone, old woman."

"That is legend. I'm not so sure. Coyote seeks out this Green-eyes. Maybe he knows something. This Coyote is not what he seems."

"If you are right," Kwahu said, "this girl can't fight your battle. She has no Power."

"I think maybe you are wrong. And maybe Coyote knows this. If it is true, she will be in it whether I want it or not."

"I don't approve," said Eagle.

Siyamtiwa smiled. "When did you ever approve? All my life, I have known eagle disapproval. When I reach the Other World, I will probably be greeted by your disapproval."

"It would give me the greatest pleasure," Eagle said.

Siyamtiwa waved her away. "Then give me peace in this world, mouse-eater. There are things I must think about."

* * *

She let the screen door slam behind her. "Stell!"

Stell started and looked up from her account book. "Jesus, I'd forgotten what the pitter-patter of little feet can do to your nerves."

"I met an old Indian woman out on the desert. She needs water."

Stell pushed her chair back and stood up. "Dying?"

"No, but I don't know why not. She's about a hundred and fifty years old. Siyamtiwa. Do you know her?"

"Can't say as I do. Might have met her, though. They don't give out their names freely." She took a glass from the cupboard, rejected it as too small, and found a quart Mason jar beneath the sink.

"She knew about the coyote," Stoner said. "Don't you think that's strange?"

"These people know things we don't. Guess it's because they look at life differently." She ran cold water in the sink. "The first couple of weeks here, I ran myself ragged trying to figure stuff out. Take my advice, go with the flow, as my son would say."

Stoner held out the doll. "She gave me this."

Stell turned it over and over in her hands. "Looks like you."

"I thought so, too." She took the doll back and leaned against the sink. "We had the oddest conversation. About sorcerers—powaqa, she called them. She said the coyote was half-man, and that he knew my heart."

Stell shook her head. "This reservation's buzzing with superstition these days. Must be the Missionary influence."

45

"Do you believe it?"

"I wouldn't say yes or no," Stell said. "But it wouldn't stand up in an Anglo court of law." She laughed. "You take a superior attitude toward things like that, next thing you know you're awake in the middle of the night with your bed levitating six feet off the floor."

Stoner took a jar of water. "Is it okay with you if we go into Beale?"

"You don't need my permission."

"We need your car."

"Take it." Stell waved her away. "We're not going anywhere we can't take the horses. If you don't mind doing some errands, there's a list of last-minute forgots on the table." She reached down a can of tomatoes. "Take these to the old lady. But don't make a show of it. It embarrasses them. Just put it on the ground and leave it behind, like you overlooked it. She'll understand your intentions."

"Thanks. Where's Gwen?"

"Last I saw, down by the barn with Ted. He said he was going to teach her to split wood. You better intervene before he turns her into a workaholic like himself. They're handy, but not much fun to live with."

She followed the sound of chopping.

Gwen stood, back turned to her, in front of a large block of wood. She lifted an uncut log, balanced it on end, stepped back, and brought the axe down with a crack. The split halves flew. Tom Drooley unfolded his legs, retrieved the sticks with a dignified air, and dropped them at Gwen's feet. She reached for another log.

"Hey!" Stoner called. "If you ever decide to quit teaching and get a *real* job, the two of you can work in a lumber camp."

Gwen turned. "Darn," she said, wiping the perspiration from her face on her shirt sleeve. "Just when we've hit our stride."

Stoner picked up a freshly-cut log and sniffed it. The sharp, resinous odor burned her nose. "Smells great. What is it?"

"Mesquite. Hard as nails. If you don't hit it just right, you can shatter every bone in your arms." She swung the axe at the chopping block, setting the blade deep into the wood. "Do you have any idea what the Yuppies back home would pay for that stack?"

"Can you take a break? There's someone I want you to meet, and I thought we could go into Beale."

"Am I decent?"

There were wood chips in her hair. Her sleeves were turned back. Dust coated her boots and the bottoms of her jeans. "You look terrific."

46

"Flatterer. How do I *really* look?"

"Your hair needs combing."

As they walked toward the bunkhouse, Gwen spotted the can of tomatoes and jar of water. "Is that lunch, I hope not?"

"It's a gift for Siyamtiwa."

"Siyamti—who?"

"Siyamtiwa. An old Hopi woman. It means Something Disappearing over Flowers."

Gwen ran a comb through her hair and picked up her shoulder bag. "Do you have the feeling you're in the middle of a John Ford epic?"

"No. A Stephen King epic. Complete with werewolves."

"This place is weird," Gwen said. She whistled for Tom Drooley. The big dog crawled, one leg at a time, into the bed of the pick-up and curled up on an old blanket.

"Think it's all right to take him?" Stoner asked.

"Ted says he goes to town all the time. He'll just hang out in back. He won't do anything."

"I believe that," Stoner said. She swung up behind the steering wheel and turned the key in the ignition. "Let's ride."

* * *

"I know this is where I left her." The desert was empty. The ground was scuffed and broken.

"You certainly made a mess," Gwen said.

"She must be around here somewhere."

"Maybe she got tired of waiting."

"Even at that, she couldn't have gone far." She turned in all directions. "I hope nothing's happened."

"Maybe she went looking for shade, or hitched a ride."

"You don't understand. This woman is *old*."

"Well, she managed to get here, didn't she? I'll bet she can handle herself on the desert better than you can."

Stoner decided not to respond to that one. Her morning experiences hadn't been anything to brag about.

She slid to the bottom of the hill and looked around. Nothing. No body, no tracks, no litter. Only a little gray spider that couldn't be in its right mind, spinning a web between two rocks.

"Want to wait?" Gwen asked.

She shook her head. She had the feeling Siyamtiwa wouldn't come.

"Tell you what," Gwen said. "We'll tuck the water and tomatoes

47

into a crannie, and maybe she'll find them." She handed Stoner the can and jar. "Careful with this. If you spill it, we could change the whole ecology."

Stoner laughed.

"I'm serious," Gwen said. "There are seeds out here that lie in the sand for hundreds of years, waiting for the exact combination of rainfall and temperature to burst into life. Maybe *you'd* like to make the desert bloom, but I don't want the responsibility."

*   *   *

Now what?

Eagle launched herself from her perch high on Big Tewa Peak as the trading post truck pulled out of the driveway.

Crazy Whites, she groused. Always moving. Afraid Masau will get them if they sit still. She circled high and watched as the truck turned south onto the blacktop.

Midday, and the sun hot as embers.

Crazy, crazy, crazy.

GO HOME! she shrieked. Sit in the shade. Count your money. Stare at your ghost boxes. Think up new ways to kill each other. But leave me in peace, for the love of Taiowa.

No doubt about it, she had always hated the Two-legs, especially the White ones. Old Man had called her a racist for that, but look where all his open-mindedness had gotten him. A tolerant dead eagle's just as dead as an intolerant one.

She could still see, in her fading ancestral memory, how it had been in the old days. The unbroken sweeps of land stretching from the dawn place to the evening place. The buffalo grass and pinyon forests, spruce and mesquite and creosote and cactus. Still canyons and quick rivers. The late afternoon parade of the Cloud People bringing rain. Long, cold, silent winters under the soft snow. The easy hunting, the clear kill. And the Dineh, *her* Dineh that the Whites called Navajo, with their sheep and dogs, their summer homes in the cool green canyons, the fragrant smoke of winter fires rising from their *hogans*. And everywhere Harmony, everywhere *hozro*.

Looking back, she could even spare a kind thought for the Hopi, those broad-nosed fanatics. She had enjoyed the many-days cere-monies, the mystery plays that told the Creation stories, the Kachina dancers with the brightly painted masks, the bells and rattles, the offerings of the Corn Mother. More than once she had made a tasty dinner of Rodent People who came to eat the lines of meal and pollen marking the trails the *Kachinas* would follow. Yes, even the Hopi had

48

their good points.

But the Whites...

White was guns and fences and pony soldiers and fighting. White was pushing and shouting, moving people here, there, always some dying. White was the iron rails with their smoke-breathing wagons, the hard black roads and tin horses, the many-wheels that roared across the land day and night and flattened the Hare People and never stopped. White was the Giant Mushrooms that brought poison rain, the big *hogans* spewing black smoke. White was machines that clawed and chewed the mountains and moved on, while the land died in their wake.

Life had been good in the old days, as long as you stayed away from Black Mesa where the Two-legs gather eagle feathers for their prayer sticks. You could pass the afternoons on a rocky crag and gossip with the wind. The Eagle people were plentiful, and while she didn't particularly care for neighbors—not like the Hopi living in one another's shadows—it was comforting to know they were there. Now the Eagle People were nearly gone, too, the nesting places destroyed, the food beasts poisoned. At her last laying time, the eggs had been sterile, the shells fragile as tissue. After that, though the mating had gone well, there were no more eggs, and she had wept over the empty nest.

And the Two-legs had changed. The dark wind blew through them. Squabbles, meanness, fights between the old ways and the new ways, between the clans, within the clans, everybody looking sideways at their neighbors.

And now here came the old Grandmother, who was maybe the oldest Indian she had ever seen, maybe older than the oldest, maybe something else altogether. Old Grandmother, talking of battles and making up to the Green-eyed *pahana.*

It made her tired to think of it.

The truck turned east, toward Beale. Not much trouble for you to make there, Green-eyes.

She swooped low, screamed an insult, and headed back to Big Tewa Peak.

FOUR

No one has ever called Beale, Arizona, the Jewel of the Desert. Founded by Lieutenant Ed Beale during his camel-train survey of the Southwest in 1857, it straddles the old Atchison, Topeka and Santa Fe rail line, and Route 66. The trains don't stop there any more, and old 66 is crumbling to gravel while tourists roar past on Interstate 40. But waxed paper wrappers and old newspapers and squashed beer cans still pile up against the chain link fence that protects the tracks, and that makes it a railroad town.

Outsiders, who are generally from the east and ignorant, claim I-40 has bypassed Beale. The truth is, Beale is studiously ignoring I-40. The main street still boasts the original black-on-white 66 shields. Every road sign within a twenty-mile radius can be shotgun blasted to Kingdom Come, but no one—no matter how restless, bored, adolescent, or liquored-up—would take aim at those road markers. The original concrete is lovingly patched each spring in a kind of community fertility rite during which men let their beards grow and women dress up in hand-sewn pioneer dresses and everyone eats fried chicken and potato salad under the blistering sun amid swarms of deer flies, and when the day's over everyone wonders secretly why the only ones who seem to enjoy it are the deer flies, but no one dares to say it out loud.

The road runs east to west straight as a ruler. So does the town. At the east end, the Church of Jesus Christ of Latter-Day Saints and Saint James Episcopal, Southwest Mission, face off like gunfighters, each waiting for the other to make the first move. Things deteriorate steadily from there. The buildings along the street are dusty stucco, and bear the original names. The Stockman's Savings and Loan has been the Stockman's Savings and Loan for over a hundred years. The gold lettering on the plate glass windows of the Waldorf Cafe is chipped but readable. McMahon's Hardware still sells pitcher pumps and barbed wire, and dry goods by the yard. Nobody remembers when the last Smith owned Smith's Feed, Grain, and Farm Equipment, but it's still Smith's Feed, Grain and Farm Equipment. According the marquee over the Roxy Theater, *3:10 to*

Yuma is still playing, but the doors are boarded up and the cracked windows of the ticket booth are reinforced with mummified scotch tape.

Beale's more modern attractions include a Western Auto Store (circa 1949), the IGA ('53), Bud's Army/Navy Surplus ('55), and the Golden Opportunity Texaco Service, which still bears the motto "Trust Your Car to the Man Who Wears the Star". During the patriotic craze of '76, the townsfolk gave a passing thought to having Beale declared a National Historic Site and restoring it. But, as someone pointed out, why invite the government to stick its nose in their business, when Beale was already in mint condition?

Beale is also hip-deep in history. There's a crumbling Cavalry Fort west of town, from which originated a score of Indian massacres and which is visible in winter when the prairie grasses die back. Two of the local boys fought in the South Pacific in World War II. One came home, the other stayed in San Diego. After some heated discussion, it was agreed that anyone who preferred California to Beale must have been driven mad by the war, and his name appears on the plaque at the Town Hall, which is also the Post Office, police station, and barber shop.

In '47 the mayor caught his wife in bed with a traveling salesman (bathroom fixtures), shot them both, and ran two successful re-election campaigns from the County Jail. A family named Clark once owned a farm nearby which burned to the ground under mysterious circumstances. The 1958 high school basketball team made it to the state quarter-finals and managed to score twelve points against the team from Holbrook, down the road. Ethel Boyd's Rhode Island Red once laid an egg with three yolks. In the late 60s a band of hippies camped for a while at the edge of town—but nothing was happening, man, and they moved on.

Nowadays there's plenty going on in Beale. You can get a decent meal at the Waldorf Cafe, or a quick sandwich at the Rexall counter. The Episcopal Church holds a bingo night once in a while, which causes the Mormons to accuse them of 'turning toward Rome'. A couple of real estate agents have moved in, but nobody knows why. You can go down to the county seat and watch the local lawyers sue each other to keep in practice. Now and then somebody claims to have heard about somebody who spotted a descendent of Beale's camels out on the prairie. Since the story is usually told well after eleven p.m. on a Saturday night at the Sheepherder Tavern, that remains an unconfirmed rumor.

Every afternoon about four, the dry wind rises and moves the

51

waxed paper wrappers around a bit.

Stoner pulled into the IGA parking lot and cut the motor. "Want to start loading, or should we see the sights?"

"From the looks of it," Gwen said, "we can see the sights without leaving the parking lot. Cute little place."

"Another in our endless succession of small towns," Stoner said as she slid to the ground. "It can't be worse than Castleton, Maine, can it?"

"If you want to see real small-town life," Gwen said, "some day I'll take you to Jefferson and parade you in front of the crowd at the A and W Root Beer stand. All the girls I grew up with will die of envy."

"Or shock." Stoner filled Tom Drooley's water dish from the emergency canteen and woke him up long enough to tell him to "Stay! Guard!"—which he probably didn't understand—and left him with his legs dangling over the tailgate. She locked the truck cab and pocketed the keys.

"Sure you want to do that?" Gwen asked. "The locals might be offended if you lock."

"If I were a teenager," Stoner said, "and lived in this town, I would steal this truck."

"And Tom Drooley?"

"*And* Tom Drooley."

She stepped out onto the pavement and looked up and down the street. Across the way, someone in a second floor apartment raised a dark green shade and peered out. Gwen waved. A figure in gray cotton bathrobe and pink foam rubber curlers waved back.

Stoner squinted against the light, felt the breeze finger her hair, smelled dust and tar. Down the street, a cluster of men in patched Levi's lounged in front of the Sheepherder and tossed pebbles at a parking meter. A black and brown mongrel dog browsed through litter in the gutter until one of the men threw a rock at it and it skulked away, casting dark looks over its bony shoulder.

Gwen paused to examine a 4-H exhibit of quilts and aprons in the bank window.

"Look at that sky," Stoner said. "I wonder what it'd be like to make love under that sky."

"Roomy, I expect," Gwen said. "Also hot."

"I *meant* at night." She ran her hand along the sun-warmed stucco wall. "This place is like something out of a movie, isn't it?"

"You mean that one where the kid wants to go to New York and study art, but his father wants him to stay home and run the Feed

52

and Grain business, and the mother ran off with a no-good cowboy and is living a life of pregnancy and oppression in Mexico while the cowboy drinks himself to death. Then the brand-new, blonde, anorexic schoolteacher shows up..."

"No," Stoner said. "The one where five murderers break out of jail and terrorize the town until this high school kid—who really wants to be a physicist but can't afford to go to college—sets up these special effects with lasers made from old telephone wires and soda straws, and explosives that are really all the pressure cookers in town rigged to boil dry and blow up simultaneously so the murderers think they're surrounded."

"What I *really* had in mind," Gwen said, "was the one about the schoolteacher who has a falling out with her family over the woman she's in love with, and runs away to Arizona..." Her voice caught.

Stoner touched her. "Gwen , it'll be... it'll be..."

"All right?" Gwen laughed bitterly. "If you can predict how this one will turn out, you can go into the fortune-telling business." She leaned her head on Stoner's shoulder. "Can we get a lemonade?"

Stoner kissed the top of her head gently. "Goodnight's Rexall is on Stell's forgot list. Want to check it out?"

The inside of the drug store was cool and smelled of marble and cherry syrup. A soda fountain ran along one wall, shelves of over-the-counter medicines and magazines along the other. A fan turned lazily in the ceiling. At the back, a pair of giant apothecary jars—one filled with red water, one with yellow—marked the limits of the pharmacist's territory. A skinny young man in a stained white uniform lounged against the soda fountain counter reading a Marvel comic. He glanced up indifferently, took one look at Gwen, and snapped to attention. "Get you something?"

"Iced tea," Stoner said as she swung up onto the stool.

"Lemonade," Gwen said. "Easy on the sugar."

"You folks ain't from around here," he said as he put the glasses down.

"That's right," Stoner plucked a straw from a stainless steel and glass container.

"Passing through?"

"We're staying with the Perkins'," Gwen said. "At the trading post at Spirit Wells."

"Mrs. Perkins is swell," he said, tossing a lock of sandy hair from his forehead. "But that rez is dead. You oughta go see the Grand Canyon."

"I'm sure we will," Gwen said.

53

"I mean it. The rez is the deadest place I ever saw."

Unlike Beale, Stoner thought. A veritable beehive of activity.

"It's a change," Gwen said. "We've never seen a reservation, dead or alive."

"Nothin' but wind and dust and Indians."

"I think it's pretty, in a strange way. I never knew dirt came in so many colors."

"It's about what we expected," Stoner added. "What do you do for excitement in town?"

"Not much," the boy said. "But at least we got TV."

"Cable?"

"Naw." He pouted. "We keep tryin', but nobody wants the franchise. Not enough population out here."

"Yes," Stoner said, "I see the problem."

"Television," Gwen put in, "rots your brain and stifles your imagination."

The boy scowled. "Jeez. You sound like a school teacher."

"I am."

"Where at?"

"Boston."

He brightened. "Hey, Boston. They got a lot of crime there, right? Mafia and stuff?"

So this is what happens to kids in small towns, Stoner thought. They grow up wanting to be the Godfather. Good thing I ran away from home. In Rhode Island, I'd have had half a chance.

"Listen," the boy said, "what's the ocean like? I never seen an ocean."

"It looks a lot like the desert," Gwen said. "Big, lots of sky, only wetter."

"Bet you go swimming all the time, huh?"

"Not too much. The Atlantic's pretty cold."

"The desert gets colder'n a whore's eye," the boy said. "But you can't swim in it. They have a town pool over at Winslow. And in some of the motels. But they don't let you swim in them unless you're from there. Some of the guys get jobs in the motels just so they can swim. That's what I'd do, if my folks didn't need me here. Bet I'd be good, too. Swimming. If I knew how, bet I'd be real good." He scooped ice into a paper cup and drew himself a Hires'. "You really gotta see the Grand Canyon. It's really big."

"I've heard that, " Gwen said.

"No, you wouldn't have heard how big it is 'cause it's too big to say, even. So big you don't even know it's big. You walk along the

54

edge, see, and feel like you're strollin' down Main Street, and you don't stop to think, if your foot slips or somethin' you'd fall a mile. A whole mile. That's no exaggeratin'. They measured it. I read about that in *National Geographic.* "

"You see?" Gwen said. "If you had cable TV you never would have read that article."

He looked at her as if she were crazy. "I read it in school, lady. Jeez." He spread a daub of egg salad on a saltine and gulped it down. "Little kids run right up to the edge and hang over. That's on account of they don't understand how *big* it is."

"Sounds dangerous," Stoner said.

"Heck, yeah, it's dangerous. You wouldn't catch me hanging over the edge of anything that big." He took another saltine and spread it with cream cheese and olive. "Give you an idea how big it is, you can stand in front of El Tovar—the hotel—and look *down* on the top of thunderstorms. You ever seen the top of a thunderstorm?"

"No," Gwen said. "I've missed out on that."

He spread another cracker with ham salad. "You oughta try and do that. It'll move you. How long you here for?"

"About two weeks," Stoner said.

"Jeez, in that time you could see the Grand Canyon two, maybe three times. Couldn't see it all, though. I'll bet nobody's ever seen it all, on account of it's so..."

"Big?" Stoner offered.

"Yeah, right, big." He leaned over the counter and lowered his voice. "There's this place, down in the canyon. A secret place, see? Where the Indians think they came up out of this hole in the ground. So it's a holy place, kind of, and they go out there and do ceremonies and stuff, and they leave things behind for their Spirits. Presents and stuff. Mr. Begay's gonna take me out there some day."

"If it's secret," Stoner asked, "how does Mr. Begay know where it is?"

"Mr. Begay knows everything, especially about the Indians. There's this other place we're gonna find, up on the rez but he won't tell me where. A long time ago the Indians buried a whole lot of stuff up there. Gold and stuff. We're gonna find it and then he's gonna help me get out of Beale for good. My Dad says that's a load of crap, but he don't like Mr. Begay much, and anyway Mr. Begay says don't listen to him, he's trying to hold me back and this is a free country, I got a right to try and make any kind of life I want for myself." He grinned shyly. "Though Mr. Begay puts it a little different. You know how Mr. Begay puts it?"

"Give me a hint," Gwen said.

"Fuck 'em hollow. That's how Mr. Begay puts it."

"Well," Gwen said. "That certainly is expressive."

"And poetic," Stoner added. "Is this the Begay that runs the Texaco Station out at Spirit Wells?"

The boy beamed. "That's him. You know him?"

"We haven't met," Gwen said. "But I wonder, if he can get *you* out of Beale, why he hasn't gotten himself out."

"I dunno," the boy said thoughtfully. "Maybe he likes it here. Bein' part Navajo and all."

Gwen looked over at Stoner. "Sounds like a credit to his race. We should pick up Stell's order."

"Right." Stoner turned to the boy. "Did Mrs. Perkins phone in an order?"

"Sure did. I got it all put up." He reached under the counter and hauled up a cardboard box. "When you see Mrs. Perkins, tell her Jimmy Goodnight says 'hey'. She's a swell lady, ain't she?"

"Sure is,"Stoner said.

He looked her up and down. "You oughta wear sunglasses out here. And sunscreen. Looka that, you're gettin' burnt already. Guess you don't have a lot of sun back east."

"Not like you have here."

"We got some good glasses over on that counter. Not too expensive. Some places, they'll try and sell you real expensive stuff, rip you off. But there ain't much difference unless you wanta get into the real highclass French stuff. We got a nice selection, though. You got your pick of brown, green, yellow. Wire rim or plastic. I'd go with the plastic. Better get yourself a tube of sunscreen. With your coloring. . ." He studied her in a deeply serious way. "...I'd say go with a fifteen, tops. You gonna be out on the desert much?"

"There doesn't seem to be a lot of choice," Gwen said, "unless we stay indoors and play double solitaire."

Jimmy Goodnight leaned forward earnestly. "I don't wanna scare you bad," he said with obvious relish, "but there's a lot of snakes out there this time of year. Rattlers and sidewinders. Tarantulas. Scorpions. You know how to take care of yourself on the desert?"

"Probably not," Stoner said.

He reached under a stack of Marvel comics and pulled out a mimeographed sheet of paper. "This'll tell you what you need to know. Most important thing is, make sure someone knows where you're going."

"I know," Stoner said.

"You ought to carry a mirror and matches," he went on, "along with your canteen. So you can signal for help." He handed her the paper. "You can have this. Part of the service. Now, if you get lost, don't wander around. Stay where you are and let them find you. Don't sit on the ground, and don't take your clothes off."

"Take my clothes off?" Stoner said in alarm. "Why would I want to do that?"

"Some folks think it'll make 'em cooler. 'Course, some folks're pretty dumb. You probably wouldn't do a dumb thing like that."

"Not like that," Stoner said.

"Not with snakes and tarantulas," Gwen muttered under her breath.

"Burning tire makes a good signal fire," Jimmy Goodnight said.

"Assuming I happen to be rolling one along with me."

"Now, if you can't find water, you can always make a solar still. Start with a sheet of plastic, about six feet in diameter..."

"Which I have tucked inside my rolling tire."

"...and a pail and a drinking tube—that should be about five feet long—and a trench shovel..."

Stoner held up her hand. "Jimmy, we're only going sightseeing, not joining the French Foreign Legion."

He raked his sandy hair. "Well, you promise me you'll read this until you understand it total, okay? No skimming. It could save your life."

"Yes, Sir," Stoner said with a smile. "I appreciate your concern."

"Hey, you're friends of Mrs. Perkins, you're friends of mine." He grinned at Gwen. "Even if you *are* a school teacher."

"Same goes for me," Gwen said, "even if you are a punk."

He blushed. "I'll bet Mrs. Perkins is real glad you're here. She's been wantin' company something awful."

"Jimmy Goodnight," Gwen said when they were out on the street, "must be the loneliest individual I ever met."

Stoner balanced the carton on one hip, put on her new sunglasses, and looked up at the sky. Through the brown tinted lenses, it resembled a bad sunset. She took the glasses off and settled them on top of her head.

"Goodnight. Do you think that's an Indian name? He doesn't look Indian."

"The Goodnights were ranchers out here in the early cattle days," Gwen said.

"What do you know about Begay's."

"The name crops up in some of Tony Hillerman's novels," Gwen said. "That's as much as I ever heard."

"If I were the Goodnights," Stoner said, "I might not be too pleased about my son hanging around with him."

"Well, you're not the Goodnights, my dear friend, and as far as we know, Larch Begay may be a cut above the general populace."

Stoner tossed the carton into the back of the truck. Tom Drooley crawled out from under a silver Windstream camper.

"Poor old dog," Stoner said, knuckling his head. "I'll bet you're hot."

"That," Gwen said to Tom Drooley, "means you get to ride up front with the air conditioning."

*   *   *

The afternoon air was brittle. The backs of her hands tingled as if tiny, invisible creatures were walking over her skin. Static electricity. She wondered if it meant rain.

Gwen pulled up to one of the two rusty pumps at Begay's Service and cut the motor.

The shack's tarpaper roof was cracked and flaking. The screen door listed drunkenly from a single hinge. Old tires and dented hubcaps littered the ground, and a junked '64 Nash Rambler was sinking slowly into the sand. Inside the garage, a vehicle of unknown make and purpose was jacked up at a crazy angle, surrounded by grease-caked tools and oily rags. Through the fly-specked windows of the room marked 'office', they could see the feeble flicker of a black-and-white television.

"Stell's nuts to do business with this character," Gwen said. "There could be *anything* in that gas."

"Yeah, but it's the only station around." Stoner got out of the truck and stretched her legs.

Climbing down from the cab, Gwen stood beside her. "He doesn't seem exactly eager for business."

Tom Drooley pressed his nose against the windshield and sneezed.

"Maybe we caught him in the middle of his favorite soap opera," Stoner suggested.

"Or he didn't hear us." She thought for a moment. "I wonder what the local customs are in situations like this. Back in Georgia, we used to honk the horn."

"Try it."

She tried it. Nothing happened.

The breeze began to pick up. The air took on the smell of ozone.

58

"Well," Gwen said, "we can't just stand here like a couple of idiots." She climbed the two rickety steps and rapped on the door frame.

From inside came a series of bangs, moans, and low curses. "Hold your piss," a man's voice growled. "I'm comin'."

Gwen jumped back as he shoved through the door.

The man was of about average height and built like a bear, stocky, short-limbed, and running to fat. His dark hair was shoulder-length and greasy. The skin of his face—what little was visible beneath an untrimmed and spikey beard—resembled a lunar landscape of pock-marks. A monstrous beer belly overlapped his belt, the tarnished brass buckle sunk deep in his flesh. He wore cowboy boots with rundown heels, jeans caked with something dark, stiff, and mysterious, a filthy undershirt. The hair on his chest was matted and wet-looking. His eyes were tiny, red-rimmed, and unnaturally bright. His eyebrows were ponderous. A droplet of spit or beer had caught on his beard. He smelled like the Celtics locker room after the NBA playoffs.

Begay looked them over, individually and slowly. He turned his shaggy head and looked at the truck. He looked at Tom Drooley. He looked back at them, and back at the truck, and generated a thought. "That the trading post vehicle?"

"Yes," Stoner said. She felt like gagging.

"What's the problem?"

"No problem. We need gas."

"That all?"

"As far as I know," Stoner said.

"Coulda got that yerself."

"I'm sorry. I didn't realize."

Begay shuffled to the pump, waving listlessly at a fly that was trying to gain a foothold on his head. He sucked from a can of Colt .45 Lager and unscrewed the gas cap. "Hear anything about Claudine?"

"She's out of the hospital," Stoner said.

He motioned for her to crank the pump. She did.

"Goddamnedest thing," Begay said, "takin' her like that. Makes you think, don't it?"

Stoner doubted that he had much experience with that particular form of exercise. "Certainly does," she said.

"'Skins are talkin' Ya Ya sickness." He took a swig of beer and watched the numbers of the pump dial. "Goddamn assholes."

"What's Ya Ya sickness?" Gwen asked.

He shrugged heavily. "What are you girls doin' out here?"

Stoner started to say "women", to correct him, but thought better of it. "We're on vacation."

He glanced at her. "Must be nuts, comin' to this hemorrhoid on the rectum of the universe."

"We have friends here," Gwen explained. "The Perkins'."

"Well, now, ain't that sweet?" Begay belched and spat in the dust. "Where ya' from?"

"Boston," Stoner said.

"Never been there."

"Have you always lived around here?" Gwen asked.

"Born on the rez. Old man was a mixed-blood. That's how I got this fuckin' Navajo name."

"If you're unhappy here," Stoner suggested, "why not move?"

"Too much trouble."

She was inclined to believe him.

"Besides, who'd buy this shithouse?" He waved toward the office and garage. "That comes to nine-ninety. Want me to put it on the tab?"

"I'd rather pay." Stoner handed him a twenty.

"Think I can change that?" He gave an oily laugh. "Sweetheart, you ain't aware of the facts of life out here."

She stuffed the money back into her pocket. "I guess you'll have to put it on the bill, then."

Begay turned his attention to the dog. "Hey, old Tom. See you got yourself a coupla good-lookin' gals to go riding with. Wouldn't like to tell me your secret, would you?"

Tom Drooley sneezed.

"Smell that old storm comin'?" Begay looked back at Stoner. "This hound's got a good nose for storms. Not much else, though."

Stoner smiled noncommittally.

"Well," Gwen said, "we'll be moving along." She started to climb back into the truck.

"Whoa, Sweetheart," Begay said. "You gotta sign for that gas."

"Oh," Stoner said. "Okay."

"Come on inside."

It was the kind of invitation responsible parents warn you against. She hesitated.

Begay grinned, revealing a row of broken and yellowed teeth that looked like a vandalized graveyard. "I ain't gonna bite."

Gwen started for the office. Stoner ran to catch up with her. The protective gesture didn't go unnoticed. Begay gave her a knowing wink. It made her skin crawl.

While the man made a great show of searching for his account book, she looked around. The inside of the shack achieved the impossible task of being even worse than the outside. A broken-down easy chair, springs sagging, rough upholstery nearly worn through, was placed directly in front of the television set. A litter of beer cans, cigarette butts, and empty Cheese Curl packs suggested that this was the spot on which Larch Begay was most likely to be found on any random day. In the corner, a sheetless cot was unmade, the blankets rumpled, the pillow stained with grease. A makeshift table held a hot-plate, several empty tin cans, and a pile of food-encrusted dishes. Behind the cash register, a shelf contained various bits of unidentifiable hardware, and one very identifiable pistol and box of shells.

She forced herself to look around the room in a casual, uninterested sort of way.

Her chest felt tight. It was hard to take a deep breath. She tried to relax her shoulders and open her lungs, but all she could manage was a quick, shallow gasp.

"That truck oughta be due for an oil and lube," Begay said.

"I'll mention it to Ted," Gwen said and signed the account book.

Begay crossed his arms and leaned against the counter. "That Stell's some good looker. You been friends long?"

"About a year," Gwen said. She looked over at Stoner. "Are you all right?"

"Sure."

"You're as white as a ghost."

Begay looked at her sharply, his eyes narrowed.

Stoner forced a smile. "I'm fine. Really." She took a deep breath and felt as if she had slammed into a door. Something coiled around her chest like a giant Anaconda and forced the air from her lungs.

"I take it back," she gasped. "Better go outside."

She tried to move. Her legs were paralyzed.

She tried to speak, but no words came.

"Your friend's offended by my house-keeping," Begay said with a laugh.

"Stoner?"

She wanted to reach toward Gwen, but the walls were receding, melting. She was in open air, in darkness. Gray clouds boiled overhead. She was falling, tumbling...

Gwen caught her. "Easy," she said, and began to lead her to the chair.

61

The feeling passed.

"Want a drink of water?" Begay asked.

Stoner shook her head. She felt completely herself. Whatever had gripped her had just as suddenly let go. She forced a laugh. "That's what I get for spending too much time in the sun."

"Are you sure you're all right?" Gwen asked.

"Positive."

Begay dragged a folding chair from behind the counter. "Here, you better set down a minute." He shoved her down roughly. "I got something to show you while you rest."

She had to admit it felt good to sit. She was so tired...

Begay opened a glass case near the door and swept out an armful of objects, spreading them on the counter.

Jewelry. Silver jewelry inlaid with turquoise and coral. Belts, necklaces, bracelets, rings, bolo ties. All obviously hand-made. Even through their patina of dust and tarnish, they were breath-takingly beautiful.

Begay folded his hands over his stomach. "Genuine Navajo."

"They must be valuable," Gwen said, one hand stroking Stoner's shoulder.

"Took 'em in pawn. Tourists go nuts for 'em." He reached into the case and drew out a turquoise and coral hatband. "Look at this. Got it from a boy up at Coal Mine Canyon. Paid twenty-five dollars for it. It'll bring me three -fifty easy."

"If it's worth that much," Gwen asked, "why would he sell it to you for so little?"

"Had something he wanted and couldn't get anywhere else." He grinned slyly. "Whiskey."

"I thought liquor wasn't allowed on the reservation," Stoner said.

Begay chuckled, admiring the hatband. "Works to my advantage, don't it?"

Gwen gave her shoulder a warning squeeze.

"Yes," she said, trying to keep the sarcasm from her voice. "I can see how it would."

He turned back to her. "Someday I'm gonna have enough to get out of this pisshole."

"I certainly hope it works out for you," Gwen said.

"It will." He gave Stoner a knowing wink. "Something tells me it won't be long now. Not long at all." He looked at her hard and meaningfully, as if they shared a secret.

She couldn't figure out what he was getting at.

Begay put the hatband back in the case and blew his nose on an unspeakable cotton handkerchief. "You want any souvenirs," he said, "you come to me. I'll give you a real good deal." He licked his lips. "On account of you're friends of the Perkins'."

"That's very generous of you," Gwen said. "We'll keep it in mind. Stoner, are you ready to go?"

Begay turned to her. "That what they call you? Stoner?"

"That's right."

"Interesting name. A person wouldn't be likely to forget a name like that."

"True," Stoner said. "I've never forgotten it." She managed to pull herself to her feet and stumble from the house.

As soon as she hit the outside air, her tiredness drained away.

Tom Drooley had jumped out the cab window and crawled under the truck to sleep. Gwen coaxed him out.

"You take care of these pretty gals, Old Tom," Begay said. "This country can get a mite rough."

Not as long as I have my rolling tire and six feet of plastic, Stoner thought. She managed to get Tom Drooley between herself and the passenger window.

Gwen climbed behind the wheel and started the motor.

Begay leaned against the side of the truck. "What's your pal's name, Stoner?"

"Oxnard," she said quickly. "Mrs. Bryan Oxnard."

"Is that a fact?" Larch Begay grinned. "Well, I'm right pleased to meet Mrs. Oxnard."

"Pleasure," Gwen muttered. She put the truck in gear and pulled away in an explosion of dust. "What's with the name business?" she asked.

"I just didn't want him to know too much."

"As my mother used to say," Gwen said, "Mr. Larch Begay is one unsavory character, sorely in need of a woman's civilizing influence." She put her hand on Stoner's knee. "What happened to you back there?"

"I don't know. All of a sudden I felt very odd."

"I thought you were going to faint."

"So did I."

"Well," Gwen said, "if this climate is going to affect you like that, we're getting out of here. You scared me half to death."

"It might be the climate, but I doubt it. Probably Jimmy Goodnight's iced tea. I never do well with tea."

She wished she believed it. Something told her the things that had

63

happened were a lot stranger—and more frightening—than that.

Over the San Francisco Mountains far to the west, a column of purple clouds had begun to form. The wind rose, hurling curtains of dust across the road. The clouds picked up and moved. Rain fell in veils behind them. The declining sun painted the tops of the clouds with gold.

Gwen glanced uneasily at the storm. "Do you think it'll reach us?"

Stoner shrugged. "Gwen, I think we should stay clear of Larch Begay."

"Granted, he's every woman's worst nightmare, but is there a particular reason?"

There was, but she couldn't put into words. Something in the way he looked at her. Something in the way he said her name. Something that told her Larch Begay had been behind the things that had happened to her at the service station. She didn't know how or why, but..."Just a feeling, I guess."

Gwen smiled. "Don't worry. I'm not tempted to seek out his company."

Stoner put her arm around the dog. "Funny, Tom Drooley doesn't seem to mind him."

"I'm afraid Tom Drooley falls a little short of being the world's smartest dog," Gwen said.

Tom Drooley reached across Stoner's lap and licked Gwen's face.

"Seems perfectly intelligent to me," Stoner said.

Gwen gagged and wiped her face on her sleeve. "Did you notice Begay's eyes? I don't know what's wrong with him, but I hope it's not contagious. The only time I've ever seen eyes like that was on one of our dogs that got conjunctivitis."

"Well," Stoner said, "we'd better keep Tom Drooley away."

The clouds were on the move, billows of smoky black, angry and boiling. Tongues of lightning flickered through the sky like probes searching for a place to grab earth. To the south, where the sun still shone, the land glowed.

Tom Drooley's ears began to twitch.

"I'm glad we're nearly home," Gwen said. "I'd hate to be stranded in this."

"Don't worry. If worse comes to worst, all we have to do is burn a tire."

"Poor Jimmy Goodnight." Gwen shook her head sympathetically. "If the best hero he can find is Larch Begay..."

The trading post came into focus behind the swirling dust. The windows showed light like strokes of orange paint. Stell was at the kitchen door.

"Put the truck in the barn," she shouted over the wind. "And close up. The horses are spooked."

The wind grabbed the truck door as Stoner opened it, and slammed it forward. The hinges made a popping, creaking sound. She reached for the handle as the first crack of thunder broke. Tom Drooley flew over her arm and into the house.

Fighting the wind, she pulled the barn door open and let the truck inside.

"Go up to the house, " Gwen said. "I'll settle the horses and be along."

She managed to slip through the banging door and headed for the kitchen. Dust scoured her nose and eyes. Grit blew into her mouth. The wind screamed past her ears.

Stell was slamming windows. "I closed up the bunkhouse," she said as Stoner shook sand from her hair. "Glad you got back in time. These storms are sudden and awful."

"Where's Tom Drooley?" Stoner asked as she drew water and rinsed the dust from her mouth.

"Under the bed."

"Darn. I forgot to bring in your groceries."

"They'll be fine in the barn until this is over," Stell said. "Take a look out the window and see if Gwen needs help."

The wind had shifted and picked up speed. The barn was barely visible through flying sand. The door blew crazily back and forth on its hinges. Gwen chased it, caught it, hung on for a second before it was ripped from her hands.

"I'd better go," Stoner said.

"If you can't get it, let it go. That truck's not worth getting killed for."

Her presence seemed to enrage the wind. It struck her in the back like a fist, and sent her stumbling forward.

"Go back!" Gwen waved her away.

She ducked the flying door and slipped inside the barn. The horses were nervous, stamping the floor sharply, kicking at the stall doors. She leaned against the wall to catch her breath.

"Stell says...leave it," she panted.

"Damn it, Stoner, I was having a good time."

"You what?"

"I was enjoying it."

"That's nuts."

"It is not."

Stoner dug grit from the corners of her eyes. "Could you enjoy it some other time? I was worried about you."

"For God's sake!" Gwen kicked the side of the barn in anger. "I'm *sick* of being worried about. You're as bad as my grandmother."

"*Gwen...*"

"I can take care of myself, Stoner."

"I didn't say you couldn't."

"Then stop treating me like a child."

She felt lost in a heavy, gray confusion. "Gwen..."

"You're so damned overprotective. I don't *need* to be protected."

"I don't understand this," Stoner said. "Everything was all right five minutes ago."

Gwen slammed her hand down on the truck hood. "Five minutes ago you hadn't come tearing out here to *worry* about me."

Frustrated, Stoner threw her arms up in the air. "Okay. Fine. I won't worry about you. Let the damn wind blow the damn door halfway to Louisiana, and you with it. God forbid I should worry. God forbid I should care. God Forbid I should *love* you."

"*Don't* love me!" Gwen screamed at her. "I don't want you to love me. I don't want *anybody* to love me, ever again."

"Gwen..."

"People say they love you, but it's a joke. A trap. Step out of line just once...just once...then you find out how wonderful that *love* is."

Stoner grabbed her shoulders and shook her. "Goddamn it, Gwen, I'm not your grandmother."

Gwen glared at her.

"Look, she's being a shit. I don't blame you for being hurt, but *don't take it out on me.*"

"I have a better suggestion," Stell said from the doorway. "Come into the house and both of you stop taking it out on the horses. They're upset enough as it is."

Gwen looked at Stell, then back at Stoner. "Oh God, Stoner," she muttered, "I'm so sorry."

"Sorry won't get this door shut," Stell said.

Gwen gave an apologetic half-smile. "You're right."

"I'm always right," Stell said as she went for the door. "Let's move it."

They managed to close and bolt the door, and were halfway across the yard when the hail struck. Ice pellets the size of mothballs

66

pummelled the ground and rattled like a snare drum on the barn's tin roof. Stell peeled off her slicker and covered their heads. By the time they reached the back porch it was coming down in golf balls. The wind shrieked. Dust swirled and scoured the buildings and blew into their eyes. The rain hit from every direction. It pounded on the windows and blew under the door. It slammed against the trading post walls and flew beneath the porch roof.

Stell shepherded them inside. The temperature plummeted. They were cold and wet, and then the electricity went.

Stell and Stoner lit the hurricane lamps. Gwen stood in the corner and looked miserable.

"Come over here," Stell said, and held out her hand.

Gwen came to her reluctantly. "I'm sorry. I didn't..."

"Hell," Stell said. She grabbed a towel from the back of the bathroom door and rubbed Gwen's hair. "We all get wretched in these storms. I'd hate to hear what the horses would say if they could talk." She gave Gwen's hair a final rub and brushed it into shape with her fingers. "One thing to say for it, though, it takes you straight down to what's ailing you." She sat on the bench at the table and patted the seat beside her. "So, while Stoner makes us a fire—which I don't know why she hasn't already—what do you say you let the weight off that particular hurt?"

Stoner grabbed a load of wood and papers and got to work.

"It's just my grandmother," Gwen said. "I try not to think about it."

"Some things," Stell said firmly, "require a certain amount of thinking. You can do it now, or you can do it later. But until you've thought all the thoughts, it isn't going to let you go."

"I don't want to bother you with it," Gwen said.

"Well, now," Stell said, and slipped an arm around her. "We have a nice storm here, the electricity's out, Tom Drooley's under the bed, and Ted's up at First Mesa on mysterious business. Seems to me you have the perfect opportunity to take advantage of my years of experience."

Gwen sat miserably inside Stell's arm. "I don't know what to say."

"Good! You can listen."

Stoner got the fire going and leaned against the wall near the stove. The heat drew the water from her clothes and turned it to steam. Lightning ran from window to window. The storm slammed against the roof and hurled water at the glass. In the light from the kerosene lamps, the gray in Stell's hair shone brass.

67

"Seems to me," the older woman said, "there's some folks in this world who find it easier to love than hate. Ted's like that, I hope I am—even though more sophisticated types might call us fools—and I expect the same holds for you. And there are others—I won't go so far as to say they'd sooner hate than love, but they do spend an awful lot of time wanting things and people to be just so. Does that describe your grandmother?"

"Yes," Gwen said. "It does."

"The problem isn't what *you* are, it's what *she* is. And I'd be willing to bet she'd find fault with whoever you decide to love."

"She has," Gwen said. "But she was right about Bryan."

"Of course she was. That's why Nature made us in two forms—so some of us could be right half the time, and the rest the other half. The problem is, her kind of bigotry has a lot of company these days." She pulled Gwen close and took her hand. "What I hope you'll stay clear on in all of this, is that it's her that's in the wrong, not you. Don't go getting down on yourself for loving. There's a lot of hurting and a lot of hating going on in this world, and I think it's time the ones that do the hating start doing their share of the hurting."

Gwen began to cry.

"The time might come," Stell said as she stroked her head, "when you feel like you want to give up on her. You shouldn't feel guilty if that happens. Your job is to care for yourself, and Stoner, and all the other people you love. It's a fine thing for you to love your grandmother, but set yourself a limit. Because if she doesn't want your love, there's plenty of folks who do, and it'd be a shame to waste it on someone who's just going to throw it away."

Gwen put her arm around Stell's neck.

"I know it's real hard," Stell said, rocking her gently, "to change how you feel about someone you've grown up loving. But that's part of growing up, too. Dogs and babies go on loving the ones that treat them mean, because they can't help it. But when you get older you learn to be a little more selective." She kissed Gwen's cheek. "And that's enough folksy wisdom for one night. Stoner, get me a paper napkin before she blows her nose on my shirt."

Gwen laughed and looked up. "You think I'd do anything that tacky?"

"You might."

Stoner handed her a napkin.

Gwen wiped her nose and eyes. "Stell, I really appre—"

"Hold it," Stell said. "I don't want to hear that, it makes me uncomfortable."

"I know, but..."

"If you want to express your everlasting gratitude, go take a shower and help me with dinner." She plucked at her damp shirt. "Jesus, if it isn't wet dogs, it's wet dykes."

"Stell!" Stoner said, and collapsed laughing against the wall.

Stell glared at her. "You wouldn't win any fashion contest yourself, Madame. You get in that shower, too. Matter of fact, the two of you get in there together."

"How can we take a shower?" Stoner asked. "There's no electricity."

"You fixing to bathe?" Stell asked. "Or electrocute yourself?"

Gwen rolled her eyes in dismay.

The storm was moving away to the east, leaving behind a purple twilight. The rain had let up, falling now in a hard drizzle.

"I'll get clean clothes for us," Gwen started for the door.

"Look out for Dineh Wash," Stell called after her. "It gets real mean after a storm." She pulled a couple of knives from the utensil drawer and tossed Stoner a cabbage.

"Thanks, Stell," Stoner said. "Gwen really needed—"

"I told you I didn't want to hear that," Stell cut her off. "That knife sharp enough?"

Stoner touched the knife blade. "Sharp enough for brain surgery."

"Forgot to tell you," Stell said as she pulled a couple of onions from beneath the sink. "Smokey Flanagan called while you were out. Said to tell you he's sorry he missed you, but he'll try you again next week."

"How's he doing?" Stoner asked, trying to cut the cabbage into very thin slivers.

"You know Smokey. All he needs to keep him happy is a crusade."

Stoner smiled. "What is it this time?"

"Buffalo. Seems the Forest Service and the Government have come to a serious disagreement over what to about the Yellowstone buffalo. He's gone up to the Park to try and swing the Park Service over to his side." She scraped her chopped onion into a bowl and took another. "If he had his way, of course, he'd throw the tourists out and turn Teton and Yellowstone back to wilderness."

"That wouldn't do much for *your* business, would it?" Stoner asked.

"Well, I suppose not. But I have mixed feelings about it these days. Seems as if people are just getting meaner and more selfish."

Stoner glanced at her. "It scares me to hear you talk like that, Stell. You're usually so optimistic."

"Oh," Stell said with a shrug. "It's probably just a passing fancy. Shoot, I have everything I ever wanted and more than I ever thought I'd have. But every now and then I get to thinking about how I was as a kid—shy and awkward and lonely most of the time, scared of people, couldn't get along with anyone but animals... You gonna finish that cabbage, or just stand there with your mouth hanging open?"

"I'm sorry," Stoner said and got back to work. "I'd never thought of you that way."

"Yeah, I was like that a whole lot."

"What changed for you?"

"Life. Age. It all changes. I sometimes find myself forgetting I've grown up, feeling like sixteen again. Sweet Jesus, that was one miserable time. And the worst of it is, once it's gone it's too late to change it." She glanced up and reached for another onion. "Not that I have regrets, mind you. Still, I do feel for that kid I used to be."

Stoner nodded. "I know what you mean."

"Every now and then, when something good happens to me, I think to myself...why couldn't it have happened back then, when I really needed it? This sound like self-pity to you?"

"No."

"I wouldn't want it to. It's just life. They save the good stuff for the end. Kind of a screwed-up way to do business, if you ask me."

"I wish I'd known you back then," Stoner said.

Stell brushed her hair from her forehead with the back of her hand. "Shoot, I'd have been scared to death of you. I was scared to death of everyone."

"So was I."

"Then I'm sorry it didn't happen. Maybe next time around."

"Maybe."

"But I'll give you fair warning." Stell said, "I'm not coming back to this planet until folks learn some manners."

* * *

Stoner pounded on the bathroom door.

"What is it?" Gwen called.

"Are you going to be in there all night?"

"I might."

"Then I'm coming in." She pushed the door open. Steam billowed out. There was a transparent curtain on the shower, and a kerosene

70

lamp on the wash stand. Stoner stared at Gwen's naked body openly and appreciatively. "Stell says I smell like a mule," she said.

"I don't know what you expect me to do about it," Gwen replied.

Stoner grinned. "Stay put," she said as she stripped off her clothes. "Here comes Pig Pen."

Gwen reached for the soap, worked up a lather between her hands, and rubbed it over Stoner's face, her hair, her body. Her hands were warm and slippery.

Stoner took the soap, ran it over Gwen's body, then pressed their bodies together, smooth breasts against smooth breasts, smooth thighs against smooth thighs. She stroked her back, her hips. She bent down and stroked her legs.

Standing, she leaned against the shower wall and pulled Gwen to her, Gwen's back against her breasts, her buttocks cupped between her thighs and stomach. She soaped her hands again and slid them over and under Gwen's breasts.

Gwen sighed and leaned back against her.

She stroked her for a long time, the water sliding over and around them.

She felt Gwen's breathing quicken, felt Gwen's hands fumbling for her. She slipped one arm around Gwen's waist, and with her free hand found the warm softness between Gwen's legs, circling and touching and stroking and teasing until Gwen's body went rigid and she gasped and clutched at Stoner's arm.

"Stop," Gwen said without conviction. "What if...someone comes...?"

"Someone *is* coming," Stoner whispered, and stroked her harder.

"I mean...if we get caught...?"

"We won't get caught. Stell's on guard."

"*Stell!*"

Stell was in the kitchen, just beyond the door. She was singing at the top of her lungs.

"Oh, Jesus," Gwen said. Her body was trembling, her knees giving way.

Stoner held her up. "Jesus?" she teased with her words as she teased with her hand. "Is this some kind of religious experience?"

"Oh, God, Stoner, I'm coming out of my SKIN!"

"I don't think so," Stoner said, touching her harder, then lighter, stroking, teasing.

Gwen's back arched. She moaned softly, fingers digging into

Stoner's arm as surge after surge went through her. Stoner felt an answering surge in her own body. She pressed her back against the wall and locked her knees to keep from falling, and suddenly her body broke out in warm, damp tingling.

She felt her muscles go limp, felt Gwen go limp against her, became aware again of the sound of water pounding on the shower floor, the gurgle of water as it swirled down the drain.

Beyond the door, Stell was bellowing out *Rock of Ages*.

"Hey, Mrs. Perkins," Gwen shouted to her, "did anyone ever tell you you have a terrific singing voice?"

"Nope."

"I can see why."

Stell laughed and started in on *The Streets of Laredo*.

"Care for another round?" Stoner asked. "That song has about twenty verses."

Gwen touched her face and looked deep into her eyes. "Stoner, my love, has it occurred to you that sooner or later we'll run out of hot water, and we're going to have to go out there and face her?"

Stoner shrugged. "So what? It's darker than night out there."

Naturally, at that exact moment, the electricity came back on.

* * *

By midnight the storm was far to the east. Water still dripped intermittently from the bunkhouse roof, to be caught and swallowed by the ever-thirsty earth. Dineh Wash raged and tossed and rattled the smooth round rocks that lined its channel. The skies cleared. The Choochokan, the Pleides, sparkled overhead.

Siyamtiwa rolled the nearly-forgotten taste of tomatoes around on her tongue, sucked the sweet-tart-salty juice from her fingers, and wondered at the ways of Spirits who send a green-eyed *pahana* to do battle with a Skin-walker.

* * *

Hosteen Coyote prowled the base of Long Mesa.
His eyes glinted silver.

FIVE

Morning sparkled like fresh laundry hung on a line. The sky was clean, the air sweet, the dust washed and settled. The scattered desert plants shone with brilliant green. The buttes and mesas stood out in sharp relief, basking in the sun.

Stoner ran. Ran because it felt good, because the desert was beautiful, because she was happy, because she knew she would see Siyamtiwa again.

An eagle soared overhead as she trotted down the road, hugging a paper bag filled with sweet rolls and water and a thermos of hot coffee. The shadows lay deep in the gullies. The road was swept clean by the rain. There were no tracks in the dust but hers. She felt her feet strike the hard dirt, breathed the pure, light air, knew the steady pounding of her heart, the pull of muscles in her legs, and thought she could run like this forever.

The breeze ruffled her hair. The desert colors flowed past. The eagle drifted lazily, keeping pace with her. Her rhythm lifted her out of her body and into the air, higher and higher until she felt herself stretch out against the wind, her soul mingling with the wind's soul, with the eagle's soul, with the soul of the dust and rain and sacred mountains. Sounds rose in her throat, singing vowel sounds. She let them come, and offered them up to the morning.

Suddenly self-conscious, she came to a stop and was silent. From nearby echoed the same rhythmic chant, and the sound of slow drumming. She looked around, and realized she had reached the spot where she had seen Siyamtiwa yesterday. Where she had known, in her first thought of the morning, that she would see her today.

There was no one here. It's not as if we made a date, she reminded herself to stave off disappointment.

But I brought coffee, and breakfast. I was so sure...

She sat on the ground and poured herself a cup from the thermos, tore a piece from a sweet roll.

She probably thinks I'm not worth her time. She probably has more important things to do.

She took a sip of coffee and watched a lizard watching her.

Her shadow shortened. She watched it slip away from one pebble, then the next, and the next...

A thought took shape in her mind. If there's nobody here but me, who was drumming? Who was chanting with me? Maybe my imagination.

A magpie eyed her from a low, straggly bush. She tossed it a crumb of roll. It thought things over for several minutes, then hopped to the ground, snatched up the crumb, and flew off.

Well, pal, you've been stood up.

It made her sad, and a little empty. She got to her feet and brushed the dust from her jeans.

"So, Green-eyes."

A grin broke across her face.

The old woman stood at the bottom of the hill, arms folded beneath a light multi-colored blanket. Her white hair was parted down the middle and drawn into two long braids, one of which hung down her back, the other over her shoulder and across her breast. "Well," Siyamtiwa said with a laugh, "what you think? Do I look enough like a Hollywood Indian for you?"

"You look great."

The old woman held up one foot. "You don't think the tennis shoes spoil it?"

"I don't care. I'm glad to see you. I thought you weren't coming."

Siyamtiwa shrugged. "You know Indians, no sense of time."

Stoner held out her hand. Siyamtiwa grabbed it in both of hers and pulled herself up the hill.

She's so light, Stoner thought. Her bones must be hollow.

She took the blanket the old woman offered and spread it on the ground.

"What you got in that sack?" Siyamtiwa asked as she settled herself.

"Coffee and sweet rolls." She knelt and passed them.

Siyamtiwa looked them over carefully. "I gotta get soft stuff," she said. "Only got a couple of teeth left." She chose one and tore it into tiny pieces. "I always liked sweet things. People used to tease me when I was a girl."

"Is there anything else you need?" Stoner asked.

"You worry too much, Green-eyes." She took a long swallow of coffee from Stoner's cup and smacked her lips.

"I brought a second cup if you don't want to share mine."

"Indians are used to sharing," Siyamtiwa said. "Whites never left us enough to go around."

"I'm sorry."

Siyamtiwa grunted. A smile played at the corners of her eyes. "Did you say that to get me to apologize again?"

The old woman chuckled and poked Stoner with her bony elbow.

Stoner laughed.

"You have a nice laugh, *pahana.*"

She felt herself blush. "Thank you."

Siyamtiwa chewed thoughtfully for a while. "What happened to you yesterday?"

Stoner hesitated, believing for a second that something important had happened which Siyamtiwa knew about, but she, herself, had forgotten...and then realized it was only residual fear and guilt, compliments of a childhood spent with parents who laid traps to catch her in lies. "Not much," she said. "We did some errands in Beale, and there was a storm—but you probably know about that."

Siyamtiwa nodded. "This friend you visit, you like her a lot, eh?"

"Very much."

The old woman seemed to think on this for a long time. "And Hosteen Coyote, did he come around?"

"Not that I know of."

"Well, that's good."

"Siyamtiwa, have you ever met a man named Larch Begay?"

The old woman seemed to search her memory, then shook her head. "Lots of Begays around here. I don't know that one."

"He runs the gas station."

"Well, I don't need that very much." She chewed on a bit of sweet roll.

"I thought...if you're from around here, you might have heard..."

"I've been away. Long time away. Things change. Hard to explain. What about this Begay?"

"He gives me the creeps," Stoner said. She glanced over. "Do you know what that is, the creeps?"

Siyamtiwa nodded solemnly. "I know creeps."

"He showed us some jewelry he'd gotten from the Navajos by selling them whisky. Do you think I should report him?"

"Leave it alone, *pahana.* When the People get tired of this, they'll handle it their own way. They ain't gonna thank you for butting in."

"Yeah," Stoner said, "that's what I thought, but it makes me mad."

"The Spirits got their reasons. Maybe they got plans for this Begay." She shrugged and drew the empty tomato can from the folds of her skirt. "You want this back?"

"No, thanks. They're not returnable."

The old woman turned the can over and over in her hands and looked at it from every angle. "Maybe I'll keep things in this. Maybe make a little stove out of it."

"A stove?"

"Sure." With her fingernail, she traced a rectangle along the top rim. "Cut a door here, punch some holes in the bottom." She turned it upside down on the ground. "Now you got a little stove. Make a fire inside, maybe cook beans, make coffee on that."

Stoner picked it up and looked it over, fascinated. "That's really clever."

"Nothing wrong with that can, no point to throw it away."

Stoner sighed. "It doesn't seem right. We throw away so much…"

"Well," Siyamtiwa said, "we each got our ways." She touched Stoner's hand. "Now don't save all your old cans and bottles to dump on this old grandmother's doorstep. I don't need a hundred little stoves."

Stoner laughed. "I wouldn't do that."

"Jesus Way people do stuff like that. You're not Jesus Way?"

"I was raised Congregationalist, but I kind of fell away from it."

"Why do you fall away?"

"I don't know. I guess their God had too many strings attached."

Siyamtiwa nodded. "This Grandmother Hermione, do you follow her way?"

"She's not my grandmother," Stoner explained. "She's my aunt."

Siyamtiwa grunted. "Grandmother is a way of saying things, a word of respect. Don't you use the word like that?"

"I don't think so."

Siyamtiwa grunted again, eloquently.

"I could call you Grandmother Siyamtiwa if you like."

The old woman shook her head. "Better not, it might take all day. How come," she asked, abruptly changing the subject, "this Begay makes you creep?"

"There was something…" Stoner frowned. "I'm not sure, but when he looked at me, I felt he was reading my mind. Or trying to

76

put something in it. I guess that sounds crazy..."

"Not crazy."

"And when I was in his house, I couldn't breathe. I felt as if I were evaporating. And I got so tired..."

"You stay away from this Begay," Siyamtiwa said sharply.

"Why?"

"I think he is dangerous for you. I don't like what I see here."

Stoner shook her head. "I don't understand."

"The things you notice, maybe they mean something." She sat quietly for a moment, sucking her cheek. "I would like to see this Begay."

"I could introduce you."

The old woman raised a hand. "There is another kind of seeing."

"Like reading his aura?"

"What is aura?"

"It's...it's kind of like the energy you put out. Sometimes you can tell what a person's like, you know, on a spiritual..."

Siyamtiwa cut her off impatiently. "Did you read this Begay's aura?"

"I didn't have to exactly. I mean, it sort of comes at you, all thick and tarry." She refilled the coffee cup. "But I'm not very good at that sort of thing."

"I think that is good luck for me. I think maybe you would read my spirit energy and not like it."

"Oh no," Stoner said quickly. "I know I'd like it."

"No tarry?"

"Not at all."

The old woman stood up abruptly. "Time for you to go. Your friend is waiting for you. She wants you to go to Wupatki Ruins. I think that is a good idea. Maybe something happens there. Meanwhile, I will try to read this Begay."

"Wait a minute," Stoner said, scrambling to her feet. "How do you know...?"

Siyamtiwa reached up and lifted a necklace from around her neck and placed it on Stoner's. "You take this."

She held it up in the palm of her hand. The necklace was made of small striped seeds, interspersed with rough black beads. "What is it?" she asked.

Siyamtiwa shrugged. "A trinket, something for tourists. Maybe good luck for you." She turned away. "Maybe you will need good luck."

"I don't understand," Stoner said. She stared, mesmerized, at the necklace. "Why would I need good luck?"

"All *pahana* need good luck. Their Spirits aren't friendly."

"But why me?"

The old woman put the thermos of coffee and remaining sweet rolls into the paper bag. "Questions. Maybe I shouldn't call you Green-eyes. Maybe I should call you Many Questions."

"It's just...I want to know things."

"You think any old person walking on the desert knows more than you? Everything you need to know, Green-eyes, comes through the *kopavi* ." She patted the top of Stoner's head. "This. The open door where the spirits come in. If you keep the *kopavi* open, you don't need anyone to tell you things. If you let it go shut, nothing you hear will do you any good." She tucked the paper bag under her arm. "You think about that. Maybe next time I see you you'll know something, eh?"

"Am I going to see you again?"

"If Masau doesn't take me first, and I don't think that's gonna happen." She held out the paper bag. "I gotta bring this back to you or you go home and say all Indians are thieves."

"I'd never say a thing like that," Stoner said indignantly.

"You shame your race," Siyamtiwa said. "No wonder you ran away from home."

She felt as if someone had punched her in the stomach. "How did you know...?"

The old woman ignored her. "You're gonna like Wupatki." She turned and walked away, her tennis shoes barely leaving a trace in the dust.

"Thank you for the necklace," Stoner called after her.

The old woman waved without turning around.

In a few minutes she was out of sight.

* * *

"I don't get it," Stoner said. "She knew you'd want to do this. How could she know that?"

"It's probably a popular tourist attraction," Gwen said.

"This place?" She looked around at the nearly-deserted parking lot.

Gwen stretched and arched her back. "I feel as if I've been run over by a sack of potatoes. We've got to stop riding the back roads."

"It's *not* a popular tourist attraction," Stoner persisted.

78

Gwen looked around. "You're right."

"So how did she know we were coming here?"

"It's a mystery." She took off the cowboy hat she had borrowed from Stell and dropped it on Stoner's head. "If you refuse to wear sunglasses, at least cover your head."

Stoner adjusted the hat. "So how did she?"

"I mentioned a lot of places, Stoner. Wupatki, Sunset Crater, Petrified Forest, Meteor Crater—everything within a half day's drive from Spirit Wells. You're the one who chose Wupatki."

"It was the first one you mentioned."

Gwen looked at her and shook her head, smiling. "Dearest, I think you're losing your grip."

"Don't you feel it?"

"Feel what?"

Uncertain, bewildered, she glanced around. It was only the desert, strange and familiar all at once. Like a place visited in dreams. Like a place seen and forgotten. Like a place she knew, somewhere deep inside where there were no words. Like...home.

It felt like something crawling under her skin.

"Let's look around," she said quickly.

"Stoner, are you okay?"

She forced a smile. "Sure." She started up the walk to the Visitors' Center. "Get us a map, will you?"

She watched Gwen at the counter, exchanging a few words with the Park Ranger, as she always exchanged a few words with cashiers, sales clerks, meter maids, postal employees, and parking lot attendants. Wupatki lay behind her, out of sight unless she turned around. She was afraid to turn around.

It's a *ruin*, she told herself. A pile of fallen-down, uninhabited buildings. Probably not even very interesting, except to archaeologists and such. Ruins are the safest places on earth. Especially nice, sunny, National Park-ized ruins like Wupatki. You want to be afraid? Go to New York. To Boston. To Providence, Rhode Island, even. Not to Wupatki, Arizona.

"Ready?" Gwen asked.

"What did you find out?"

"She's from Nevada. This is her first year here. Last summer she was at Cedar Breaks. She'll be staying here over the winter, and isn't looking forward to it but it'll give her time to think about whether she wants to marry Michael. I recommended against it."

Stoner grinned. "About Wupatki."

"It's a National Monument, not a National Park. For our purposes, the distinction is irrelevant. It was occupied by the Sinagua Indians from 1120 to 1210 A.D., and nobody is certain why they left. Which is ominous. There are about eight hundred ruins in the Monument—some Sinagua, some Anasazi. The building blocks are Moencopi sandstone. It seems to have been a town of some importance, having both an amphitheater and a ball court. The New York of its day." She held the door open. "Shall we?"

Wupatki looked, at first glance, like a pile of giant Lego blocks, surrounded by sandstone dust and scaly chips of rock. The edge of the lava flow from Sunset Crater lay just beyond, dotted with saltbush and Mormon tea. The ruin itself was roofless, some walls fallen in, a jumble of doorways and angles. The rooms were tiny, low-ceilinged, and practically windowless.

"According to the guide book," Gwen said, "during its hey-day, as many as two-fifty to three-hundred people lived in this. I wonder if they had rent control."

The light, Stoner thought. How did they bear the light? It was everywhere, bleaching the sky, pounding at her from all directions. She felt a pressure behind her eyes and across the bridge of her nose. Like the onset of a sinus headache. Except she didn't get sinus headaches...

Anxiety fluttered moth wings against her fingertips.

"What do you think?" Gwen was asking.

Think? Can you really think about this? How can you think about light, and sky, and...

A large, flat disk detached itself from the sun and hurtled toward her. A face. Horizontal lines for eyes and mouth. Vertical lines like tears beneath the eyes. Bright, blinding colors—red and white and black and yellow...

She covered her face with her hands, felt a jolt of electricity as the object passed through her.

"Stoner?"

"Did you see that?" Stoner asked.

"See what?"

"That...thing?"

"I didn't see anything." Gwen touched her arm. "Are you sure you're all right?"

Stoner nodded. "It must have been an optical illusion. The sun."

"Want a drink of water?"

"I'm fine. It's gone." But it wasn't gone. The *feel* of it wasn't gone. The *feel* of it was all around. In the sky, in the ground, in the crumbling sandstone...

Once, when she was a child, she had stayed up late on Christmas Eve. Long after the house was silent, long after her parents were asleep, long after the traffic no longer moved on the packed-snow streets...

There had come such a stillness, a calm, a sense of waiting for something wonderful...as if the universe had stopped to listen, to hear the sound of Creation.

She could almost hear it now. In the sky, in the ground, in the crumbling sandstone...

"This is a holy place," she said in a whisper.

Gwen knelt in the center of the room, examining a firepit. "In that case, it can't be New York."

"I mean it," Stoner said. "I don't think we should be here."

Gwen glanced up at her. "Want to go?"

"No, but..." Something didn't want her to go. There was some-thing she had to do. "Don't you feel it?"

"I'm not tuned in to these things," Gwen said as she brushed the red dust from her knees. "I wish I were, but the Spirits seem to find me lacking in some way."

"Are you being facetious?"

"I'm completely serious."

"Well, I wish they'd find *me* lacking."

"I'd think they would," Gwen said, "since you don't even believe in them."

"I believe..."

"If you really believed in Spirits," Gwen laughed gently, "you wouldn't look so embarrassed every time the subject came up."

From beyond a hill off to the side there came an explosion of raucous voices. Stoner looked up sharply. "What's over there?"

Gwen consulted the map. "According to this, a ball court."

"Softball?"

"It doesn't say, only that the games had religious significance."

"Gosh," she said. "A dyke softball diamond."

Gwen laughed. "Now that I've come out, will I have to play softball?"

"The urge can strike at any..."

IT ISN'T A BALL COURT! The thought slammed into her con-sciousness.

IT'S A SACRED PLACE. THEY'RE DEFILING A SACRED PLACE.

Another burst of girlish shrieks and boyish curses reached them.

"Sounds like Mets fans," Gwen said.

They have to be stopped. Before it happens again.

"Stoner?" Gwen said.

The last time it happened...

"Stoner."

The last time, the rain died, and the land died, and the People died, and the world came to an end. The last time...

She took off running down the path.

As she rounded the corner, she saw it. Two waist-high walls, like cupped hands, open at either end. She stared at it, fascinated, and knew that what was happening here was wrong...

Terrible...

A violation of sacred things.

This place was no place for games. It was a place of mystery and secrets, of sacrifices and silent prayers. Here Spirits lived below the ground by day, to rise with the moon and restore the balance man had upset. Here the People met. All the People. The Old Ones and the New Ones. The tribes that had gone, and the tribes yet to come. It all spiralled to this place...

...this place where Whites were playing.

"Stoner!" Gwen called sharply.

She stopped in her tracks.

"Dearest, what do you think you're doing?"

Stoner gestured toward the ball court. "I have to break that up."

"I don't think that's a good idea," Gwen said. "You're outnumbered."

Stoner shook her off.

As she crested the rise, she saw them. A family of six, all looking remarkably alike, between the ages of twenty-five and forty. Assorted spouses. A mother who sat to one side guarding a large wicker picnic hamper and drinking something from a thermos. The father had organized the troops into a rollicking game of touch football, family versus in-laws. They cavorted on the field, tossing a chartreuse Nerf ball. They probably wouldn't leave home without it. Probably carried it on the dashboard like a plastic Jesus. If it was left behind, they probably went back for it, no matter how far.

"God damn it!" she shouted from the top of the hill. "Stop that!"

The game came to a screeching halt. They all looked at her.

"This isn't the Super Bowl. It's Holy ground."

"Yeah?" One of the women stepped forward. She was short, stocky, sweaty, and obviously annoyed. "You a Ranger?"

"No."

"Then buzz off."

Her rage exploded. *"The world was not created for your personal pleasure !"*

"It's a free country," Stocky-sweaty said.

"Want to bet?" She headed for the ball court.

Gwen jumped her from behind. "Let the Rangers handle it, Stoner."

Stoner shook her off. "Why do they have to take *everything*?"

"Calm down."

Anger coursed through her like fire. "It never stops. Killing. Taking. Destroying..."

Gwen held her shoulders. "There's nothing you can do about it, Stoner."

"It has to stop. Right now. *It has to stop!* "

"All right," Gwen said. "We'll find a Ranger..."

"You don't understand."

"I do. Really. But you can't ..."

"It's been like this for three hundred years, *Three hundred years.* "

"I know. Please let it go for now. We'll find a Ranger..."

She tried to pull away.

"Stoner," Gwen said firmly, "there are at least twelve of them down there. There is one of you. Now let it go."

She took a deep breath, forced her fists to unclench, forced her heartbeat to slow, forced her rage to subside. She looked down into the ball court and sent a few dark thoughts in their direction.

"You okay?" Gwen asked.

Stoner nodded. "I cursed them with the McTavish Curse."

"And what is that?"

"For sudden and complete enlightenment. The McTavish Curse has sent people to the brink of suicide."

Gwen smiled and brushed Stoner's hair back from her forehead. "Want to get out of here?"

The game seemed to be breaking up. One of the women—an in-law, she guessed—had decided to drop out. Pressure was exerted on all sides. The woman held her ground—or rather, her stomach—and indicated cramps. With great reluctance, the family resigned themselves and stood about with their arms hanging at their sides.

Stocky-sweaty had a sudden burst of inspiration. "Yo!" she shouted in Stoner's direction. "Either of you play touch football?"

Stoner stared down at her, her mind turning to white noise.

"Are you seriously inviting us to play?" Gwen called.

"Yeah, why not?"

83

"Because we're on our way to report you to the Park Service."

Stocky-sweaty shrugged. "So come play football instead."

Gwen grabbed Stoner's wrist and dragged her back along the path, saying, "Get me away before I do serious damage."

*　　*　　*

The road to Lomaki Ruin was nearly deserted, the last mile unimproved dirt. They decided to walk it. "We're pretty vulnerable out here." Gwen said. "I hope The Family doesn't catch us."

"Don't worry," Stoner said. "I fixed them."

Gwen stopped walking and looked at her. "You what?"

"Stopped them."

"How?"

"It doesn't matter, I just stopped them."

"Stoner McTavish," Gwen said in a menacing tone, "what did you do?"

"Nothing much. I just bent the exhaust pipe on their van. They should be breaking down just about now."

Gwen's eyes widened. "You did what?"

"Bent the exhaust pipe." She shrugged. "Only a little."

"How do you know it was their van? It could have been anybody's van."

"Are you kidding? The thing was littered with sports equipment and empty beer cans. They even had back-up Nerf balls. And the bumper stickers. 'Go Mets.' 'Nuke Jane Fonda.' 'I Heart Pit Bulls.' " She laughed. "If it wasn't them, it was someone just as worthy."

Gwen shook her head. "One of these days you're going to get us into serious trouble."

"I'm working on it."

Dust had begun to build up in the air. It softened the edges of the distant mountains. The ground underfoot was black with volcanic ash. The sun was bright, the shadows impenetrable. Everything was still. And silent.

The crumbling wall was warm and hard. From the slight rise where she stood, she could see across miles of valley. Smudges of green marked the spots where precious rain collected, or ground water seeped to the surface. The ruins of smaller pueblos lay scattered about, a day's walk distant, seeming close enough to touch. Several yards behind the ruin, the earth's surface had cracked. Gwen wandered off to inspect it.

Stoner sat in the dirt and rested against the sandstone wall. She closed her eyes. The sounds of long-past life came to her—the scrape of grinding stones as they crushed the dried corn kernels, low talking voices, water splashing in an earthen jar, brittle rustle of reeds being woven into mats, the clatter of digging sticks against the pebbly ground.

She felt the summer's driving heat, the bitter wind that blew the snow across unbroken deserts. The icy fall of silver rain. The prickle of rough wool blankets. Felt the wonder of bright parrot feathers, traded up from the south. The hard obsidian arrowheads, black as death. The smell of sagebrush after the rain. The sharp, crusty odor of earth during the years when the rains never fell. Heard the tinkle of pottery shards discarded on the trash pile.

They buried the dead children under the floors of the houses, so their souls could enter the bodies of babies yet unborn. But the People had to move on, and the homeless souls stayed behind.

She could sense them now, whispering around the doorways, slipping through shadows. They played on air currents, and made dust devils to ride across the desert. Curious but shy, they came close to her, and touched her hair and arms. She tried to sit very still, barely breathing, not wanting to frighten the little homeless ones. Giggling, they played peek-a-boo among the shrubs and rocks. A few of the braver ones danced up to her as she pretended to sleep. She opened her eyes and sent them laughing and scattering like sparrows. A baby, brown-skinned and black-eyed, crawled between her knees and stared up at her, sucking its thumb. She winked at it, and they laughed together.

She sensed the Old Ones watching. Waiting.

Waiting for...what?

They want something from me, she thought.

Unconsciously, she reached up, touched Siyamtiwa's necklace.

The Old Ones drew closer.

She looked down at the beads. She hadn't noticed the carvings before. Each one different. Bear and badger claws. Clouds that rained. Stalks of corn. Snakes and birds and spirals and dog-like animals. Arrows, rainbows and hump-backed flute players. Tiny, intricate carvings. Too small, it seemed, for human hands to make.

These are the marks of the People, she felt the Old Ones say. The People need your help.

Me?

When the time comes, you will know what has to be done.

But...

"Hey." It was Gwen. "Wake up. You'll get sunstroke."

She opened her eyes and looked up. On a wall above her head sat a small, long-tailed lizard. Its eyes were silver.

She shivered and felt fear.

"What's the matter?" Gwen asked.

"That lizard. Look at its eyes."

Gwen looked. "Seem like ordinary, garden-variety lizard eyes to me."

"They're silver."

Gwen looked again. "I can't see it. Must be the angle you're looking from."

Or maybe it only shows the silver eyes to me.

"Gwen," she said, "do you believe in ghosts?"

"In the theological sense?"

"In any sense."

Gwen sat down beside her. "I guess I do. Why?"

"Do you ever have the feeling there are...human souls around?"

"My father? My ex-husband?" Gwen shuddered. "I really need *that* ."

"Not like that..." She groped for words. "Like maybe souls that just hang around being helpful. Watching, sort of."

"It's a comforting thought."

"Well," Stoner said, "I think there are a few hanging around here."

Gwen looked over her shoulder. "This place is weird."

"You feel it, too?"

"I feel we're not alone. Should we be frightened?"

Stoner shook her head. "How come you can accept things like this, and I have such a hard time with it?"

"I'm Welsh. We practically invented mysticism."

Stoner pressed her fingertips to her temples. "There's something they want me to do."

"Well, do it," Gwen said as she got up, "and let's hit the trail."

Stoner pulled herself to her feet. "Are you afraid?"

"You bet. Afraid we'll miss dinner."

When they reached the car, she looked back. Lomaki Ruin seemed to glow and throb in the slanting light.

* * *

It was nearly dusk by the time they reached the trading post. A small circle of Indian women in light plaid cotton dresses lounged on the porch drinking sodas from the machine. One of the youngest women, a girl of about fourteen, got up and approached the truck.

"Are you Stoner?"

"That's right."

"Mrs. Perkins asked would you look after the store? She's not feeling so good."

Apprehension gripped her stomach. "What's wrong?"

The young woman shrugged. "She didn't say. Just that she was going to lie down for a little."

"Oh, God. Gwen, take over." She left the motor running and raced into the house.

Stell was drinking water by the kitchen sink, her feet bare, a light cotton blanket tossed over her shoulders. Her face was gray, her hair stringy and lifeless. There were dark pockets under her eyes.

"Stell, what's the matter?"

Stell looked up, her eyes glassy and a little out of focus. "Calm down," she said with a faint smile. "I'm just tired. Too much horsing around last night."

"You look *awful*."

"Where'd you get your manners, girl? You don't go around telling folks they look awful."

"But you *do* ."

Stell refilled her water glass. "Thank you very much."

"You should lie down."

"I just got up."

"Come on, Stell." She shoved her toward the bedroom door. "If you feel as bad as you look…"

"Now that you mention it," Stell said, "I do feel kinda like something the cat dragged in and wouldn't eat."

"What is it?"

Stell drained her water glass. "We can rule out premenstrual tension. Beyond that, it's anybody's guess."

"I'm going to get you to a doctor."

"Whoa," Stell said, and put a hand on her sleeve. "This isn't Boston, kid. It's a forty-mile drive to Beale, which has no doctor, and another twelve to Holbrook. I think we should wait and see what develops."

"At least lie down, okay?"

"Gladly." She put the glass on the lamp table and stretched out on the bed. "Lordy, it's cold in here. Get a couple of blankets out of the bureau, would you, Stoner?"

Frantically, she pawed though the drawers, found the blankets, and spread them over Stell. She touched her face. Her skin was dry as paper and hot.

"You're burning up."

"Figured."

Stoner sat beside her. "Isn't there anything I can do?"

"I'll be all right," Stell said, and patted her hand. "It's probably just a summer cold."

"Sure." She toyed with Stell's fingers. "Where's Ted?"

"He rode over to the Lomahongvas' with Tomás. Their grandmother died last night. Had to get the coroner from Holbrook. Dealing with Anglo law, it helps if there's someone around they know." Her voice trailed off. Her eyes drifted shut.

"He left with you feeling like this?"

"Didn't feel like this when he left. Not this bad." She opened her eyes. "Heck of a thing to do to you on your vacation."

"That doesn't matter." She massaged Stell's hand. "Are you sure I can't do anything? Get you some aspirin?"

"Already did that." Her eyes drifted shut again. "Don't know why I'm so sleepy."

"Because you're sick, idiot," Stoner said gently. She tucked the blankets around the woman's shoulders, pulled the blinds, and refilled the water glass. By the time she had returned to the bedroom, Stell was asleep.

She put the glass down and stood for a moment, looking at her. Please, Stell, don't let it be serious. If anything happened to you...

Don't be ridiculous, she told herself fiercely. It's a summer cold, like she said. It isn't...

Stell stirred beneath the covers. "Dinner."

"We'll take care of it. Lucky for you you've got two able-bodied women around. You know how helpless men are in a crisis."

"Guests."

"Family, Stell. Remember? If you're going to think of us as guests, I'll tell Gwen to be polite to you. And, lady, you ain't seen polite until you've been on the receiving end of that one's Southern charm."

Stell's mouth twitched into a smile. "Chili."

"I take it chili is on the menu. Or is that a comment on our early autumn?" The inside of her head trembled in a high-pitched whine.

"Talk too much," Stell mumbled.

"You're absolutely right. If you need anything, throw this glass at the door. I'll check on you later."

Gwen was in the store, talking with the Indian girl. She looked up as Stoner came in. "How's Stell?"

"She looks terrible." She punched her hands into her back pockets to keep them from trembling. "She's asleep."

The Indian girl shot Stoner a knowing, penetrating glance.

"Fever?"

Stoner nodded.

"Skin gray and dry?"

"Very."

"Not good," the girl said.

"What do you mean?"

"I think you know."

Stoner shook her head. "No, I don't."

"Ya Ya sickness."

"This is Rose Lomahongva," Gwen explained. "She says her grandmother just died of it."

"Stell told me. I'm sorry to hear it." Stoner held out her hand. "Stoner McTavish."

The girl gripped her hand without shaking it, exactly the way Siyamtiwa had. "Yes," she said.

"Yes?"

"We know about you." Abruptly, she turned back to Gwen. "As soon as the Anglos leave, we will have our celebration."

"Death is a happy thing for you, then?" Gwen asked.

"My grandmother was an old woman. Now she's with her friends. Yes, it is a happy thing. Why not? We'll miss her, but to ask her to stay here for us wouldn't be right." She frowned thoughtfully. "We're going to need a lot of food. If you have trouble here, maybe we should hitch into Beale to shop."

"Tell you what," Gwen said, "when you're ready, give me a list of what you need and I'll take the truck in for it. Something tells me Whites are treated better than Indians in that town."

A smile lit Rose Lomahongva's broad face. "We have a couple of days. People have to come from a long way off. We'll see how things are, okay?"

"Okay," Gwen said. "But don't you hesitate. Stell says they even have different prices for Whites and Indians."

"Well," Rose said, "that's how it is with them. I'll get these old ladies out of here." She went to the door, said a few words in Hopi. The women got up silently and filed off toward Long Mesa. Rose Lomahongava followed them.

"You're not going to believe this," Gwen said, "but when they saw how Stell looked, these women came over here to make sure no one broke in before we got back. They've been sitting there all afternoon. She's really bad, huh?"

Stoner nodded. "I haven't seen anyone look that awful in a long time." She ran her thumb nail along the edge of the counter. "I'm scared, Gwen. It happened so fast."

"Hey," Gwen said, "it might not be serious. Maybe she always looks worse than she feels when she's sick. When my grandmother gets a cold, you'd think it was the Black Plague."

"Not Stell."

"You don't know that, Stoner."

"And what about what Rose said?"

"Frankly, several things Rose said made no sense whatsoever to me. *You* know what's wrong with Stell? *They* know about you? Do you have any idea what that's about?"

Stoner shook her head. She couldn't think about it now. "Gwen, I have a bad feeling about this."

Gwen squeezed her hand. "Let's not go off half-cocked. Ted can tell us more when he gets home. For all we know, she might be up and dancing the *pax de deux* from *Swan Lake* by then."

* * *

But she wasn't.

By the time Ted got home, she was worse, her skin hotter and dryer. When she tried to drink water, her hands were too weak to hold the glass.

Stoner held it for her, and gritted her teeth to keep from screaming.

Ted watched for a while, then tightened his jaw and went behind the barn with a Coleman lantern and started restacking the wood pile into a perfect rectangle.

By the time dinner was over, which didn't take long since no one felt like eating, she was drifting in and out of sleep. She refused a bowl of chili, even refused a slice of bread and butter, and muttered something about 'getting up in a while and fixing myself a bite'. Her fever hovered around one hundred and three degrees. She asked for more blankets.

Gwen brewed her hot lemonade with brandy, an old family remedy, which she hated but it made her sweat so that she was more comfortable and her fever went down a little.

She agreed to eat canned soup, after Stoner convinced her it was easier to do than try to win a battle of wills with *her*. It seemed like a major victory, until Stoner remembered that, for Stell, a light breakfast consisted of eggs, bacon, juice, and pancakes, with sour dough biscuits on the side.

The effort seemed to tire her more.

Ted washed the dishes, one dish at a time, scraping, soaping,

90

rinsing, drying, putting away before he reached for the next. Gwen said it had crossed her mind to make coffee, but if she had to watch him wash one more cup they'd have to cart her away in a rubber U-Haul.

Tom Drooley crawled under Stell's bed and refused to come out, even when they tried to bribe him with last night's chicken.

Stoner mostly sat beside the bed and held Stell's hand and tried to make her body hard and frozen inside so she could do what she had to do. Every now and then, when she couldn't stand it any more, she got up and wandered—through the kitchen to the sitting room, into the store, back to the kitchen. After about ten minutes out of Stell's sight, she'd find herself in a panic and rush back to the bedroom.

"Darnedest thing," Stell murmured after one of her wanders, "every time you come back in, I feel better."

She knew it was a lie.

Ted decided to balance the books. Gwen took one look at what he was doing and allowed as how he was going to make a total mess, and talked him into a game of gin.

Around midnight, it seemed they might as well go to bed. Stoner thought about moving into the guest room, to be close by. But Gwen pointed out that, if Ted were going to get any sleep at all, it'd have to be in there.

They all agreed Gwen was the only one capable of rational thought.

The last thing Stoner did before she left for the bunkhouse was give Stell a backrub, which Stell declared—weakly—had prolonged her life by a good five years, thank you, and fell asleep. Stoner sat by her for a while, touching her hot, tight, skin, watching for each breath. She couldn't shake the idea that Stell's life was being measured, not in years, but in hours.

She pulled herself together, kissed Stell's forehead, arranged the blankets, whispered, "I love you, Stell, " and left.

She walked slowly back to the bunkhouse through the cold night.

She didn't see the coyote.

The coyote saw her.

Around two in the morning, she gave up trying to sleep. There was a light in the kitchen. She could see Ted's silhouette, hunched over the table. Gwen had finally drifted off. Carefully, she slipped out of bed, eased her feet into her boots, and picked her way back between the white-washed rocks.

Ted was fully dressed and staring into a cup of cold, oily coffee. He glanced up. His eyes were bleary and red-rimmed.

"How is she?" Stoner asked in a low voice.

He shook his head.

She peeked through the bedroom door. In the dim light, she could barely make out the rise and fall of Stell's chest as she breathed. Her skin was even more ashen than before. Her hands, moving restlessly along the edge of the blanket as she slept, looked like birds' claws, the fingers long and bony, the skin between translucent, and loose as webbing.

She poured herself a cup of coffee and sat down at the table. "You should try to sleep, Ted. You look worse than Larch Begay."

He ran his hand over his cheeks and chin. His beard stubble sounded like corn husks.

Stoner sipped her coffee and shuddered. "I've had bad coffee in my time," she said, trying to cheer him up, "but this belongs in Ripley's *Believe It or Not.*"

He looked at her pleadingly. "What's wrong with her?"

"I don't know."

"It's like someone went and sucked all the life out of her."

She stood up. "I hate to hurt your feelings, but I can't drink this straight."

As she was returning the milk carton to the refrigerator, she heard a low sound—a hiccupping sound like a gas motor that won't catch. She turned.

Ted sat with his face in his hands, sobbing.

It tied her stomach in knots.

She went to him, touched his shoulder. "Ted."

"I don't know what to do," he choked.

She put her arms around him. He cried into her shoulder. "Yeah," she said. "Stell's a pretty neat lady."

"I gave her a hard time about young Ted," he mumbled. "Jesus, wish I hadn't."

Stoner stroked his hair. "The way I heard it, she gave you a pretty rough time, too."

He wasn't listening. "And Smokey Flanagan. The Ranger back home. When he first came around, I was real jealous. I could see he loved her and she loved him. It made me mean. I didn't care if she slept with him, I just didn't want her to love him." He ground his knuckles into his eyes. "Shit, Stoner, I was a real son-of-a-bitch about that."

"It's okay, Ted."

92

"Wouldn't talk to her, wouldn't listen to him."

"Stell told me all about that," Stoner said. "It's in the past."

"All it meant was," he rambled on, ignoring her, "Stell's got room in her heart for a lot of folks." Tears spilled from his eyes and trickled through his beard stubble. "That woman's got room in her heart for the whole human race. I'm so damn grateful she married me."

"She married you because she loves you. You don't have to be grateful for that."

He twisted his hands around his coffee mug. "She wanted a daughter, and all I gave her was boys."

"For God's sake, Ted, that wasn't anybody's fault."

His chest and shoulders shook with little jerking spasms. "She works so damn hard at that lodge, and I can't even give her woman-talk. Jesus, I wish I wasn't a man."

"All right," Stoner said firmly. "Now you've passed best. Get a grip on yourself."

He straightened his back and fumbled for a handkerchief.

"Stell loves you the way you are. I don't know why, since your mind works in mysterious ways, but she does."

He gave her a weak, watery smile. "That sounds like something she'd say."

"I need your help with this, Ted."

"Let me have a minute," he said. He went to the sink, splashed water on his face, took a few deep breaths. "Damn. I haven't been right since we went on that marriage encounter weekend."

Stoner couldn't help laughing.

"You and Gwen ever get in trouble, stay away from them things." He shook the water from his hair. "Jesus."

She glanced toward the bedroom, where Tom Drooley had grown sufficiently curious to stick his nose out from under the bed. "Ted, do you have any idea what's wrong with her? Did anything happen while we were away?"

"She was fine this morning. After you gals left, I went out back and did some work for a while. When I came in for lunch she was lying on the bed. She said she was just tired. It wasn't like her, but I didn't think much of it, what with the heat and all. Then when Rose and Tomás came by about their grandma, she said she was all right."

"Well, she'd do that."

"I figured maybe she'd got bit by a spider or something, but she claimed not."

"She might not have noticed," Stoner suggested.

"I thought of that. Checked her over, didn't find anything. Besides, the poisonous insects we got out here, one bites you, you sure as hell know about it." He blew his nose. "Shit, Stoner, men are constructed all wrong for this kind of thing. Don't know what to do about trouble we can't punch in the face."

"You're doing all right." Something occurred to her. She hesitated to ask it, but… "Rose Lomahongva mentioned Ya Ya sickness. Do you know anything about it?"

He shook his head. "No more than you do. Think there's anything to it?"

"I don't know…" She heard Stell stir, and went to stand in the bedroom doorway.

"Little Bear?"

"Right here."

"Don't believe that marriage encounter story," Stell said, barely audible. "He's always been foolish."

She went over to touch her face. "How are you feeling, Stell?"

"Like sand blowing away in the wind. Think I'm in trouble, Little Bear."

That made up her mind. She went back to the kitchen. "We're getting her out of here."

"She's too weak to move."

"Well, she's not getting any better. She *won't* get any better."

"Moving her might—"

"Damn it, Ted," she said angrily. "This doesn't make sense. That woman needs help, and she needs it now. And all we've done is stand around and feel pitiful. If you won't do anything, I will."

She grabbed Stell's jacket and the truck keys from the coat hook by the back door, and slammed out.

Gwen was running down the path. "I heard shouting. Did something happen…?"

"Ted's frozen. Stell's fading. I'm taking her to Holbrook, and if he wants to stop me he can get a court order."

"Right," Gwen said, and shoved open the kitchen door.

By the time she had started the truck, emptied the front seat of trash and litter, and backed out of the barn, Ted stood on the porch with Stell in his arms. He opened the truck door and slid her inside. "You stay here," he said abruptly. "Gwen's calling the hospital so they'll be ready for us. I'll phone you as soon as I know anything."

Tom Drooley bounded into the truck bed. Stoner dragged him out and leaned in the window. "Stell…"

"She's unconscious," Ted said as he rammed the truck into gear.

94

The rattle of the receding motor was swallowed up in the night.

She sat at the table, afraid to look across the room to where Stell's rumpled bed lay just beyond the door.

Not Stell. Please, God, not Stell.

"They're waiting for her," Gwen said as she hung up the phone in the sitting room. "God only knows what they call medical care out here, but I'll bet it's better than the assembly lines we have back home."

She cleared Ted's cup from the table and straddled a chair. "Hey." She tugged lightly at Stoner's sleeve. "It's going to be all right."

"Is it?"

"I know it. Pisces are never wrong about things like this."

Stoner forced as smile. "Sure."

"I mean it. Nobody just ups and dies, here one minute, gone the next."

"Ted thought it might be an insect bite, but she'd be dead by now, wouldn't she?"

"Absolutely."

"Go on back to bed if you want," Stoner said, her eyes drifting to the bedroom door. "It'll be a while before we hear anything."

"I guess I'll stay up." Gwen looked around the room. "Too bad Stell's such a good housekeeper. If we were home, I'd pass the time waxing the floor and cleaning the oven."

A chilly draft reminded her that they hadn't bothered to light the fire. She got up, crumpled the morning newspaper, and tossed on a few sticks of kindling. Matches. She spotted them on the bedroom bureau.

She hesitated.

"I'll get them," Gwen said.

Stoner shook her head and forced herself to go into the bedroom. It smelled of camphor and pine, and very faintly of yeast. Stell's flannel shirt was tossed over the back of a chair. She touched it, stroked it, picked it up and buried her face in it.

She felt sick, and frightened down to her bones.

Gwen took the shirt from her and held it out. "Put it on," she said.

She slipped into the sleeves and buttoned it. It made Stell seem closer. "Gwen, I'm sorry about this…"

"Oh, for God's sake," Gwen said. She took Stoner's hands. "I'm with you for better or worse, my love. And if that means sitting through the night with you until we find out what ails that crazy lady, well...I'm pretty fond of her myself. And I know, as surely as I've ever known anything, she's going to be all right."

She thought of Ted, driving through the lonely night, with nothing to keep him company but fear.

*   *   *

The sun was coming up. It touched the clouds with pink and turned them to cotton candy. Birds sang their songs to Talavai. Desert mice licked the last of the dew from low-growing grasses and scurried away to their cool tunnels.

Stoner opened her eyes.

The fire had nearly gone out. Her joints were stiff from the cold. She pushed herself out of the armchair and untangled the blanket from around her legs.

Gwen was talking on the phone.

Suddenly she remembered what had happened. Her stomach tied itself in knots.

Gwen glanced at her, nodded, and flashed a 'thumbs up'.

She couldn't help grinning.

"She's going to be fine," Gwen said when she hung up. "She started to pick up the minute they crossed the reservation line. She has to stay in the hospital a couple of days, but we can visit this afternoon. Ted'll bring the truck back and look after things here."

"She's really all right?"

"Just fine." Gwen rubbed the back of her neck. "Lord, I feel gritty. Think I'll have a shower and a nap. We don't have to open the trading post until eight." She put her arms around Stoner's waist. "You look pretty ragged, too. Why don't you join me?"

"In a minute. I want to change Stell's bed and pick up a little in there. Ted's had a hard enough time."

She waited until she heard water running in the shower, and went into the bedroom. She took off Stell's shirt and sat on the edge of the bed.

Tom Drooley crawled out and looked at her. His ears lay flat along his head. His forehead was smooth with dog-worry. The veins in his face stood out. He looked totally exhausted.

Stoner knelt and put her arms around his neck. "She's going to be all right, boy. In a few days she'll come home and yell at us all for making such a fuss. And everything will be just the way it was."

Tom Drooley rested his head on her shoulder and heaved a deep, moaning sigh.

She let herself cry.

SIX

News travels fast in isolated places. By ten o'clock they had had a visit from Larch Begay, who had seen the truck lights go by in the night, and stopped up to find out what was wrong and what he could do to help out. The gesture should have made her feel more kindly toward him, but it didn't. And she couldn't get past the feeling—through the *kopavi*, Siyamtiwa would say—that he actually took some pleasure in their trouble.

Jimmy Goodnight called from Beale, in a state bordering on panic. He'd heard about it from Larch Begay. Stoner reassured him that Stell would live.

Someone named Martha Hunnicutt, who happened to be in the Rexall picking up her month's supply of insulin when Begay called, phoned and offered to run over to Holbrook with magazines.

One of the local lawyers phoned saying he'd heard Mrs. Perkins had come down with food poisoning after eating in a restaurant in Winslow. He offered his services.

The Ministers of both the Mormon and Episcopal Churches called with their sympathy and concern, even though Mrs. Perkins wasn't a member of their flock, but she'd certainly be welcome if she cared to drop in.

Tomás Lomahongva came by, hung around for a while without saying anything, split two bushels of kindling, and left before anybody could thank him.

A tourist couple—woman in skin tight pink polyester pants and black patent leather high heels, man in Bermuda shorts and sandals—stood uncertainly on the porch until Gwen assured them, yes, the rumor they'd heard at the IGA in Beale was true, Mrs. Perkins was a little under the weather, but everything was fine now and the trading post was officially open for business.

The Social Service Department at the Navajo County Memorial Hospital in Holbrook called to see if they could find Stell's Blue Cross number.

Ted showed up, bearing steaks and wine, and fell asleep across the bed without bothering to undress.

97

A cluster of elderly Navajo women came and sat on the porch to gossip and await further developments.

The Pepsi distributor arrived to restock the soda machine. He decided to spend his lunch break sitting on the window sill and trying to flirt with Gwen.

A Yuppie family, with their children Melissa and Jason, couldn't *believe* there was no place in the area to pick up the *New York Times* and a croissant. Gwen suggested Begay's.

"If we could keep up this pace for one week at Kesselbaum and McTavish," Stoner said to Gwen, "we could retire from the travel agency."

Gwen who was trying to explain to Jason that, no, she wasn't an Indian—and, no, he could *not* take a picture of the ladies out front without asking them—didn't answer.

Melissa told Stoner to "put your eyeballs on your nose, put your nose on your back," and fell to the ground laughing hysterically.

Stoner hoped Armageddon would arrive before Melissa grew up to be President.

Jason announced that he was going to hold his breath until they let him take pictures of the ladies out front. Gwen told him he could hold his breath until he burst, it didn't matter to her, as he was certainly not the center of her universe.

Jason expressed his outraged Yuppiedom by shrieking at the top of his lungs.

Stoner told him to shut up or she'd cut out his tongue, and went to the kitchen to make lunch before she did something she could get arrested for.

As she was trying to decide between BLT's, and ham and swiss on rye, she happened to glance toward the back door and saw Siyamtiwa standing patiently in the yard holding the thermos.

She opened the screen door. "This is a surprise."

"Not to me," Siyamtiwa said.

"Would you like to come in?"

The old woman shook her head. "I came to see how it goes with the *pahana*."

"This place," Stoner said, "reminds me of my home town, the way the rumors fly."

"I don't know rumors. My news comes from my friend *Kwahu*."

"Who's *Kwahu* ?"

The old woman smiled. "Nobody you know. Is it not true? Your friend isn't sick?"

"It's true, but she's better now."

Siyamtiwa smiled in a`puzzled way. "So soon? I heard she was very sick."

Stoner sat on the edge of the porch. "She was. Very sick. I thought she was going to die. But Ted took her to the hospital and she's all right."

"Pretty good," Siyamtiwa said. "Must not be a Bureau of Indian Affairs hospital." She spread her blanket on the ground and sat down.

"It's a funny thing," Stoner said. "Ted says she started to get better as soon as they left the reservation."

The old woman looked up sharply. "Tell me this again."

"Ted, her husband, drove her to Holbrook last night. Says she felt better the minute they crossed the reservation boundary."

Siyamtiwa sucked air. "Listen to me, Green-eyes," she said harshly. "When you see your friend, you must tell her to stay away until this thing is settled."

"Why? What thing?"

The old woman stood up. "I have to think on this. You do as I say."

"I'll try, but..."

"Make this promise," Siyamtiwa snapped. "Make this promise in the name of whatever Spirits you pray to. She must stay away."

"I can't just tell her not to come home without..."

Siyamtiwa stamped her foot. *"Make her stay away."*

"But..."

"I will not argue with you, Green-eyes. If your friend comes back here now, she will die."

"I..."

"This is not a game, *pahana*." The Indian woman was very angry. "This is the life of your friend. If she stays away, she will live. If she comes here, she will die. It is up to you."

"Okay," Stoner said placatingly. "I'll do what I can."

"Not 'do what I can'. You will set your heart to this. You will do it. If you don't, you will never see her again. And you will never see me again. And maybe nobody will ever see *you* again." She turned abruptly and began to walk away.

Stoner followed her. "I said I'd try. I can't do more than that."

"The Anglo says he'll do something, and maybe he does it. If he promises to 'try', it doesn't get done, you bet."

"I'm not *like* them," Stoner said impatiently.

"So you say." She turned away again.

Stoner ran after her, touching her arm. "Wait a minute..."

99

"What is happening here I have been waiting for for more years than you can count. I have no more minutes to wait. If you don't convince your friend to stay away, we will have plenty of time for talking. At her Burying Ceremony. Now I have other things to do."

"Damn it!" Stoner shouted. She pounded her fist against her leg in frustration. "You're a stubborn Indian."

"And you're a stupid White. I will have answers for you when I have answers, not before."

Gwen appeared on the porch. "What's going on out here, a race riot?"

"This woman of yours," Siyamtiwa snapped, jutting her chin toward Stoner and addressing Gwen, "has the character of a mule."

"I know," Gwen said. "She's a Capricorn."

"And *you*," Stoner fumed at Siyamtiwa, "think just because you're a hundred and fifty years old..."

Siyamtiwa laughed. "A hundred and fifty years! I don't even remember a hundred and fifty years. At a hundred and fifty years, I was young like you, but not so foolish."

"Children, children," Gwen said. "Suppose you tell me what this is all about."

"She..." Stoner gestured in the old woman's direction. "... doesn't want Stell to come back here, but she won't tell why."

Siyamtiwa folded her arms across her chest. "If you were of the People, you wouldn't need all this explaining."

"Well, I'm not of the People."

"You Whites have no respect for your elders. That is what is wrong with you."

"Thank you very much," Stoner said sarcastically. "I'm glad there's such a simple solution to our problems."

Gwen gripped her shoulder hard. "Stop that this minute and apologize."

"Why should I apologize? All I want is a simple explanation."

"Because we're guests on these people's land," Gwen said. "Apologize."

She realized Gwen was right. The anger drained out of her. "I'm sorry." She held out her hands to Siyamtiwa. "Please, Grandmother. I'm really sorry."

The old woman turned a hard face away from her. "You should be more like your woman. She has good manners."

"She was brought up better than I was."

Siyamtiwa contemplated the horizon.

"Grandmother, I know I was rude. But I've had a terrible

twenty-four hours. My friend nearly died, I was so worried, I've hardly slept. Look, I promise. I won't let Stell come back until you say so. I don't know how the hell I'm going to manage it..."

"A mule like you," Siyamtiwa said. "How could you not manage?"

"You haven't met Stell."

The old woman grunted. "Fine pair."

"I'll keep her away," Stoner said. "I don't break promises, do I, Gwen?"

"Never," Gwen said.

Siyamtiwa looked a Gwen. "I believe *you* tell the truth. Does Green-eyes tell the truth?"

"Always," Gwen said. "It's gotten her in no end of trouble."

"I can't believe it," Stoner said. "You think I'm a *liar.* "

"I think you're White."

"Gwen's White. How come you trust her?"

"She has respect."

"She has diplomacy."

"Well," Siyamtiwa said, "you catch more flies with honey than with vinegar, eh?" She looked hard at Stoner. "You're fond of this Stell?"

"Very."

The old woman turned to Gwen. "You don't mind this?"

"Of course not," Gwen said. "I'm her lover. I..." She caught herself.

Siyamtiwa nodded. "Lover. Okay."

"You know about things like that, don't you?" Stoner asked.

Siyamtiwa glared at her. "You think I never set foot off the mesa? You think I'm some ignorant savage like you have in your movies? I know things you'll never know, Green-eyes. And I have done things you would blush to speak of."

"I'm sure you have," Stoner said awkwardly.

"I am an old woman," Siyamtiwa said. "I am trying to keep something terrible from happening. Do you think I have time to worry about what goes on in your bedroll?"

"Too bad that attitude isn't more widespread," Gwen said.

"What something terrible?"

"When I know how big this thing is, I will tell you." Siyamtiwa turned to go. "You be careful, Granddaughter. Someone is watching you."

* * *

"KWAHU!"

101

The call reached her where she rested on the air.

Now what?

"KWAAA...HUUU!"

The urgency of the summons stopped her in mid-grumble. She quickly scanned the ground, spotted the figure of Old Woman Two-legs standing, arms outstretched.

She folded her wings and let herself drop.

Siyamtiwa grunted as the claws closed gently around her wrist.

Eagle swiveled her head around and preened modestly.

"Pretty good," Two-legs said. "For an ancient relic."

Eagle fixed her with a golden, one-eyed stare. "If you have business with me, say what it is. I have things to do."

Siyamtiwa laughed, then took on an air of great solemnity. "Thank you, Grandmother, for visiting this poor, wretched old Indian."

Kwahu pretended not to notice she was being mocked. "Well, well, what is it?"

"About the *pahana*. The sickness." Siyamtiwa lowered herself to the ground. "We have to talk about this. I think maybe it is the Ya Ya business."

Eagle paced in an irritated circle. "I told you before, the Skin-walkers are gone. Sorcery is forbidden among the People. You know that."

The old woman snorted. "If we could get rid of evil by passing a law, we would have one fine world, eh?"

Caught in a foolishness, Eagle spread her feathers. "What have you seen that makes you think this? Or do you feed on rumor in your old age?"

"This sickness has taken many this summer, and not all old like the Lomahongva woman. The two white women left the reservation and got well. This is a funny business."

"The Whites have medicine."

Siyamtiwa shook her head. "I think not. The first white trader suffered for many weeks, in spite of their medicine. Until the Green-eyes came. Now the second white trader recovers." She contemplated the ground. "And think of this, Grandmother Kwahu: all who have had the sickness have been women."

Eagle thought that over very carefully.

"All summer I have felt something in the air. Now the waters clear and I can almost make out the shape of it." She gave Eagle a moment to digest this. "Now here is what I know. The Dream People have spoken to me of Green-eyes, and told me to make the doll."

Eagle strutted back and forth angrily. "You and your Dream People. If your Dream People are so fond of giving orders, why do they never speak to me?"

"Because," Siyamtiwa said, "your *kopavi* is closed."

"So you say."

"So I know. You are an arrogant, ill-tempered old bird. Why would the Dream People want anything to do with you?"

"Well," Eagle snorted, "I'm sure they come to you only as a last resort."

"You know what I am, Grandmother," Siyamtiwa said softly. "Let us not argue. I need your help. Somewhere out there..." Her gesture took in the land from horizon to horizon. "...is a *powaqa* , a Skin-walker, a Two-Heart. With your strong wings and eyes..."

"So," said Eagle, with just a hint of smugness, "now you need me, you decide to try flattery."

"There is no flattery in truth," Siyamtiwa said. "I must know more about this *powaqa*. Who is he? How great is his power? What does he want? What does he know of Green-eyes?"

Grandmother Kwahu stood still and stared out from under her fierce eyebrows. "I'll see what can be done," she said at last. "But you don't give me much to go on."

"Only this: He is a Coyote Man. And he knows Green-eyes is his enemy. This is why he has made the trader sick. It is how he shows his power." She hesitated for a heartbeat. "Next, I think, he will take the friend."

Eagle shuddered as if a shadow had passed over her. She tasted iron on her tongue. "If Green-eyes is smart, she will take her friend and leave this place."

"I think not," Siyamtiwa said. "My heart tells me, when she understands the danger, she will not turn her back."

"Then why not tell her all of it now?"

"Her thinking is White. Her mind would reject it."

Kwahu rocked from foot to foot. "I don't have a hopeful feeling about this, Grandmother."

"You know how it is with us," Siyamtiwa said. "We can only play our part. Only the Spirits know how it will come out."

A sharp breeze came up, good flying weather. "We'll meet here at twilight," Eagle said. "And tell each other what we know."

"Good."

Grandmother Eagle flung herself into the morning air.

* * *

Stoner sat in the hospital waiting room, surrounded by salmon walls and green vinyl furniture. Sunlight poured white through dusty windows. She crossed her legs, recrossed them, got up and went to stare down into the black-topped parking lot, returned to her seat, and picked at a loose thread on her jeans.

"She's not having a heart transplant," Gwen said. "We're only waiting for visiting hours, which we wouldn't even have to do if you weren't so rigid about the rules."

"I can't help it," Stoner said. "I know we'd get caught sneaking in, and they'd throw us out, and I'd never get to see her."

"Well, *relax*, for Heaven's sake. You're making *me* nervous, and there's nothing to be nervous about."

She paced to the door and looked down the hall. The clock above the fire stairs read two-fifty-five digital. Five minutes.

"I hate hospitals," she said, striding back to the couch and flinging herself down. "They're so sterile."

Gwen patted her arm reassuringly. "They're supposed to be sterile."

"People *die* in hospitals."

"People also die on the highways, in the ocean, jumping out of airplanes, and in the privacy of their own bathrooms. The worst is over, remember? She's getting better."

"Right." She went back to the window and toyed with the Venetian blind cord. "How am I going to convince her to stay here if she wants to come home?"

"Tell her she'll die if she doesn't."

"It's crazy. None of it makes sense. Do you know how this is going to look to someone as down-to-earth as Stell?"

"Crazy," Gwen admitted.

"How can I explain it to her?"

"Don't explain. Ask her to trust you."

"Why would she do that?"

"Because," Gwen said, "she loves you. And when people love each other, they quite often trust each other."

Stoner glanced over at her. "You think I'm silly, don't you?"

"No, dearest, but if you don't stop blinking out an S.O.S. with those blinds, we're going to have the local SWAT team on the scene any minute."

A soft chime sounded in the hall.

Stoner jumped down from the window sill. "Visiting time. Ready?"

"You go along. I'll finish this excellent institutional coffee and join you in a few minutes. I imagine you and Stell have some private things to say."

She hesitated. "What if she looks really awful or something? What do I do?"

Gwen took her hand. "You say, calmly and in a cheerful manner, 'Jesus, Stell, you look like shit. Are you sure these assholes know what they're doing?'"

Stoner laughed. "Thanks a lot."

"Just get in there, will you?"

Stell was sitting up in bed reading the February *Family Circle*. There were still dark smudges under her eyes, but her eyes were blue again. Her face was pale, but there was life in her hair. She wore a white chenille robe over a powder blue nightgown that complemented her eyes and revealed a fair amount of cleavage. She started to turn a page, sensed someone in the room, and glanced up.

"Stoner." She held out her arms, nearly detaching the IV that ran into the back of her hand. "Lord, Lord, the sight of you's more fun than amphetamines."

Stoner grinned. "Is that what you're mainlining?"

Stell scowled at the IV. "I don't think it's anything. Just one of their little tricks to let you know who's boss."

Stoner embraced her carefully, unable to forget the feel of her hot, dry skin, the brittle-feeling bones, the muscles too weak to return her slightest pressure.

"Hey," Stell said, and tightened her grip, "I'm not going to break."

"You scared me, Stell." She held on hard. "I thought we'd lost you."

"Scared myself, and that's a fact."

Stoner stood back and looked at her. "That's a swell outfit you have on."

"Isn't it?" Stell said. She plucked at the sleeve. "Ted went out and got this as soon as the dry goods store opened. Said that hospital nightie looked like a shroud." She laughed. "This little number ought to cause talk, if nothing else."

"A lot of people have been asking about you," Stoner said as she sat carefully on the edge of the bed. "Larch Begay, among them."

Stell grimaced. "You certainly know how to lift a gal's morale."

"Stell," Stoner said quietly, picking up Stell's glasses and fooling with them, "do you know how sick you were?"

"I know how sick I felt."

"Has anyone told you what was wrong?"

Stell shook her head. "They claim they don't know. Find out if that's the truth, will you? Or if I have something terminal and incurable and they're just trying to soften the blow?"

Stoner felt a tight band of fear around her chest. "Do you mean that?"

"Heck, no. I have whatever Claudine had, and from what I hear she's raising three kinds of Hell in Taos at this very minute. It might have something to do with something around the trading post. You watch yourself out there, hear?"

"Stell, about the trading post..."

Stell covered Stoner's hand with her own. "I know, this is supposed to be your vacation. Ted can handle things for now, and I'll get back as soon as..."

"That's not what I mean, for God's sake." Stoner said indignantly. "Don't you know me better than that?"

"Well, then, what's the problem? Didn't burn it down, did you?"

"No, it's just...well...this is kind of crazy."

"I expect crazy from you," Stell said, retrieving her glasses from Stoner's hands. "What's up?"

Stoner looked up at the corner where the walls and ceiling met. "Siyamtiwa said to tell you not to come back. She said, if you did, you'd die." She glanced at Stell. "She was very firm about it."

"I'll be damned," Stell said, "they've finally started to fight back. Haven't taken Tom Drooley hostage, have they?"

"Stell, darn it, listen to me. There's something funny going on, and you getting sick is part of it, and if you come back now it's going to start all over again only this time we won't be able to save you."

Stell laughed. "Want to run that by me again?"

"Something's going on. Something dangerous."

"*What's* going on?"

Stoner raked her hand through her hair. "I don't know. Nobody tells me anything. I was ordered to order you to stay away or you'd die, and I'm doing it."

"I can't run out on the trading post. It's my responsibility."

"And you're *my* responsibility."

"Since when?" Stell huffed.

"I love you. That makes you my responsibility."

Stell shook her head in bewilderment. "Why would anyone want to kill me? I'm from Wyoming."

"I don't *know!*" Her voice rose. "I don't understand any of it. But I don't want anything to happen to you. Is that clear, Stell? *I don't*

106

want anything to happen to you!"

The door flew open. "Ladies," a woman's voice boomed, "this is a hospital, not a Sheepherder Saloon."

She turned around. In the doorway stood a nurse. About twenty-six. Average height, slim, black eyes and hair, skin the color of a polished pecan. And clearly someone who intended to be in control of the situation.

"I'm sorry," Stoner said.

"Mrs. Perkins, I have strict orders that you are to rest. Rest, Mrs. Perkins, is *not* defined as participating in a verbal melee, no matter how vital the issue or provocative your guests. Your recovery is in *your* hands, Mrs. Perkins. Are we communicating?"

Stell grinned. "Stoner, this is Laura Yazzie. Laura, Stoner McTavish, my friend from Boston."

"Hi," Stoner said.

Laura Yazzie looked her up and down. "Is this the way one behaves in hospitals in Boston?"

Stoner looked at the floor.

"There are sick people in this hospital, Ms. McTavish. There are sick people in this very room. Mrs. Perkins may or may not be delirious, and therefore not entirely responsible for her behavior. That remains to be seen. You, however, seem relatively healthy."

"I said I was sorry," Stoner said, slipping her hands into her back pockets. "I was trying to tell her..."

"I don't care what you were trying to tell her," Laura Yazzie said. She turned away and stuck a thermometer in Stell's mouth. "If you can behave yourself, you may stay. If not, you'd better leave before I lose my temper."

"Before?" Stell mumbled around her thermometer.

"Don't give me a hard time, Mrs. Perkins," Laura Yazzie said, taking her wrist and looking at her watch. "Just because you're back from the brink doesn't mean you're out of the woods."

"Laura Yazzie," Stell said when she was allowed to speak, "is a Navajo. A marauding, thieving, warlike race, feared and hated throughout Navajo County Hospital."

"If you're this difficult when you're sick," Laura said as she made a note on Stell's chart, "I'd hate to see you when you're healthy." She arranged Stell's pillows and bedclothes, checked her IV, and somehow managed to ease her back onto the pillows without letting on she was doing it. "Temp's one hundred, pulse up a bit. I assume we can blame your company for that."

"Will she be released soon?" Stoner asked.

"Not if you keep upsetting her."

"I'm not upset," Stell said.

"If I had my way..." Laura made an adjustment in the IV. "I'd keep her around to brighten up the place. Unfortunately, I don't have my way."

"I don't know why not," Stell grumbled. "Half the doctors in the place are afraid of you."

Laura Yazzie laughed. She had a very nice laugh, rich and full and genuine.

"Look," Stoner said, "this is really serious about Stell coming home."

"Well, they sure won't keep her here any longer than necessary. The way she's coming along, you should have her back in a couple of days."

"But I don't want her back," Stoner said.

Laura Yazzie raised an eyebrow.

"Kids," Stell muttered. "You try to raise them right, sacrifice for them, what happens? First chance they get, they ship you off to be looked after by strangers."

Stoner looked at her. "You don't have to stay here," she said. "You can go to a motel, or take a trip. You just can't come back to the trading post."

Laura Yazzie shook her head vehemently. "She can stay here or go home. No motels, and no trips. Her system's had a nasty shock. She ought to take it easy for a couple of weeks, at least."

"In that case," Stell said, "I'm coming home. I'm sorry, Stoner, but that's how it is."

She had an idea. "I wonder if I could talk to you privately," she said to Laura Yazzie.

"Stoner..." Stell warned.

"I'm sorry, Stell. I have to do this."

"You're putting a strain on our friendship."

"If the situation were reversed," Stoner said, "you'd do exactly what I'm doing."

"Okay," Laura put in. "You've got me curious and I'm due for a break." She tossed the chart on the bed and headed for the door. "Happy reading, Mrs. Perkins."

Gwen was working the crossword puzzle in the morning paper. Stoner introduced them, and figured it took Laura Yazzie about fifteen seconds to size up their relationship.

"It's about Stell," Stoner began.

Laura poured herself a cup of coffee from the urn in the corner.

"I didn't think you wanted to discuss the Texas Rangers' chances of winning the American League pennant." She added a packet of Sweet'n Low and stirred. "They're lousy, by the way. What can I tell you?"

She decided to ease up to it. "Do they know what's wrong with her?"

"Nope." Laura perched on the edge of the window sill.

"Don't you think that's odd?"

"Yep."

Stoner cleared her throat. "There's been some talk, out on the reservation..."

"Rez gossip is as common as sand."

"Well," Stoner said. "there might be something to it. It's the best explanation I've been able to get."

"For what?"

"What happened to Stell."

Laura turned her head away quickly and unknotted the Venetian blind cord. "Kids," she muttered, "always monkeying with these things."

Stoner knew avoidance when she saw it. She decided to plunge in. "Do you know anything about Ya Ya sickness?"

Laura glanced at her, and back to the window. "Maybe I heard of it. A long time ago."

"There's talk of it on the reservation."

The woman looked down into her coffee cup. "There's always talk of something."

"Do you think that could be what's wrong with Stell?" Stoner persisted.

Laura's eyes flicked toward the hall, in the general direction of Stell's room. "I'm a professional. I don't deal in mysticism."

"But if you did, is it possible?"

"What are you?" Laura asked with a laugh—a forced laugh. "Wannabee?"

"I beg your pardon?"

"Wannabee. White person that wants to be Indian."

"No," Stoner said patiently, "I just want to understand what's happening."

"So you figure, because I have brown skin, I must know all about this mysterious sickness." The woman's face was closed, her voice hostile.

"Look, this whole thing has me scared. If you'd seen Stell when Ted brought her in here..."

"I did," Laura Yazzie said softly.

"Then you must know how I feel."

The woman sipped her coffee. Her face was unreadable.

"All I have to go on," Stoner said, "is what Siyamtiwa told me. And she sure didn't tell me much."

"Who?" Laura asked sharply.

"Siyamtiwa. An old Hopi woman."

"My God," Laura whispered, "I thought she was dead."

"You know her?"

"She and my grandmother walked around together."

"Walked around together?" Gwen asked.

"They were friends. Close. Like sisters. But I haven't seen her since I was a kid, and she was old then."

"She's *very* old now," Stoner said.

"She's always been very, *very* old." Laura Yazzie began to look a little frightened. "What did she tell you?"

"To keep Stell away from the reservation, or she'd die."

Laura crumpled her paper cup and hurled it angrily into the wastebasket. "Damn it!"

"What's wrong?"

Laura rubbed at her forehead. "Leave me out of this, okay? That's behind me."

"I don't..." Stoner began.

"Look. I grew up on that reservation. Grew up afraid to close my eyes at night, or leave the *hogan* after dark because there might be ghosts or sorcerers out there. Grew up believing in nature spirits, and healing with chants and sings. Then they sent me to the white schools, and *they* taught me to laugh at that stuff. Half the time I was afraid, and half the time I was ashamed. Jerked around between the white world and the reservation. They really know how to mess up a kid's head."

She was silent for a moment, gazing out the window to where the desert stretched on forever.

"I knew I had to get out," she said at last. "Get out or go under. Mary Beale had gotten out, back when it was a lot harder than it is now. I thought, if I could walk in Mary Beale's path..."

"Excuse me," Gwen said, "but who's Mary Beale?"

Laura Yazzie shrugged. "Just a reservation Indian. Just another poor, miserable redskin trying to make it in the world. But Mary Beale did it. She got her nursing certificate, and her college degree, and she made it through graduate school. And now she has respect, and she doesn't worry about ghosts and sorcerers." She turned back

110

to the window. "Mary Beale says you can get away from it," she said in a low voice. "But it comes back. It always comes back."

"What comes back? Stoner asked.

"I don't want to be involved in this," Laura said, ignoring her question. "I don't know anything about Ya Ya sickness. I don't live here any more. I don't belong here any more. This is a summer job, that's all."

"Where do you live, then?" Gwen asked.

"Montreal. I'm working on my doctoral dissertation. At McGill."

"I see," Gwen said. "And you take this job for tuition money; am I right?"

"Right. I have a marketable skill. Big deal."

Gwen got up and poured a cup of coffee and handed it to Laura Yazzie. "Are you a good nurse?"

"Damn right I am."

"Well," Gwen said. She sat on the edge of the sill and looked out at what Laura Yazzie was looking at. "Funny, isn't it?"

"What's funny?" Laura asked.

"That you couldn't get a single job anywhere between here and Montreal."

Laura didn't answer.

"I grew up in Georgia," Gwen said. "We didn't have ghosts or spirits or healing chants. But we did have prejudice, and bigotry, and all the other things that make small-town life such fun. I certainly was glad to get out of there. And you know what? I think about that town at least once every day. Sometimes it's thank-God-I'm-not-there. But most of the time it's little memories—like walking through my neighborhood on summer nights, with the sound of the sycamore leaves moving in the breeze, and dark shadows on porch swings. Or the silence at three o'clock in the morning. Or seeing a light on in a farm house on the other side of the valley, and wondering if there's someone sick in there, to be burning the lights so late." She paused for a moment. "It stays with you."

Laura sighed. "Yeah, it's the old story. Can't wait to get away, then feel like you left half of yourself behind." She looked over at Stoner. "So I might as well tell you what I can. Old Siyamtiwa'd come and get me if I didn't, anyway."

Stoner sat on the couch and folded her hands between her knees. "What do you know about her?"

"There was talk when I was a kid...sorcery talk." She got up and got another packet of Sweet'n Low. "Some folks swore they'd see her

111

disappear over a hill and the next thing you knew, there was a lizard or something sitting on a rock, and old Siyamtiwa nowhere around. So they'd figure the lizard *was* her and the stories'd start about sorcery."

"Are you saying," Stoner asked, "they thought she was a sorceress?"

"I guess there were folks who thought that. Times were pretty desperate. You take desperate times, plus things maybe not going well for you personally, and maybe your sheep start dropping dead for no reason you can find—next thing you know, you're thinking about sorcerers, or aliens, or maybe seeing Jesus Christ taking a shower in your bathroom." She stirred her coffee. "So, yeah, there was talk. But then my grandmother died, and I went off to school, and when I came back she was gone. Folks even stopped talking about her, except now and then in bedtime stories to scare little kids."

"What's the situation out there now?" Gwen asked.

Laura thought it over. "Tense. But it's politics, mostly. Not the kind of thing to start sorcery talk. If there's Ya Ya sickness..." She shrugged. "The Ya Yas go way back. Started out as just one of the Hopi Societies, who believed they drew their power from the animal world. Some of them got too caught up in it, and started using their power in wrong ways, so the society was abolished."

"I don't understand," Stoner said, "what that has to do with sickness."

"According to some of the legends, the Ya Ya could drain the energy from women and use it for their personal benefit."

"That doesn't sound like sorcery," Gwen said. "It sounds like marriage."

"So," Laura Yazzie went on, "if you have a debilitating illness going around, and it seems to be hitting women selectively..." She shrugged. "You see how it happens."

"From what you've observed," Stoner said carefully, "do Stell's symptoms fit the pattern?"

Laura's eyes flicked to the side again, then back to Stoner. "Could."

"Do you think Siyamtiwa could be behind it?"'

"Absolutely not. There's not a bad bone in that woman's body. Only stubborn ones."

"Have you ever known anyone who was involved with the Ya Ya?"

"Hardly," Laura Yazzie said with a laugh. "The Ya Ya were Hopi.

I'm Dineh, Navajo. Oil and water. The Dineh have sorcerers, Skin-walkers we call them. But they don't cause Ya Ya sickness. So, if you're going sorcery-hunting, my guess is you'll find what you're looking for on the Hopi Reservation." She stood up. "I better get back to work. God knows what Mrs. Perkins has done to doctor her chart by now."

"I need a favor," Stoner said. "Siyamtiwa doesn't want her to come back to the trading post right away. But Stell won't listen to me. Is there any way we can keep her here?"

Laura thought it over. "I guess I could fake her fever, but it's not exactly kosher."

"Well," Stoner said, "neither is Stell."

"We might get away with it, but the other nurses will record her normal. It might buy us a few days, though, if no one looks too closely."

Stoner grinned. "Us."

"Us." She glanced over at Gwen and shook her head. "Boy, I've met manipulators in my life, but that one takes the cake."

"Who, me?" Gwen asked, all innocence.

Laura Yazzie turned back to Stoner. "If you plan to spend much of your time with her, maybe *you'd* better learn a little sorcery. Otherwise she'll have you admitting stuff you didn't want to admit to get you to do stuff you swore you'd never do again."

"She already does," Stoner said.

* * *

Stoner sat on the bunkhouse steps and tried to cope with a world gone haywire.

Ya Ya sickness.

Ya Ya sickness? Sounds like something little kids would make up. Billy's got the Ya Ya. Nyah, nyah, Nyah-nyah, nyah. Dear Ms. Jones, Please excuse Susie from gym today. She has the Ya Ya sickness.

Hey, Ern, wait'll you hear this one. I'm sittin' at the dispatch desk, right? And it's about two a.m., and this call comes through on the 911 line. And it's this old codger, yellin' how we gotta' send the wagon 'cause his wife's got the Ya Yas. What're they puttin' in the booze down at the Sheepherder?

Good afternoon. I'm collecting for the Mother's March on Ya Ya. The Surgeon General has determined that Ya Ya causes heart disease, emphysema, birth defects, and premature baldness. However, studies in this month's *New England Journal of Medicine* show that, used in moderation it may prevent varicose veins.

113

She pressed the heels of her hands into her eyes until she saw little red blobs of floating light. Ya Ya sickness.

At this moment, Stell is languishing in a hospital room in Holbrook perhaps because some Hopi sorcerer—or sorcerers—she has never met have put a curse on her.

Four million years of evolution, and we come to this? But there was no getting around the fact that Stell had been sick. Desperately, dangerously sick. She had gotten sick fast, and recovered fast. And none of the doctors could say what was wrong with her. The only people who *could* say were an old Hopi and a Young Navajo. A young Navajo who was not at all happy about talking sorcery.

She wondered what her friends back home would say.

Aunt Hermione would believe it, of course. Aunt Hermione was quicker to believe in the occult than in the evening news.

Marylou? Marylou would probably wonder which wine was appropriate to serve with Ya Ya sickness.

Edith Kesselbaum—the eminent Dr. Edith Kesselbaum, her former therapist and Marylou's mother—might, at one time, have expounded at length on the primitive mind and superstitious thinking. But Edith was in the process of converting from Freud to Jung, and anything was possible.

Unconsciously, she reached up and touched the necklace Siyamtiwa had given her. Which was probably the only thing that was standing between her and a terminal case of the Ya Yas.

Siyamtiwa. Whatever was happening here, Siyamtiwa seemed to be the pivot point.

And Siyamtiwa was drawing her in.

Into what? And why me? Because I happen to look like a doll she happened to carve? That's crazy.

The whole thing is crazy. I mean, what do I have to do with sorcerers and Native Americans and mysticism and…

She looked up to see Gwen coming along the path from the trading post. Gwen stopped, studied the ground for an moment, then bent and picked something up, frowning a little in a puzzled way.

"Look at this." She handed the object to Stoner. "Have you ever seen one of these before?"

It was a lump of natural stone, embedded in a matrix of hardened clay. She rubbed off the clay to reveal a bright blue background criss-crossed with thready streaks of rust in a spider-web pattern.

"Turquoise?" Stoner asked.

"Looks like it."

"Funny markings." She turned it over in her hands. The stone had a warm, living feel to it. "I hope it isn't radioactive."

Gwen laughed. "You *would* think of that."

She started to hand it back. "Keep it," Gwen said. "Maybe it'll bring you luck."

Stoner winced. "That's what Siyamtiwa said when she gave me the doll. And the necklace. What am I going to need all this luck for?"

"You could put it all together and win the lottery."

"Seriously, what do you think of all the things that are happening?"

Gwen sat down beside her and hugged her knees. "I'm keeping an open mind. What's on yours?"

"Nothing that makes any sense."

"Well, considering that it's happening in three languages and as many cultures, maybe you should wait for more information."

Stoner drew meaningless pictures in the dust. "Siyamtiwa wants something from me, I can tell."

"You're worn out, Stoner," Gwen said, reaching out to massage her shoulders. "It's been a hard couple of days. Why not get some sleep before you try to figure it out?"

"You're probably right." She turned and stretched out on her back, her head propped on Gwen's legs.

Gwen stroked her hair and eyelids.

"Remember last summer," Stoner said, "when I had just met you? We took that trip to Yellowstone?"

"I remember."

"On the way back, in the bus, you fell asleep in my lap." She smiled. "You were married, and I was so in love with you. I thought I was going to explode. I'd have done anything for you then, even if you'd been straight forever. I still would."

"I know," Gwen said, "you've been a good friend, as well as a good lover."

Stoner opened her eyes a little. "No regrets?"

"None." She took Stoner's hand. "You're not very good at letting me take care of you, but that's my only complaint."

"I don't know why it's so hard. I've always been that way. The frustrating part of it is, I hate it as much as you do."

"Well," Gwen said, and squeezed her hand, "we have a lifetime to work on it."

The setting sun drew heat from the air and washed the sky a pale, misty blue. Long Mesa began to lose its definition as the dust caught bits of angled light and spread a dry haze across the landscape.

Stoner sighed, feeling the touch of Gwen's hands on her face, and fell asleep.

* * *

Grandmother Eagle settled on the ruined wall and watched the sun go down over the rim of the world.

"So," Siyamtiwa said, "any news?"

"Maybe." She strutted in a self-important way.

"Well?"

"I find footprints where there have not been footprints in many winters. Where footprints are not supposed to be." She paused for dramatic effect.

Siyamtiwa waited.

"Deep in Hisatsinom Canyon, where Tsaveyo Mesa and Lost Brother Butte embrace one another's shadows."

Siyamtiwa sucked in her breath sharply.

Eagle gave her a cagey look. "This is interesting, is it not?"

"Maybe. Do you know whose they are?"

Eagle shook her head. "The canyon walls are high. They stayed in shadow. I would have to drop down close to see. I must try to be there when they are."

"There is more than one, then."

"Two men. One heavy, one light. Both wearing boots."

Siyamtiwa stroked her chin. "In the old days, boots would tell us something. Now everyone wears them."

"I can keep watch," Kwahu said, "now that I know what I'm looking for."

"If they go by day."

"There is plenty of sleeping time ahead," Eagle said with a shrug. "I can watch by night."

"You know how we are," said the old woman. "At our age, we nod and don't know it."

"What do you think they're looking for?" Eagle asked, trying not to reveal her curiosity.

Siyamtiwa shrugged. "Maybe gold. Maybe the hot stones that bring gray sickness."

"Maybe something more powerful than that, eh?"

"Some things may only be known to the People," Siyamtiwa said, and turned her head away.

"Some things are maybe already known to these men who may not be of the People," Eagle said. "We are old, you and I. We need each other. It is not a time to stand on differences."

116

Siyamtiwa nodded reluctant agreement. "Here is what I think. I think these men seek the Ya Ya medicine bundle."

Eagle stared at her wide eyed. "That terrible thing was destroyed."

"No," Siyamtiwa said. "That was legend. It cannot be destroyed. The bundle has been sealed in a cave deep inside Pikyachvi Mesa."

"Hard Rock Mesa?" Kwahu said. "There are no deep caves in Hard Rock Mesa."

"There are many caves. Hidden entrances. When do you think these men will find the place?"

"They are very near. If they know about the hidden entrance, if they don't go past it...three days, maybe."

Siyamtiwa sucked in her cheeks. "So soon?"

"They look hard, and they look carefully."

"My Green-eyes has much to learn," Siyamtiwa said. "And not much time."

"She better learn fast."

"She can learn fast, if she makes up her mind to listen."

Eagle spotted a small desert rodent hiding beneath a fallen chunk of wall. "Are you fond of that mouse?"

"Help yourself."

Eagle pounced and snapped the mouse's backbone with one sharp bite.

"I see you're as blood-thirsty as ever," Siyamtiwa said wryly.

"You never turned down meat when you could get it."

"That is no longer true. My teeth crumble. My bones crumble. Even my skin is tired."

"Lucky for you this thing will happen soon," said Eagle as she tossed away the mouse's tail.

"Lucky for me." The old woman shook her head. "Not so lucky for my *pahana* friend."

117

SEVEN

The rented Jeep bounced along the road, sounding like the advance troops of Patton's Army. Stoner gripped the wheel and thought her teeth were going to crack. The muscles of her arms were being ripped to shreds. "My God," she shouted over the wind and rattles, "this thing should have been recalled by the manufacturer."

Gwen had belted herself in, but was hanging onto the roll bar just in case. "We should have put the top up," she shouted back. "I'm freezing."

"What top?"

"You mean this thing doesn't have a top?"

"That's right."

"What if it rains?"

Stoner glanced over at her through the darkness. "Worried about the upholstery?"

The upholstery had once been black vinyl, but now looked as if it had recently served as a trampoline for goats.

"Never mind," said Gwen.

"They only had two cars. You should have seen the Dodge station wagon. At least this one runs."

"I'm not sure that's an advantage," Gwen said. "Can you slow down?"

She lifted her foot from the accelerator, slowing to twenty, which was quieter and a little less bumpy but just as cold. Darkness transformed the experience of the desert. Night pressed close against the road, cutting off the vast, sprawling flatland. Bits of mica and the eyes of small animals flashed briefly in the headlights' glare, and disappeared just as quickly into the black. The night sky seemed to funnel down to a tube of inky air that tried to lift her toward the stars.

"I'm glad Ted decided to stay in town," she said. "Do you mind us taking over for the next few days?"

"Of course I don't mind," Gwen said between chattering teeth.

"I should have asked you first."

"I don't mind."

118

"But we'll have plenty of time to travel around later, and Ted said it was okay to close up in the middle of the afternoon because nobody in their right mind goes out then, anyway."

"*We* will," Gwen grumbled. "Count on it." She unbuckled her seat belt and leaned over into the back. "There must be *something* warm back here. An old horse blanket'd do."

"Next time we leave during the day and plan to stay away for a while, we've got to remember how cold it gets at night."

"I'll remember,"Gwen said.

Stoner peered at the cluster of lights ahead. "Larch Begay's hovel coming up."

Gwen shuddered.

"He's lived out here all his life," Stoner said. "I wonder what he knows about Ya Ya sickness."

"As I recall, his opinion was that it's superstition."

"That's his *opinion.* I'd like to know what he *knows.*"

"With people like that," Gwen said, "their opinion is *all* they know."

The lights fell behind them. Darkness settled in again. The moon began its rise behind Tewa Mountain. A night bird dipped low over the jeep and kept pace with them for a while, then veered upward and out of sight. At the edge of the head lamps' pillar of light, a scrawny gray animal perched beside the road.

"Slow down," Gwen said. "I want to see if that's what I think it is."

The rabbit was knobby, bony, and pitiful. Two large translucent ears protruded from its head like miniature dunce caps. It froze for a second, then leapt straight up, made a quarter-turn in mid-air, and darted off into the night.

"Jack rabbit," Gwen said. "Isn't that about the most miserable looking creature you ever saw?"

"Nope," Stoner said. "The most miserable looking creature I ever saw was you, when you came back from McDonald's with that burger and fries for Stell. You'd been crying, hadn't you?"

Gwen shrugged. "A little."

"Was it your grandmother? Or has McDonald's reached new heights of horrible?"

"I wish I'd hear something. It's as if she disappeared off the face of the earth—or I did. I don't know if she misses me, or doesn't give me a thought from one day to the next."

"Why don't you call her?"

"I told her to call me, remember?"

"Well," Stoner said, "that was then. If you're only going to worry yourself crazy, call her."

"I said that to her to make a point."

"This is life, Gwen, not a classroom. Do what'll make you feel better."

"Maybe." She was silent for a moment. "It's hard to believe this is happening," she said quietly. "All my life, she was the one I could count on. Before my parents died, when she'd come to visit us, I'd feel as if I had someone on my side. She didn't care what I did, as long as I was happy. If I was late to supper or got dirty playing, my mother'd have a hissie. But Grandmother always stood up for me."

"I know, Gwen. It's hard."

"I guess being a lesbian's different from being late to supper."

"I guess."

"If we're such low-life, it's a wonder dogs don't attack us on the street."

"Dogs are more highly evolved." Stoner said. She smiled. "Actually, I heard the Righteous Right was training Dobermans to sniff out queers in airline luggage."

"At last," Gwen said, "an issue every good American can rally behind."

Stoner felt a brief, sharp pang of guilt. "Sometimes I think it would have been better if I hadn't gotten you into this."

Gwen looked over at her. "Stoner, that's ridiculous. This is who I am."

"I know, but..."

"My dear friend, a lot of things go on in this world that are not of your doing. I hope that doesn't destroy your delusions of grandeur."

"All I know is," Stoner said. "I must have done something terrific in a past life, because I sure don't remember doing anything in this one terrific enough to get you as a reward."

Moonlight illuminated the weathered boards of the trading post. It glowed gray against the desert. She pulled into the driveway.

"This truly is a beautiful place," Gwen said. "Weird, but beautiful."

"Yes, it is." She could feel invisible things moving around her in the night. Whispers. Emotions. Centuries past, drifting away on Time's river. The future almost coming into view around the bend. If she sat very still...

"Are you all right?" Gwen asked.

Stoner nodded. "Everything's just so strange. Do you feel it?"

120

"I think so."

"The land is alive."

Gwen pushed open her door. "Well, my love, alive is what we're not going to be if we don't get dinner. Who's on KP tonight?"

"Me."

"Perfect. I can finally have a long, leisurely bath without wondering who else is waiting to use the bathroom. Is Ted coming for dinner?"

"He'll drop in to pick up some things, but I don't think he plans on staying."

Gwen touched her hand. "Stell will be fine. Don't worry."

"Sure." Stoner slid from behind the wheel to the ground. "This whole thing will be cleared up in a few days." She looked up into the dark sky and wondered what was out there, and why, and what part in it had been chosen for her.

* * *

As she tossed the potatoes into the stewpot, she had the feeling she was being watched. It was impossible to see beyond the window, of course, but if there was someone out there. . . *they* could see *her* as clearly as day.

Play dumb and casual, she told herself, though it went against her instinct—which was to shout., "I know you're out there. Who do you think you are, you lousy coward?"

She peeled two carrots with excruciating slowness, chopped them, and added them to the sliced scallions and spinach leaves in the salad bowl. She set the table—better make it for three so whever was watching would think they weren't alone in the house, or at least would think they were expecting someone any minute.

She washed a small stack of dirty dishes, the leavings of the day, mostly coffee mugs and spoons.

She rinsed out the dishtowels and hung them to dry by the fireplace.

She scrubbed the sink with Bon Ami.

She got a pan of water and a sponge and washed down the chairs and benches.

She still had the feeling there was someone out there.

She went into the store and looked around, but it was secured for the night, the cash register locked, the shutters closed, the latch firmly on the door.

Through the sound of Gwen's running bathwater, she thought she heard a footstep, but couldn't be sure.

121

Finally, she couldn't stand the tension any longer. Taking a flashlight from the shelf over the sink, and pulling on one of Stell's sweaters, she wandered out onto the back porch.

As she played the light slowly over the bare yard, it occurred to her it would have been safer to wait for Gwen to finish her bath, and search together.

Well, too late now.

There didn't seem to be anything around the barn. It was shut tight. Bill and Maude made little thumping and munching sounds from the paddock.

The whitewashed stones leading to the bunkhouse glowed like fluorescent mushrooms in the moonlight. The path was deserted. Everything was quiet.

Too quiet.

It felt as if something was missing.

Something *was* missing.

Tom Drooley was missing.

She remembered seeing him when they came home. He had crawled out from under the barn and sat and made fans in the dust with his tail until they fussed over him, then dug his way back under the barn.

If Tom Drooley were a normal dog, he'd make fierce, threatening sounds if a stranger were wandering around.

No one had ever pretended Tom Drooley was a normal dog.

Tom Drooley was, in fact a sitting duck for anyone with evil intentions.

She swung her light back toward the barn, half expecting to find the big brindle dog's mangled, blood-spattered corpse.

Nothing.

"Tom Drooley," she called softly. "Come on, boy."

No answering bark or sound of flopping feet.

She decided to try the one thing no dog could ever resist, the one thing that would bring him running if he were within twenty miles and had a single breath of life left in him. "Tom Drooley," she shouted. "Dinner!"

She thought she heard a whine nearby, and swiveled her light around. The darkness ate the flashlight beam. If there was anything or anyone out there...

"Hey, there, little lady."

She jumped and nearly dropped the flashlight.

Larch Begay stood at her elbow, close enough to touch. Tom Drooley panted happily at his side. "Hope I didn't scare you," he said with a grin that told her that scaring her was exactly what he had hoped to do.

"Startled," she said, feeling the adrenalin course through her body and puddle up in her throat. "How long have you been out here?"

"Long enough to know what you're havin' for supper."

That made her angry. "Well, that was rude, " she snapped. "You could have knocked. Or was the point to spy…"

"Whoa." He laughed, holding his hands in front of his face as if to defend himself. "Guess you don't know how we do things out here."

"I guess I don't," Stoner said, still annoyed. "And if creeping around in the dark and peering in windows is part of it, I don't think much of your local customs."

"The 'Skins, you see, don't go barging up to a body's house banging on the door and making a ruckus. They sit real quiet in the front yard until you decide if you're set for company."

"Well…" Stoner said, at a loss.

"So, I figured that'd please you, seein' as how you're so cozy with our red brothers…or should I say sisters?"

The hair on the back of her neck crawled. "What do you mean?"

"Way you're hangin' around that old Hopi woman."

'Careful', something told her, 'don't give anything away.' She smiled. "This reservation is like a small town, isn't it? Is there something I can do for you , Mr. Begay?"

"Hey," he said, and pointed skyward. "Look there!"

She looked up. A large bird circled overhead. Light from the crescent moon painted its wingtips with silver.

"Son-of-a-bitch," Begay said. "Don't think I've ever seen an eagle at night, and sure not this close to the ground." He stared. "Jee-*sus!* Look't that fucker move. Must be a hundred years old."

Stoner watched the bird. It seemed to hang in the air directly over their heads.

Begay whistled softly. "That's some bird."

"Yes," Stoner said in a business-like way. She had better things to do tonight than bird-watch with Mr. Larch Begay. She couldn't actually think of anything, but it had to be better. "You were going to tell me what I could do for you," she reminded him.

He grinned at her. "Nothing. But I could do somethin' for you."

She didn't like the grade-B horror movie sound of that.

He crossed his arms, leaned lazily against the side of the building, and let his gaze sweep slowly over the surrounding darkness. "Ted

Perkins gone in town?"

There wasn't any point in lying. "For a while."

"See you got yourself a jeep."

"That's right."

"Rent 'er in Holbrook?"

"Yes, we did."

"You got took."

"It seems to run all right," Stoner said.

"For now, maybe."

"Mr. Begay..."

"Call me Larch, Sweetheart. Everybody does. Stands for Lars. Swedish or somethin'."

"That's nice." She wished Gwen would finish in the bathtub.

The corners of Larch Begay's eyes—red rimmed and rheumy even in the moonlight—crinkled. "Kinda tough for you gals, Stell takin' sick like that."

"We're doing all right." She rocked back and forth on the balls of her feet in what she hoped was a casual, self-assured manner.

"Betcha get kinda nervous out here all alone."

She made herself laugh. "Not at all. Gwen has a black belt in karate." Which wasn't exactly the truth. Gwen had taken a self-defense course that involved some karate, but she sure wasn't the Karate Kid.

The man drew a crumpled pack of unfiltered Camels from his pocket, stuck one in the corner of his mouth, and sucked on it. "That a fact? Little bit of a thing like her? Ain't that a wonder?"

"Oh, I've gotten used to it," Stoner said. "You just learn not to make her angry. Still, life *is* full of surprises."

Begay considered that for a moment, and nodded. "Truly is."

"Mr. Begay—Larch—Ted's going to be here any minute, and I have to get dinner..."

The man roused himself with a little shake. "Damn Sam," he said. "It's so pleasant passin' the time with you, I clean forgot why I came." He went to his truck, reached in through the window, and pulled out a brown paper bag. "Got your mail here."

"Thank you," Stoner said as she took it. "It was considerate of you..."

"Ordinarily, Ben Tsosie hauls it over," he cut her off. "But he's doing a Big Star Chant up by Tuba City. You ever been to a Big Star Chant?"

"I'm afraid not," Stoner said. She hadn't the vaguest idea what a Big Star Chant was.

124

"Oughta do that while you're out here. It's a lot of damn voodoo, but kinda colorful." He lit his cigarette from a turquoise-encrusted Zippo. "I'll track one down for you if you want."

"Thank you," Stoner said, "but I imagine something like that wouldn't be open to Whites, would it?"

He shrugged carelessly. "That doesn't matter. I can get you in. Half the local Dineh owe me up to their loincloths." He glanced up as a shadow fell across the steps. "Good evening, Sweetheart."

Gwen pulled her bathrobe tighter with one hand while she rubbed at her wet hair with a towel. "Good evening, Mr. Begay." She turned to Stoner. "What's in the sack? Rattlesnakes?"

"Mail." She didn't like the way the man was leering at Gwen. Didn't like it at all.

Begay dug at his eyes with a grease-stained finger. "When's Mrs. Perkins comin' home?"

"Pretty soon." Stoner said.

"They ever figure out what ails her?"

"Gall bladder," Stoner said quickly. "It turns out she has a history of it."

"That's rough." Begay scratched at his head. "I knew a fella had that once. Said it was like pissin' fire." He dropped his cigarette to the ground and mashed it under his heel. "Well, you gals need anything, you give me a call. I can be here in two shakes."

"Thank you for bringing the mail," Stoner said.

He gave Tom Drooley a quick pat and hauled himself up into the truck cab. "No problem. Let me know if you wanna see a Big Star Chant."

She watched him drive off in a cloud of dust, exhaust, and darkness.

"What's a Big Star Chant?" Gwen asked as she took the bag and rummaged through the mail.

"Some kind of ceremony. Navajo." She peered at the letters in Gwen's hand. "Anything?"

"Not for me." She handed Stoner an envelope. "Marylou." She turned and walked quickly into the house.

"Gwen," Stoner said as she followed her, "I'm sorry you didn't hear from... "

Gwen cut her off. "Read your mail. I'll get dinner on."

Dear Stoner,

How's the food out there? Is Tex-Mex really as vile as I suspect? Have you eaten toad yet? Rattlesnake? Bacon and beans? How do you bear it?

125

Not much to report from here. I told Mrs. B. about Gwen's defection from Boston per our plan. She appeared unmoved. Quite unmoved, and unmoveable. I won't distress you with direct quotes, but the gist of her message was: I could care less. I swear the woman makes me ashamed to be straight. Do you think it's too late to change? Or does heterosexuality become a permanent condition if not treated promptly? Can I qualify for a handicapped parking sticker?

Seriously, Pet, the woman is bonkers on the subject. I'm not getting to first base. My friendship with you effectively invalidates anything I might have to say to her. Have called in the heavy artillery. Even as we speak, the eminent Dr. Edith Kesselbaum is racing through the night in her white Chrysler Convertible to take up our cause with all her credentialed might. I have promised to spring for dinner at Pizza Hut, an act of conciliation which may put the mother-daughter relationship on an entirely new level. Who but your oldest and dearest friend and colleague would make such a sacrifice?

I assume you'll share all this with Gwen. Tell her I'll write again, or call, as soon as I have news. Hope you're having a fabulous time and staying out of trouble.

DON'T DRINK THE WATER!!!

Love and kisses (Preferably Godiva),

Marylou

She handed the letter to Gwen. "Nothing new, I'm afraid."

Gwen glanced through it. Read it. Reread it. Folded the letter and placed it carefully back in its envelope. Placed the enveloped carefully on the table. "Is dinner ready?" she asked in a soft voice. "Or do I have time to dress?"

"Whatever you like. Gwen, I wish..."

Gwen held up her hand. "Don't."

She got two bowls, served up the stew, poured water. "Would you like anything else?"

"No, thanks." Gwen toyed with her dinner, impaled a potato. "When I was a kid," she said, treating her salad rudely, "my mother and I were downtown one Saturday morning, shopping. That's what you did in Jefferson on Saturdays. You got all gussied up—hat and white gloves and white shoes if it was between Memorial Day and Labor Day—and you went downtown and shopped. Sometimes you stopped in at the lunch room at Bailey's Department Store for tea."

She punctured a chunk of beef. "Anyway, this particular Saturday we left the car windows open—you could do that back then, especially in a little one-horse tank town like Jefferson. When we got back to the car, a mongrel dog had jumped through the open win-

126

dow and taken possession of the driver's seat. My mother shrieked and waved her arms around and made a fool of herself, and a couple of the local boys tried to coax or threaten him out of the car, but he wouldn't move until I asked him very nicely to please get in the back with me, and he did."

"I would have, too," Stoner said, and wondered where this was leading.

"He was a mess, matted and dirty and flea bitten. It looked as if he'd been beaten. I didn't want to advertise for his owner because of how he'd been treated and because I'd already fallen a little in love with him, but my folks said we had to. But nobody showed up, and he refused to run away. Everytime I got in the car, he'd jump behind the steering wheel until I asked him politely to get in the back with me. If you left the windows down, he'd get in whether anybody was going anywhere or not, and sit there in the driver's seat, and that why we called him Driver."

"Well," Stoner said lamely, "I guess you always knew who was in charge." She passed the rolls.

"He was a good dog," Gwen said. "I'll bet he wouldn't have cared whether or not I'm a lesbian."

Ah. "Dogs are like that. Too bad people can't learn from them."

Gwen put her fork down. "I wish I could get angry. I mean, I do, for moments at a time. But I can't keep it up." She pulled tiny chunks off the roll and crumbled them between her fingers. "Every time I try to think about it, my brain turns to pinwheels."

"I know what you mean."

Gwen looked up. "I'm sorry, Stoner. I just can't seem to make any sense of this."

"I know. It's all right."

From the yard came the bang of a car door. Tom Drooley's ears flew skyward.

Gwen sighed and pushed her chair back. "That's probably Ted. Why don't you give him a hand, and I'll do the dishes."

*   *   *

Another sleepless night. The guest room clock was old and loud. Each tick sounded like someone dealing from a deck of new cards. She found herself counting, a guaranteed no-sleep situation. She tried to focus on other, less rhythmic noises, and picked up the low rumble of the old refrigerator. After a few minutes it, too, settled down to a steady and countable throb.

A night creature called and was silent.

127

Called again and was silent.

Called again...

She threw back the covers, slammed her feet into her boots—remembering at the last minute that scorpions were fond of hiding in shoes, and getting away with nothing worse than a flood of adrenalin-pumping, sleep-destroying panic—and stumbled out to the sitting room.

She closed the guest room door—quietly, she hoped, without waking Gwen—and flicked on the table tamp.

The pine board walls glowed with a soft ocher light. The store and kitchen were caverns of darkness on either side. The bookcase was inviting.

She scanned the shelves. Most of the books were old, their titles faded, their content Victorian. She wasn't in the mood for Victorian. On the bottom shelf lay a stack of Harlequin Romances, next year's Victorian no doubt. She wondered if Claudine read them. Or Gil. Or if they read them aloud to each other on long, cold winter nights. She was pretty sure they weren't Stell's. But anything was possible.

She missed Stell. Glad she wasn't here and in danger, but it was lonely without her. The world was a diminished place without Stell Perkins.

Tom Drooley, as if reading her thoughts, crawled out from under Stell's bed and came into the sitting room and threw himself down with a pitiful moan. Stoner knelt to stroke his head, and found herself looking at the spine of a well-thumbed paper back called, *Walking in the White Man's Shoes: A study of the impact of White contact on Hopi and Navajo customs and ceremonialism, University of Southern Arizona Press.*

If *that* didn't put her to sleep, nothing would.

She turned to the back cover. There were the usual words of praise. "Great contribution..." "The definitive work..." "Only a handful of books on the market today match the thoroughness, accuracy of detail, and readability of Mary Beale's..."

Mary Beale? The name rang a bell. Mary Beale.

Laura Yazzie had said she "Walked in Mary Beale's path".

Mary Beale was an Indian woman, who had left the reservation and made a name for herself in the White world.

She curled up in an easy chair.

Let's see if Mary Beale has anything to say about the current goings on.

She flipped to the glossary. *Powaqa*, a witch, may be good (healer) or bad (sorcerer).

Ya Ya, Hopi Ceremony, now outlawed, which forms the basis for modern sorcery. Originally associated with the Fog Clan.

Not very helpful.

Skin-walker, Navajo sorcerer, also called Two-Heart. Believed to possess two hearts, one human and one animal. Not to be confused with 'to have a divided heart', a White expression.

Big Star Chant, one of the Evil Way ceremonies used to exorcize evil spirits. Navajo.

And Ben Tsosie had been called to Tuba City for a Big Star Chant. Interesting.

She wondered if there could be any connection between that and the Ya Ya sickness. Or was it purely coincidental?

Laura Yazzie had seemed certain the Hopi and Navajo Ways were separate. But wasn't it possible, especially with modern communication and transportation, that there might be a point at which they intersect? If not in the tribes as a whole, at least between individuals? After all, the Hopi sickness was affecting whites. Why not Navajos? And wouldn't that require the services of a Hosteen Tsosie?

And who was to say Laura Yazzie was telling the truth? She could be a Two-Heart herself.

Or Siyamtiwa. Or Rose and Tomás Lomahongva.

Even Tom Drooley could have two hearts.

Feeling a little foolish, she reached down and rested her hand on the sleeping dog's side. His heartbeat was strong and sure. And there was only one.

"Well," she said half-aloud, "at least we can trust Tom Drooley."

She let the book's pages sift through her fingers, glanced at the inside back cover, and caught her breath. The photograph of Mary Beale—a middle-aged, dark-haired woman with sharp black eyes, small mouth, broad nose, thin lips, high cheekbones...Siyamtiwa.

It couldn't be.

She read the biographical note:

Mary Beale, PhD., is a full-blooded Native American, born and raised in the Laguna Pueblo near Santa Fe, New Mexico. Educated in the Santa Fe Public Schools and the University of New Mexico, she earned her degree in Cultural Anthropology from McGill University, and is currently the curator of the Pueblo Collection of the Kearney Museum of the North American Indian in Omaha, Nebraska. *Walking in the White Man's Shoes* is her doctoral dissertation.

The book was published in 1981. Stoner looked at the picture again. Now it didn't resemble Siyamtiwa at all. She shook her head. Stereotypes.

A high-pitched, siren-like sound brought her out of her thoughts and made the hair along Tom Drooley's spine stand up.

The sound came again, this time preceded by puppy-like yipping. Coyote?

She went to the door and listened.

The cry was repeated, distant and tantalizing.

Tom Drooley stuck his nose into the night and whined.

"Come on," Stoner said.

She stepped outside.

The desert glowed with its own faint light, a dull blue so dim it might be an illusion. It swirled around her ankles like mist.

She walked to the road and looked out over the Painted Desert.

It lay lifeless and empty as the moon, bathed in moonlight.

A dead, alien, terrible place.

A place of hidden danger and invisible moving things.

An old place, old as the universe. A place built on the skeletons of long-dead sea creatures. Built on jungles turned to stone, built on desiccated plains and sandy beaches, on exhausted volcanoes. Built by time and wind and blowing dust.

Built by the Spirit People.

Spirit People? She rubbed the back of her neck. "I don't know about any Spirit People."

She looked around. Damn it, there's something here.

Tom Drooley pressed against her legs.

She could hear her own heartbeat, quick unsteady, tentative.

The coyote's cry came again, closer now.

She looked toward Long Mesa and thought she saw...something ...hunched against the sky.

She squinted, thought she saw it move, decided she hadn't.

Tom Drooley sat on her foot.

She closed her eyes for a moment, then looked quickly, hoping to catch and identify the object through her peripheral vision. She recognized the shape...a clump of mesquite, or juniper, or rabbit brush, or some other bushy plant.

Maybe.

So what? So what if it's a plant, or a coyote, or even a Great White Buffalo? Why are you making yourself crazy with this stuff?

A second heartbeat joined her own.

She turned quickly.

No one was there.

A third heartbeat kicked in, this one high and sharp, dancing through and around the other, grace notes to the stronger beats.

"Who is it?" she whispered.

The heartbeats quickened, her own and the Other's.

She rubbed her arms to still the trembling in her hands.

"Look, I know you're out here. Show yourself."

Silence answered her.

"Damn it, either tell me what you want, or *leave me alone.*"

Something padded away into the darkness.

EIGHT

Morning arrived fast and hot.

By sunrise, the humidity had risen to an all-time record twenty percent. Which would have brought a breath of relief from Massachusetts dampness, but by the time that bit of moisture connected with the Arizona sun, the result was worse than midday in July on the Boston Common. Heat built up on the roads and spilled over into the shade. Lizards panted. Flies hung suspended in the air, or crawled lazily across table tops and windowsills. Men mopped sweat from their faces with wrinkled bandannas. Women fanned themselves with magazines. The faces of children ran with mud.

Gwen grumbled over morning coffee.

Stoner made an attempt at being cheerful, gave up, and grumbled back.

She opened the store for business and wrote inane postcards to the folks back home, and then couldn't find stamps.

Around nine-thirty, a couple of Indians dropped by to trade for coffee and roofing nails.

A contingent of Navajo and Hopi women—Rose Lomahongva among them—held what seemed to be a prearranged meeting on the trading post porch. When Rose came in for change for the soda machine, she mentioned that there had been two more deaths on the reservation since yesterday. Both had been women.

Gwen swept out the kitchen, which improved her mood.

It kept getting hotter.

Stoner hid in the sitting room, the darkest room in the house, and told herself it was cooler there, although there was really no noticeable difference anywhere except inside the refrigerator. She made another stab at *Walking in the White Man's Shoes,* but decided it was too esoteric for the climate. Even the Harlequin Romances were too esoteric for the climate. She stared at the picture of Mary Beale, and wondered how she could ever have mistaken her for Siyamtiwa.

She settled for rocking and waiting for the heat to lift.

Gwen, meanwhile, had worked herself into a frenzy of cleaning, beginning with the kitchen and progressing through the bathroom, guest room, and Ted and Stell's bedroom in record time. She approached the sitting room with a fierce and determined gleam in her eye.

Stoner tried to make herself invisible.

"Are you doing anything in here?" Gwen demanded, hands on her hips and dustcloth dangling from her pocket.

Stoner got up. "Nope. I'll clear out of your way." She headed for the kitchen.

"Don't make a mess. I just finished out there."

She looked around for a book to take with her. "What's with you, anyway? This is a killer."

Gwen attacked the book case. "Must be premenstrual." She yanked books out by the handful and dusted them viciously. "What time does the mail come?"

"When Larch Begay gets around to delivering it, I guess." She rescued an old photograph album which would never survive Gwen's assault.

"Maybe we could pick it up." Gwen slammed books back onto shelves. "Save him a trip."

The mail. The grandmother. Of course. "We could do that. When you run down."

Gwen waved her off. "I might as well finish this room now that I've started it."

Stoner poured herself a glass of iced tea and wandered around to the group of women on the porch. All conversation ceased immediately. She smiled apologetically and went back to the kitchen.

The photograph album aroused her curiosity. Most of the pictures were old sepia prints of Model A Fords, men in large sweeping moustaches and wide-brimmed hats. Groups of Indians in ceremonial dress. A smiling priest. A picnic. A Mexican fiesta. All of the pictures labelled in a spidery, deeply-slanting script.

Toward the back were treasures. Claudine as a child, playing on the trading porch with 'Cousin Stell'. Cousin Stell in Levi's and plaid shirt and a cowboy hat three times too big for her. Cousin Stell at ten, bareback on a pinto pony. Cousin Stell as a teen-ager, lounging on the porch in penny loafers, circle skirt, and crinolines. Gil and Claudine's wedding, with Stell in a puff-sleeved bridesmaid's dress and Ted looking—in his rented tuxedo—as uncomfortable as a kid forced to play the violin for guests.

Then snapshots of babies, some with Claudine, some with Gil, some held by a Hispanic nursemaid named Maria Hernandez. Maria was a stocky, middle-aged woman...

...who looked exactly like Siyamtiwa.

Stoner rubbed her eyes. Either my racism has taken a giant leap forward and every non-white in Arizona looks the same to me...

...or something very strange is happening.

Events of the past few days led her to lean strongly toward the "something strange" hypothesis.

She called Gwen over and pointed to the better of several pictures. "Doesn't that woman remind you of Siyamtiwa?"

Gwen looked hard at the snapshot, then shook her head. "I don't know, Stoner. I only met her once."

"Well, it does look like her. Exactly like her. Doesn't that strike you as odd?"

"I guess so."

Heat and apprehension made her petulant. She went to the sitting room and snatched up Mary Beale's book. "Look." She put the book and photo album side-by-side. "Look at these two women. They look exactly alike."

Gwen pulled her reading glasses from her pocket and slipped them on and took an eternity staring at the faces. "They don't look alike to me."

"Of course they do. Clean your glasses."

"I just did."

"Gwen..."

Gwen glanced at her, then back at the pictures. "Well maybe."

"Don't placate me."

"For heaven's sake, Stoner, what difference does it make? You'll probably never meet either of these women."

Stoner raked her hand through her hair. She felt slightly hysterical. "Hah. Heavy irony. I've already met them. They're Siyamtiwa."

Gwen smiled uncertainly. "It's too hot for this."

Unsure of herself now, she looked at the pictures again. The photo of Mary Beale was posed. The photo of Maria Hernandez was old and faded. Well, maybe...

Suddenly she didn't want to think about it any more. "You're right," she said, and closed the book and album. "Let's ask Rose to look after things, and go for the mail. Maybe a drive'll cool us off."

* * *

Grandmother Eagle felt the bottom fall out of her stomach and snapped awake just as the ground raced to meet her. Her eyes were sore and puffy. It was an effort to lift her wings. She searched for an air current to rest on, but the day was too still. Sleep became a gnawing hunger. The sun pressed her toward the earth.

Big Tewa Peak beckoned seductively. There would be coolness there, among the canyons and junipers. Maybe water in a high lake. A rock ledge which faced east, away from the brutal sun. At least a bare, dead tree in shadow, a shady spot for a little nap.

She tried to shake off the temptation. Old Woman Two-leg will have much to say to you if you let trouble slip in the back door.

Old Woman Two-leg is probably having a lovely rest for herself at this very minute.

The sun caressed her back hypnotically.

Old Woman Two-leg expects me to do everything. Did I volunteer for this? I did not.

She smelled the sweet, sharp odor of cedar rising from the mountains.

This is Two-leg business, not Eagle business. What did Two-legs ever do for us? Nothing but kill my Old Man. Nothing but poison my babies. Nothing.

A sparkle of blue from below. Water, reflecting the sky.

I'm an old bird, and the Two-legs would begrudge me even an hour's rest at the end of my life.

She flew lower over the mountains, feeling the coolness.

A drink of water.

Fish drifted in the shallows. She ate her fill.

The rock ledge lay in shadow, just her size, just right for a little nap.

Eagle yawned. Skinwalkers walk by night, not day.

She folded her tired wings and closed her burning eyes

Down on the desert floor, the coyote roused itself...

...and walked.

* * *

Stoner felt it as soon as they got back to the trading post. Something had been here. Was still here.

She looked around, but there was nothing to see. Because whatever it was, it couldn't be seen.

"I can't believe it," Gwen called from the front porch. She waved a brown paper bag. "It was here all along."

No, Stoner thought, it wasn't here all along. Because I checked before we left for Begay's and there was nothing on that porch. And we didn't pass him on the road.

Rose Lomahongva strolled by, on her way home. Stoner called her over. "Would you like a ride?"

"No, thanks," the girl said. "If I walk, I can feel the breeze."

135

"While we were gone, did anyone come by? Like Larch Begay?"

Rose shook her head. "Nobody came by."

"Do you know how the mail got on the porch?"

"Nope. The women left, and I went inside, just like you asked. Didn't see anything." She started to turn away. "Have a nice evening."

Stoner caught her arm. "Rose, have you noticed anything...well, strange going on around here?"

The girl looked at her with a puzzled smile. "Sure."

"What is it?"

"Siyamtiwa didn't explain?"

Stoner shook her head.

"That old woman," Rose said with a laugh. "Never tells anything." She turned and walked away.

So great, great. Another of life's little unexplained mysteries.

I didn't ask for this. I came out here for a vacation, a break from the pressure, an escape from screwed-up travel vouchers and homophobic grandmothers. And what do I get? My good friend nearly dies, coyotes stalk me at night and try to make me lose my way in the desert. Old Indian women appear out of nowhere and give me gifts and orders—mostly orders. And Spirits, living, dead, and otherwise, feel free to prowl around in my personal space whenever the urge strikes.

And all I can do is piss my life away here in Tarantulaville while I wait for something to happen.

She slipped a hand into the pocket of her jeans and felt the bit of turquoise Gwen had found. It was warm from her body heat or from the sun, or...

Swell. Living rocks. This fits right in with petrified trees and Yellowstone Park and plants that wait a hundred years to germinate and three-headed goats, and other wonders of Nature.

She kicked dust and slammed the bunkhouse door behind her. The necklace Siyamtiwa had given her lay on the dresser. "Maybe it brings you good luck," the woman had said. "Maybe you need it."

She slipped it on. Yeah, I need it, all right.

There was a tentative knock on the door. She opened it. "Jimmy Goodnight."

"Hiya," the boy said. He peered through the screen expectantly.

Stoner hesitated. What's Western etiquette in this situation? Would it be rude not to ask him in? Or would entertaining him in what was essentially her bedroom lead to loose talk—older woman/younger boy stuff?

Well, she wasn't planning on staying in town—such as it was—forever, and Jimmy Goodnight's reputation could probably profit from a little color enhancement. "Come on in," she said.

He sidled into the room and looked around. "This is neat." He surveyed the array of articles on the dresser. "Is all this your stuff?"

"Mine and Gwen's." She laughed. "You sold me most of it, remember?"

His fingers lingered on the green-eyed doll. "That's a funny thing, huh?"

"Funny?"

"Yeah, funny to have around, like."

"A friend gave it to me. What are you doing so far from Beale?"

He put the doll down. "Rockhounding. With Mr. Begay." He picked up a comb, turning it over in his hands. "He knows where there's this vein of turquoise, just laying on the ground almost. We're gonna find it."

Sure, Stoner thought, just like he's going to get you out of Beale. "If he knows where it is, why not just go and get it?"

"We will," Jimmy Goodnight said as he inspected her snakebite kit. "Like, he pretty much knows where it is, but not exactly."

She sat on the bed to change from boots to sneakers. "It's an awful hot day to go tramping on the desert. I hope you went prepared."

"It's not real hot down in the canyons." He grinned at her in the mirror. "Anyway, you don't hardly notice the heat when you're hunting for treasure."

Stoner felt a little tug of sympathy for him. "You'd really like to get away from here, wouldn't you?"

"Yeah." He looked down at the floor and shuffled his feet. "My Dad says I don't have the brains to go as far as Holbrook, much less some city. And I'm no good at sports, so nobody's gonna give me a scholarship or anything. But Mr. Begay, he says it ain't so hard to get out, you just have to want it bad enough, and get a kinda push."

"If it's all that easy, don't you think it's odd he hasn't gotten out?"

"Heck, no." He turned back to the dresser and took inventory again. "He can't go. Folks around here need him, 'cause his Dad had the service station and it's the only one around and folks depend on it. And the Indians wouldn't know what to do if he left. He says half of them would just roll over and starve to death. He says it's an awesome responsibility."

"Awesome," she muttered. "You know, Jimmy, Indians are just like the rest of us. I'll bet, if Mr. Begay *really* wanted to get out of here,

137

he could find someone to buy the station."

"But he really *cares* about them."

She decided not to argue the point. "Where is he now? At the trading post?"

"Naw, he had to get back."

"How will you get home?"

"Hitch."

"That's kind of dangerous," Stoner said. "Why don't I give you a lift?"

"Dangerous?" He looked at her quizzically. "I hitch all the time."

Right, boys do that. This is, after all, the United States, where boys—particularly boys over fifteen—can do pretty much what they want, when they want. It's girls who have to be careful. Girls who can't do things like hitch hike across the country meeting interesting people and having adventures. Because of the boys.

She noticed him staring at her necklace.

"Where'd you get that?" he asked.

"From a friend."

"Can I see it?"

She took it off and handed it to him. He gave it a cursory glance, and looked up at her. "I'm awful thirsty. Could I have a drink of water?"

"Sure. Come up to the kitchen." She held out her hand for the necklace.

He seemed reluctant to part with it. "It's pretty," he said. "Must be real valuable."

"I don't think so. It's mostly sentimental value."

He appeared uncomfortable, blushing and hesitating, as if uncertain what to do. Did he want to steal the necklace? She found that unlikely. Her instincts told her Jimmy Goodnight wasn't a thief. He looked...almost as if someone had *told* him to take it.

He shoved it at her, and smiled a little apologetically. "I really just came by to see how you are," he said as he followed her up the path.

"We're doing very well. Thank you for asking."

"Mrs. Perkins okay?"

"Much better."

"That was pretty scary, huh?"

"About as scary as I can stand," Stoner said.

He hesitated at the kitchen door. "I really oughta get truckin'."

"At least stop and say hello to Gwen."

138

He turned as pink as the undersides of the clouds out where the sun was setting. "Oh, gosh, I don't know..."

Gwen appeared at the door. "Well, James, what brings you into this neck of the woods?"

He darted her a glance. "Could-I-have-a-drink-of-water?"he mumbled.

"Certainly. Want to come in?"

"Can't."

Gwen brought him a glass. He swallowed it in three gulps, his Adam's apple bobbing like a buoy.

"Thanks-I-gotta-go."

"Wait a minute," Stoner said. "Did you happen to bring the mail?"

"Me?" Jimmy Goodnight said. "Naw."

Before she could repeat her offer of a lift, he was gone.

Stoner watched him go. "I think you have an admirer," she said to Gwen.

"It's being a teacher. It sends them into paroxysms of ambivalence."

Stoner went inside and picked up the pile of first-class mail. "Anything from your grandmother?"

"Not a word." She sighed. "Guess it's time to call." She glanced at her watch. "It's two hours later there. I could do it any time."

Stoner looked at her. At her soft, waving hair. At her strong, sure hands—hands that moved with unconscious grace. At the startling depth of her dark eyes. How could anyone, she thought, want to do anything to hurt her?

She found her voice. "What are you going to say?"

"I don't know. Play it by ear, I guess."

"Want to have dinner first?"

Gwen shook her head. "I'd only pick at it. The truth is, I'm all of a sudden terrified."

Stoner touched her. "I wish I knew what to do."

"Tell me I'm not being ridiculous."

"You're not being ridiculous."

"Tell me there's a chance..."

"There's always a chance." She tilted Gwen's face up and looked into her eyes, holding them with her own. "I promise you, Gwen, whatever happens, whatever she does, whatever you do, I'll stand by you. Always."

Gwen rested her head against Stoner's chest. "I love you so much. Why does it have to be such a problem?"

139

Stoner stroked her hair. "Because we live in an imperfect world."

"That," Gwen said with a small laugh, "is not a comforting thought." She pulled herself together. "Care to listen in?"

"I don't know."

"I would." She went into the sitting room. "I'll call from the store. Use the extension in here."

Stoner stared at the phone. Maybe this is a mistake. Maybe it would be better not to know. Maybe... She saw Gwen gesture, and picked up the receiver.

Eleanor Burton's phone rang once, twice, three times. Not home. She started to hang up.

"Hello?" Mrs. Burton's voice was far away and staticy.

"Hello, Grandmother."

A pause. "Gwyneth?"

"Yes."

"Where are you?"

"Still in Arizona."

"Are you having a nice time."

"Yes, we are."

"I'm so glad," Mrs. Burton said.

Hope began to stir. She could see it in Gwen's face.

"How is Stoner?"

"Fine. Stell was under the weather for a while, but she's feeling better." Gwen was grinning from ear to ear.

Don't jump to conclusions, Stoner thought cautiously. One of the games played around this is: Pretend Nothing Ever Happened and Hope It'll Go Away. Then you have to go through it all again.

"Well," Mrs. Burton said, "I hope you're having a wonderful, wonderful time out there."

"We are," Gwen said. "Grandmother, are you all right?"

Eleanor Burton laughed. "Of course, dear. Whatever would make you think..."

"We didn't exactly part on a friendly note."

"I know. And I'm so sorry about that, I could lie down and die. It's been an absolute nightmare."

Gwen's eyes were shining.

Stoner had a distinctly uneasy feeling.

"I miss you, Grandmother," Gwen said, her voice husky with emotion. "I love you."

"And I love you too, Gwyneth. How long are you planning to be away?"

Gwen glanced at her. Stoner shrugged.

"We're not sure. Stell isn't ready to take over the trading post yet, and we want to do some sightseeing after she gets back. A couple of weeks, I guess."

There was a brief pause. "Dear," said Mrs. Burton, "do you suppose you could be home by the twenty-seventh?"

"I guess so, if we cut it close. Why?"

"You have a doctor's appointment."

Gwen frowned. "I do? I don't remember that."

"You didn't make it." Mrs. Burton sounded flustered. "I did it for you. Not with a real doctor, just a psychologist, but he comes very highly recommended..."

Stoner felt the blood drain from her face.

"Grandmother," Gwen said, "I don't understand what you're saying."

"He's a very nice young man, Gwyneth, and he's had a great deal of success with cases like yours. The minister says..."

"With cases like mine?" Gwen interrupted.

"Well...people who are...confused."

"I'm not confused."

"Of course you are, dear."

"Did you talk to Edith Kesselbaum about this?"

"That dreadful, dreadful woman," Mrs. Burton said. "Not only does she condone—*condone*, mind you—this terrible thing, she had the nerve to suggest that *I'm* the one with the problem."

"Good for her," Gwen snapped.

"It's all right, dear," Mrs. Burton said placidly. "Dr. Paul warned me you might react like this."

Gwen's face was scarlet. "It is not all right. I'm very happy with what I am, Grandmother. So you can tell your Dr. Paul to take his successful cases and shove them. And you along with them."

She slammed down the receiver.

Stoner hung up silently.

"Well," Gwen said, "now I know where we stand." She walked slowly into the kitchen.

"Gwen..."

"Think you can handle supper? I don't trust myself." Her face was unreadable.

"*Gwen...*"

She was calm, too calm. "I think I'll take a walk."

"It'll be dark in half an hour."

"I'll be back by then." She started out the door.

Stoner caught her arm. "I can't let you go off like this. Please tell

141

me what's going on."

"I'm fine. I need to be alone for a while, okay?"

Stoner didn't know what to do. She felt large and awkward.

"I'll walk up past Long Mesa, that's all. I won't leave the road."

"I don't think you should."

Suddenly, unexpectedly, Gwen's eyes flashed fire. "Leave me alone!" She yanked her arm from Stoner's grasp. "Damn it, just *leave me alone!* "

The door closed behind her.

Stoner watched through the window until she was out of sight behind the mesa.

Clouds had gathered over the mountains, high and puffy. The setting sun painted them with blood.

I shouldn't have let her go, Stoner thought.

She's not a child. She has the right to be alone if she wants. Gwen Owens is a perfectly mature, sensible adult.

A sensible adult who married a man who wanted to kill her and nearly succeeded. Who got herself beaten up in a dark alley in Maine. Who decided to come out to her grandmother on the hottest night of the year after they'd lost two straight rubbers of bridge.

This perfectly mature, sensible adult is now wandering somewhere out beyond Long Mesa in a land full of snakes and Skinwalkers and sorcerers and Larch Begays and ghosts and the spirits of homeless babies and women dying of the Ya Yas—and God only knows what else.

And all I can do is stand around wondering what to have for dinner. Chicken? There's a chicken in the freezer. But it would take all night to thaw, and it's too hot to cook chicken.

She scanned the refrigerator and shelves. Chili? Hot dogs and beans?

Damn you Eleanor Burton. You must know what this does to her. You must hold love in very low esteem, to throw it away so easily.

I could make an omelette, but I've never seen Gwen eat an omelette. Maybe she doesn't like them. I don't like them, but if I don't chew it too much, and swallow real fast, and try not to think about it, and forget they have the texture of slimy cotton, I might be able to handle it.

There are a thousand different ways to love, but hate is hate no matter how you slice it.

This has the makings of a hard-rock-heavy-metal-Motown-rap-protest song.

Come on, all you dykes and tykes, let's all get down and boogie

142

to the Homophobia Blues.

The clouds had turned from red to gold, with silver only minutes away. The sky took on a lavender tinge.

> *Whatever happened to Lavender Jane?*
> *She's perfectly well and she hasn't a pain,*
> *And they've closed down the Lesbian Disco again.*
> *Oh, whatever happened to Lavender Jane?*

Make dinner, not war.

This occasion calls for something disgusting. Depression food. Like Sweet and Sour hamburger with pineapple chunks and coconut topped with pecans and mushrooms braised in white wine, served on a fluffy mound of Minute Rice with peppers and snails. And for dessert, the head of Eleanor Burton *a la mode*.

She scrubbed at her face with the palms of her hands. This is not healthy behavior. This is behavior of a useless and futile variety. This is behavior for which one is looked at strangely on the street, while small boys point grubby fingers and chant cruelly as you pass by.

Damn it, she thought as the twilight deepened, why does it have to be so hard? Lovers of women. We can't change that, wouldn't change it if we could. But we're not asking for medals, only to exist without having to justify our existence.

Small destructive children exist. Adolescents on skateboards exist. Politicians, TV Evangelists, bus exhaust, skunks, the National Rifle Association, players of loud rock music, the Christian Broadcasting Network, stock brokers, Yuppies, professional wrestlers, door-to-door-salesmen—*they're* all allowed to exist, and those are only the everyday horrors.

When the sky turned purple, she began to feel uneasy. She turned on a few lights and went to stand on the porch, peering up the road, searching for Gwen in the near-darkness.

An hour later, night had settled in for good. Fighting off the fear that turned her stomach into a swarm of stinging bees, she took a flashlight and went looking.

*   *   *

Grandmother Eagle opened her eyes. The night silence hummed around her. She fluttered her wings anxiously. She had only meant to nap, to wake before dusk, before the Danger Time. Sleep and dust made her tongue as dry as an aspen leaf in October, but she didn't dare take time to drink.

Tight with apprehension, she hurled herself into the night sky.

She picked up the glow of Green-eyes' flashlight on the north side of Long Mesa. The Two-leg walked slowly, searching the ground.

143

She stopped and knelt, and Kwahu's sharp eyes saw what she saw—two sets of foot prints, one belonging to the companion, the other the prints of Hosteen Coyote.

Green-eyes stood, puzzled, looking here and there in the darkness. She called the companion's name, waited, and called again.

Eagle circled high, scanning the desert for movement. She saw a handful of Night People—mice, she thought—near Dinnebito Wash. A fox prowled and sniffed among the rabbit brush on Black Mesa. Two young Dineh, newly married, made love under the stars near Betatakin. But no Hosteen Coyote, and no companion.

Green-eyes was still calling, her voice rusty with fear. Kwahu swooped low over her head, and let the air whistle through her feathers. The woman looked up. Their eyes met.

Eagle sent her words. "The companion isn't here. Go home and wait. I will do what I can."

She pumped against the air and went to find Siyamtiwa.

* * *

Stoner stood alone in the desert, fear running through her in waves. The footprints, Gwen's and the coyote's, had disappeared on rocky ground. And the bird—the bird had seemed to know what she was doing, which was ridiculous. It was only fear making her mind play tricks.

Gwen must have wandered off the road, anger propelling her in random directions. The coyote? Who knew how long those tracks had been there? Probably since the last rain. This wasn't a fairy tale. Gwen hadn't gone off for a stroll with a coyote.

Had she?

And was it only a coyote? Or a Skinwalker? *Powaqa.* Werewolf. Stephen King Time.

One thing was certain, she wouldn't do Gwen any good if she got lost on the desert herself.

* * *

"Grandmother," Eagle said, "I've done a terrible thing."

Siyamtiwa held out her wrist. Eagle landed on it and turned her head away in shame.

"Well?"

"I fell asleep this afternoon. When I woke, it was night and something had happened to the White woman."

The old woman frowned. "Green-eyes?"

"The companion of Green-eyes. I am a useless old bird, Grandmother. I deserve your anger."

144

"Silence," Siyamtiwa said. "We have to think about this." Still holding Kwahu on her arm, she sank cross-legged to the ground and sucked at a tooth. "Tell me about this falling asleep," she said after a while.

"I tried to stay awake, as I had promised. But the sun was so warm, and the shadows on Tewa Peak so cool. And when I found the blue water, and the small dark cave…"

Siyamtiwa cut her off with a gesture. "Blue water?"

"A lovely pond, the water clear and clean, with fishes …"

"There is no little pond on Tewa Mountain," Siyamtiwa said. "You have lived your whole life there. Have you ever seen a little pond?"

"I saw it. I drank from it. I ate the fishes…"

"Think hard," Siyamtiwa said. "Is your belly full?"

Eagle thought. "No."

"Is your tongue damp?"

It was dry as the desert. "No, Grandmother."

Siyamtiwa nodded knowingly. "You did not eat, you did not drink. There is no water on Tewa Mountain. Someone has gotten inside your head, my friend. Someone wants you to stop watching, so they can bring trouble."

Eagle shook her feathers. "How can this be?"

"This is the Ya Ya. Two-Heart knows you are my eyes and ears. He fools you into sleep, and while no one is watching…"

She stood up suddenly. "We must go to Green-eyes."

* * *

She called the Navajo Tribal Police.

Sergeant Dave Shirley told her to stay at home, they would look for her at first light. Meanwhile, it wouldn't do anyone any good to have *two* missing persons.

"But something might have *happened* to her," Stoner insisted.

"She probably found someplace to sleep. Don't worry, Ma'am, she's safer on the desert than she would be in her own bed at home."

"I certainly *hope* so. We're from the city. Nobody's safe in their beds in the city."

"Well," Shirley said laconically, "we haven't lost anyone out there in four-five years."

"How do you know? Maybe they're so lost you didn't even know they were lost. Maybe the whole area out there's littered with the bones of people you didn't even know were lost."

145

The man chuckled. "That's good, Ma'am. Keep up your sense of humor."

"I'm serious!"

"We'll have the patrols keep their eyes open," Shirley said. "But I'll bet you dollars to doughnuts you'll be calling here within the hour, feeling foolish because she just stopped off somewhere for a while."

"Stopped off?" Stoner shouted."Stopped off where? We don't know anyone out here. There aren't any movie theaters, or ice cream stands, for crying out loud!"

"Well, we got the Hopi Cultural Center."

"What time does it close?"

"This time of year, around nine, more or less."

She looked at her watch. "It's nine-thirty now."

"Look, Ma'am…"

"It's twenty miles from Spirit Wells to the Cultural Center. She didn't have a car and there were coyote tracks…"

"Spirit Wells?"

"Yes, I'm calling from the trading post."

There was a long silence. "Well," the Sergeant said at last, "they say there's been a bug around there. Maybe your friend felt a little unwell and sat down for a rest."

"The kind of sickness we've had out here," Stoner said, "is not the kind you 'sit down and rest' with. It's the kind you never get up again with."

"Look, you don't want to get yourself all worked up over…"

"There were coyote tracks. What do you make of that?"

"I would say," the man replied patiently, "if there were coyote tracks, there's probably a coyote around somewhere. But I wouldn't worry, coyotes don't attack people."

"And if this coyote happens to be a Skinwalker?"

Another silence. "Skinwalker?" he said, at last his voice hard. "Ma'am, has someone been telling you stories?"

"Did you know Ben Tsosie has gone to Tuba City to perform a Big Star Chant?"

His laugh lacked sincerity. "Excuse my bluntness, Miss, but we have our ways out here. You have to be born here to understand. But there are still pockets of superstition…"

"Really?" Stoner asked dryly.

"I'm sure your friend will be back soon," he said quickly, cutting off further discussion. "I'll call around and let you know if we hear anything. Meanwhile, you give me a call if she comes in." He hung

146

up without waiting for an answer.

Stoner stared at the receiver. Superstition? Sergeant Dave Shirley may claim not to believe in Skinwalkers, but I sure rattled his cage when I brought it up.

But he's right about one thing. There's not much anyone can do until morning. And it's possible—barely possible—that Gwen really did stop off somewhere and lost track of the time.

No, Gwen wouldn't do that. Gwen wouldn't leave her worrying. Not if she had a choice.

She went out and stood on the porch until the silence began to break into sounds that teased and frightened her. She thought about taking the jeep out and driving up and down the road, looking, keeping busy. But Gwen might call, and there would be no one here to answer. She was trapped.

She found herself reaching for the phone, realized there was no one she could call. She didn't know where Ted was staying, and there was no point in upsetting Stell, who would only feel helpless or maybe get up and come out here against both the doctors' and Siyamtiwa's orders. She didn't care to tell her problems to Larch Begay. Aunt Hermione and Marylou were probably asleep, or out, and there was nothing they could do, anyway.

She could call Eleanor Burton and tell her what had happened, then hang up and let her chew on it. But that wouldn't solve anything.

She felt herself wanting to cry, and rapped her knuckles rhythmically against the tabletop.

The desert was so big.

The house felt so empty and lonely.

She glared at Tom Drooley. If you were a *real* dog, you'd be out there picking up her scent, tracking her down, rescuing her. But, no, you have to be a totally useless, afraid-of-the dark mutt.

He tucked his tail and slunk into Stell's room, sighing heavily. Stoner called him back. "I'm sorry, old fellow." She knelt to look into his eyes. "I didn't mean to hurt your feelings. I'm just so scared."

Tom Drooley put his paws on her shoulders and licked her face.

"How can you stand to do that?" she asked, wiping the dog-lick off on her sleeve. "You don't know where my face has as been."

She sat on the floor, one arm around the dog, and wondered how to pass the time.

Read? Aunt Hermione would read at a time like this. Read the Tarot. Maybe she should call and ask her to do a reading.

Not yet. If she doesn't come back in the next half hour, I'll call

Aunt Hermione.

The house ticked as it cooled.

The silence was beginning to get on her nerves.

Laura Yazzie! She knows the reservation. Maybe she'd have an idea.

I don't even know where she lives. And she won't be in the phone book because she's only here for the summer, but the hospital should have her home number.

She used up twenty minutes looking for the phone book, and found it didn't cover the Holbrook area. She called Directory Assistance, which was taking a coffee break. She let it ring.

Directory Assistance returned from the Ladies' room on the twenty-seventh ring.

She got the number and called.

The switchboard operator gave her Laura Yazzie's home number.

Laura Yazzie's roommate said she was working three to eleven at the hospital and wouldn't be back until near midnight.

She called the hospital again and spent another ten minutes trying to talk the operator into having Laura paged.

When she threatened to call every fifteen seconds throughout the night, thereby tying up the switchboard so no calls could come through, so that at least three people would bleed to death because they couldn't reach the ambulance and she, Stoner, would personally go to the media—and the insurance companies—and explain how that happened simply because the operator was too lazy to page Laura Yazzie...

The operator agreed to connect her with the third floor nurses' station, and was heard to remark "some crazy woman wants to talk to Yazzie," before she turned over control of the phone to Stoner.

"Third floor nurses' station, Ms. Yazzie."

She was so glad to hear a familiar voice, she nearly broke down. "Laura? This is Stoner McTavish. You probably don't remember me, but..."

"Remember you? How could I forget the greatest con artist between here and Montreal?"

"Laura, I need help."

Laura Yazzie sighed. "When I was eight years old, I accidentally disturbed a Blessing Way. I must be paying for it now."

"I'm serious, Laura. I need...Gwen's gone."

"Gone?"

"Disappeared. She went for a walk at least two hours ago. She said she wouldn't be long, and I haven't seen her since. I know she didn't stop off and visit someone because we don't know anyone and besides, there were coyote tracks..."

"Hold on," Laura Yazzie said, her voice deadly serious. "Did you call the Tribal Police?"

"Yes, but they can't do anything until morning." Her voice began to shake. "Laura, I don't know what to do."

"Well, look, I don't get off here for another hour, but I'll come out there right after that, okay?"

"You don't have to..."

"It'll take about an hour to get there, so expect me around midnight. If you hear anything before eleven, call me here."

"Laura..."

"We'll figure something out. Don't worry, Stoner, she's probably lost her way. I know that rez like the palm of my hand and I used to be a pretty good tracker."

"If I'd known you were going to rearrange your life for this, I wouldn't have called. I just needed someone to talk to." But her relief was tremendous.

"Don't be silly."

"I'd rather Stell didn't know about this, okay?"

Laura Yazzie laughed. "Don't worry. She'd get up and walk out of here, and that'd be heap big trouble for this Injun, you betchum." She hung up before Stoner could respond.

Ten-fifteen. Where is she? Oh God, where *is* she?

She paced the length of the building from the kitchen through the sitting room to the store and back again to the kitchen. She froze and listened, then paced again. Fear was a solid thing that filled her and wouldn't let go. She tried to relax, told herself everything was being done that could possibly be done, that she didn't really know anything yet, only that Gwen was missing—no, not missing, overdue—not officially missing—right now, at this moment, there was only uncertainty...

She tried holding her breath and letting it go all at once.

She tried making coffee.

She tried thinking of something else.

She decided to work a crossword puzzle in the newspaper, to pass the time. But the only paper she could find was written in Navaho, which might as well be Hebrew.

She tried to think positive thoughts, to send positive energy out into the night as a beacon to guide Gwen home.

None of it worked. She was afraid, and she'd stay afraid until

Gwen was back with her.

She started to go out to the porch again...

When Tom Drooley, for perhaps the first time in his life, bared his teeth and growled.

Half frozen with anxiety and hope, she waited for a sound.

A soft footstep, a soft tap at the door.

She opened the door.

Larch Begay stood on the step.

"Mr. Begay, I'm sorry, but you've come at a bad..."

"I think you'd better let me come in," he said gently.

She hesitated, but there was nothing threatening about him now. He seemed worried, embarrassed.

She stood back to let him pass.

He looked around. "Ted Perkins here?"

She shook her head.

"Maybe we oughta sit down," he said.

Whatever he has to say, she thought as she sat across the table from him, I don't want to hear it.

"Couple of Navajo boys from over at Sand Springs come by. They'd been out on the desert, they said, practicin' tracking at night. I don't give that much credence, but it ain't important. They found something, see, and..."

Someone inside her head started screaming.

Begay rammed his hand into his pocket and brought it out, his hamlike fist wrapped around an object. "I gotta ask you...do you recognize this?"

He held up a thin silver chain, a necklace. In the center of it dangled a rough stone. She had given it to Gwen last year, before they were lovers, before they were even close friends.

Stoner nodded. "It belongs to Gwen," she said. "I appreciate you bringing it back. It was kind of you. She'll be so relieved..." She knew she was talking fast and loud, trying to build a different reality between herself and what she knew was coming next.

"I'm sorry," Begay said. "She was wearing this when they found her. I figured you could identify it."

A high buzzing began in her ears. She held out her hand. He dropped the necklace into it. She stared at it, then looked up at him. "Is she all right?" she asked in a thin voice.

Begay shook his head. "I'm sorry," he repeated. "There's been a rock fall. I'm afraid your friend's dead."

150

NINE

She stared at him, her mind turning to cement.

"The way it looks," Begay went on, "she wandered out on the edge of a mesa and the rim gave way under her. They can be tricky that way. Sandstone caps look solid enough, but there's not much holding them up."

"She's dead?" Stoner asked in a whisper.

He nodded. "Could've happened to anyone. Dark as a witch's cunt out there."

"Are you sure it's her?"

He rubbed a hand over his chin. "I didn't want to think so, seein' how I know you gals and all. But there weren't no mistakin' it looked like her, and you say that's her jewelry…"

She grasped at straws. "There wasn't any other identification?"

"You mean a wallet or driver's license or something? Not a thing."

Of course not. Gwen had run off in a surge of emotion. She hadn't taken…

She knew she was in shock, her feelings shut down. She knew pain would come later, and it would be unbearable. "Where is she?"

"The Navajo boys that found her took her in to Holbrook. I certainly am sorry about this." He peered at her. "You gonna be all right?"

Dead. Gwen dead.

"Anybody I can call for you?"

She was here two hours ago. She was alive two hours ago.

"Miss."

She forced herself to concentrate. "Thank you for telling me," she heard herself say. "I'm sure you have other things to…"

Begay rested his elbows on the table and folded his hands. "I ain't leavin' 'til I'm sure you're looked after."

She had to get him out of here! "I'll be all right, really. I have a friend coming out tonight."

"I'm mighty glad to hear that. Thought maybe you was all alone

151

out here, not knowin' anyone and all."

"I'll be all right," she repeated. It was all she could think to say.

"They gonna be here soon?"

"Any minute."

"Feel like I oughta stay 'til then."

Please, please, go away! "Everything's under control, Mr. Begay. You can go…"

"Well." He looked at her hard, assessing her emotional state, then pushed away from the table. "You need anything, I'm right down the road." He went to the door, patting her shoulder awkwardly as he passed. "I surely am sorry about this. Wish I knew how to make it not so."

"Thank you."

Then she was alone.

Gwen's dead. What does that mean, Gwen's dead?

First she was married, and then we were friends, and then we were lovers, and now she's dead.

How do I think about that? I've never known anyone who was dead before.

Well, there was my dog Scruffy. After he was dead, I couldn't touch him or talk to him any more. Is that what it means? I won't be able to touch or talk to Gwen any more?

Not talk to Gwen? Not touch her? Before we were lovers, I couldn't always talk to her or touch her, but she wasn't dead. I could always maybe talk to her tomorrow.

Now I can't talk to her tomorrow.

But she's my lover. You can always talk to your lover, can't you? Even if it's hard? Even if you're having problems? Because it hurts both of you to be having problems, so you both want to be able to talk.

But if you're dead you don't want to talk. So it's like you're having problems, only one of you doesn't care.

Is that what it's like when your lover's dead? Like one of you doesn't care?

Maybe I did something wrong, and that's why she's dead. Maybe I did something so awful she never wants to talk to me again. Maybe that's why she went out and died.

Stoner looked down at the necklace in her hands.

She sent it back. I found that stone on a perfect day, and I gave it to her because I love her, and she took it because she loved me. She cried that day, because she loved me. And now she sent it back.

I wish she'd told me what I did wrong, not just gone out and died.

152

If she'd told me, I'd have changed it, whatever it was. I didn't want her to go and do this.

The keys to the jeep lay on the table.

I'll go to Holbrook and find her. We can talk about what I did wrong, and maybe I can convince her not to be dead any more.

Dead any more.

She grabbed the keys and got to her feet. Her knees buckled beneath her. She was shaking. A drop of wetness splattered on the table top. She touched her face, and realized she was crying.

I'd better stop. If Gwen sees me, she'll be upset.

But Gwen won't see me...

...because Gwen is dead. And dead is forever.

No matter what I say or do, she'll never respond to me again.

Panic swept over her. She looked around the room.

I can't stay here.

She started for the door. Have to get out, get out, get out...

She plunged into the darkness, and nearly ran into the old woman holding the eagle.

"Oh," she said, startled.

The eagle flew away.

"Now what?" Siyamtiwa asked.

"She's dead."

"Who?"

"Gwen. My lover. He told me."

Siyamtiwa frowned. "Who told you?"

"Him. Larch Begay."

"Here is this Begay again. What is he to you?"

"Nobody, just... "

"You are related to this Begay? He is your clan?"

"Of course not. You know that."

"And you believe what this man says?" Siyamtiwa shook her head. "You *pahana* have very strange customs."

Stoner grabbed the old woman's arm. "Listen to me! Gwen is dead!" She realized she was screaming—or someone was screaming.

"You have proof this man tells the truth?"

"Yes." She dragged Siyamtiwa into the kitchen, snatched up the necklace. "This. I gave it to her. He took it off her body and brought it to me."

"He is a Begay?"

Stoner nodded.

"Then I do not believe he did this thing."

153

"He brought it to me. It's hers."

The old woman held the necklace in her hand for a moment, her mind turned inward. "This does not belong to a dead person," she said at last, and handed it back. "Your friend is alive."

Stoner shook her head.

"This man," Siyamtiwa said heatedly. "This man you hardly know, who is not related to you or part of your clan, holds this thing in his hands and says, 'Your friend is dead', and you believe him. I hold it in my hand and say, 'Your friend lives', and you do not believe me. Why is this?"

"You want to make me feel better." Stoner brushed at tears that ran down her face. Tears she couldn't feel or stop.

"You think I would lie to make you feel better? Maybe I tell you, 'A wonderful thing is going to happen. Tomorrow the sun will rise in the west and nobody will ever make war any more'. And when tomorrow comes and the sun does not rise in the west, what will happen to all your feel good?"

"You're confusing me."

"But if you are sad and I say, 'Life has many sad things, but once a hummingbird came and drank from your plate and this was a magic thing'—if this is true, then when you are sad you will remember magic. Then your feel good will not go away." She crossed her arms. "But if it pleases you to think your friend is dead, you will think it. For myself, I will wait and see."

Stoner took a deep breath and felt hope flicker. "Why would Larch Begay lie about it?"

"When we know that, we will know many things." The old woman shoved back the curtains covering the kitchen shelves. "You have coffee in here?"

Stoner handed her the can and watched as Siyamtiwa shuffled to the sink, filled the coffee pot and dumped at least a cup of grounds into the water. "Where did you learn to make cowboy coffee?" she asked irrelevantly.

"From cowboys."

Siyamtiwa lit the fire under the pot and came back to the table. "You wear that necklace I gave you. That's good."

"Right," Stoner said dryly, "it's brought me untold quantities of good luck." She could feel desperation pounding at her consciousness, fighting its way back in. "I'm sorry I shouted at you."

"If you were Hopi, you wouldn't have to apologize. You wouldn't shout at me in the first place."

Stoner leaned against the sink. "Siyamtiwa?"

154

"Hoh."

"Hoh?"

"'Hoh' means 'I listen.' Now you know some Hopi. You have something to say?"

She hesitated. "Do you really believe Gwen's...alive?"

"I said the stone is not a corpse stone. I said I would wait and see."

Despair formed a white-hot ball in the pit of her stomach. "If I lose her..." She began to cry, feeling it now, her body cracking like rock, shedding rock-hard tears.

Siyamtiwa held out a hand to her. Stoner took it, startled to feel the strength in the rough skin, in the small, brittle bones.

"It has been a long time," the old woman said, "since I have held someone in my heart that way."

Stoner wiped her eyes on her sleeve. "I don't know if I envy you, or pity you."

"Well," Siyamtiwa said, "that's how it is with me." She squeezed Stoner's hand. "We'll know more about this dying business when your Hermione calls."

"Aunt Hermione isn't going to..."

The phone rang.

Siyamtiwa chuckled. "Now you will say I make magic, like the Ya Ya." She shuffled over to tend the coffee.

Stoner went to the sitting room and picked up the phone. "Hello?"

"Stoner," Aunt Hermione said, her voice sharp with alarm, "what in the world is going on out there?"

"How did you know anything's..."

"My dear, its the middle of the night—two a.m. here, in case you're curious—and I was sound asleep when suddenly I received an absolutely terrifying barrage of energy from you. Dark energy. Clouds and clouds of it. And then a voice, as clear as a bell but with an accent I can't place, ordering me to call you."

Stoner glanced at Siyamtiwa, who was stirring sugar into her coffee, an expression of angelic innocence on her face.

"Aunt Hermione, something's happened to Gwen."

Her aunt was silent for an instant. "Yes, I can feel it has."

"She's disappeared. A man told me she's dead. Aunt Hermione...Aunt Hermione, do you think..." She couldn't bring herself to ask.

Siyamtiwa came into the room and gestured for the phone. Stoner handed it to her.

"Grandmother Hermione," the old woman said, "this niece of yours is a very stubborn woman. I tell her her friend is okay, but she doesn't believe me. Maybe she believes you. What do you think?" She listened.

"What's she saying?" Stoner whispered.

Siyamtiwa put a finger to her lips. "She talks with her Spirits. Show some respect."

Stoner rammed her hands into her pockets.

Siyamtiwa listened and nodded and grunted and nodded. "Okay," she said at last. "You better tell her yourself. Your Green-eyes doesn't trust Hopis."

"That's not true," Stone protested. "I trust..."

Siyamtiwa turned to her. "She says to tell you the medicine cards say your friend is alive. She says she sees darkness, a cave, cold there. Something magic around. Not bad, not good. Gray magic."

Stoner bit her lip. "What does that mean?"

"It means your friend is alive and we got things to do." Siyamtiwa turned back to the phone. "Grandmother, do your Spirits teach you to wind-walk?" She listened. "Too bad. It would be good to sit down with you. We have many things to teach each other, eh? Maybe we even straighten out this young one."

She handed the phone to Stoner and went back to her coffee.

"Goodness," Aunt Hermione exclaimed. "What an amazing person. I can feel her aura right through the phone."

"Aunt Hermione, do you really think Gwen's all right?"

"I didn't say 'all right', dear. I said 'alive'. But she's uncomfortable, and frightened, and in a very dangerous situation. It will take great strength of character to get her out."

"Aunt Hermione, I don't think I'm up to this."

"You really don't have a choice, Stoner. You've been chosen."

"Chosen by whom? For what? "

Her aunt was silent for a second. "I really can't make it out. But I suppose all will be revealed in good time."

Stoner sighed. "Okay, thanks for calling."

"I know that tone of voice, Stoner. Five minutes after you hang up, you'll have yourself completely turned around again."

"I guess so," she admitted grudgingly.

"Sometimes I don't know what I'm going to do with you. Well, I suppose you're my *karma*. I do love you, Stoner. Take care of yourself." The line went dead.

Siyamtiwa looked a question at her.

"I don't know," she said. "The trouble is, I want so much to

156

believe you."

"Good. You get smarter, "said Siyamtiwa.

"But I might believe you, not because I believe you, but because I want to."

The old woman threw her hands in the air. "I will never understand White thinking."

A car pulled up by the kitchen door. Stoner glanced at her watch. Twelve-fifteen. That would be Laura Yazzie.

The woman entered without knocking, still in her white uniform. Her eyes lit up when she spotted Siyamtiwa. *"Yah-tah-hey,* Grandmother."

"Yah-tah-hey, Headpounder."

Laura Yazzie laughed. "Don't start that." She turned to Stoner. "Headpounder is an old Hopi insult for Navajo. We try to rise above it. What's up?"

"Larch Begay came by. He told me Gwen's dead." Stoner held out the necklace. "She was wearing this. He brought it to me."

Laura took the necklace and studied it. She looked up at Siyamtiwa. "How do you read this?"

"That stone has never touched a corpse."

"Good." Laura turned her attention to Stoner. "What did this Begay guy tell you? Exactly."

She could feel the black knot tightening in her stomach. She couldn't say it.

"She's afraid," said Siyamtiwa, "if she says words she makes them true."

Laura shook her head. "Whites are so superstitious." She took Stoner's shoulders in her hands. "You have to help us with this, Stoner. There are things only you know and we need to know them."

"He...he said some Navajo boys found her over by Sand Springs. Or they were from Sand Springs, I can't remember which. He said they told him she'd fallen off the edge of a mesa in the dark." She rubbed her arms. "That's all I know."

"Did you see the body?"

"No."

"Did Begay see the body?"

She nodded.

"And he removed the necklace?"

"I don't know. Maybe one of the others did."

"I doubt that," Laura said. "Where is the body now?"

The body. The Body. It used to be Gwen. She could feel herself begin to tremble, fear and loss curling up her spine like a snake.

"There she goes again," Siyamtiwa said.

Laura Yazzie gave her a little shake. "Answer me, Stoner."

"He said..." She gulped air. "He said they took her to Holbrook."

Laura Yazzie glanced at Siyamtiwa, who nodded knowingly. "Think about this very carefully," Laura said. "Who took her to Holbrook?"

"The boys that found her."

" Hopi or Navajo? "

Stoner looked up. "What?"

"The boys from Sand Springs, were they Hopi or Navajo? Be absolutely certain."

She thought hard. "Navajo."

"Are you sure of that? That's Joint Use Area over there. They could be either tribe. This is very, very important."

"Navajo." He said 'The Navajo boys that found her took her to Holbrook.'"

Laura Yazzi's face broke into a smile. "Did you hear that Grandmother?"

Siyamtiwa grunted.

"Please," said Stoner, "tell me what this is all about."

"Okay." Laura Yazzie sat down at the table. "In the first place, Sand Springs is about fifty miles from here. If they found her there, your friend was taking quite a hike. If they found her here, those Navajo boys are pretty far from home. That's possible, but not likely. And, since this supposedly took place on the rez, they'd have reported it to the Tribal Police, who would have called you by now since they know you're looking for her. But, even if all those things were the way he said, there's one aspect of this that makes me know for sure it's a lie."

"What?"

"Navajos," Laura Yazzie said, "won't touch corpses. It's a thing that runs deep with us. We believe, when a person dies, their bad spirit, *Chindi*, hangs around the body after their good spirit has left. It takes some complicated rituals to get rid of it, and it's hard to find a Singer who knows them any more. I've worked in hospitals for years, and I still have a hard time with corpses. If Larch Begay told you some Navajo boys took a dead body to Holbrook, he was lying."

"Gwen didn't—doesn't have any bad spirit," Stoner said.

Laura Yazzie laughed. "This presents interesting possibilities. I wonder if the Church is prepared to deal with a self-avowed lesbian

158

saint." She turned serious. "But just to make sure we have all our bases covered, I'll call the hospitals and police." She got up and went into the store.

"So," said Sityamtiwa, "you feel any better?"

Stoner nodded.

"Then have coffee."

She looked down at the muddy sludge in Siyamtiwa's cup. "Later, maybe. Siyamtiwa, why would anyone want to do this? I mean, even if Gwen's alive, she's still missing. Where is she? And why would Larch Begay tell me those lies?"

The old woman sipped her coffee. "Long story."

"I don't mind."

"Wait until your Headpounder friend finishes her calls. You don't listen so good when you're worried."

Stoner managed a smile. "I guess you're right."

"For the *pahana*, the big reality is up here..." Siyamtiwa tapped her forehead. "For us, is in here." She pointed to her heart. "I think I trust our way better. Not so easy to fool."

* * *

Laura Yazzie's half hour of calls turned up no trace of new White female corpses within a hundred-mile radius of Spirit Wells. It didn't completely relieve Stoner's anxiety, but it came close.

"Now," Laura said as she threw out the coffee Siyamtiwa had brewed and made a fresh pot, "it's time we got down to what this is all about."

"Might as well start with me," Stoner said. "I don't know anything."

Siyamtiwa rolled her eyes in a long-suffering way.

"You might know more than you think," Laura said. "Tell me what's happened to you since you got here."

She didn't want to. She wanted to run off into the night to find Gwen. But she knew that would solve nothing, and Laura Yazzie was probably right. So she forced herself to tell it all—the funny feeling in her stomach when she first crossed the reservation boundary—the sense that there were ghosts in the air—the coyote—the meeting with Siyamtiwa—the doll that looked a little like her...

"A lot like you," Siyamtiwa corrected.

Laura Yazzie dug a felt-tip pen from her pocket and started making a list on the back of a brown paper bag.

Stoner told them about Wupatki Ruin, the people on the ball court and her unreasonable rage. About falling asleep at Lomaki—

159

or not falling asleep—and about the spirits of the homeless children.

"Lomaki," Siyamtiwa interrupted, looking hard at Laura. "You know what goes on there."

"What goes on there?" Stoner asked.

Siyamtiwa shrugged. "Not much. Some old ancestors hang around."

"Many of the ruins in this part of the country," Laura explained, "were built by Anasazi, ancestors of the Hopi."

Siyamtiwa made a disgusted noise.

"Excuse me," Laura said. "Anasazi is a Navajo word. The Hopis call them Hisatsinom."

"That's their name," Siyamtiwa muttered.

"Yes, Grandmother." Laura turned back to Stoner. "Anything else?"

"Well, I still have that funny feeling, but I've gotten used to it. After that, Stell got sick, and that's really all we've been able to think about."

Siyamtiwa nodded and sat quietly for a moment, sipping her coffee. "Now," she said at last, "we will speak of this Begay." She looked at Laura. "You know his family?"

"I know a lot of Begays," Laura said, "but I never specifically heard of a Larch Begay. Still, that station's always been Begay's and it's a pretty common name. He could be a cousin from over in New Mexico."

"He claims it was his father's before him," Stoner said.

"Unfortunately, that doesn't help us much. If we knew his mother's clan, we might have something to go on. That's how we sort folks out." Laura chewed on the end of her pen. "Even at that, I might not recognize it. I've kind of lost touch..."

"You don't lose touch," Siyamtiwa said sharply. "You fear, if you remember too much, you will go back to the blanket."

Laura Yazzie blushed deeply and was silent.

"Go back to the blanket?" Stoner asked.

"When an Indian goes out into the White world, but the reservation haunts her heart until she returns, we say that Indian went back to the blanket." Siyamtiwa stared deeply into Laura Yazzie's eyes. "Maybe that Indian finds she has no soul in the White world."

Laura got up and carried her coffee cup to the sink. "That's beside the point," she said, her back to them. "The point is, what's with this Begay?"

"I think he is after the Ya Ya bundle," Siyamtiwa said.

160

Laura turned quickly. "That thing was destroyed."

Siyamtiwa shook her head. "A thing like that doesn't die. It can only be put somewhere safe. Someone has been looking for it."

"How do you know all this?" Laura asked.

"It is my business to know," Siyamtiwa answered softly. "It has always been my business."

Laura drew in her breath sharply. "Then the old stories about you were true."

"Maybe."

"What stories?" Stoner asked.

They ignored her.

"You are..." Laura began.

"I am what I am, nothing more."

"Of course." Laura Yazzie lowered her eyes. "The bundle, do you think this Larch Begay is the one who's looking for it?"

"Maybe."

"A Dineh, after Hopi magic?"

Siyamtiwa shook her head. "This is what I don't understand."

"If it's valuable," Stoner suggested, "maybe he wants it for the money."

Siyamtiwa glanced at her. "No money in that thing. Lot of rags and feathers and stuff you pick from the ground."

"Some people would pay a lot of money for a thing like that," Stoner said.

Siyamtiwa gave her a puzzled look.

"Because it's the only one of its kind. Some people would feel...important to have something like that."

"We handled the Anglos all wrong, long time back," Siyamtiwa said. "Should have realized they're crazy."

"Look," Stoner said to Laura. "Maybe you don't recognize this Larch Begay's name because he isn't Navajo. Maybe he's white. Have you ever seen him?"

Laura Yazzie shook her head. "This is the first time I've been out this far since..."

Siyamtiwa smiled at her. "Afraid you might find where you left your soul?"

"Maybe," Laura said. She turned back to Stoner. "You've seen him. Does he look White to you?"

Stoner shrugged. "He's kind of brown, but...to tell you the truth, I couldn't tell for sure if he's brown from the sun, or a mostly White Native American, or..."

Laura Yazzie threw up her hands. "Never mind."

"Has a Dineh name," Siyamtiwa offered.

"But he might have just taken that name," Stoner said. "People do that all the time."

Siyamtiwa sighed and shook her head. "Crazy people."

"So maybe it's not really magic at all." Stoner found herself laughing with relief. "Maybe Begay takes a Navajo name so the Indians will trust him and he can exploit them. Then he hears about this Ya Ya medicine bundle, and knows a good thing when it crosses his path. If he can find it, he can sell it to a collector. He sees Siyamtiwa and me together, realizes that she's Hopi and probably knows where the bundle is, and takes Gwen to get to Siyamtiwa through me. He holds her hostage, and the ransom is the location of the bundle." She laughed again. "See? It explains everything."

"Everything," Laura said, "except your funny feeling and ghosts and the Ya Ya sickness and coyotes that call you awake in the middle of the night and dolls that look like you." She doodled on her paper bag. "That certainly does clear it up, all right."

"Oh, "said Stoner.

Siyamtiwa crossed her arms over her chest. "I say Green-eyes is right, but it is also more than a money thing. It is a *powaqa* thing."

Stoner waited for her to go on. She didn't. "So that's it? That's the sum and substance of your explanation?"

Laura made another doodle. "Stoner, in the times you've seen Larch Begay, have you noticed anything wrong with his eyes?"

"He probably watches too much television. Or maybe it's hay fever, or he drinks too much."

"Explain that," Siyamtiwa said.

"His eyes are red and runny and sore-looking. Why?"

"*Powaqa*," Siyamtiwa said. "Two-Heart."

Laura Yazzie nodded. "Skinwalker."

"I beg your pardon?" Stoner asked.

The two Indian women began talking rapidly in Navajo or Hopi or both.

Laura turned to her at last. "The Dineh believe sorcerers can see in the night, like animals. They use their animal spirits to do magic. But it affects their eyes."

"*Powaqa*, too," Siyamtiwa said, "change shape, become animals. Have the heart of man, and the heart of animal. Two- Heart."

Stoner raked her hand through her hair. "Well, surely that's only metaphysical…"

"When *powaqa* walk in animal form, most often become wolf. Next most often coyote." She nodded abruptly and leaned back in

162

the chair, as if that ended the discussion.

"You think that coyote that's been prowling around here is Larch Begay?" Stoner asked. "That's ridiculous!"

Siyamtiwa narrowed her eyes. "Why ridiculous?"

"Because...people can't change themselves into animals."

"You have werewolf. Vampire."

"Those are *stories*."

"Okay." The old woman got up. "You don't want to believe, don't believe. I got other things to do."

Laura Yazzie stopped her. "Grandmother, we need her." She turned to Stoner. "And you need us. So why don't we all make an effort to see things from one another's point-of-view?"

"Ha!" Siyamtiwa said sharply. "For three hundred years we have looked from the *pahana* point-of-view. Time we tried something better."

Laura sighed. "You're a stubborn old woman, Grandmother. My grandmother said it, my mother said it, and I say it. And I also say there's trouble in this place, and we can't solve anything by fighting among ourselves."

Siyamtiwa stood her ground, silent, arms folded, looking out into the night.

Stoner decided she'd better make the first move. "Siyamtiwa, friend, please forgive me."

The old woman glanced over her shoulder, mouth turned down like a crescent moon resting on its points.

"I know I was rude. But I'm frightened. Everything is strange here. I don't understand it. My good friend nearly died, and now my lover... Grandmother, please don't turn away from me."

Siyamtiwa looked closely into her eyes, searching for lies. She nodded, and went back to the table. "We will look at what we know, see if it makes a picture."

Stoner looked at Laura.

Laura Yazzie looked at Stoner.

They both looked at Siyamtiwa.

"I say this," the old woman began. "There is here the White man's greed. But there is more. Back in the old days, before we learned to read the truth in the White man's heart, we shared many of our secrets. Now people know things it is dangerous for them to know. I think this Begay has learned enough of sorcery that he knows the bundle will give him great Power. If he finds the bundle, he will know how to use it." She turned to Stoner. "This is why you must stop him."

163

"Why me?" Stoner asked. It seemed like a reasonable question.

"You were chosen."

"Who chose me?"

Siyamtiwa shrugged. "I was told. I made the doll. You saw it."

"But..."

"Maybe because he's White, and you're White," Laura Yazzie said. "You might have that in common. Or maybe because, being a lesbian, you don't let men into your heart to mess up your head. Or for some other reason we'll never know. Does it really matter?"

Stoner ran her finger around the top of her coffee cup, and remembered it was a gesture she had picked up from Gwen. "I guess not, as long as nothing happens to..."

"She will be okay," Siyamtiwa interrupted, "if we do this thing properly." She stood up. "You come with me. Things you gotta learn."

"But..."

The old woman snatched up Gwen's necklace. "This is the challenge. We got four days to get ready."

"Why four days?"

"That's how it is."

"But what if this was a normal everyday kidnapping? What if he asks for ransom? And what's going to happen to Gwen in those four days?"

Laura Yazzie pressed her shoulder gently. "Don't worry. I'll be here all the time. If he wants ransom, he can deliver the message to me. Meanwhile, I'll let our brothers in the Tribal Police know Mr. Begay bears watching. I know where to find you now that I know what Siyamtiwa is. We won't let anything happen to Gwen."

"What do you mean, know what Siyamtiwa is?"

Siyamtiwa moved toward the door. "You come now."

"But if I can't stop him, if he gets the bundle..."

"Trouble," Siyamtiwa said. "Long time trouble. Could be very bad."

"And what if I'm not ready in four days?"

"I think he will kill your friend, and then he will kill you. Because you stand between him and me, and I am the one he wants."

"But why didn't he go after you directly?"

"He knows my power is too great for him,"Siyamtiwa said simply. "I am born to the Fog Clan."

"The Fog Clan," Laura Yazzie explained, "were the old Ya Ya clan."

"Then why don't you..."

164

"Because I am old and tired," Siyamtiwa snapped. "My power cannot help me to walk across the desert, or stay awake through the night, or think like a White man."

"I can't think like a man, either. I'm a woman."

"You do better than I do."

She felt trapped. "But why me? Why Gwen? We don't know anything about all of this. We came out here for a vacation, and all of a sudden we're in the middle of something I don't even understand. We don't know anything about Ya Yas and *powaqas*, and I'm not Shirley MacLaine, even if the doll does look..."

"If you were Shirley MacLaine," Siyamtiwa interrupted, "you would do what I say and know it is right. You wouldn't argue, or ask questions all the time."

Stoner pushed herself away from the table. "This whole thing is crazy. Why should I trust you?"

"Because this woman," Laura Yazzie said, and gestured toward Siyamtiwa, "is not like anyone you have ever met, or will ever meet again. Because you should be honored to do as she asks." She held up Gwen's necklace. "And because of this."

Suddenly she didn't care. Didn't care about Ya Yas or strange sicknesses, or Skinwalkers, or Two-Hearts. She wanted Gwen, and she'd do anything to get her, and if it didn't make sense...

"I'll get my things," she said, and ran from the trading post, down the path to the bunkhouse.

It was a mistake. Gwen's presence was everywhere in the room. Her clothes, the plaid shirts and light khaki slacks and worn, pale jeans, her rain coat, her pajamas—all smelled of her. The pillow on her side of the bed bore the imprint of her head. Her toothbrush lay on the dresser. The book she had been reading was turned face down on the bedside table, her reading glasses marking her place.

Anything could be happening to her, out there in the dark.

I might never see her again.

Or I could look out the door and there she'd be, ambling up the road, wondering what the fuss was about, laughing her velvet laugh, saying "My goodness, Stoner, I only went for a little walk..."

But it wasn't a little walk. It was hours ago, and Larch Begay had returned the necklace, and...

Anxiety paralyzed her, and made her want to run.

She couldn't just stand there. She pressed her face against the east window, searching for a hint of morning.

Out among the buttes and mesas, a coyote sang.

In her heart she knew it was Larch Begay.

The squeak of the screen door made her blood race. She whirled around. "Gwen?"

Siyamtiwa stood in the doorway, books in her hand. "Only me," she said. "I got something to show you."

Stoner held the door for her.

The old woman placed the books carefully on the bed. "You see this?" She held up *Walking in the White Man's Shoes.* "You have touched this book. Your spirit energy is on it." She turned to the inside back cover. "This is me. Mary Beale." She opened the photo album to the pictures of Maria Hernandez. "This is also me, Maria Hernandez. Now you understand?"

Stoner looked at the photos. "I suspected this, but it didn't..."

"So you know this thing is not just about you and me, Green-eyes. Or about the Two-Heart. It is about magic."

"I suppose."

"Laura Yazzie says I gotta tell you everything. I think maybe she is right, even if she is a Headpounder."

Stoner smiled weakly. "It would be helpful."

"You try to keep an open mind, okay?"

Stoner nodded.

"If you don't understand, pretend you do. Maybe you get used to it."

"All right."

"A long time ago when the People came up into the Fourth World—this world—Masau said they had to go in all directions and then they could come home and live on the Black Mesa land. But before that some of them were living over by Canyon de Chelly and they had a hard time because the rain had gone away so nothing grew and they had to eat wild grain. They were very hungry. One day a girl went to look for grain and she found a lot but the place was too far away so she had to be there all night. In the dark a man came and gave her meat and stayed with her but they didn't have relations.

"The girl went home the next day, and after a while she had a baby. People looked at her sideways, but she knew she hadn't had relations and her parents knew it, too. They called the little baby Siliomomo and he was Yucca Plant Clan because of his mother.

"One day Siliomomo went to hunt and there was the place where his mother had met the strange man, and the man came and took him to where there were lots of people in the *kivas.* They went down in the *kivas* and the people put on different animal skins and they were those animals. And he told him they got their power from animals

166

and they called it Ya Ya power because when Somaikoli—who is the chief Ya Ya God—when he comes around everyone says, 'Yah-hi-hi. Ya-hi-hi!' So Silimomo made a ceremony of the Ya Ya and everywhere his clan went there were animals to hunt and help them.

"By the time they got to Walpi, over on Black Mesa, the Ya Ya ceremony belonged to the Fog Clan. They could go around and you wouldn't see them because they knew how to make fog come around them. They could see in the dark and make things move across the room and walk over fire without getting burned. People say they could jump off the top of the mesa and land at the bottom and be okay, but I never saw that so I don't know if it's true.

"There was a lot of power in the Ya Ya. Lot of magic. But then some people wanted to do bad stuff with it and everybody got afraid so they made them stop the ceremony and the ones that wouldn't stop, they made them leave. But first they took all the fetishes and the pahos and baskets and other stuff and put them in a cave and that's what Begay wants to find." She looked at Stoner. "So now you understand?"

"Perfectly," Stoner said a little wildly. "It clears it all up."

Siyamtiwa got to her feet. "Good. We go now."

"But I don't know how to fight *powaqa*," Stoner protested.

"Not hard. Just a brave heart."

She cringed. "I don't have a brave heart. I never had a brave heart. Even my blood is yellow."

"That's okay," Siyamtiwa said. "We fix."

"I don't know if I want to be fixed. I mean, maybe the smartest thing about me is my natural inclination to run like hell in the face of danger."

"You ready to go now?" Siyamtiwa started for the door.

Stoner buried her face in her hands. "We only wanted a vacation."

Siyamtiwa grunted. "Life gave you lemons. Make lemonade."

She felt as if the entire inside of her body was populated by hyperactive centipedes. "I have to pack. What do I need?"

"Everything you need, I got."

"If I have to stay overnight, I want a change of underwear." Stoner realized she sounded ridiculous. "And my toothbrush. I won't go without my toothbrush. And my knapsack, and first aid kit…" She knew she was stalling. "And clean socks."

"Okay."

Great. Now that I've agreed to get myself killed, or worse, she's all generosity. "Will I need a book?"

167

"Book?"

"To read. In case I have time on my hands."

"We only got four days. No time on your hands."

"Can I be ready in four days?"

"Maybe," Siyamtiwa said with a shrug. "Maybe not."

"Stop that! Don't tell me maybe-maybe not. I need to know the truth."

"The truth," said Siyamtiwa placidly, "is maybe, maybe not."

Stoner sighed. "Well, will I need my pocket knife?"

"Is this a magic knife?"

"No, it's a Swiss Army knife. Aunt Hermione gave it to me for Christmas."

"Better bring that. Maybe she put magic in it."

Stoner stuffed a few belongings into her knapsack. "I guess that's it."

"You're gonna need the doll."

"Right." She looked over at the dresser. The doll was gone. She pulled out the drawers, searched the floor. "I don't understand. It's been here all along."

"Maybe your Gwen took it."

Stoner shook her head. "I doubt it." She searched under the bed, the closet floor, her suitcase. "It's not here."

"This is not good."

"Well," Stoner said, "I didn't expect you to give me a medal."

"Anybody else been in your room?"

She started to deny it then remembered the afternoon. So long ago. "Jimmy Goodnight."

"What is a Jimmy Gooodnight?"

"Larch Begay's friend."

Siyamtiwa turned on her heel and stomped out the door and off through the darkness toward Long Mesa, muttering to herself in Hopi.

Stoner, hurrying after her, knew better than to ask her what she was saying. She knew it wasn't good.

TEN

Purple dawn lightened to red, then yellow. Night chill clung to rocks and shadows. Stoner panted and stumbled her way up the steep slope. It seemed as if they had been walking for days, always uphill. Siyamtiwa's pace never lessened or quickened. She was a machine.

Maybe, Stoner thought, as she winced against the burning knots in her calves, she isn't human. Maybe she only tricks me into thinking she exists. Maybe this whole place is a dream, and I've blundered into the Spirit World. Maybe it rises once every hundred years, like Brigadoon.

The ache in her side was no dream. Neither was the trembling in her knees. Her knapsack felt as if it were full of rocks. It scraped and bounced against her back. Her feet burned until she was certain she could count the stitches in her socks.

"Go on without me," she called ahead as she shrugged out of her knapsack and collapsed on the ground. "I'm going to die here."

Siyamtiwa turned and padded back down the barely-visible trail. "I forget," she said as she squatted beside Stoner, "*pahana* don't go so much without cars."

"And you say you're too old to walk across the desert, but I'm not?"

Siyamtiwa smiled. "You want water?"

Her mouth tasted like chewed aspirin. "Yes, but we didn't bring any."

"There is water near here," Siyamtiwa said and sniffed the air. "Smell."

"You can't smell water," Stoner protested. "Only Boston water smells."

Siyamtiwa gripped her arm and shook it. "Smell."

She took a deep breath. Dust. A faint suggestion of sage. Overtones of creosote. And something...cool and silver. "You're right!"

"When I can be right and not amaze you," the old woman grumbled, "then you will have learned something."

Stoner grinned sheepishly. "You're very patient, to put up with me like this."

"Not patient, just old. When you're old you know things take as long as they take."

She propped herself up on her elbows and looked around. They seemed to be on top of a large mesa. Below, canyons cut deep through layers of multicolored rock as if scratched by giant claws. Clumps of vegetation sprouted here and there. A pencil-thin line, probably a dirt track, ran along the base of the cliff. None of it was familiar. She ought to be able to spot the San Francisco Mountains that dominated the desert to the west. But there were no mountains in any direction. For all she knew, they had, during the night, slipped into a parallel universe.

"Please don't think me rude," she said to Siyamtiwa, "but how old are you?"

Siyamtiwa looked inward for a long time. "Old," she said at last. "Probably the oldest person you know. The oldest I know, anyway. How many years?" She gestured, palms up. "I don't remember. I remember lots of stuff, but not how many years. After this, I think I will retire."

Stoner smiled. "I think you've earned the right."

"Earn? When the Spirits want you to do something, they call. When you have done it, when they don't want you any more, you can go. What does this have to do with 'earn'?"

"Sorry." Stoner fiddled with a bit of dried grass. "Laura Yazzie says I should try to think like an Indian. I think maybe Laura Yazzie expects the impossible."

"She is young." The old woman chuckled. "You complained of thirst. Do you want the water to come to you? Even I don't have that much magic in me."

Stoner scrambled to her feet. "Which way?"

"Close your eyes and open your nose and tell me."

It was totally confusing. Odors came from everywhere, mixing and swirling around her. She strained and tried to sort them.

"You work too hard," Siyamtiwa said. "You scare the Water People away. Make a picture in your head."

She imagined water. Water in a glass. A lake. The ocean. A brook. Bathtub.

Settle *down*.

Okay, a waterfall. Might not be appropriate out here in Sandland, but go with what you can get. She closed her eyes.

A compass formed on her mind's screen. The needle swung rapidly and came to rest. "That way," she said, and pointed.

Siyamtiwa stood aside and let her lead.

She found the little spring in a deep and narrow crevice cut into the mesa wall. A pencil-thin stream of water trickled over rocks and disappeared into the sand. Not exactly a waterfall, but it was water. Falling water. "Hey," she said. "It works!"

Siyamtiwa rolled her eyes.

"Is this how we'll find Gwen?"

"Got a better way to do that. Eagle will find her."

Yeah, right. Why didn't I think of that?

The old woman knelt by the spring and drank from cupped hands. She wiped her mouth on her sleeve and sat back. "Now I will tell you something that you will not believe. Or, if you believe it, you will forget it." There was something close to affection in her voice. "Magic is not a thing for which you must grunt and strain. Magic is a bird that comes to you if you are very still and very quiet in your heart. But if you try to grab it, it will fly away."

"I'll try to remember that. I really will."

"Yes," said Siyamtiwa. "No doubt you will grunt and strain with trying to remember."

Stoner laughed. "You're very wise."

"Well, I had a lot of experience."

"There's something I don't understand," Stoner said hesitantly, wondering if she were treading on taboo ground.

"Lots of things I don't understand. What troubles you?"

"It's about Mary Beale. And Maria Hernandez. What did you mean when you said they were you?"

"What I said. They and me, same person."

"You mean, sometimes you've called yourself Mary Beale, and..."

"No, Green-eyes," Siyamtiwa said firmly. "I *am* Mary Beale and Maria Hernandez. Not sometimes, all times."

Oh, boy. Multiple personality. "I see."

"You don't see. You want life to be like soldiers in a straight line, first one thing, then the next, then the next. It makes you feel safe, but it is not how things are."

"Okay," Stoner said carefully. "How are things?"

"Everything goes at once, in a big mish-mosh." She chuckled. "Now you really think I'm crazy, eh?"

"I didn't say that," Stoner said, and blushed guiltily.

"That's okay. Maybe, if you think I'm crazy, you humor me more. Don't argue with me so much. Then maybe we get something accomplished." She got up, went back to the path, and disappeared over a gentle rise.

Stoner ran to catch up. "Don't leave me here!"

"You think I'm going to vanish into thin air?"

She realized that was exactly what she had been thinking, and laughed.

"I sure do like your laugh, Green-eyes. Too bad you take life so seriously."

"I know." She walked along silently for a while. "Darn it, Grandmother, it's hard being young."

The old woman looked off toward the horizon, where an eagle circled a pile of fallen rock. "Well, maybe I don't make it so easy for you, either. Ask a lot of you." She glanced slyly at Stoner. "Don't get big in the head. I said *maybe*."

"May I tell you something personal?" Stoner asked.

The old woman nodded.

"I like you."

Siyamtiwa looked away, her face softening.

Spears of sunlight found the spaces between the eastern mountains and flooded onto the desert, chasing away the last of the dawn twilight.

"If you have a morning song." Siyamtiwa said, "time to sing it."

* * *

The outside of the village made Wupatki Ruin look like the Hyatt Regency. Crumbling red rock. Mortar long ago eroded by time and blowing sand. Doors fallen in. Windows fallen out. The wall that had once surrounded the town a pile of rubble. The plaza choked with dead and drifted tumbleweed. Pottery shards and chipped stone tools scattered over the ground like smashed Christmas tree ornaments. The silence whispered 'old' and 'gone'.

Stoner stood in the middle of the plaza and sensed the loneliness. "What is this place?" she asked.

"No name," Siyamtiwa answered. "Long ago forgotten."

"I wonder why the people left."

"Drought. Whites. Navajos." The old woman shrugged. "Maybe the Spirits said go."

Stoner knelt and picked up a piece of broken pottery. It was part of a bowl, black paint in geometric designs on white clay. She held it up. "Do you know what this is?"

Siyamtiwa gave it a cursory glance. "*Hisatsinom*. You like my town?"

"To tell you the truth, " Stoner said hesitantly, "it looks as if

172

someone's been chewing on it."

Siyamtiwa chuckled.

"How long have you lived here?"

"Long time. Too long to remember."

"Time doesn't mean much to you, does it?"

"I'm here, long time here. Someday gone. How many years doesn't matter."

Stoner brushed her fingers over the broken pottery gently. "Did your people live here?"

"Some."

"This was a Fog Clan town?"

"For a while."

Stoner picked up what looked like the broken head of a terra cotta bear.

"Siyamtiwa, are you a sorceress?"

"*Powaqa*? No. Like your Hermione. *Tuhikya*, Healer."

Stoner stirred through the shards. They made a sound like tiny bells. "Do you have as much power as Begay?"

"Not if he has the bundle."

"If he doesn't?"

The old woman shrugged.

"If I can't do what you need me to do, what happens?"

"Nobody blames you. You do what you can."

"But...in general, what will happen."

"Pretty bad stuff." Siyamtiwa said.

"How bad?"

"Some legends say all the *powaqa* from all over the world meet at *Palangwu*, over by Canyon de Chelly. Maybe true, maybe not. If true, and they get the bundle...could be a lot of trouble."

"Trouble?"

"Land dies. People die. Maybe even the sun dies."

"Are you talking about Nuclear War?"

"Mushroom bomb," said Siyamtiwa, "is the White man's Ya Ya bundle."

Stoner mulled it over. "You really think I can stop him?"

"*He* thinks you can stop him. So he takes your woman. He read something in you, Green-eyes. He is afraid of you."

Stoner laughed humorlessly. "He has a funny way of showing it."

"He shows it in the man's way." Siyamtiwa thrust out her chest and pulled her skirt up between her legs to form trousers. "Big man here," she shouted, swaggering around the plaza. "Everybody get out of the way of big man." She dropped her skirt. "When man starts kicking stuff around, that's how you know he's afraid."

"Hey," Stoner said with a grin, "we may not speak the same language, but we have the same politics."

"Frightened man is a very dangerous man. You gotta be extra careful."

"If I'd known I had all this scary power," Stoner said, "maybe I could have done something about the '84 election."

"Everybody drunk in '84. Gonna wake up to big hangover, eh?" Siyamtiwa perched on an intact section of wall and swung her legs. "We got some ways out here you *pahana* women oughta think about. Our women own everything. All property. Man and woman marry, he joins her clan. She gets tired of him, one night he comes home and all his stuff is on the front porch. He's gotta pick it up and go away." She crossed her arms over her chest. "I got rid of three, four that way."

"Too bad Gwen didn't know about that," Stoner said. "We had to kill her husband to get rid of him."

The old woman looked at her sharply. "You have killed?"

"It was self-defense. It took two of us and a horse." She glanced up. "Does that disqualify me?"

"I've been too easy on you," Siyamtiwa said. She hopped down from the wall and started across the plaza. "You come," she tossed over her shoulder. "We begin."

*   *   *

From the outside, Siyamtiwa's house had the same crushed-graham cracker look as the rest of the village. Inside, it was a different story. A single room of whitewashed adobe walls, the roof supported by rough log timbers, the windows without shades or glass. The first impression was light, light pouring through the doorway, light reflecting from the walls, light broken into colors by the bits of crystal and tinted bottles that sat on a high shelf opposite the windows and turned the rough wall into a mosaic of rainbows and hues. The second impression was coolness, as the thick clay absorbed the sun's heat, storing it by day to release it by night.

A rough cot-like bed lay against the north wall, the head facing east. It was covered with a woven blanket of natural, earth-tone dyes. Other blankets covered the dirt floor. Near the door stood an ancient wood-burning stove, in another corner an open fireplace with raised hearth. A large, hand-made basket held scraps of material and dried yucca leaves. On a table against the wall sat a kerosine lamp, tin plate

174

and eating utensils, and a pottery mug that looked as if it had been salvaged intact from the shards in the courtyard.

Stoner touched it. "This is beautiful. Is it a copy?"

"No copy," Siyamtiwa said.

"How old is it?"

The old woman shrugged. "Seven hundred, eight hundred years. Hard to remember."

"It survived that long," Stoner said wonderingly. "It isn't even cracked."

"I take good care of stuff," Siyamtiwa said.

"Even so, it must have been lying around a long time before you found it."

"You act like one of the museum people. Maybe you'll steal my stuff and sell it."

"If I were thinking of that," Stoner said, "I'm sure you'd know it before I did." Talking about museums made her think of Mary Beale. "Siyamtiwa, about Mary..."

"Mary Beale retired now, couple of years ago. Living in Albuquerque. Out Chamayo Road. House with light blue door, lots of sunlight. You want to visit?"

Stoner rubbed the back of her neck. "Well..."

"Bet you're sorry you asked," Siyamtiwa said with a sly look.

"You know how it is with me."

Other pieces of pottery and scraps of woven blanket lay on the floor, up against the walls. Siyamtiwa pointed them out. "Hohokam, Sinagua—all old stuff. Some from Wupatki, some from Chaco, some other places. All a little different. Mary Beale gets mad I keep this around. Should be in museum, she says. Under glass, she says. I think maybe Mary Beale got too much education. Next thing she'll want me under glass."

Stoner decided to ignore that in the interest of her own sanity. "This place is wonderful," she said, and meant it.

"It's okay. Got no cable hook-up or VCR, though."

"I'm sure you get plenty of entertainment."

"Sure," Siyamtiwa said. "Lotsa ghosts to talk to, tell stories. Sometimes animals come along. Sister Angwusi—Sister Crow—she makes good gossip. Other things happen, too, but I don't want to make you nervous."

"Good idea," Stoner said, feeling as if a cold breeze had just drifted through the room. She slipped out of her knapsack. "Well... uh...where would you like me to put my things?"

"Come look around. Find something you like." She led the way

175

past the blanket door and around the plaza. What had seemed before like piles of rubble took on the shapes of rooms.

Some were unusable, roofs fallen in, a wall collapsed. Some were already occupied by mice or snakes or things that lived in holes in the ground that she'd rather not observe too closely. Others were piled with broken pottery and had apparently served as the *Hisatsinom* version of a dumpster. But the most remarkable thing about the place was the absence of litter. No paper scraps. No mangled foil, shredded styrofoam, candy wrappers, cigarette packs. No yellow film cartons.

As she walked and looked, she began to feel sleepy, a slight, pleasant dizziness, as if she were slipping backward and down. She leaned against a wall. The sun washed over her in gentle waves, stroking and soothing. Dust gave the air a burnt smell. Silence formed a dome around her.

"Come," Siyamtiwa said, and took her arm.

Her feet barely seemed to touch the ground. Then there was shade and coolness all around. She felt her knees give way beneath her. "I'm sorry," she murmured, and sank to the ground.

"You sleep now, that's good," Siyamtiwa said. She slipped a soft pillow beneath Stoner's head.

As she drifted off, she could hear the old woman nearby, chanting.

*   *   *

It was dark when she awoke. For a moment she was afraid. She sat up, joints complaining. The ground was hard, and cold. Beneath her head, her knapsack was stiff and lumpy as a sack of potatoes. She struggled to her feet and went to the door. Across the plaza, a faint light marked the window of Siyamtiwa's room. On the ground by her own doorway she found a candle and matches. At least Siyamtiwa didn't expect her to see in the dark like a Two-Heart. She lit the candle and looked around.

The room was small and perfectly square. The dust of dead years had drifted into piles where the walls met the floor. The sandstone blocks smelled dry and red. Overhead, a roof constructed of dried cornstalks—some with small ears attached and hanging down—made a zig-zag pattern.

Had that roof been there before? Had she, by accident or manipulation, fallen asleep in front of the one roofed room in town? Or had Siyamtiwa levitated those corn stalks and spruce beams up there while she was unconscious?

Maybe the old woman had conjured up a platoon of beavers.

Chisel-tooth Construction Company. No job too big or too small. We work while you sleep.

She decided not to look too closely at the cut ends of the stalks. There might be toothmarks.

She dripped wax to secure the candle to a window sill and sat down, back against the wall. Well, here I am—wherever here is.

Loneliness flooded in to fill the silence. And longing. And fear.

Oh, God, please let Gwen be all right.

The fear rose and expanded in her like yeast. It traveled outward from her heart and filled her legs, her arms, her mind. She saw Gwen broken, dead, her body crushed, her clothing torn, and blood...so much blood.

She tried to push around the fear, to sense what was true. To get behind the picture with a clear mind.

But fear held tight.

I'm never going to see her again.

Never.

Don't give in to this, she told herself roughly. The truth is, nothing is definite.

I'm never going to hold her again.

You have to fight. Don't let it take your strength.

The one person in my life who ever made me feel understood, and we only had five months together.

I never loved anyone the way I loved her.

Stop! Someone's putting those thoughts in your head. You can control it.

She thought of advice Dr. Edith Kesselbaum had given her once. "Turn your emotion into a person. Sit down and talk to it. Ask it what it wants from you. And don't you dare tell anyone I told you this. If the insurance company finds out I'm handing out New Age advice, my malpractice rates will skyrocket."

Stoner closed her eyes and tried to make a Fear person.

It turned out to be huge, mean, clumsy, and hairy, and said its name was Kurt. It said it liked to see her cringe. It said it liked to trample her into the ground and turn her into a spot of grease. It said it liked to be In Charge. It said it was going to get inside her and stay there. It said...

She asked if they could make a deal.

Kurt said no deals.

She pointed out that he was merely a psychological exercise.

Kurt said he didn't give a shit.

She threatened to send a small, yappy dog with tiny sharp teeth

177

to nip at him and drive him crazy forever.

He said if that was the best she could do, she might as well pack it in.

Okay , asshole, she thought. Okay, hang around, see if I care.

She heard Edith Kesselbaum's voice telling her this wasn't what she had in mind, exactly. What she had in mind, exactly, Stoner, if you don't object to a teeny suggestion, is that you try to make *friends* with this person.

Hey, Kurt, wanna make friends?

Kurt roared a laugh drenched in halitosis.

Sorry, Edith, he's not interested.

Nonsense. Everybody wants a friend, it's human nature.

What say, Kurt? That true?

He laughed again, and the ground trembled.

This one can't be helped, Edith. I think what we have here is your basic psychopath.

Anti-social personality, Edith said. The terminology's been updated.

Right.

She turned back to Kurt. Buzz off, buzzard-breath.

He roared and beat his chest and started toward her.

The energy-knot in her stomach began to glow. She concentrated on the warmth, on gathering it and sending it toward him. She breathed deeply, pulling energy from the air, building a shining gold cord that reached out...

Kurt took a step backward.

She kept on sending.

He backed up a little more.

Okay, she thought as she held him at bay, let's see if Gwen can slip through.

She squeezed her eyes shut and strained. Part of her mind reached out like a hand.

Come on, Gwen.

She clenched her fists.

Come through, Gwen. Please come through.

"My goodness," she heard a velvet voice say. "What in the world are you doing?"

Her eyes flew open. "Gwen!" She scrambled to her feet and started toward her.

Gwen backed away. "I don't think you'd better touch me."

"Why not?"

"I don't know exactly how I got here," Gwen said, " but I don't

178

feel very substantial." She held her hands up and looked at them. "I think I might be an out-of-body experience."

Stoner ached to touch her. "Are you all right?"

"Sort of. I mean, where I am...was...whatever...it isn't the Waldorf Astoria."

"You're with Larch Begay, aren't you?"

"Not willingly, Stoner. You don't have to make it sound like an accusation."

"Can you come a little closer?"

Gwen took a couple of steps forward.

"Are you sure I can't touch you?"

"You better not. If I wake up or something, I'll be back in that cave."

"You're in a cave?"

"It's what we call home. God, Stoner, when am I going to get the men out of my life?"

"Are you alive?" Stoner asked.

"What do I look like? The Ghost of Christmas Past?"

"Is he treating you okay?"

"Well, it isn't exactly Disney World, but he's not into rape. Yet." She held out a hand, then jerked it back before Stoner could take it. "Look, I might fade any minute. Can we talk fast?"

"Do you know where you are? The part of you that's not here, that is?"

Gwen shook her head. "It was dark when he brought me here. I don't know how he managed it. I didn't see him or hear him or anything. One minute I was walking along, and the next thing I knew I was in a cave, tied up. I'm sorry I stormed out like that, Stoner. It was really stupid."

"You couldn't help it."

"Were you terribly worried?"

"Of course I was, for God's sake."

Gwen sighed. "I hate this. The wrong people are getting hurt."

"I'm all right now," Stoner said. "Gwen, are you sure you don't have any idea where you are?"

"I'm in a cave. That's all I know. There's something in here that Begay wants, but I can't figure out what it is. I think he's planning to trade *me* for *it*."

Stoner nodded.

"Do you know what it is?" Gwen asked.

"Yes, but it's pretty complicated."

"Well, if you have a chance to get a message to whoever thought this up, I hope you'll express my undying indignation."

"It has to do with Spirits," Stoner said.

"Lovely. Listen, I don't care if it's about the Second Coming. I have *had* it with being the victim."

Stoner smiled.

"One of these days," Gwen went on, "it's going to be *my* turn. And there are going to be a lot of unhappy people in the world." She was taking on an opalescent quality. She looked down at herself. "Listen, do you think many folks know this trick?"

"I don't know," Stoner said.

"Well, I hope they don't. I can just see uninvited guests dropping in at all hours of the day and night." She shuddered. "What if my grandmother could do it. We'd never have a moment's peace."

Either the light was fading or Gwen was.

"Don't go," Stoner begged. "Please."

"I can't help it. I think I wore myself out. Literally. Come get me soon." She held out her hands. "I love you. I miss you. I'm so afraid." She was gone, and left behind a great, aching emptiness.

"Don't leave me Gwen. GWEN!" The sound of her own shout woke her. She rubbed her eyes and looked around, dazed. The sky beyond her window was black.

Only a dream.

Except for the candle that burned on the window sill.

But Siyamtiwa could have placed it there while she slept.

She got up, rubbed the stiffness from her knees and hips, and started across the courtyard.

Someone had covered the earth with a gigantic cobalt cup filled with stars.

Words drifted through and around her mind. Strange words, in a strange language.

Ghosts, no doubt. Old Spirits loitering around downtown waiting for a little action.

Could Gwen see the night sky where she was?

Stoner didn't think so.

God, I hope I did the right thing, coming here.

Of course you did. Laura Yazzie is looking for her back at Spirit Wells. The police are looking wherever police look. You're doing the only thing left to do...

...warp off and check out the Twilight Zone.

She smelled smoke, light, sharp with a touch of sweetness, and realized she was hungry.

I wonder what Siyamtiwa eats. Probably not much.

What if it's something exotic, like raw rattlesnake, or fried iguana? Or something occult, like newts' tongues and boiled bat wings?

Wish I'd picked up a couple of Hershey bars.

A whole trading post stuffed with canned and wrapped and plastic food, and I didn't have the sense to pick up a few Hershsey bars.

The aroma grew stronger, richer.

Heck, anything that smells that good can't be too bad.

She stood outside the blanket-covered doorway and wondered what the local custom was for making your presence known in the dark. If Siyamtiwa followed Navajo etiquette, which necessitated waiting until she was noticed, and if her advanced age had affected her hearing, it could be a long, cold night.

She cleared her throat softly.

Nobody stirred.

She vaguely recalled—from a book she'd read as a child—that Indians asked permission to enter a tepee by scratching on the cloth. Maybe...

"*Hai*," Siyamitwa said.

Stoner brushed the blanket aside. "All right to come in?"

The old woman gestured her forward. "Next time don't stand out there like a bad ghost."

"I was trying not to disturb you," Stoner said, miffed.

"Why? You been making noise all night, you and that other one."

Stoner felt her skin crawl. "I...I guess I talked in my sleep."

"That must've been it." Siyamtiwa turned back to her cooking.

There was a fire in the raised fireplace. Siyamtiwa spread a thin batter on a large flat stone that rested on the fire. She watched it for a few minutes, then peeled it off. It looked like a sheet of marbleized tracing paper.

"*Piki*," she explained as she rolled it into a cone. "Pretty good stuff."

"It certainly smells good."

Stoner sat cross-legged on the floor and looked around. More cones of *piki* lay piled in a yucca leaf basket. A pottery bowl held a stew of meat and beans. The teapot steamed, and a freshly cut melon soaked in its own pink juice.

"This is quite an array," Stoner said, wanting to fling herself into the middle of the meal like a pig in garbage and disgrace herself.

"Don't have company so much any more," Siyamtiwa said. "Big

181

feasts in the old days. Ceremonies. People come from a long way, stay a week maybe. Eat and sing, gossip. That was good."

"I guess you've seen a lot of changes," Stoner said.

The old woman nodded. "That's how it goes. Things change. Got to be like Changing Woman, go along, not fight." She peeled off a sheet of *piki* and spread more batter. "But it's good not to lose the old ways, too." She pointed her chin toward the food. "You eat. I don't get hungry so much any more."

Stoner looked around. "This is all for me?"

"You gonna need it. Won't eat again until you're with your woman."

"Do you really think I'll see her again?"

Siyamtiwa sighed. "Always doubts. I bet your Hermione has a bad time with you."

"Not really."

"I better find out how she does that."

Stoner smiled. "She doesn't pay any attention to me."

"Pretty smart woman."

"I wish you could meet her," Stoner said, "I know you'd get along."

"That might be rough on you, Green-eyes. Two against one."

Stoner nibbled on a piece of *piki*. "This is good. It tastes like corn."

"That's right,"Siyamtiwa said. "Corn's very big magic out here. Keeps away bad stuff."

"Like evil spirits?"

"And hunger. This is blue corn. Hopi corn." She got to her feet and poured them each a cup of tea. "Drink this. Don't taste so good, but good for you."

It had a smoky, bitter taste. Not really unpleasant. The kind of taste you might acquire a liking for. "What is it?" Stoner asked.

"Some herbs. Some other stuff. Make you sleep good."

"I've already slept a whole day away."

"That's okay."

Stoner realized, with surprise, that Siyamtiwa was looking at her affectionately. It embarrassed her a little, and made her feel childishly proud.

She picked up the bowl of stew and worn tin spoon. "What do we have to do to get ready?"

The old woman got to her feet. "I got something to show you." She scrounged in several baskets, at last drawing out a length of snow white woven material. She placed it in Stoner's lap.

182

Stoner touched it carefully. The weave was complicated and hard to read in the candle-and-fire light, but it looked and felt as if each thread had been put there with great care and purpose,as if—if she only knew the language—the shawl would tell stories to her fingers.

"Unfold it,"Siyamtiwa ordered.

She hesitated. "I'd hate to damage it, or get it dirty."

"If I gotta tell you everything two-three times, I'm not gonna live long enough to see the end of this."

"Sorry," Stoner muttered. She spread the cloth between them. It was larger than she expected, nearly the size of a bed sheet. The whiteness of it was blinding. It seemed to glow with its own light.

"This is my burial robe," Siyamtiwa said. "You think Masau will like it?"

"I'm sure he will." Stoner looked up at the old woman. "You're not afraid of death, are you?"

"I don't think about death like you do. Not the Big Silence."

Stoner found herself transfixed by the cloth. The pattern of thread almost spoke to her. "You believe in reincarnation, then?"

"Hard to explain," Siyamtiwa said. "I think only one life, sometimes here. Sometimes somewhere else. Sometimes one way, sometimes another. But only one life all the time." She pulled the robe onto her own lap. "You eat now."

The stew was lamb, and delicious. She tried not to wolf it down.

"Pretty good, eh?" Siyamtiwa asked.

"Wonderful."

"I cook okay. Not like Maria Hernandez, though. She was best cook in Navajo County."

Stoner swallowed hard, cleared her throat, and forced a smile. "Is she still alive?"

Siyamtiwa shook her head sadly. "Gone a long time now. Gray sickness got her. Came and took away her strength and ate up her insides. Wouldn't let her die easy. Lots of months she lay on her cot in her little house and waited for Masau to come."

"I see,"said Stoner.

"One day it was very hot, so hot it was like wet cloths in your nose and mouth, hot like bricks on your chest. Someone came to see her—maybe grocery boy, maybe her nephew Pete, she couldn't see so good by then. When he went away he didn't close the screen door right, left a little space, maybe half an inch. So the flies wanted to come in, but Maria didn't like flies, made her mad, worse than skunks and rats maybe. So she was there on her little cot and

183

watching the flies come in and walk on her white porcelain sink and taste the fruit she couldn't eat any more and it made her mad. Lightning in the brain mad. So mad she got up and thought she'd kill those flies, but she fell down on the floor and it felt so good and cool her spirit could go away."

Stoner scooped up the last drips of gravy on a scrap of *piki*. "But if what you say is true, about one life and all, then she must be around somewhere."

"Well, I got some. Not cooking, though. Mary Beale got that, I guess. Maybe someone else. Hard to tell."

"Grandmother," Stoner said, "forgive me if this is rude, but do all Hopis believe the way you do?"

"Probably not. Why? You wanta join up?"

"No, thank you," Stoner said with a laugh. "I have enough problems."

Siyamtiwa cleared her plate away. "Yeah, you gotta figure out that '84 election stuff."

"I wish I could. It's the women I don't understand."

"White women got their heads all mixed up. Can't think clear. Tell 'em you're gonna pass a big law, make 'em equal with men, makes 'em nervous." She held up a bit of her skirt between two finger and minced around the room. "Ooooo, don't make that big law. I don't wanta marry my girlfriend and go in Army and make pee-pee with men. I'm a lay-dee!"

Stoner fell back on the floor.

"White people always afraid. Afraid of strangers, afraid of friends, afraid of everything. Must be because their Spirits aren't friendly." She sat down and held up a corner of the white cloth. "See that?" She pointed to a tear in the material, a rip about three inches long and unraveling at either side. "This thing got torn. My eyes don't see good enough to fix it. I don't want to go meet Masau looking like a beggar. Think you can mend it?"

"I can try."

The old woman handed her a bone needle and a length of cotton thread.

"I'm not very good at this sort of thing. Will it matter if I break the pattern?"

Siyamtiwa seemed to find that amusing.

"Did I say something stupid?"

"You think things are all stop and go, like traffic signals. I think maybe more like a river." She tapped Stoner's hand. "You can't break pattern, only make new pattern. You understand?"

"I think so." She took a stitch. The cloth felt soft and alive to her touch.

"So," said Siyamtiwa, "each time you draw the thread through, you change the world. How do you like that?"

"Frankly," Stoner said as she bent closer to the work, "it's terrifying." She made a few more changes in the world.

Siyamtiwa took a small pipe and a bit of tobacco from a little box. "I'm gonna make some smoke now. Okay with you? "

"Sure." The rip was closing slowly beneath her fingers. The stitches did seem to make a pattern—nothing that would win any prizes, but distinctively her own.

She heard a soft drumming, and looked up. Siyamtiwa sat cross-legged on the floor. She tapped lightly on a piece of leather stretched over a bone hoop. Designs were painted on the drum—spirals and turtles, rabbits, snakes, stylized deer.

"This bother you?" the old woman asked.

"Not at all. It's kind of relaxing." Between the meal, the tea, the soft light, and the rhythmic pat-pat of Siyamtiwa's fingers on the drum, she was beginning to feel calmer than she could remember feeling in a long time.

She worked for a while, not thinking, listening to the drumming, breathing in the mingled odors of corn and mesquite and tobacco. This is a story, she said to the thread, of a White woman who comes out here from the east and gets mixed up in something about sorcerers and Ya Ya sickness, and mends a burial robe for old Siyamtiwa, and who means well even though she doesn't know what in the world she's doing.

"That's a pretty good story," Siyamtiwa said, drumming. "Hope it comes out okay."

Stoner looked up. "How do you do that, know what I'm thinking?"

"Not hard. A trick. You can do it real easy."

"How?"

"Empty your mind and I'll put something in it."

She did, and came up with nonsense. "I can't do it."

"Why do you say that?"

"Because I heard you invite me to go down a hole in the ground, and I'm not Alice in Wonderland."

"I'm not a white rabbit, either," Siyamtiwa said. "You want to see this hole in the ground?" She stood and took the burial robe. "Come with me. Finish this later."

The plaza was black as ink. Overhead, the stars seemed very far away and very cold. The silence was tangible.

"Watch how you go." Siyamtiwa reached for her hand, and led her to a break in the packed ground, a round opening the size of a man-hole. A ladder of raw pine trunks protruded from the opening.

"This wasn't here when I came through earlier," Stoner said.

"Weren't supposed to see it." She touched the ladder. "This goes down into *kiva*. Did secret ceremonies down there in the old days. Whites not allowed, but it's okay now. Nobody down there now but ghosts." She stood aside to let Stoner precede her.

Nobody but ghosts. Very comforting.

She felt as if she were climbing to the center of the earth, from darkness to darkness. The blackness reached up and lapped around her ankles, her legs, her hips. Like warm water. She let herself sink into it. When her foot touched ground she stood away from the ladder and listened to the shape of the room. The ceiling arched overhead in a dome that amplified the sound of her breathing, her heartbeat, even the blood churning in her veins. Beyond that sound she could hear the air moving, and whispers in the air, old whispers like dry leaves blowing over sand, tumbling end-over-end, the hiss of sand falling into the depressions left behind. Grains of sand falling one-by-one with a papery, ticking sound.

The ladder creaked. She reached up to help Siyamtiwa down the last few rungs. The old woman leaned on her arm, as light and hollow-boned as a sparrow.

A candle flame illuminated the *kiva* and set the ladder's shadow dancing.

It occurred to Stoner that she hadn't heard a match strike.

There was only the sudden light.

She put the thought from her mind.

Ahead she saw what looked like an altar. Elaborately carved sticks placed upright in the ground. Smaller sticks with feathers attached by cotton threads. Brightly painted dolls that resembled the *kachinas* in Mary Beale's book. A flat basket piled high with blue corn.

Beside her, Siyamtiwa mumbled a prayer.

Stoner waited.

The old woman placed a small deerskin pouch in her hand. "Take this. Keep you safe."

It contained a soft, slightly gritty substance. Corn meal. She clutched it tight.

Siyamtiwa led the way, once slowly around the circle and toward a shadow-darkened hole, a tunnel behind the altar.

Stoner could have sworn it hadn't been there before.

The old woman was nearly out of sight in the shadows. Stoner hurried to catch up. Siyamtiwa moved along smoothly but evenly, almost as if she floated.

Stoner drew back against the wall, reluctant to go on.

Siyamtiwa turned and motioned to her. There was reassurance in her eyes.

Now it was as if she were being carried along by the tunnel itself, or the tunnel was moving past her while she stood still. She was aware of motion, but not of causing motion.

The glow of Siyamtiwa's candle grew brighter.

The tunnel walls were white, like whitewashed rock. Cracks in the paint came toward her slowly, resolved themselves suddenly into strange symbols, and sped past.

She wasn't afraid any more. But she was light-headed, dizzy from the motion of the walls. She closed her eyes for a moment...

...and opened them in bright sunlight.

They were outside the tunnel. Cliffs rose steeply on all sides, layered in gray and red and yellow, high into the far blue sky, high enough to touch the sun. The ground beneath her feet was sandstone dust. Tufts of coarse grass broke through the packed earth. A river, choked with mud, rolled by sluggishly. She heard the sound of quick running water and looked up to see, beyond the river, a waterfall as fine and clear as spun glass. Trees and brush grew around the base of the falls. The water collected in terraced pools and reflected the blue of the sky. The air was silver-pure.

"It's beautiful," she said in awe, and turned to Siyamtiwa.

There was no one there.

"Grandmother?"

The only sounds were the fall of water and the river's low, sucking murmur. "Grandmother! Siyamtiwa!"

Still no answer.

Don't panic, she told herself. She's probably hiding to test you. Sit and be calm, and she'll show up sooner or later.

She found a flat rock, warmed by the sun, and eased herself down on her back. The light and warmth were good after the darkness.

If I have to be lost for the rest of my life, this is as good a place as any.

In the distance someone began to play a wooden flute. The bright, hollow notes rose into the air like larks. Relaxing, feeling the sun, she watched questions float through her mind—where am I, how did it get light, what's happening, why?—and released them.

Something nudged her arm.

She opened her eyes.

And found herself staring into the gentle face of a little burro.

"Well, hi, there."

The donkey turned and walked away, then stopped, looked back.

It wanted her to follow.

She hesitated. She was already lost enough without...

The little gray animal trotted back to where she sat, lowered its head, and pressed its forehead lightly against her face. Its fur was soft and dusty, its eyes round and gentle. It made little snuffing noises deep in its throat.

Come, it said.

She got up and let it lead her. Over powdery, pebbly ground, along the river's edge, past cottonwoods and willows, along the canyon walls where fossils of trilobites lay embedded shoulder-high in ancient rocks.

They came at last to a sandy area, stripped of vegetation, a cleared circle.

This is as far as I'm allowed, the donkey said. You have to go to the center alone.

Will you wait for me?

The animal shook its head.

Then I won't go.

You'll see me again. Go.

She took a step into the circle. When she looked back the burro was gone.

The ground inside the circle rose slightly, too gradually to see, but her feet could read the change. When the rising stopped, she knew she had come to the Place.

Now what?

A movement on the ground, at the corner of her eye, caught her attention. She knelt.

A small brown spider scurried busily back and forth among the sand and pebbles. It stopped and looked up at her, its black eyes seeing through to her mind. Then it backed slowly into a tiny hole, a hole that seemed to go straight down forever.

It came back out into the sun. Then returned to the darkness.

Three times it repeated the dancelike movement. Then it was gone.

She stared down at the tiny hole, puzzling.

And suddenly she knew, the knowledge slipping into her head, that this—spot—was the center of the world, the beginning of it all, the Place of Emergence.

She was filled with a sudden joy, and awe, so complete, so deep it lifted her out of herself and she thought she could soar with eagles and dance on the air. She spread her arms to welcome the sun.

A red-tailed hawk flying overhead dropped a single feather. It landed in her outstretched hand.

"That looks pretty good," Siyamtiwa said.

Stoner blinked in confusion. She was back in the night, in the pueblo room, the burial robe stretched across her lap. The rip was closed. She looked up.

Siyamtiwa nodded. "Pretty good, " she repeated.

"Did you see what happened?"

"You bet. You sewed that real good."

"No, I mean..."

"When old Masau sees that, he's gonna think he got one hot chick old lady, eh?"

Stoner ran her hand through her hair, front to back. "You mean we've just been sitting here, like this, since... Did you put peyote or something in the tea?"

"No phoney-baloney loco plants. We made a little magic, you and me. I think maybe you're gonna be okay."

Oh, boy, here we go. Dancing down the line between illusion and reality. Life on the terminator. Did we travel, or didn't we? What's behind the door, the lady or the tiger?

"Look what you got there," Siyamtiwa said, pointing to Stoner's chest.

She looked down and saw the deerskin pouch that hung around her neck. She pulled it open, peeked inside. Corn meal. A long strand of hair from a burro's tail. The wing-feather of a red-tailed hawk.

"That's your medicine bag," Siyamtiwa said. "Protects you, like Grandmother Hermione's good magic. Burro and hawk give you presents. They're your Power Animals, gonna look after you. When you need spirit, you can call on burro spirit and hawk spirit." She chuckled. "Burro. If you asked me, I'd guess Brother Wolverine was your spirit animal, all the time grumbling and looking for fights."

"I thought you had to go out in the desert and fast to find your totem," Stoner said. "I thought you had to be half dead or something."

"Well,"Siyamtiwa said, "that's a good way, but takes a long time,"

Great. I've just been treated to the Reader's Digest Condensed

Version of a vision quest.

Siyamtiwa laughed. "That's pretty funny. Reader's Digest."

"Don't read my mind," Stoner said irritably. "It's rude."

The old woman thought that over. "You got a point there. Big surprise for me. You teach me something." She sucked meditatively at a tooth. "This Larch Begay, this *powaqa*, you better watch out. Maybe he can read your thoughts, too, find out things you don't want him to know."

"It's entirely likely," Stoner said.

"So we better mix him up. You know how to make a cloud come around you?"

"Of course I don't know how to make a cloud come around me."

"Think about cloud," Siyamtiwa said.

She thought about a cloud.

"Now put him in that corner over there."

She looked at the corner and thought 'cloud'. The edges of the shadows took on a slightly weakened look.

"Good. Think harder."

She thought harder. The corner turned foggy, smeared. The fog coalesced into a cloud.

"Now make him come over here to you."

Cloud she thought, come.

Nothing happened. Come on, cloud. Good cloud. Here, boy. The cloud seemed to move forward a little.

Come on boy. Go for a walk?

"Crazy woman," Siyamtiwa said. "You call a *cloud*, not a dog."

"I've never called a cloud before."

"Watch me." She stood up, hands on hips, and glared fiercely into the corner.

COME! The unspoken word filled the room.

The cloud drifted forward and hovered just beyond Stoner's reach. She was surprised the dishes and furniture and bottles and bits of crystal, everything that wasn't nailed down, didn't come with it.

"Now," Siyamtiwa said, "you call the rest of the way."

She cleared her throat and thought of herself as a magnet, or a vacuum, pulling the cloud forward. She closed her eyes and waited.

The air around her face turned cooler. She opened her eyes. The room was filled with a swirling fog. "Hey, I did it."

Siyamtiwa nodded. "You said it. We got enough cloud in here to make desert bloom."

"How do I get rid of it?"

"Release him. Tell him to go."

Stoner broke contact between her mind and the cloud. It receded, disappeared. "That was fun. What else can I do?"

Siyamtiwa shook her head in amusement. "That's enough for tonight. You gotta be careful how you use that stuff. Could do a lot of damage."

"Yeah," Stoner said gleefully.

Siyamtiwa frowned. "Am I gonna have to worry about you?"

"No, but there have been a few people in my life I'd really like to scare."

"You wait, maybe I teach you some real scary stuff." Siyamtiwa yawned and stretched. "Go now. We got a lot to do tomorrow."

"Like what?"

"Like you learn right attitude about this stuff. "

"I'll be all right, really. I just feel kind of fired up."

"You're getting some power, Green-eyes. Makes you feel like that. But remember your animal spirit, use your Power that way."

"Okay."

"Now go to bed. You're gonna use me up in one day."

"Siyamtiwa?"

"*Hoh.*"

"Why won't you call me by my real name?"

"Because we do an Indian thing here. I use Indian name. When it is done, I will call you by your White name. Okay?"

"Okay."

She strode across the plaza, past the point where the *kiva* had been but of course wasn't now. The air had the heavy, unmoving feel of three a.m. As she approached the door to her hide-away, she realized she was exhausted. The rush of excited energy drained from her like water through sand.

She wished she had taken the time to fashion some kind of bed. She dreaded the hard ground beneath her body. The lumpy pillow of her knapsack. She glanced back toward Siyamtiwa's room, but her window was dark. Oh, well what's one more sleepless night?

She lit the candle. In the center of the room lay a rough bed of juniper branches covered with soft animal hide. She stretched out on it. The fit was perfect, indentations for her hips, extra height for her head and shoulders.

Siyamtiwa must have made it while she was—wherever she had been.

191

She luxuriated in the springiness, and the sharp, fresh odor of forests. A woven blanket lay beside her. She pulled it over her and blew out the candle and fell asleep.

So deeply asleep she didn't see the paling of the darkness, the fading of the stars...

...or the large gray coyote that circled the plaza and sniffed dark doorways. It stopped outside hers and stood for a moment, listening to her deep breathing. The hairs along its backbone rose. Its silver eyes glowed. Then, sensing the coming light, it turned and trotted away from the Village-That-Has-Forgotten-Its-Name.

ELEVEN

Grandmother Eagle perched on the top rung of the *kiva* ladder. "Where's your Green-eyes this morning, old woman? Sleeping her life away?"

Siyamtiwa went on with her sweeping. "She brings wood and water."

"Is that so?" Eagle spread her wings and admired the shadows they cast on the packed earth. "I flew over the wood place, and the spring. No Two-leg there, only some Fog People."

The old woman smiled to herself.

Kwahu furrowed her brow and thought hard. "You taught her the Cloud game?"

"I did," Siyamtiwa said.

"Foolish old woman!" Eagle thrashed her wings. "You teach our tricks to the Whites? Aren't they bad enough when we can see them?"

"This one is all right."

Kwahu touched the tiny oil sacs at the base of her feathers with her beak and stroked the oil along her wings. She starts to like the Anglo, she thought to herself. This is dangerous. She glanced secretly at the old woman. Tired old grandmother. It would be good for her to end this now, before her old heart has to break.

"I hear you," Siyamtiwa said over the rustle of her sweeping. "You waste your time on me. Save it for our Skinwalker."

"This thing is hopeless," Eagle said.

"Not so hopeless. Already she has a Power Animal."

"Which one?"

"The little wild horse of the canyons."

Eagle threw back her head and laughed so hard she nearly fell from her perch. "Some Power Animal. All Brother Burro knows is to plod along and look sad."

Siyamtiwa stopped sweeping and glared at the bird. "I have enough to concern myself with, Kwahu. Must I hear your complaints as well? Maybe you try to defeat what we do here. Maybe you make a treaty with the Skinwalker, eh?"

Grandmother Eagle clacked her beak in anger. "My people make no more treaties with Two-legs. Never again."

"Well, it's a mixed-up world," Siyamtiwa said thoughtfully. "I trust this one. The Spirits sent her, and my heart tells me she is okay."

"You better be right." She paused for dramatic effect. "The Begay has found Pikyachvi Mesa."

Siyamtiwa drew in her breath sharply. "The cave? The bundle?"

"He knows it is there, but it hides from him. He is angry and impatient. Already he has sent the ransom note to the trading post, making his demands. Tomorrow I think he will begin to hurt the White woman."

Siyamtiwa looked up at the sky, where the sun was beginning to slide toward the Sacred Mountains. "This thing is supposed to happen in four days. Tomorrow is not four days."

"The man is White." Eagle cocked her head and looked at Siyamtiwa sympathetically. "We may be in for hard times, Grandmother."

The old woman set her jaw. "I don't give up. Neither does my young friend. This much I know." She dismissed Kwahu with a wave of her hand. "Go. Rest. I will need you tonight."

The eagle flapped her wings and rose steadily into the air. Siyamtiwa watched her thoughtfully.

Tomorrow.

She went to the section of broken wall overlooking the spring. She could see Green-eyes below, playing with her cloud, sending it away and calling it back, wrapping it around herself, tossing it in the air.

Siyamtiwa shook her head. Foolish *pahana*, magic is not a toy. It is a serious, deadly business.

Then she smiled, remembering how—in her long-ago young time—she had played with each new trick until she tired of it. But there had been time, then, to play with magic. She had a lifetime, many lifetimes ahead before she would need to test herself.

Oh, Granddaughter, I wish you had more than this old bag of bones to help you.

She folded her arms and wondered what to do.

* * *

"PA—HA—NA!"

The call rolled down the mesa side and caught her at the edge of the spring. She looked up, squinting against the sun. The cloud dissipated as she withdrew her attention.

194

"Here, Grandmother." She lifted the clay water jug and trudged up the path to where the old woman stood. "I filled the jars. I'll start on the wood…"

Siyamtiwa cut her off with an impatient gesture. "No more work. We got to take a trip."

"But…"

"Don't argue. We got a lot to do and not much time. Tomorrow you face the *powaqa*."

Stoner felt a sudden rush of apprehension. "Tomorrow? That isn't four days. How can I be ready?"

"The ransom note has been delivered. If you don't go there tomorrow, it will be bad for your friend."

She turned on her heel and strode toward the plaza.

Stoner trotted after her. "Grandmother, what happens if I don't do this right?"

"Maybe you die."

Well, that's wonderful. Very encouraging. You really know how to cheer a person up. "And Gwen?"

"Maybe she dies, too. Maybe the *pahana* Perkins dies. Maybe all the women die. You oughta think about that. "

"I think about it," Stoner said irritably. "This isn't exactly a picnic for me, you know."

Siyamtiwa walked on ahead of her, not speaking. The tattered blanket trailed in her wake.

I could get out now, slip away while she's not looking. Go back to Spirit Wells, let the police handle this. For all I know, Gwen's been found by now and the whole incident's closed. For all I know, there never was a Ya Ya sickness, just virus and superstition. For all I know…

"For all you know," Siyamtiwa tossed over her shoulder, "the sun will not set tonight."

"Stop reading my mind."

Siyamtiwa gave a sharp laugh. "You think so loud, I'd have to be deaf not to hear you." She stopped at the entrance to Stoner's room. "You go in there now. Travel back to the place you went yesterday. I will meet you there."

"What do you mean, travel back? I didn't…"

Siyamtiwa didn't answer.

Siyamtiwa was gone.

Stoner kicked at the dirt floor of her cubicle. Mystics. Do this, do that, travel here, travel there, make clouds. But do they tell you how to do all this wonderful stuff? Hell, no. They're too busy with

195

important things, like talking to eagles and making *kivas* appear and disappear, and reading your mind. "Reading someone's mind," she grumbled to herself, "is an invasion of privacy. A violation of guaranteed Constitutional rights." She kicked another clod of dirt. "Do you hear that, old woman? You violate my Constitutional rights."

"I hear you." Siyamtiwa's voice drifted across the plaza. "Constitution is for White man. Got nothing to do with me. Nothing to do with you, either, woman. Travel."

Stoner leaned out the door. "I don't know how," she called.

Siyamtiwa stood in her own doorway, a shadow against the dark. "How come you knew yesterday, and you don't know today?"

"*You* did that yesterday."

"And you gotta do it today." She stepped back into the shadows and disappeared.

Okay, Stoner thought, I'll give it a try. You'll see how far I get.

She crossed the plaza to the *kiva* entrance.

The ground closed. The ladder melted away into air.

All *right*, damn it. I'll do it your way.

She went back to her room, sat in the center of the floor, and closed her eyes.

Nothing happened except that she got a few minutes older.

She took a deep breath, cleared her mind, and tried again.

A fly buzzed over her head. A large, green, fat fly. The kind that makes a wet, cracking noise when you step on it. It landed in her hair. She could feel it crawling around, tickling against her scalp. It made her feel like a hunk of rotting meat.

Go away, she thought.

The fly launched itself into the air, circled once, and went away.

Some trick, huh? Hot stuff. I can get a lot of mileage out of a trick like that.

She settled herself down again.

How am I supposed to do this by myself? Last night I had drumming, and smoke, and maybe the tea. And all of a sudden I'm on my own? How fair is that?

But I'm going to be on my own tomorrow, aren't I? Completely on my own. So I'd darn well better be able to do this, or we are in deep trouble. Deep terminal trouble. The kind of trouble after which you never have trouble again, because there isn't any you to have it.

Go over the steps you followed last night.

Imagine yourself crossing the plaza with Siyamtiwa. Step onto the ladder. Climb down, one rung at a time, into the darkness at the bottom. Feel it. Feel the room, the coolness, the vibration of air.

Now see the altar, lit from behind you. Walk around the room, all four directions.

Now to the right.

The opening.

The tunnel.

It pulled her along. The odd markings and symbols sped by. The speed made her dizzy. She held tight to her medicine bag.

Then she was at the mouth of the cave, in sunlight. The canyon walls rose to the sky. Clouds raced overhead, their shadows speeding along the ground. The river mumbled and shook the stones along its bank.

If this is a dream, she thought, it could win an Academy Award for cinematography.

She saw movement in the distance, down the length of the canyon, and went to meet it.

Siyamtiwa came toward her, leading the little gray burro. When it saw her, it left the old woman's side and trotted to her, pushing its nose against her shoulder.

She stroked its neck. It gazed at her with its round, liquid eyes.

She glanced at Siyamtiwa.

The old woman nodded. "Nice Power Animal. Eagle doesn't think so, but eagles don't know everything. Does it please you?"

Stoner rubbed her knuckles against the burro's forehead. "Very much."

Siyamtiwa motioned her forward. "Come. We take a walk."

The donkey plodded along behind them.

"Some people say," Siyamtiwa said as they walked along the river, "this is the place where the People go when they return to the world of the Spirits. I think I will soon come to this place for the last time."

"I'm sorry," Stoner said.

Siyamtiwa took her arm. "This is not a thing to be sorry for. It will be good to rest on the wind."

They walked in silence for a while. A cactus wren chattered among the mesquite. Lizards darted back and forth across the canyon wall, chasing insects. The burro's hooves made ticking sounds against the round river rocks.

"I will tell you about this medicine bundle," Siyamtiwa said. "This thing was here long before the Ya Ya society. It will be here always. And always there will be those who must protect it, and those who must try to find it. That is how it is. Do you understand?"

197

She understood, not in ways she could explain, but somewhere deep inside where everything that was, was—and magic was an everyday thing.

"When you're gone," she said, "who will guard the bundle?"

"Rose Lomahongva will be ready soon."

"And who will try to find it?"

Siyamtiwa shrugged. "Hard to tell. Maybe this Jimmy Goodnight who took your doll. Maybe not."

"I hope not," Stoner said. "He seems like a basically good kid, just misguided and not too bright."

"Then I don't think the Spirits will find him worthy."

"Worthy?" She was surprised. "You call Larch Begay worthy?"

"His heart is dark but pure. It flies like the arrow. There is no hesitation in him."

Stoner laughed without humor. "And you think there's no hesitation in me? Grandmother, your Spirits have made a serious error in judgement."

"You got your opinion, I got mine."

"Your opinion could get me and Gwen killed."

"I will tell you something." Siyamtiwa pointed to the canyon walls. "These cliffs are here, and this river is here. This stuff we are walking on, this is about two billion years old. And that little bit of green up there..." She indicated the tree and brush cap at the rim of the canyon. "That's only an inch deep. These walls are a mile deep. If these walls were all the time the earth has been going around, that little green inch is all the time people have been here." She stopped and looked at the sky. "What happens to you tomorrow, it doesn't make so much difference in that inch of green. It is a speck of dust on these rock walls."

"Thank you, "Stoner said dryly. "But I've never found much comfort in my insignificance."

Siyamtiwa nodded. "I forget a lot how it was to be young. Tell me what you want from this thing."

She thought it over carefully. "I want to get Gwen back. I want to stop the Ya Ya sickness for all the women. I want to keep Begay from the medicine bundle."

"And for yourself alone?"

She hesitated. "I want my part of the pattern to be correct."

The old woman smiled. "My friend Kwahu will be annoyed. She doesn't like to lose an argument." She pressed her hand onto Stoner's arm. "Tomorrow, when you go to meet the *powaqa*, remember your medicine bag and your little horse. Remember this place and how

you got here. Use what you know…" She touched Stoner's heart. "…
in here." And the top of her head. "And through the *kopavi*. Maybe
things will be okay."

"I wish you could come with me."

"I'll be there, but you won't see me. I'll help you if I can, but I got
other stuff to do."

Stoner shrugged. "Well, that's how it is with you."

"I think maybe you're getting too clever for me. Maybe the Spirits
should have sent me someone not so clever."

"I still can't believe I was sent," Stoner said.

"Why not?

"It was a coincidence. We happened to come here on vacation
because this is where Stell is. If her cousin hadn't gotten sick…"

Siyamtiwa shook her head. "Every minute of your life had to be
just so for this to be. And the *pahanas*. Even the grandmother of your
friend, who made you want to go away. Maybe even your parents,
and your grandparents. One little thing different, you not here.
When you get home, ask your Computer God what were the chances
you would be on this spot at this time. Ask him the chances you
would *not* be on this spot at this time. Then tell me you believe in
coincidence."

Stoner smiled. "You always win."

"I'm one of the People," Siyamtiwa said. "I got the advantage."

The donkey made little snuffling noises behind her. Stoner
turned to rub its soft velvet nose. When she turned back, Siyamtiwa
was gone.

"Well," Stoner said, "what do we do now, little friend?"

The burro tossed its head and started off at a fast walk. Stoner
followed. It led her down a narrow, sun-filled box canyon. At the end
hung a pale blue waterfall, fine as mist. Water dripped from the
surrounding rocks into a clear pool. The burro bent its head and
drank, inviting her to do the same. She cupped her hands and
scooped up the icy water. It tasted of purity and clean air. She
splashed it on her face and arms, and felt her skin drink thirstily.

A shadow slipped down the canyon side and told her it was time
to leave. The donkey sensed it, too, and walked ahead, leading. At
the entrance to the cave, she turned and embraced the little animal,
then stepped into the darkness.

*   *   *

She stretched, got up lazily, and strolled out into the plaza. From
Siyamtiwa's doorway came the sound of drums and rattles, and a

199

high, strong chanting. In the west, the sun touched the peaks of the San Francisco Mountains. She leaned on the village wall and watched it go down.

Somewhere out there. Gwen is somewhere out there, and tomorrow I must go to find her.

Tomorrow I go out to face a *powaqa*, armed with a bag of corn-meal, a burro's hair, a hawk's feather, a necklace of seeds and beads, and a couple of magic tricks.

I'd feel a lot more comfortable if I had a gun.

The wind toyed with her hair and reminded her of Gwen's fingers.

The drum beat faster. The dried gourd rattles clattered like a hailstorm. She wondered how Siyamtiwa could beat the drum and shake the rattles and dance and chant, all at the same time. Either she was doing some serious levitating, or she looked like a one-man band at a country fair.

The thought made her smile. She leaned back against her arms and looked up into the sky. An eagle circled overhead. She wondered if it were Siyamtiwa's Kwahu.

She supposed the eagle was the old woman's Power Animal. Well, some of us get eagles, and some of us have to settle for donkeys.

Some of us soar and some of us plod.

I am a plodder.

Hey, not to be embarrassed. History is full of good, old, relentless plodders. Like...

...like inventors. I'll bet the really good inventors are plodders.

And scientists.

And Ants.

The Ant People, Siyamtiwa had told her during one of the endless succession of stories she had spun through half the day. The Ant People had taken care of the Hopi when Topka, the Second World, was destroyed by ice. The Ant People had sheltered them in their tunnels and starved themselves to feed the Two-legs, pulling their belts tighter and tighter, until their waists were as small as they are today.

Speaking of which, she was so hungry she was ready to chew her shoe soles. Siyamtiwa hadn't been kidding about the stew—it was the last food she had seen for two days, except for endless amounts of sweet bitter tea and two slabs of *piki*.

She wondered for a moment about the tea.

Siyamtiwa was pretty close-mouth about that tea, except to say it wasn't any phoney-baloney loco weed.

Anyway, she was fairly sure she wasn't getting any mind-altering drugs. Not out here. Out here, life itself was mind-altering.

The eagle still circled. Maybe it was always there, keeping an eye on the old woman. Maybe your Power Animal looked out for you all through your life, only you couldn't see it unless you went through mind-altering experiences like vacationing in Arizona.

Quite a handsome creature, the eagle. Very impressive. Nobody'd mess with you if your Power Animal was an eagle. On the other hand, you couldn't hug it or pet it. Probably couldn't even look it in the eye for very long. And you certainly couldn't lean on it, or take a walk with it, or generally behave in a casual and friendly manner.

Burros had their good points.

Yah-tah-hey, she said silently to the eagle, and hoped it spoke Navajo since she didn't know Hopi for 'Hi'.

It dipped lower and glared at her with a fierce expression.

She spread her hands. No offense. I'm cool, okay?

She could have sworn the eagle answered "okay."

Sure, Dr. Doolittle. Let's talk to the animals. I mean, as long as we're chatting with ghosts and becoming an out-of-body Frequent Flyer, what's talking to animals? Small time stuff. Weird 101.

Siyamtiwa was working herself up to something of major importance out behind the pueblo. Her drumming and chanting had reached a frenzied pitch.

I ought to give her a hand, Stoner thought with a mixture of laziness and guilt. Then remembered she had been ordered to do nothing but 'prepare' herself.

Prepare myself. For what? How?

After all, chances are the Great Begay Encounter could end up being nothing more than a very mundane, physically exhausting knock-around.

So what's with all the 'prepare yourself' stuff? Kung Fu for the masses? New Age 'get in a good space'?

Back in the Good Old Days, 'Prepare yourself' meant 'Make your will, Buster.' Ah, the Good Old Days.

Should I concentrate on thinking only pure thoughts? If I do, my unconscious will deluge me with such an outpouring of obscenity as hasn't been seen since *The Exorcist*.

Should I focus my mind on True and Lofty things? Pray? Write my congressman? "Dear Mr. Kennedy, I have gotten myself into a terrible situation out here. Please use your considerable influence…"

I could take another of those Super-Saver mind-trips to the bottom of the canyon. But if Siyamtiwa wanted me to do that, she'd have said so, no bones about it.

I guess I'm supposed to do whatever I do to get ready for major events. Major events.

The first major event I remember was running away from home. I prepared for that by stealing fifty dollars from my mother's handbag.

Meeting Gwen was a major event. For that, I overdosed on sugar in my coffee.

High school and college graduations. They came with built-in rituals.

When Marylou and I opened the travel agency, we planned to celebrate, but it rained, the paint was still wet on the walls, the carpeting was lost somewhere south of Gardener. We couldn't get the cork out of the champagne bottle, and we both ended up being violently ill with oil-based paint poisoning.

Becoming lovers with Gwen? I didn't do that, she did. And then she got beaten up by two hoods in a dark alley.

Face it. As far as Major Events go, I have a lousy record.

We used to do energy-raising circles at the Cambridge Women's Center. Not practical, there being no one but me, Siyamtiwa and the Enemy within a ten-mile radius.

Aunt Hermione would light candles and burn incense and toss a little oil around. At the very least, gather flowers for an altar.

Flowers. It would take me a week to find a decent altars-worth of flowers out here. You got yer cactus, you got yer mesquite, you got yer creosote—altar-worthy flowers, you ain't got.

What would I do if I were home, and had to pass some time but didn't want to get too nervous?

I'd sort M&M's.

But we don't have M&M's. No flowers, no M&M's.

On the other hand, we do have rocks. Big rocks, small rocks, medium-sized rocks, rocks of unknown origin, rocks of indeterminate age, rocks of dubious composition. What we have got in Arizona, folks, is ROCKS!

She sat on the ground and scooped up a handful of pebbles.

First, by color. Yellow, grey, tan, ocher, pink. She placed them in neat piles.

Okay, now by size.

And texture. Smooth, grainy, powdery.

"That a game?" Siyamtiwa asked, coming up behind her.

202

Stoner looked up. "Not really. Sorting them calms me down, but it's better with M&M's."

The old woman squatted beside her and studied the pattern she was forming with the pebbles. "M&M's? You expecting E.T.? Better get Reese's Pieces."

Stoner laughed. "You know the strangest things."

"I get around. Sometimes I go to the Hopi Cultural Center, watch some TV." She placed a stone in the design. "Let tourists take my picture, only a dollar. Listen to White talk. Pick up a lot that way." She placed another stone. "Mary Beale, she likes movies. Goes two, maybe three times a week. Calls it 'research'. Mary Beale very La-De-Dah."

"I see," Stoner said uneasily.

"That still make you nervous. Bet you got two-three different lives going on, only you don't know it 'cause you don't want to."

"Well, I have as much as I can handle with this one."

Siyamtiwa studied the pattern and put in another stone. "One time I went to Beale. People push you around, say 'Move along, old woman.' Sometimes they say worse."

"I know how it is," Stoner said.

"'Look at that drunk Indian', they say. Whites, they think if you're standing around, you gotta be drunk."

"That's because *they* usually are," Stoner said.

Siyamtiwa nodded. "Indians not the only ones that don't hold liquor so good, eh?" She looked down at the circle and spokes Stoner had built. "Now you got a medicine wheel. That's good."

Stoner remembered the turquoise stone she was carrying in her pocket, and dug it out. She placed it in the center of the wheel.

"Hunh," Siyamtiwa said, "you find my stone."

"Your stone?"

"Got my mark on it." She picked it up and traced the gold web-like lines with a cracked thumbnail.

"Gwen found it, " Stoner said. "We didn't know it was yours. Take it."

"Left it for you. You carry it around, makes you think of me when you need to." Siyamtiwa stood up. "You come now. Got something for you to see." She started off across the plaza.

She may be old, Stoner thought as she stumbled to her feet and ran after her, but once she gets started there's no slowing her down.

The *hogan* stood beyond the walls of the town, to the east. A small, round house, it was built of rough logs and chinked with mud. The roof was thatched. A door, covered by a Two Gray Hills rug, faced the sunrise. There were no windows. A ragged stovepipe protruded from the center of the roof. The wind blew sand in the corners where the logs joined.

"This is some Navajo stuff," Siyamtiwa said. "Use lots of People's different magic, makes us good and strong, eh?"

She drew the blanket aside and motioned her in. The walls were covered with hides bearing painted symbols—bear prints, arrows, coyotes, rain clouds and stalks of corn. There were picture stories of hunts, and raids against cavalry forts, long winters in which many died, the burning of a village. One hide held pictures of masked dancers, brightly colored, shimmering even in the dull light.

Fascinated, Stoner moved closer.

"You like that?" Siyamtiwa asked.

Stoner nodded, transfixed. They were compelling.

"Kachinas," Siyamtiwa said and named them. "Soyokwuti, Ogre Mother. Kotori, Screech Owl. Tunukchina, Careful Walker. Somaikoli, you know him, eh? Ya Ya Spirit. Tawa, that's the sun. Pretty nice, huh?"

"They're a little frightening," Stoner said.

"Supposed to be. Spirits are serious stuff."

Stoner looked around the room. "Did you paint these?"

"Not me. Got from other people. Some from other tribes. Got a little bit of everything around here."

A fire pit in the center of the *hogan* was lined and encircled with rocks. Bowls of corn meal and herbs marked the four directions. Branches of cedar were scattered about. A bed of corn husks and blankets lay against the wall.

"Here's what we gonna do," Siyamtiwa said. "You stay here tonight. We wash your hair with yucca and make some steam and you can have a bath."

"I'll bet I could use one."

Siyamtiwa nodded. "You smell White. Begay will know you're there. You got to see him before he sees you."

She decided to make one last try. "Siyamtiwa, Grandmother, I really don't think I'm the best person for this."

"Get a good rest," Siyamtiwa said, ignoring her. "No food, just tea. In the morning, Angwusi comes for you."

"Who is Angwusi?"

"Sister Crow."

Stoner sighed. "Right."

"I got some stuff for your medicine bag here." Siyamtiwa took a small bowl from the altar. "This is important stuff, magic stuff. Stuff you oughta remember." She picked out a small white bone. "This is foreleg of rabbit. Rabbit runs like the wind and jumps up, turns in mid air. Even Brother Coyote doesn't catch rabbit, because rabbit has wisdom in his legs. But if Brother Rabbit does not listen to the wisdom in his legs, if Brother Rabbit sits and thinks like a man, that is one dead Brother Rabbit. This will help you remember."

She poked among the objects in the bowl and brought out a stone. "Stone is patient. Waits. Endures. It does not hurl itself into danger. When you need to know that, think of stone." She added the stone and bone to the medicine bag and held up a snake skin. "Brother Snake is silent. Doesn't chatter and announce his presence to his enemies. Think of how many snakes you have seen in your life. Think of how many you have *not* seen because they lie beside the path and do not speak. Remember that." She placed the snake skin in the bag and drew the bit of turquoise from her sleeve. "And remember me." She dropped the turquoise into the bag, pulled the string tight, and handed it to Stoner. "Any magic you got I don't know about, put in there. Now go bring your things from your room. You won't need it any more."

Well, that was ominous enough.

She trudged up the hill and through the village. Night was coming on fast.

She stuffed her belongings into her knapsack, hooked Gwen's necklace around her own neck. By the time she was finished it was purple dark. The moon was no more than a pin-scratch. Tomorrow night there would be no moon at all.

Overhead, the Milky Way formed a glittering bridge across the heavens.

The coyote was out there.

She couldn't see it, but felt its presence. The hairs on the backs of her hands prickled.

Hosteen Coyote, she thought, it seems you and I have some serious business to do.

She waited, half expecting a reply.

The night was silent.

*   *   *

When she got back, the *hogan* was dimly lit and smelled of sage and burning cedar. Siyamtiwa had built a crackling fire in the rock-lined pit. She sat beside it, tossing bits of fresh herb and pine boughs into the scarlet coals. She got up and reached for Stoner's knapsack, dropping it at the head of the corn husk bed. "You sleep with the corn tonight. Brings you good luck."

Oh, great. We're reduced to *luck.*

"Take off your clothes," Siyamtiwa ordered. "Give to me."

"Wait a minute," Stoner said, blushing. "I didn't know this was going to involve nudity."

"If it is your way to bathe with your clothes on," Siyamtiwa said, "you're crazier than I thought."

Stoner fumbled with her buttons. Siyamtiwa took her shirt and tossed it into the fire.

"Hey, I kind of liked that shirt."

"No magic in it." She waited for her jeans.

"But these clothes make me feel strong," Stoner said as she stripped them off.

The old woman threw her jeans into the fire and motioned for her underwear.

Stoner watched it break apart into black ashes. "I was fond of those socks," she said wistfully.

Siyamtiwa wrinkled her nose. "*Powaqa* could smell you coming a mile away, even if you were down-wind." She pointed to a deep pan of water and a bowl of milky suds. "Wash yourself with that stuff. I come back when you're through." She picked up the knapsack and left.

The air of the *hogan* was chilly in spite of the fire. Shivering, she contemplated the bowl of suds. It looked almost like dish water.

Oh, well. Probably has deep ritual significance.

The soap had an astringent quality. It made her skin tingle, sensitive to the slightest draft and movement of air. She washed quickly, rinsed in the lukewarm water from the basin, and huddled close to the fire to dry.

Okay, here we are, clean as a whistle and naked as a jay-bird. Now what?

The fire collapsed in on itself. She looked around for more wood and found a stack in a corner, or what passed for a corner in a round house. On the wall above the wood hung four sticks, each decorated with soft gray feathers. They were painted in the colors of the four sacred directions: red-east, blue-south, yellow-west, white-north. At the corners of the wood pile sat four woven plates filled with corn meal. She hesitated. What if it wasn't a wood pile? What if it was an altar? Under the circumstances, desecration didn't seem like a good idea.

She hugged herself and jumped up and down to keep warm. It made her feel like a jerk, hopping around in the nude, everything loose, jiggling. It made her feel as if the whole world were watching.

206

Hey, there's nothing wrong with nakedness. It's natural, right?

For new-born babies, frogs, and earthworms, it's natural. For me, it's not natural.

"If you're embarrassed," she remembered Gwen telling her once, "close your eyes."

She closed her eyes, which helped a little. But it still didn't help with what to do with her hands. If Nature had intended us to be naked, she would have given us pockets in our skin.

Something poked her roughly in the shoulder. "Don't get so nervous about your shell," Siyamtiwa said. "It's only something to get you around, so your spirit doesn't blow away."

"Stop reading my mind," Stoner muttered.

The old woman glanced down into the fire pit. "You let the fire go out." She gathered an armload of wood from the altar and tossed it onto the coals.

"I was afraid to use it," Stoner admitted as she edged closer to the fire. "I thought it might be sacred."

"Everything's sacred." Siyamtiwa said. "Air, water, earth, food, all sacred. What you gonna do, stop eating, stop breathing, die?"

Stoner sighed. "I don't want to discuss it."

Siyamtiwa raised an eyebrow. "You don't want to discuss? You not feel good?"

"I'm fine. Just in a bad mood."

Siyamtiwa stood back and looked at her. "This isn't good. What troubles you, Granddaughter?"

Granddaughter. The term of affection and familiarity did her in. "I don't like being naked," she said as tears made her vision go blurry. "I'm afraid. I don't know what you want me to do. And I don't think I'll ever see Gwen again."

The old woman took her hand. "Your friend's okay. Kinda scared, I'll bet, but okay."

"You say that..." Stoner brushed at her tears with her forearm. "But you don't know it's true."

"Sure, I know it. Know it in here." She touched her heart. "You're gonna be okay, Green-eyes. I couldn't have done any better." She chuckled. "Begay sends note, says we gotta give answer tomorrow. We have answer, all right." She went outside and returned carrying fresh jeans and underwear. "Put these on, maybe you don't feel so crazy."

Stoner slipped into them gratefully. She looked around for a shirt.

"Here," the old woman said. "I got a present for you."

The shirt she held out was a soft, much-washed denim, embroidered with beads and porcupine quills. There were designs of suns and bear claws, clouds and snakes, spirals, arrows, forks of lightning, corn stalks, and hump-backed flute players. And across the back, linking a stylized mesa and burro, a rainbow of brightly painted quills.

"You like it?" Siyamtiwa asked.

"It's beautiful. Did you make it?"

"Well, I had something to do with that. See this?" She pointed to the rainbow. "This is strong magic, so your Power Animal, the little horse of the canyon, brings you back safely."

"Grandmother," Stoner said, at a loss for words, "It's...it's the loveliest thing I ever saw."

Siyamtiwa gave the shirt a critical frown. "Not so good as I used to do when my eyes were sharp. But got lots of heart. Maybe it'll do okay." She hung the shirt on a pine peg set in the wall. "Now we gotta wash your hair."

She laid out a woven rug and brought fresh water and yucca suds from the shadows. She motioned for Stoner to kneel on the rug. "Your hair's nice and short, won't take long."

Stoner covered her eyes against the suds, feeling calmed by the touch of the old woman's fingers. "Is this a ritual?"

"Would be if you were gonna get married. You gonna get married?

"Not if I can help it."

The old woman chuckled and massaged her scalp. "The Dineh, you know, they like women like you. Let you bring your friend into your mother's clan, even let you be a warrior sometimes. Maybe you oughta think about that, eh."

Stoner shuddered. "I don't want to be in my mother's clan. Except for Aunt Hermione, it's as bad as Gwen's grandmother's clan. And, frankly, this is as close to warriorhood as I care to get." She brushed soap from her eyes. "If the Spirits had wanted me to be Dineh, the Spirits would have made me Dineh."

"You're catching on," Siyamtiwa said, and dumped cool water over her head. "Now you smell better." She handed her an old rag for a towel.

Stoner rubbed her hair. "Should I put the shirt on?"

"Better not. It's gonna get pretty sweaty in here." She built up the fire again, adding bits of sage and juniper. She indicated a bucket and gourd dipper. "I'm gonna leave you now. You have to do this yourself. Make steam in here until you feel like you got all the *nuk-*

208

pana, all the bad stuff out of you. All bad thoughts, too. Okay?"

"Okay."

"You probably get sleepy pretty soon. Do what your body says. Maybe some interesting things happen, maybe not. If you get hungry or thirsty, there's *ngakuyi*, medicine water, in that jug. Tastes kinda funny, but it's okay." She took the blanket from around her own shoulders and handed it to Stoner. "I gotta go now."

Stoner looked at her with a sinking feeling. "Will I see you again?"

"Maybe. Maybe not. Maybe you see me and don't recognize me. When Sister Angwusi comes for you, you follow."

Stoner pulled the blanket tight around her shoulders. "All right."

"You remember what I said, about the *kopavi*. The Spirits will talk to you through there, but you got to listen."

"I know. I'll keep an open mind."

Siyamtiwa smiled. "Not too open. Don't want your brains to fall out." She turned to go.

"Grandmother."

Siyamtiwa turned back. "*Hoh*."

"I...I hope I weave the right pattern."

The old woman touched Stoner's face. "No right or wrong patterns, Green-eyes. Things are gonna happen how they happen."

Feeling awkward, Stoner looked at the ground. "I wish you had someone better than me to do this."

Siyamtiwa stroked Stoner's hair. "Well, I wouldn't have met you, would I? That would have been too bad."

She looked up. The old woman was gone. The blanket that covered the door moved softly in her wake.

TWELVE

The night was as dark and still as Tokpela, First World, Endless Space World. Sotuknang the Air Mover held his breath, while Spider Woman Kokyangwuti paused in her weaving. At the poles, Poqanghoya and Palongawhoya turned the earth trembling on its axis. The planets and constellations slipped noiselessly through the sky, and worlds were born and worlds died and comets leapt like flying fish, and there was no sound anywhere except the song of Palongawhoya that is the song of the Universe, the song of Taiowa the Creator.

In her room, Siyamtiwa wrapped herself carefully in her white shawl, blew out her candle lamp, and began to compose her Song to Masau.

Kwahu, in her aerie high on Big Tewa Peak, shifted uneasily in her sleep. "Soon," she crooned to her little lost ones. "Soon."

The little horse of the canyons raised its head from drinking and listened to the silence. Droplets of water fell like tears from his soft muzzle. Deliberately, he stretched and shook each muscle, then began picking his way east, up out of the canyon.

Larch Begay scratched his stomach and looked down at the sleeping Gwen. "Fuckin' bitch," he muttered. "Your friend better come through tomorrow. I ain't a patient man."

Her face was ruby in the dying firelight. He hungered to strip that soft woman body naked, to crush it beneath his own, to feel her frantic, useless struggle.

The old taboos held him back. They might be a crock of shit, but he thought he just might wait until he had the bundle. Once it was his, he'd be beyond taboos, beyond laws. Once it was his, there'd be no stopping Larch Begay.

"*Mister* Begay to you," he said to Gwen and the mesas and the stars and the universe in general.

He drained the pint bottle of cheap bourbon and hurled it into the darkness. It shattered on a rock, the sound of destruction giving him a deep and sincere sense of satisfaction.

Stoner built up the fire again and made more scented steam.

Deep beneath Pikyachvi Mesa, in the secret cavern, the *Kachinas*

210

began to gather.

Jimmy Goodnight, keeping an eye on things at Begay's Texaco, got tired of tossing his pocket knife at mice and popped the cap on a Coors.

Laura Yazzie stepped outside to look at the stars. She remembered some ancient Dineh prayers she'd thought she'd forgotten.

In her hospital room, Stell stared into the darkness over her bed and swore, if anything happened to her Little Bear, someone'd pay for it, and pay big.

Tom Drooley dreamed ancestral dreams of cold and hunger.

Stoner drank the last of the medicine water and rinsed the sweat from her body. Her pores felt exhausted. She had stripped away her clothes long ago, and wrapped herself in Siyamtiwa's blanket. Going back to the blanket, she thought. Her old friend Insecurity stopped by for a visit, bringing greetings from Kurt. Ineptitude and Inadequacy joined the party. Together they poked and taunted until her brain felt like bacon on a griddle.

She told them they could come along for the ride, since she didn't know how to get rid of them. But she had to do what she had to do, regardless.

Loneliness wrapped a fist around her heart and began to squeeze.

Over on Pikyachvi Mesa, Gwen, hovering between sleep and waking, slipped out of the ropes that bound her wrists and ankles, and began to walk on the wind.

*   *   *

"Stoner."

She thought she had been dreaming, but she was wide awake. A hissing ember? A falling log? Breeze through the rough mud chinking?

"Stoner."

It came from just outside the *hogan*. She held the blanket aside and peered out into the night.

"Thank the Goddess," Gwen said. "I thought I'd never find you." She brushed past and went to huddle by the fire. "Would you ever believe it could get so cold in August?"

"Gwen..."

"If you ever go out of body be sure you have your destination clearly in mind. Otherwise you could wander in the ether for an eternity." She moved closer to the fire. "Of course, I *did* have my destination clearly in mind, you just happened not to be there." She

211

looked up and swallowed Stoner with her eyes. "Next time, Dearest, please leave a forwarding address."

Stoner knelt beside her. "Gwen, doesn't this strike you as odd?"

"Naturally." Gwen rubbed her hands together. "Or should I say *un*-naturally?"

"This place is so *strange*."

"Maybe it's one of those mystery spots where nothing grows and water runs uphill."

"Nothing grows, that's for sure."

Gwen sat back on her heels. "Stoner, my love, getting here wasn't the easiest thing I've ever done in my life. Believe me, sailing through the sky at high midnight is thrills and chills galore. At least you could *pretend* to be glad to see me."

"I *am* glad to see you."

Gwen glanced at Stoner's hands. "I don't have the bubonic plague, you know."

"I know." She was beginning to shake. With wanting her, with needing her, with longing for the feel of her. She got up and walked to the other side of the fire.

"Well," said Gwen sadly, "I guess I'm kind of disheveled. We're a little short on the amenities over at Casa Begay..." Her voice caught.

"It's not that Gwen. The last time you were here, you said, if I touched you, you might disappear."

"I don't care," Gwen said. A tear slipped from the corner of her eye. "I miss you. I need you. Isn't this ever going to end?"

Stoner went to her, reached out a tentative hand. "Tomorrow. I'm coming for you." She touched her face, expecting to feel...she wasn't sure what.

Gwen's skin was warm and soft and very, very real.

It made her want to hold her tight, but she was afraid. She needed her here, needed to look at her even if she couldn't hold her. She couldn't risk...

"What's wrong?" Gwen asked. "Do I feel like ectoplasm?"

Stoner shook her head.

Gwen hugged herself and looked down at the ground. "I'm frightened, Stoner. I don't understand what's happening."

She didn't know what to say. "Is... is Begay nice to you?"

"*Nice* to me?" Gwen looked up, eyes blazing. "Larch Begay is a wad of humanoid scum. Of course he isn't nice to me."

"Has he hurt you?"

"He offends me."

That sounded like the real Gwen, all right. Stoner smiled.

Gwen got up and looked around the *hogan*. "If you won't touch me," she said tightly, "at least you can feed me. I'm starving."

"There's nothing here to eat. Siyamtiwa has me on some kind of fast."

"I might as well go back to the cave, for crying out loud."

Gwen's back was to her. She looked so small, and so lost... She couldn't let her stand there like that, alone. Even if it made her disappear, she had to break that loneliness.

She went up behind her, slipped her arms around her.

The feel of Gwen's body against her own sent eddies and currents of excitement up and down her skin. She ran her fingers over Gwen's face and felt the warm dampness of tears. Over her hair, and felt the silky softness. Over her shoulders, and felt the worn chambray of her favorite shirt, the firmness of her muscles underneath. "I want to make love to you," she whispered, "but I've never made love to an astral body."

Gwen turned in her arms and laughed. "I've never made love *in* an astral body."

"I probably shouldn't," Stoner whispered without much conviction as she pulled the blanket around them both. "I'm in training."

Gwen snuggled against her. "What were your exact orders?"

She scanned her memory. "I'm supposed to...get rid of bad thoughts. And do what my body tells me."

"And is your body sending any messages at the moment?"

"As a matter of fact," Stoner said with a delicious shudder, "it is."

Gwen's hands touched her naked skin, stroking, gentling. Not ghost hands or spirit hands or astral hands, but very clear and very present.

"Gwen, I... "

She let herself be eased backward to the ground. Gwen's hands, her soft, sure hands... touched, and touched, and...

I ought to stop this, she thought as her own hands, of their own volition, fumbled with Gwen's clothes and sought her private places. At least I ought to think about it first. It might not be the right thing to do.

After all, tomorrow's an important day. I can't afford to make a mistake.

After all...

Gwen was completely naked now, lying along her, touching at every point. She was warm, she was smooth, and she was...

213

Her mind lost control of her body.

Gwen's hands moved over her and over her and set up warm, damp quivers.

"I love you," Gwen whispered, and her head found Stoner's chest, her mouth found Stoner's breast.

We...

Her mind turned to water.

*　*　*

"As long as you're here," Stoner said later, "why not stay? Then I won't have to worry about you *and* the Ya Ya Bundle."

Gwen finished buttoning her shirt and shoved it into her jeans. "I don't think it works that way. Sooner or later, like Marley's Ghost, I'd just fade away."

Stoner sat up and pushed her hair into a semblance of order. "Do you have any idea where you are? I mean, where the rest of you is?"

"Not in the slightest. I was thinking about you, and suddenly I was on my way. I guess I use the same method to get back." She slipped into her shoes. "How will you find me?"

"Well..." She hesitated. "It's kind of bizarre."

Gwen brushed dust from her shirt sleeve. "The only thing that would be truly bizarre out here would be a fast food restaurant."

"A crow is coming for me."

Gwen stared at her. "I take it back. That's bizarre. Should I worry?"

"Probably."

"Try not to be late, okay?" Gwen said as she started for the door. "Despite my jocular façade, I'm scared to death."

"Gwen..." Stoner stopped her. "When we... I mean, just now... did you...well, was it out-of-body?"

"No, Dearest," Gwen said. "It was most definitely in body." She stepped through the door and disappeared.

Stoner scrambled to her feet and ran outside, but Gwen was gone.

The night seemed a little softer. Over in the east, she thought she could make out, barely, the outline of a hill.

Oh, Lord, she thought, I probably smell white again.

She hurried back inside and built up the fire.

*　*　*

Angwusi the Crow awoke in the Purple Dawn time, vaguely re-

214

membering that she was supposed to do something today. Something important. Too early in the season to check the corn for ripeness. Another moon at least. Though it wouldn't hurt to peck at a few ears, just to annoy that old grouch of a farmer over by Shongopovi on Second Mesa. Peaceful People indeed.

Something important, something important.

She scavenged for delicacies among the weed seeds.

Something to do with...rituals? Dances? That's not it.

She glanced uneasily at the sky. Yellow Dawn was coming on fast.

Better get your act together, kiddo. Once that old Tawa-sun comes creeping over the horizon, it's gonna be hotter'n the rear seat of a buckboard.

Buckboard. Travel. That's it. I'm supposed to pick up a party of one, out at the Village-That-Has-Forgotten-Its-Name and take 'em to Pikyachvi Mesa. Village-That-Has-Forgotten-Its-Name, for the love of Angwusnasomtaqa Crow Mother, what kind of a name is that, Village-That-Has-Forgotten-Its-Name? Why can't they call it something sensible like... Hoboken? Hoboken is a name you can sink your teeth into.

And why me? What's wrong with this Two-leg, can't read a map? Anybody who can't read a map has no business hanging around out here in the Petrified Desert.

She hopped to the spring and drank a little water to wash the dust from her throat.

It's the People. The People and their damn rituals. For everything they have to have rituals. Can't even brush their teeth without making a ritual of it. And when you have rituals, you have to get everyone involved--birds, plants, snakes, you name it. Everybody's got to be part of the *ritual*. Whoop-de do!

Next year I get smart. Next year I take the Central Am Flyway down to Ole May—hee—co for the winter, hang out with the other señoritas on the beach, then take the Eastern route north with the spring. Once you make it past Kentucky, they say, it's smooth sailing straight up to Heaven. Of course, Kentucky can be a serious problem. They have a sincere dislike of blackbirds and their relations down in my old Kentucky Home. Like to blast 'em out of the sky, poison 'em on the ground and fry 'em on the barbed wire. Step right up, folks, for some good old Kentucky Fried Crow.

But I sure would like to see New Jersey, I sure would. Life in the fast lane on the Garden State Parkway, pecking among the food wrappers with the traffic going by and little kids yelling, "Daddy!

Daddy! Lookit that *Big Bird.* " Now, that's living.

She shook out her wing feathers. Meanwhile, we got the party of one to get to Hard Rock Mesa from Village—Et. Cetera.

* * *

If anybody ever says 'As the crow flies' to me again, Stoner thought, I'll rip out their throat. She felt as if she'd been following the wretched bird for days. Up the sides of mesas. Down the sides of mesas. Across hundred-year-old wagon ruts. Down canyons—big canyons and little canyons and canyons that twisted and turned like mazes. Along dry washes. Across flat-out, dry-and-dusty desert. Through the heat and blinding sun.

Her tongue was cracked. Her jeans were torn. Bits of sage and creosote caught in her hair. She had fallen once and bruised an elbow. Once she had seen a patch of shade and stumbled into it to rest, only to find tarantulas already in residence. Her boots were scuffed beyond saving, and her right foot was working on a blister.

And still the bird went on. If she fell behind, it perched on a rock and harangued until she caught up. If she sat to catch her breath, it flew around her head in tightening circles until its wing tips touched her face and forced her up. Once they passed by a spring. Before she could reach it, the bird had flung itself into the water and stirred up mud until it was undrinkable.

All the while the sun throbbed. And throbbed. And throbbed.

She stumbled, fell to her knees.

The crow flew back and landed on a nearby mesquite bush. "Walk," it nagged. "Walk, waalk, waalk."

Stoner glared at it. "I'm not Lawrence of Arabia, you know."

"Waaalk."

She pulled herself to her feet. "I don't have to do this. It's a free country."

"Waaalk."

She trudged forward. "How do I know you're the right crow? I haven't seen any credentials."

But of course it was the right crow. It was exactly the kind of crow Siyamtiwa would use. Persistent, demanding...

Angwusi flew to the next mesquite bush and waited.

"If you're ever in Boston," Stoner panted, "and you need a good meal, don't come pecking around *my* back porch."

"Waaalk."

"We have *cats.*" she shouted. "Hundreds of cats. Mean cats. Hungry, killer cats. Genuinely nasty cats..."

"Genuinely nasty cats." It sounded like something Gwen would say. Which reminded her that last night she had made love to—and been made love to by—an hallucination, or a ghost, or Ms. Psilocybin of Spirit Wells, AZ. Zip code 860-whatever.

Or, if it really *was* Gwen, a wind-walker.

She plodded on. A valuable skill, wind-walking. If Siyamtiwa wanted to teach me something truly worthwhile, she could have taught me that. But that would make things easy, and making things easy is *ka-Hopi*, not the Hopi Way.

According to the legends—about which she now knew more than she knew about Judeo-Christian tradition, more than she wanted to know, more than she had ever wanted to know about anything—according to the legends, all the Peoples were given a choice of which corn would be their corn and signify their way of life. The Hopi chose the short blue corn, smallest of the corn ears, so that their life would be hard and pure.

Which certainly was reflected in the current situation.

I mean, face it. Going off into the desert, armed with nothing more than a pretty shirt and a handful of corn meal and trinkets, guided by a foul natured crow, is hardly the Rambo approach to saving the world.

She was willing to bet Larch Begay hadn't chosen the Short Blue Corn Way, either. He probably had enough fire-power at his command to put a sizable dent in the Defense Budget.

Plus he might already have the Ya Ya bundle and access to its magic.

And a hostage.

Hostage.

Maybe I should call the TV networks. Hostages are big business these days. Or, as they are euphemistically called, 'hostage situations'. Not to be confused with 'everyday life situations', or 'gusty winds and rain, clearing by morning situations'.

Yep, what we have here is a real hostage situation.

A crisis situation.

A hostage crisis situation.

The operative question is, what the hell do I do when I am finally face-to-face with this actual hostage crisis situation? Siyamtiwa believes I will know what to do when the time comes. Siyamtiwa believes the Spirits will open a trap-door in the top of my head and shout down instructions. Siyamtiwa also believes that animals can talk, that people can change themselves into coyotes at will. Siyamtiwa also believes she is three different people at the same time, one

217

of them dead.

Siyamtiwa is not playing with a full deck.

Stoner stumbled a little and slowed her pace. The crow flew back to her and nagged.

I mean, look at this thing objectively, if you dare. A few people are going to a lot of trouble over a bunch of old artifacts even the Hopis don't seem to want.

A sudden realization stopped her in her tracks.

Larch Begay wants the bundle.

Larch Begay will not be scared off. If he loses this round, he'll try again, and again, and again.

The bundle is supposed to stay exactly where it is.

Therefore, the only way to keep Larch Begay from ever getting that bundle...is to kill him.

Which is why Siyamtiwa was glad to hear I'd killed a man.

Which is probably why the Spirits picked me in the first place for this hostage crisis situation.

She kicked the ground. Listen, Taiowa and Sotuknang and Kokyangwuti and all you other Spirits, I heard your legends. You're a blood-thirsty bunch. Three times you wiped out the entire world. *Three times.* Once wasn't enough. And, if the prophecies are right, you're working up to doing it again. So where do you get off calling me a killer when all I ever did was help rid the world of one sleazebucket. And I didn't have any choice in the matter. It was him or me, and if I'd made the noble sacrifice, you wouldn't have old Greeneyes to kick around. It's your world, folks. You clean it up.

She looked around quickly, and hoped they hadn't heard her because she happened to be standing in a dry wash. And dry washes were known for turning themselves into raging torrents suddenly and horribly.

Okay, she thought as she pulled herself together, you've had your fit. Now can we get down to business?

She went back to putting one foot in front of the other.

* * *

Jimmy Goodnight blinked the sweat from his aching eyes, peered through the binoculars, and began to wonder if Mr. Begay was using him. He'd let him hunt for the treasure all along, when it was hot and boring, and now that they were within striking distance, all of a sudden he was stuck out here in the sun while Mr. Begay got to poke around in a nice, cool cave. Matter of fact, ever since they'd found this big entrance hidden behind some fallen rocks and bushes, Mr.

218

Begay had turned kind of unfriendly. Wouldn't let him come in the cave at all, not even stand at the entrance and look in. Just made him stay outside and watch for intruders.

Jimmy Goodnight had the uneasy feeling that Mr. Begay might not be planning to split the treasure with him at all.

He wiped his eyes on his t-shirt and squinted toward the sun, measuring its height above the San Francisco Mountains, estimating the time left before sunset. About an hour, he guessed, not much more. Then what? His Dad'd skin him alive if he was out after dark on a Sunday night. He was already ankle-deep in shit for skipping dinner. To make matters worse, the Padres were playing a double-header on TV and he'd missed the whole thing. Missed the last Sunday double-header of the season, probably. Wasted a whole day staring at the horizon and getting sun-burnt and watching a dumb old eagle circle around and around and around, stupid bird with a one-track mind, made him wish he'd brought his .22.

Jesus, he had to get out of Beale. He wanted to see things, do things before he got worn out and discouraged and giving-up feeling like his Dad. Before he spent the rest of his life going around in circles like that old eagle.

Jimmy Goodnight snapped to attention. Something was there, out on the desert, to the southwest. Something that moved, something that wasn't a heat-shimmer or a dust devil.

He put the binoculars to his eyes and made out a figure, too far away to identify but coming this way for sure.

He licked his parched salty lips and dove for the cave entrance. "Hey, Mr. Begay! Someone's coming!"

*   *   *

Stoner walked along muttering to herself and kicking rocks. It had become mechanical, this trudging along. She'd been walking downhill for more than an hour now, down into a canyon that wound back on itself and twisted and turned and finally flattened out to the west like a river delta. She was hungry and thirsty and tired and anxious and just plain all-over miserable. The blister on her right food burned like acid every time she put her weight on it. Her stomach crawled with emptiness and fear.

Something in the distance caught her eye. A flash of light, a wink of silver like sunlight striking glass. It came from near the top of a mesa. She realized she was completely exposed, no shelter anywhere nearby. Her fingertips tingled.

She had the feeling she'd found what she was looking for. The crow seemed to know it, too. It turned in mid-air, gave a final hoarse cry, and took off to the east without waiting for her thanks.

*   *   *

Grandmother Eagle observed it all and went to make her report. She found the old woman sitting on a wall, her face to the west, her back against the remains of a ruined house. Her skin had taken on a translucent, waxy quality, as if she were fading away. She held a homemade drum between her knees and tapped it rhythmically with her fingertips. On the roof of her house, a handsome giant of a man sat patiently.

Masau waits on the roof. The old woman is dying, Kwahu thought. We'll argue no more in this world, old friend. Now is the time for kindness and good manners.

She settled quietly on the wall and waited for Old Woman Two-legs to finish her prayer.

Siyamtiwa opened one eye, grunted. "You got news? Or are you just goofin' off."

Kwahu told her what she knew.

The old woman nodded and drew her white shawl closer around her frail shoulders. "Good. It begins."

*   *   *

Begay found himself dead-ended again, and cursed. He played his flashlight over the tunnel walls, looking for an opening, even a suspicious pile of rock. Anything that might lead to another room, another tunnel.

He knew the damned thing was in here. Even now, if he switched to his animal senses, he could feel the pulsing vibration on the air. The trick was pinning it down. But every time he thought the sound gathered in one direction, it hopped to another and left him going in circles.

Sometimes he wondered if the whole thing was a joke. Maybe there was no Ya Ya bundle. Maybe it was something the damn Hopis made up like they made up stories to fool the anthropologists. They were known for that. Ask them a question, you'd get an answer. Trouble was, the answer'd be made up right then while they were talking, tricky bastards.

But this story was one he'd heard all his life, and no matter where he heard it, most of the details were pretty much the same. Even down toward Winslow, where he had grown up, where his dad had run a trashy souvenir stand—even down there, there were whispered stories about the hidden Ya Ya medicine bundle and what it could do.

After his old man drank himself into bankruptcy and ended up janitoring at the Indian school, the bundle had become his own obsession. If his no-good old man wanted to spend his life cleaning up after them damn Indians, that was his look—out. Lars Mueller was going to be in charge of things, by God. He'd seen enough of the world on the TV screen to know that Power was where it was at.

He had wheedled a job helping out at Begay's Texaco, and when Frank Begay had a car he was working on fall off the jack and crush his chest, Lars Mueller took over the service station and the Begay name, and before long nobody cared to remember that Larch Begay had started out as the very white son of a very white seller of cheap imitation Indian trinkets. Not that White law would have given a damn, anymore than it gave a damn that Frank Begay was a very careful man who was not likely to have a car slip off a jack and crush his chest.

Larch Begay laid low for a long time, working at the station, cozying up to the Indians, and keeping his nose clean. And all the while he was picking up hints and scraps of information, piecing them together until he'd tracked the bundle to the Coal Mine Canyon area. After that, it was just a matter of walking up and down the canyons, keeping his eyes open and using a few tricks he'd picked up from some Navajo sorcerers who knew all there was to know about calling up the animal Spirit. He'd narrowed it down to Hard Rock Mesa, or Pikyachvi Mesa, if you wanted the Hopi word.

Hard Rock or Pikyachvi, what was hidden inside that pile of sandstone and caves would give him Power. If not actual sorcerer-power, there were plenty of superstitious 'skins around who would be so afraid of him they'd piss their pants at the sound of his name. And who'd stab each other in the back for the honor of keeping him supplied with silver and turquoise jewelry and handwoven rugs. Shit, he'd have them heathens turning it out so fast they'd be afraid to sleep nights for fear Hosteen Begay'd catch them napping and steal their souls. Give him a year, he'd have it nailed down so none of the local 'skins would deal with anyone but Mr. Hosteen Larch Begay. Then watch the money come his way.

And if the bundle brought real Power...well, Mr. Larch Begay wasn't beyond thinking Big.

But he had to find it first. He couldn't fake that. They'd know. Sometimes it gave him the willies, the things they knew.

He knew a few things, too, children. He knew that the white

221

broad from the east was working with the old Hopi.

He knew she'd be along pretty soon now, looking for her girl friend.

He knew neither of those white bitches would leave here alive.

* * *

The figure on the top of the mesa turned and ran. She had to find cover.

The arroyo tempted her, in spite of the danger. It was, simply, the only place to hide between here and the mesa. Even at that it was tricky, the banks eroded to a height of no more than a foot at times. Still, it was better than walking up to the place fully exposed. All she needed to attract even more attention was a brass band.

She slipped down the bank and pressed close to the sides. Crouching, she eased forward, and risked a peek over the edge of the ground. Now there were two figures on the mesa, a sure indication she had been seen. And she was rapidly reaching the limits of her protection. Time for a little thinking and planning.

She found a niche in the bank just large enough to let her disappear from sight, and pressed into it.

The important thing right now was to take the offensive. Begay had the advantage of strength—which was a pretty big advantage, as any woman in an abusive heterosexual relationship could tell you. It was also safe to assume he was armed.

She, on the other hand, was smaller, quicker, and—she hoped— smarter. And she had the advantage of Right, if not Might, on her side. Which seemed to count for very little in today's world.

She knew where Begay was, and he probably knew she had arrived. So they were even on the surprise factor.

Normally, the wise thing to do would be to wait for darkness. But Begay was a Coyote-man, and his animal vision would spot her before she saw him. Or his Coyote ears would hear her. Or his Coyote nose would smell her. Or he would pick up her presence on his animal radar. Darkness definitely gave the advantage to the Coyote-man.

So the man could see her in daylight, the Coyote at night. Which left her with twilight, a confusing time for both humans and animals.

And which, out here, at this time of year, with no moisture in the air to hold the light, lasted about as long as a heartbeat.

Certainly not long enough to cover that open, flat half-mile-at-least between here and there.

She rested against the crumbly stream bank and invited the Spirits to drop a few ideas into the suggestion box in her head. The Spirits, apparently reluctant to intrude on her Personal Space, maintained an eloquent silence.

Well, that's how it is with Spirits. What they do best is set up interesting little problems and sit back to watch us mortals bumble through. "Hah! Let's see you get out of *this* one, Oedipus!"

She was thirsty. Very thirsty. Her tongue felt swollen with thirst, her lips cracked and parched. The sun pulled water from her, drying her skin to brittleness. She was almost afraid to move, for fear she would crumble like an autumn leaf.

Look, she told herself firmly, the only way you're going to get water is to whistle up a cloudburst, and that would be more water than you're prepared to handle. So you can't have water. You also can't have a car, a steak dinner, a good book, or a movie. What you can have, however, is patience. So let us concentrate on that. Let us get into Being Here Now. She closed her eyes and felt the warm sand around her.

Her ears picked up the slack. She could hear a pebble fall from the edge of the bank, the tick of a desert insect, the faint sigh of air moving past a blade of grass.

And the sound of footsteps!

Two pairs of footsteps.

Coming her way.

She pressed against the earth wall and held her breath. But there was no way they could miss her. Not if they checked out the stream bed. And since they were looking for her and not taking a Sunday stroll, they would certainly check out the stream bed.

She thought about the cloud trick. She wished she'd practiced it more. But a cloud? Here in the middle of the desert? It would be as eye-catching as a Christmas tree in July.

The footsteps drew closer.

Stopped.

She waited.

The intruders were silent, as if trying to sense where she was. Maybe hesitating in case she was armed.

The silence grew longer.

She wanted to scream.

They came closer. She could hear breathing.

Seconds passed.

A klaxon siren split the air and sent adrenalin exploding through her body.

Something touched the top of her head and tugged gently at her hair.

She looked up.

The donkey blew air at her through its big oval nostrils.

Stoner laughed in spite of her fright. "Boy, am I glad to see you."

The animal backed away and gazed around nonchalantly, then bent its neck and began to pull up tufts of dried grass.

Okay, things are looking up. She could use him for cover. As soon as twilight closed in, she could crouch beside him and make her way up to the mesa. It might even mask her smell.

The trouble was, the burro was moving away from her, grazing upstream. "Hey," she whispered, "don't go. I need you."

It twitched its ears as if it understood and kept on walking and grazing.

Something told her it wanted her to follow.

All right, she thought with a sigh of resignation, crazy time again. She got slowly, carefully to her feet and crept after him.

When the cave entrance was out of sight, the burro tossed its head, telling her to climb out of the dry wash. She scrambled up the bank.

The setting sun touched the highest peak of the Sacred mountains as the donkey turned north on a path that would take them around the mesa.

She decided to let it lead, and ran to catch up.

"Listen," she said, "I know this is a crisis, but I've been wandering around out here all day following a crow…"

The burro looked at her sympathetically, as if it understood all too well how difficult crows can make your life.

"I'm awfully tired, to say nothing of thirsty, so could we slow the pace a little?"

It turned and nudged her with its side, inviting her to get up.

She thought about it. It wouldn't be like riding a *horse*, after all. The burro wasn't ten feet tall like most horses. And probably not particularly fast. Certainly not mean-tempered. Burro was just a soft little chunky thing with round brown eyes and a gentle spirit.

On the other hand, friend Burro was awfully small.

"Thanks, anyway," she said, slipping one arm across the donkey's back. "I'll just lean."

As they walked…and walked…and climbed…and walked and climbed some more…it occurred to her that it would be pitch black by the time they reached the cave. And Siyamtiwa had not thoughtfully provided a flashlight, or taught her how to light a stick without matches. She opened her medicine bag and probed inside with one finger. Corn meal, turquoise stone, bit of bone, feather. Nothing to make light.

All right.

She supposed she could wait until morning.

On the other hand, inside a cave it didn't matter if it was night or day.

Burro veered to the left, toward a pile of rocks lodged in a hillside. She caught a glint of lavender, and realized it was a reflection of the evening sky. A reflection in water.

A tiny spring bubbled from the ground, waist high, the water momentarily trapped in a shallow depression in a rock—a natural catch basin—before it spilled onto the sand and trickled away. Prayer sticks, brightly painted and decorated with eagle down, surrounded the pool of water.

A shrine. She hesitated, then remembered Siyamtiwa's words. "Everything's sacred."

Burro waited as she knelt and drank from the spring. The water was cool and bright, and tasted a little like the tea Siyamtiwa had been serving her. Probably some dissolved mineral. Whatever it was, it made her senses come alive, her body feel rested and alert, her mind clear.

She offered up a prayer of thanks to the Water People.

By the time they reached the top of the mesa, there was nothing left of the day but cardboard cut-out silhouettes of mountains against a thin mauve line of sky. The mesa top was studded with clumps of rabbitbrush, stunted juniper, and mesquite. Burro seemed quite pleased, and immediately began to graze.

Stoner looked around. He wouldn't bring her here on a whim. There must be something she was supposed to find.

They were above the mouth of the cave now, above the spot where Larch Begay searched the desert through binoculars and thought about switching to his Coyote senses. She could see him, many yards below. Possible to slip up on him from behind, but there was no path to take her down, and the drop was sheer. She'd never make it without attracting attention, if she made it at all.

She sat on the ground and chewed her lip. She knew there must be an answer here, if she could only...

A rear entrance into the mesa!

Of course. That made sense. That would be what Burro—who was certainly not an animal given to tricks and frivolity—wanted to show her.

She gazed around. It must be a very small opening. Or hidden. Hidden behind one of those coarse, tangled clumps of mesquite.

There were hundreds of them, and the light was going fast. It would be turning cold soon, the air...

Air! The air inside the cave would be a different temperature from the outside air. Cool air from inside the earth would flow outward, setting up drafts. So it should be possible to feel the cave entrance.

Except at the instant when the outside air had cooled to the temperature of the inside air.

Which was in serious danger of happening at any moment.

She got to her feet and went from bush to bush, feeling for drafts.

Darn. If it was there, it was too slight to feel.

Smoke would respond to even to faintest air current. But she had no way to make smoke.

But she did have a feather, a hawk feather in her medicine bag.

She took it out quickly, held it over each mesquite bush, and let it drop.

It floated to the ground, straight and true as a stone. Once, twice, three times.

On the fourth drop it wavered, then floated horizontally for a moment, and came to rest on the twisted stack of green mesquite.

She moved closer, reached into the bushes with one hand, and hoped there were no rattlesnakes taking the evening breeze on that particular spot.

A faint, cool draft caressed her fingers.

She had found the back door.

Now, Friend Begay, we'll see what is what.

The grin that was forming on her face died away. Assuming the entrance to the mesa was large enough for her to slip through, she now had to crawl, climb, or slither down into the ground, in total darkness. With no idea where she was going or whether she'd find the way out. With no guarantee the whole thing wouldn't fall in on her.

She'd never crawled into a tunnel in the earth before. For one simple reason...

She'd always been afraid of dark tunnels and underground caves. Freud could make whatever he liked of it, the fact of the matter was dark places under the earth made her breath stop and her heart pound, and liberated the more morbid elements of her imagination.

She didn't like the idea of doing this.

In all probability, she wouldn't even enjoy reading about it.

But she didn't have any choice.

Stars began to show in the eastern sky.

She started to dismantle the pile of mesquite. The bushes were intertwined and spiny. It was like trying to untangle barbed wire. And it was hard to see. By the time she had cleared an opening, her hands were covered with tiny, itching, burning punctures and her nerves were completely shredded.

She sat down to rest and try to pull herself together. As far as she could tell, the tunnel entrance was a narrow shaft, just large enough for her to slip through—lucky her. Whether it narrowed, and just how far it went, whether it sloped or dropped, whether it was empty or full of crawling things, she wouldn't know until she was in it.

The one thing she could tell was that it was very, very dark.

But it would soon be dark outside anyway. Dark is dark, right?

Wrong. There is night-in-the-open dark, with room to breathe and the stars all twinkly and friendly overhead. And there is cold, claustrophobic, chest-pressing, tons-of-earth-ready-to-fall-on-you, not-knowing-where-you're-going-or-what's-going-to-meet-you-or-if-you'll-ever-get-out darkness. This is not the same commodity. This is definitely the Short Blue Corn Way.

Smoke drifted upward over the rim of the mesa. Wood smoke, smelling of meat. Dinner time below. It made her aware of her own hunger, which was considerable.

She took a moment to indulge in self-pity.

Voices. Begay, grumbling or complaining, angry and a little drunk. And the other...familiar...young. Jimmy Goodnight, of course. It didn't surprise her. Jimmy Goodnight was the kind of kid—not to bright, eager to please, easy to flatter—that was always taken advantage of by the big kids. Set up to do their dirty work, and to take the rap when they got caught. Anything to belong.

It did surprise her, though, that Jimmy Goodnight had been in on kidnapping Gwen. If he had been. He had seemed fond of her, in the shy awkward way most adolescent boys seemed to be attracted to her. Which Gwen said was a good thing, even though it was some- times a pain in the neck. Because, if you don't generate some kind of emotion—be it fear or attraction—in adolescent males, they can make your classroom a living hell. The worst thing a teacher can do, Gwen said, is lose control of an adolescent male.

Stoner thought it applied to more than teachers.

So why was Jimmy Goodnight doing this? Or did he even know what was really going on? Maybe he didn't. Maybe what he had told her was all he knew, that Larch Begay was taking him to find a treasure.

That made Jimmy Goodnight a potential ally. But not one she really wanted to count on.

He had, after all, stolen the doll.

This is hardly the time to be obsessive, she told herself. Now the brightest planets burned cold holes in the western sky, and the constellations began to take shape around them.

Time to get going.

She felt among the mesquite bushes and found the opening again, all too easily. She went down on her knees and stuck her head and shoulders inside.

She fit, damn it, and barely.

She took one last look back at her friend Burro.

He bobbed his head in a happy, optimistic sort of way.

It was strangely comforting.

She stretched out on the ground, closed her eyes, and crawled into the opening.

After a few moments she opened her eyes. The darkness was solid. And it was quiet. Completely quiet. Dead space.

She took a deep breath and crawled forward, grateful for the slight breeze that touched her skin and reminded her that there was air here.

The tunnel slanted down gradually, like a coal chute. If she shifted her shoulders, she could feel the walls. But it wasn't too bad. If fact, the worst of it so far was that if she had to turn around...

She decided that this was one of the things it was better to do without thinking.

The trouble was, it was hard not to think.

Maybe she should try a quick psychic scan of the area. She wasn't quite sure how to do that, but...

She focused on the knot of energy she still carried in her stomach. Maybe this was what it was good for.

On the other hand, it might be something she should have looked into when she got home.

She gathered up the threads of concentration and brought them to rest around the knot.

Okay, now, spread out.

Nothing happened, except she realized she had stopped crawling.

Not good. The point of this little exercise is to take your mind off what you're doing.

She put herself in motion again.

Okay, from the top. Pull the energy in...

From the fingers and toes and arms and hands and legs and shoulders.

And send it down to the energy-place.

Keep moving.

Now, release it. Send it out like sonar. Wait for echoes.

She sensed something off to her right and ahead. A slight answering tingle.

Gwen.

From straight ahead there was nothing, which could be meaningless, or dire. If it meant there was only solid rock ahead, and this tunnel didn't turn before then, and she was stopped dead with rock all around and a couple of tons of earth on top of her, and no way to turn around, and the air starting to go, and maybe somebody going up top on the mesa and finding the Burro and putting two and two together, and blocking up the entrance, out in the middle of nowhere with nobody to hear if she yelled...

A sudden blast of energy from her left took her breath away. It struck like lightning, then rattled through her in echoing, pulsing waves.

Jesus!

It stretched her flat on the ground, rolled over her, and spread like ripples up and down the tunnel.

What was *that*?

"What the fuck?" Larch Begay grunted as the wave of vibration hit him.

Jimmy Goodnight gave a frightened squeak.

The campfire shrank to embers, then exploded in a tower of flame. Begay reached for his bottle of cheap bourbon.

Gwen stopped fighting the ropes that cut into her wrists and ankles, and looked up into the darkness. "Stoner?" she whispered.

The little Burro stepped away from the tunnel entrance to let the shock wave pass, and went back to eating.

Siyamtiwa smiled to herself. So. Green-eyes has found the bundle.

229

THIRTEEN

She thought she could see light ahead. Distant, flickering, yellow light.

It might be an hallucination. It felt like hours since she had entered the tunnel. It may have been minutes. She had lost all sense of time and space.

It was light, all right. And growing brighter. She stopped to listen. A male voice, low, rumbling. The light was from Larch Begay's campfire.

If the tunnel kept going staight ahead, it would dump her right at his feet.

Which was, under the circumstances, a terrible idea.

Moving very slowly, scarcely breathing, listening for signs of discovery , she inched her way forward.

She could see the fire now. And Begay. And Jimmy Goodnight. Their backs were to her as they lounged against opposite sides of the cave entrance, looking out toward the desert. If they were expecting her, they were expecting her to come from below.

Larch Begay was fooling with a gun, a pistol. It looked like the kind of six-shooter you saw in cowboy movies.

Between her tunnel and the campfire was a small antechamber-like room. If either of them turned around they would certainly see her. But, with luck, she might be able to slip into the darkness away from the entrance.

She decided to call up a cloud. In the shadow-laced, wavering, reflected firelight, it wouldn't stand out, and might give her a bit of added protection.

This time it was easy, though she had to fight a desire to hurry. Gwen was there somewhere. She might be hurt or worse. Before she went looking for the bundle, she was by-God going to find Gwen.

The cloud enveloped her like a fog. It made her job more difficult, trying to see through a heavy mist, but it made her feel safer, too. At the moment, safer was what she needed.

Her knees were wobbly when she tried to stand. Too much crawltime. She stretched her legs, did a few knee-bends. Her joints sounded like popcorn.

She stopped her breath, afraid Begay had heard, but his grumbling went on uninterrupted. Jimmy Goodnight answered in a scared, whiny voice. Begay barked an obscenity.

Everything normal out there.

She looked around the antechamber. More tunnels, dozens of tunnels. Some tall enough to walk through, some too small even to crawl. No wonder he hadn't found the bundle yet. It would take weeks, months to travel down all those passageways. Pikyachvi Mesa was like a gigantic ant farm.

She groped her way through the semi-darkness, keeping her back to the wall, her eyes on the cave entrance.

Far around to the right, the antechamber opened into a second room, a low-ceilinged compartment no bigger than a closet.

"Stoner?"

She strained to see. "Where are you?" she whispered.

"Down here. Don't step on me."

She dropped to her knees and felt her way around the floor like a dog sniffing for tell-tale scents. A cup. A tin plate, tangled pile of rope. A foot.

A foot. She groped her way up Gwen's leg.

Something huge and tight in her chest gave way. "Gwen, are you all right?"

"Just get me out of here," Gwen whispered.

She ran her hands down Gwen's arms, her legs, and found the knots that bound her. They were tight. Very tight. Gwen's wrists and ankles were swollen, the rope cutting into her flesh. Her skin was cold.

Stoner swore under her breath. Digging her knife from her pocket, she sawed at the knots.

Gwen gave a little gasp of pain.

"I'm sorry,"Stoner whispered. "Did I hurt you?"

"I'll be okay."

At last she had her free, and tossed the ropes away angrily. She rubbed Gwen's hands, felt her wince as feeling returned.

"Oh, God," Gwen said, her voice shaky with fear,"I don't think I can walk."

Stoner slipped an arm around her shoulders. "You will. I have a lot to do before it comes to that, anyway."

Gwen fumbled for her hand. They sat for a moment in silence, watching the firelight flicker on the wall.

"This is a mess, isn't it?" Gwen asked at last.

231

"Sort of."

"What are we going to do?"

Stoner scrubbed at her face with her free hand. "I guess the first thing is to find the Ya Ya bundle…"

"The what?"

My God, she doesn't even know what this is all about. "I'll explain everything later." She moved to get up. "Stay here. Pretend you're still tied. That might buy me a little time before Begay knows I'm here." She felt for the cut ropes and handed them to Gwen. "What's the story on Jimmy Goodnight?"

"I don't know."

The reflected fire-light cast a rusty glow on Gwen's face. In spite of the artificial reddish tint, she looked tired and sick and frightened. She looked the way Stell had looked the night she had gone to the hospital.

Oh Jesus, Stoner thought. He's drawing energy from her, probably to fuel his Coyote side to help him find the bundle.

She leaned over, gave Gwen a quick kiss, and got to her feet. "Things might get a little strange. Be cool, okay?"

"Sure. Yell if you need help."

She forced a quick and—she hoped—reassuring smile and slipped out into the antechamber where the tunnels converged. Begay was standing up, his back to her. She couldn't see Jimmy Goodnight.

Keeping her eyes on Begay, she felt the wall behind her for her entrance tunnel.

It was easy to see why he hadn't found it. She couldn't find it, herself. Of course, it was dark…

She had the unsettling thought that it wasn't because of the darkness, that even with a spotlight she wouldn't find it, because that tunnel had sealed itself and disappeared.

She told herself that was ridiculous, but she couldn't shake it.

She slid along the wall, feeling the openings of other tunnels, each of which probably led to other tunnels and other tunnels and other…

The chances of getting lost multiplied geometrically.

She dreaded going back into the dark.

Come on, she told herself firmly, stop fiddling and get the show on the road. She took a deep breath and steeled herself for her plunge into blackness.

The familiar klaxon bray sounded from the cave entrance.

She looked out. Jimmy Goodnight was there, with the burro on

232

a rope.

"Lookit, Mr. Begay. There wasn't nobody out there, just this old donkey."

"Lemme see that." Begay snatched the rope from the boy's hand and yanked the burro to him.

The little animal's eyes rolled in fear.

Stoner tensed.

"Hang on to the son-of-a-bitch,"Begay snapped at the boy. He thrust the rope toward him, grabbed the burro's neck, and tried to mount.

The burro danced sideways out of his reach.

"Hold still, Goddamn it." He tried again.

The animal kicked out with its hind legs.

Begay swore and reached for a heavy stick of firewood. He waved it threateningly. "When I say hold still, I mean hold still." He raised his arm to strike.

Blind rage wiped all other thoughts from her mind. "Stop that!" she shouted, and hurled herself at his legs.

Begay was slow-moving, half drunk, and out of shape. He went down like a palm tree in a hurricane.

Jimmy Goodnight jumped back and covered his face with his hands. He dropped the rope.

The donkey whirled and high-tailed it back down the path and out into the desert.

Stoner scrambled to her feet. She figured she had about a five second head start.

She backed into the cave and slipped down the nearest tunnel. She heard Begay drag himself up, cursing and start after her.

She didn't dare run. In the pitch blackness, she might smash into a wall, or hit her head on a low-hanging rock. At least it was easy to hide in the dark. Until it occurred to him to go back for his flashlight.

The sound of his breathing, heavy and angry, filled the silence. She held her breath. She could almost see him in her mind, heavy head swaying back and forth, his eyes trying to penetrate the dark. If he decided to switch to his Coyote side...

"Goodnight!" she heard him yell, "get the lantern."

It was almost a relief. As long as he stayed human she had a chance. Gwen had a chance. But it had taken only hours for him to drain Stell to the point of death. And Gwen was already halfway there.

She understood now. All summer he'd lived on the women's

233

energy, using them like dry cell batteries to power his transformations, to nourish his animal spirit. Without woman energy he was helpless, his magic reduced to tricks. But once he had the bundle, he would be free of his dependence on women. Once he had the bundle, nothing could stop him.

She saw the balance now. Woman spirit kept him going. Woman spirit had to end it. *She* had to end it. Because she was woman. Because she was a woman who's spirit no man had ever used. That was why Siyamtiwa—or her Spirits—had chosen her. No man had found the pathway to her soul. Her doors were closed to them.

Her hand reached up and clutched her medicine bag. Oh, Grandmother, help me to weave the proper pattern. Help me to restore the balance. And if I fail, please know I did my best.

Light danced on the tunnel wall, coming her way. She pressed deeper into the shadows. The light paused.

"Come on out, Sweetheart."

She waited.

"You don't want to make me come after you," Begay said. "You really don't."

She eased along the wall, found another passageway, and slipped inside. The beam of light swept over the spot where she had just been.

"We can do this the easy way," he called. "Or we can do it the hard way. It's up to you, Sweetheart."

Slowly, carefully she backed down the narrow passage.

"I got your girl friend. You wouldn't want me to do anything to her, would you?"

She froze.

She had to divert him from that line of thinking, to keep him coming after her. She bent down and fumbled for a rock. She found one, and threw it blindly toward him.

His light followed the direction of the sound.

"I don't have to come after you. All I have to do is start cutting the bitch."

Stoner gritted her teeth. "Screw you, Begay. I knew you were chicken-shit."

She scooped up a handful of rocks and tossed them, one after another, to her right. She hoped they sounded like running.

The beam of light shifted away from her. In the second before it shifted back, she dove for the tunnel on her left.

She took a long breath. She was drawing him deeper into the mesa. Where she could get as lost as it was humanly possible to be.

Where there might be bats and scorpions and other unpleasant things. Where she could starve to death, or die of thirst. Where she'd never see daylight again.

But, by God, neither would he.

Begay was coming back.

First things first. She forced herself to go on, sliding her hands along the wall, feeling overhead for hanging rocks, moving carefully and silently.

It occurred to her that it would take a very long time to die, here in the darkness.

She could hear Begay, stumbling and cursing as he searched through the dark corridors and dead-end passages.

He stopped cursing, began walking slowly but steadily in her direction. Pausing, moving forward, pausing. As if he were following a trail.

What?

She bent down and felt the ground. Dust. She had been walking in dust, leaving a path even a baby could follow, and he had found it.

She could keep running, and he could keep following. Endlessly.

Maybe it would come to that, but not yet. First she would stand and fight.

But not here, not in a hard rock corridor where there was no place to hide and Larch Begay carried the only light.

She stumbled on through the blackness.

If only she could see.

Suddenly she remembered the night Siyamtiwa had shown her the *kiva.* It had been dark then, at first. But she had *felt* the size and shape of the room.

She stood and quieted her heartbeat, turned her attention to the surfaces of her skin, waited for impressions. She picked up a closeness to her right and forward. Walls. But on the left...

She sensed an opening. No, two...three openings.

Her mind told her this was insane. There was no way to see without seeing. Not with such accuracy. Not without years of practice.

Her instincts told her to trust her impressions.

Her practical side decided she didn't have a whole lot of choice.

She reached out and felt air, then rock, then air again, rock again, air.

Something drew her to the center opening. She ducked inside.

"What the fuck?" Begay's voice was puzzled.

From where she stood she could see his flashlight beam, pointed at the ground.

There was only solid rock beneath her feet.

He had lost her trail. He began sweeping the walls with his light.

She took a lesson from Brother Snake and stood very still.

Begay and his light disappeared into the left-hand tunnel. Okay now what?

If she had the means, she could seal off that passageway, locking him away forever inside Pikyachvi Mesa. But, of course, she didn't have the means.

She tried to think, was distracted by a feeling of warmth high on her chest. Heat, coming from her medicine bag. She grasped it in one hand.

It might be her imagination. She might be picking up her own pulse through her fingertips. But it felt as if the medicine bag were beating like a heart.

She held her breath and tried to make out the meaning.

Something made her want to go deeper into this tunnel. A gentle tug at her mind, an idea. A message through the *kopavi*.

She followed it. Into the darkness. Deeper and deeper, beyond any turning back.

Now she was hopelessly lost.

She kept on going, into the heart of the mesa, where only magic could ever get her out.

She tripped, stumbled, and glanced down. A stumplike formation, a stalagmite.

She went on.

Wait a minute. There was only one way she could know that was a stalagmite. By *seeing* it.

She looked around. It was lighter here. Softer, the darkness less brittle.

She walked faster.

Now the light was turning gray. It must be another entrance. She had come out on the other side!

Something wrong about this.

Light does not come through cave entrances in the middle of the night. In the middle of *moonless* nights. Of course, it could be dawn. But somehow she knew it was something else.

She kept on going forward, toward the light...

The shock wave knocked her back against the wall and rolled

236

away down the tunnel.

Her heart pounded.

What is going on here?

Slowly, she started forward again, closer to the source of the light, ready for another silent explosion.

She passed through a doorlike opening...

... and caught her breath.

She was in a deep chamber, as wide and high as a cathedral. Stalactites dripped from the vaulted ceiling. Stalagmites formed rows of dragons' teeth around the room's perimeter. Stone draperies decorated the walls. Flowerlike formations of white and blue and pale green blossomed on the cave floor.

And in the center of the room, glowing as if phosphorescent, lay the source of the light.

A rough pile of sticks and cloth and indefinable things.

The Ya Ya medicine bundle.

She stared at it.

If it weren't for the light, it would be only an accumulation of litter, dusty and moth-eaten, something to be passed by and left for the street-cleaner.

She got on her knees to look closer.

The decaying cloth that covered it revealed, through holes and tears, yucca leaf baskets containing corn in many colors. Carved fetishes in the shapes of bears and deer and birds lay scattered among the kernels. Beads and bits of turquoise. Prayer sticks. *Kachina* dolls carved from cottonwood. Small bones and feathers and pottery bowls. A wooden mask, large enough to fit over a man's head. A kilt-like skirt of hide. Rattles and shell bracelets. A necklace of bear claws.

She shuddered and reached into her own medicine bag, bringing out a pinch of corn meal and dropping it onto the bundle.

The light grew stronger.

She got to her feet and walked a circle around the bundle and sealed it with corn.

Then she sat against the wall to wait.

Nothing happened.

Lowering her head on her arms, she pulled her concentration into the energy knot in her stomach.

It began to grow.

Lightness spread out and through her, filling her body and arms and legs. She felt strong and whole, and unafraid.

Power radiated from her.

Come on, Begay. We have things to settle.

She looked toward the ceiling and saw...

Movement.

Not objects in motion but pure movement. Movement seen out of the corner of the eye. Movement like ice melting, like rising steam, clouds forming and reforming, drifting fog, the turning of the tide.

Now the stalagmites that ringed the chamber seemed to melt, to broaden, to grow taller, to take on color. As she watched, they became...

Masks.

Huge wooden masks, larger than life and each one different.

Faces painted black and red and white and yellow and blue.

Faces with noses, with beaks, with dog-like snouts.

Faces crowned with feathers and juniper sprigs.

Faces surrounded with sun-like rays.

Faces with yarn hair and cornhusk hair and human hair.

The masks of the Spirits.

And suddenly the bundle was no pile of decaying litter at all, but color. Vivid, vibrant, living color. Corn yellow and turquoise blue. The orange of flames. Red brighter than the brightest rose and richer than blood. Spring green and autumn brown. White of snow and ermine. Colors so brilliant they seared her eyes.

Then the sounds began. Drums. Rattles. Bells. The rhythmic thud of dancing feet on hard-packed soil. Her heart beat in time to the drumming. Power pulsed through her in time to her heartbeat.

The masks began to move, motion no longer imagined but real. They rose into the air, trailing mists of color. Reaching higher, higher to the vast dome of the ceiling. The drumming grew louder and the masks circled, dipping and twirling in dance.

Stoner watched them open-mouthed, transfixed.

A beam of yellow light cut through the room.

She blinked.

The masks were gone, the stalagmites mere stalagmites, the bundle a dusty pile of rubbish.

"Well, well," Larch Begay said. He turned his light on the medicine bundle. "Led me right to it, didn't you?"

"Leave it alone, Begay."

He looked at her and laughed.

"You don't know what you're dealing with here."

"Wrong, little lady. *You* don't know what *you're* dealing with."

She moved and placed herself between the man and the bundle. "I mean it. I can't let you take it."

"Is that a fact?" He took a step toward her.

She held her ground. "It's a fact."

He came nearer. "I wonder what I'm going to do about that." He smiled.

Stoner watched his eyes. They were growing larger, flatter. The pupils dilated. The irises turned a pewter gray.

His hand shot out and clutched her shirt front. He dragged her to the side, slammed her against the cave wall. A bolt of pain shot through her as her shoulder and head struck rock. He held her there, one hand at her throat, and turned the flashlight on her face.

Blinded, she tried to twist away.

He pulled her forward and slammed her against the wall again.

"This is gonna give me a whole lot of pleasure," he hissed. His breath was rancid with stale bourbon. His eyes met hers and held.

She could feel herself grow weaker, her energy draining away like water. She tried to struggle, but could barely move her arms. Terrified, she kicked out. Her legs refused to move.

Break his hold on your eyes, she told herself. But she was paralyzed. Begay was feeding from her spirit, sucking her dry like a vampire.

She felt like sand blowing away in the wind.

Travel, something told her.

But she couldn't let go, was afraid to let go. If she stopped struggling, if she let her consciousness turn inward, those hands would press the last breath from her.

GRANDDAUGHTER!

Siyamtiwa's command grabbed her mind.

The pain in her shoulder and head faded. Begay's hand left her throat. She breathed air, fresh air. She gulped it hungrily, and felt energy flow back into her body.

She looked around. She was lying in the canyon, in the circle at the Place of Emergence. Warm sun caressed her arms and face. The waterfall sang. The river tossed round rocks together and made them talk. A hawk soared overhead.

She lay in sunlight until her body was warm, until her blood flowed smoothly once more. Until her heart pumped stong and sure.

Too strong.

Strong and loud as drumbeats.

It frightened her. She tried to calm it.

The beats grew stronger, faster. They pounded in her head and battered her rib cage. My heart's going to burst, she thought. He's caught my heartbeat and he's going to make it burst.

Help me. Grandmother!

There was no answer.

Only the hawk, circling overhead.

Suddenly it folded its wings and plunged earthward toward her. Faster than an arrow, it came at her.

She cringed. No time to step away.

The bird spread its claws. Its talons glistened like razors.

Her heart beat faster.

Inches from the ground the hawk broke its dive and soared upward. A rattlesnake twisted in its claws. Higher and higher it circled. Its claws opened. The rattlesnake fell. The body smashed on a boulder.

She looked at the ground, where claw and wing-marks left a pattern in the dust.

Inches from her leg. She hadn't seen the snake. It would have killed her.

Now she knew what she had to do.

Attack, as the hawk had attacked. She closed her eyes and thought herself back to the cavern room.

A jolt of electricity shot through her as she slammed back into her body.

Begay laughed and tightened his grip on her throat.

Attack.

She focused her energy on his brain. Thought fire into it. Thought burrowing worms into it. Sent thought-explosions and knives and razors and hands that gripped his mind and squeezed, and squeezed, and squeezed...

He let her go and stood back, a look of bewilderment crossing his face.

She fell to the ground. Her breath came in gasps, her lungs and throat on fire, her chest aching. She rested on her hands and knees and panted, head hanging, like a dog.

She looked up. He was coming for her again.

And something was coming for him.

It stood behind him, a giant, covered with the skins of animals, its head black and bloody. One hand carried a burning torch. The other reached out to touch Begay.

"Behind you," Stoner warned.

Larch Begay opened his mouth to laugh.

The creature touched him. His shirt and hair burst into flames.

He screamed and tried to run from the room.

240

The *Kachina* blocked his way.

Begay's eyes bulged with terror.

From high above the medicine bundle, the masks drifted toward him.

The flashlight fell from his hand. She crawled forward and snatched it up.

He pressed against the wall, beating at the flames with his bare hands.

The masks silently drew nearer.

He fell to his knees and began to crawl toward the entrance.

The masks encircled him.

His whole body seemed to be burning. She could smell the charred clothing, the searing flesh.

He looked at her. "Make them stop!" he pleaded. "For God's sake..."

His words were cut off as a trickle of blood bubbled from his mouth. He wiped it away with the back of his hand. His eyes began to turn milky.

The masks closed in tighter.

A stream of dark liquid oozed from his ear.

He screamed again.

She knew something had burst inside his brain.

"He's dying," she said softly. "Please let him go."

The masks drew back.

Begay flung himself to his feet and plunged into the tunnel. She ran after him. He was a silhouette in flames, stumbling, crashing from wall to wall, faltering then going on, propelled by fear and pain.

His speed and endurance were amazing.

Stoner raced after him. Idiot. You let him go. He has a gun, and you let him go!

He burst out of the tunnel and into the firelight at the cave entrance. Jimmy Goodnight stood there, holding the gun.

"Shoot!" Begay ordered, his words spattered with blood.

The boy hesitated. His hand trembled.

"Fucker!" Begay screeched. "Kill her!"

Jimmy's hand came up. Firelight flickered on the gun barrel.

She looked around for somewhere to hide. There was only the tunnel, and she'd never make it...

Jimmy Goodnight took a deep breath and aimed.

Stoner froze.

"Hey!" Gwen barked beside her.

The boy looked at her, bewildered. "How'd you...?"

"Get back!" Stoner whispered frantically

"Come on," Gwen challenged the boy. "Take your best shot, you little creep."

"Shoot, Goddamn it!" Begay shouted. He started toward him.

Jimmy Goodnight fired. Flame spurted from the gun's muzzle. She heard a high-pitched whine as the bullet shot past her ear and ricocheted from the cave wall.

"GWEN!" She looked around. Gwen was gone.

She saw the look of horror on Jimmy's face. His eyes were riveted to a point above Stoner's head. The color drained from his face. He dropped the gun.

Stoner dove for it.

The boy turned and ran, down the path and into the night.

She aimed the gun at Begay.

He stood paralyzed, his clothes still burning, his eyes bulging with terror, staring at something beyond her shoulder.

She felt movement behind her.

Begay stumbled backward.

The campfire roared in a fountain of sparks.

Begay whirled and hurled himself off the edge of the mesa.

Something followed him. Something large and black and human-shaped. Something covered with raw skin and a blood-drenched mask. It hovered for a moment over the fire.

The fire rose and fell.

Rose and fell

Rose and fell.

The thing from the cave was gone.

She heard a soft thud as Begay's body hit the ground far below.

Clutching a burning stick for light, she went back into the room where she had left Gwen.

Jimmy Goodnight had tied her again.

"I'd always heard astral projection was fun," Gwen said as Stoner undid her ropes. "They never told me it was practical."

They held each other for a long time.

FOURTEEN

The rising dawn chased night over the western horizon.

Stoner kissed the top of Gwen's head and got up. There were still things to do.

"Did you see it?" Gwen asked.

"See what?"

"That...thing, whatever it was."

Stoner nodded. "I don't think we should talk about it with anyone. Maybe not even ourselves."

"But what *was* it?"

"Only Masau," Stoner said. "It won't come back."

She went to the cave entrance and whistled. The burro brayed an answer.

She turned back to Gwen. "How do you feel?"

"I've been better. Stoner, I don't think I can walk."

She knelt and felt Gwen's legs and ankles. "Nothing's broken. It's probably lack of circulation. It's going to hurt like anything when you get it back."

"Thank you very much," Gwen said with a grimace.

Stoner could hear the burro grunting—hunh, hunh, hunh—as it trudged up the path to the cave. "Here's your transportation." She pulled Gwen's arm across her shoulders and lifted her to her feet.

Gwen gasped. Tears sprang to her eyes.

"See?" Stoner said. "You're recovering already. The human body is a marvelous thing."

"I can't stand it. Let me die."

"Never." She kissed Gwen again.

The Little Horse of the Canyons waited patiently. She helped Gwen climb aboard, then reached up and took Gwen's necklace from around her own neck. "Here," she said as she fastened it on Gwen. "Next time I give you something, try not to lose it."

Gwen managed a pained smile. "Can we go now? I'm not real crazy about this spot."

"In a minute." She turned the donkey toward the path and gave him a push. "Wait for me down below, and don't worry when you hear me shoot. I have to seal off that chamber."

"What chamber?"

"I'll explain later." She laughed. "I have a lot to explain later. You probably won't believe most of it."

Finding the bundle was easier this time. She let the room pull her forward, through the tunnels, deep into the earth. She was surprised at how far she'd come before, how far Begay had run with his clothes on fire and his life bleeding away. She felt now as if she were walking forever between walls of rock.

At last she was there.

The Ya Ya medicine bundle lay bathed in gray light. Around the chamber's walls, the masks kept watch. The circle of corn meal was undisturbed.

She stood in front of it for a while and felt its energy.

"Well," she said at last, "I don't know exactly what went on here but I guess it turned out okay."

The energy knot in her stomach glowed briefly and went out. She took the medicine bag from around her neck and placed it on the ground. "Just to be on the safe side," she said with a smile, "a little *Pahana* magic." She looked around at the Kachinas. "Thanks for your help. Too bad you weren't around for the '84 elections."

Begay's flashlight still lay on the ground. She picked it up and shook it. The beam sprang to life. She left the room without looking back.

Outside in the tunnel, she searched the ceiling until she found what she was looking for, a vulnerable point, the rocks tumbled together, already leaking sand. She backed away as far as she could, and still hit her mark.

Very carefully, she took aim and fired.

The explosion deafened her for a second. Then she heard it, the hissing whisper of falling sand, the low rumble of rock beginning to move.

She tossed the gun into the path of the rock slide, and ran.

Through the tunnels and passages for the last time, pursued by a cloud of dust and falling rock. It felt as if the whole mesa were caving in behind her.

She ran, and ran, and ran.

Daylight at last.

She hit the outside path and slid, barely standing, down the side of the mesa to where Gwen and the burro waited.

*　　*　　*

244

They watched from the desert floor as billows of sand poured out the cave entrance. The crash and thunder of collapsing tunnels echoed up and down Hisatsinom Canyon, bouncing from wall to wall, rolling off at last into the sky and desert.

As the sounds died, the first rays of the sun appeared in the eastern sky. The shapes of mountains revealed themselves, then buttes and mesas, sage and mesquite. And, finally, the shape of Larch Begay, lifeless and twisted as a cotton doll lying among the rocks.

Curious, Stoner went to look at him.

He had died open-eyed, his lips stretched in a scream. Already the insects were at work on him. But it was his skin...his skin was papery and wrinkled and brown, like leather, like the skin on a mummy.

Larch Begay had died very, very old.

As old as Siyamtiwa.

In that moment she knew that Larch Begay had been a pawn, as she herself had been a pawn, and Siyamtiwa, and everyone whose lives this thing had touched. They had all acted out their roles in a mystery play that had been written a long, long time ago. Before anybody's memory.

It had been Begay's part to tip the balance, and now the balance was restored.

White and Navajo and Hopi, the cultures intersected.

Male and female.

Black magic and white magic.

She knew all this, then, and one more thing...

...That she would never see Siyamtiwa again.

She looked up to where Gwen waited, and the Little Horse of the Canyons. Ready to take them home.

*   *   *

Kwahu the Eagle sat beside the old woman and looked down at her sleeping face. She was smiling. In the faint dawn light, her burial shawl glowed white as a summer cloud. Her iron and silver hair was freshly washed and perfectly arranged. She was ready.

Her chest rose and fell, gently, softly, slowly. Then more slowly. Then not at all.

Masau, tall and proud and handsome, stood high on the rooftop and waved an arm in welcome.

Kwahu the Eagle waited for the Gold Dawn. Carefully, she removed four of her flight feathers and offered them to the four

Sacred Directions.

Kwahu the Eagle sang her song:

> *Old woman, my friend,*
> *In the days of fire, you were here.*
> *When the thunder of giants shook Mother Earth,*
> *You were here.*
> *Through the nights of water,*
> *Through the years of ice,*
> *When the People came from below to start their wanderings,*
> *You were here.*
> *When they came home to the mesas,*
> *You were here.*
> *Through the Spanish soldiers and the Missionaries,*
> *Through the wars and the Long Walk,*
> *When the giant mushrooms bloomed,*
> *You were here.*
> *Always you have been here.*
> *Always you will be here.*
> *With Beauty behind you,*
> *With Beauty before you,*
> *With Beauty above you,*
> *With Beauty beneath you,*
> *In Beauty you walk.*
> *In Beauty it is finished.*

She folded her wings, stepped into the crook of Siyamtiwa's arm, and closed her eyes.

*   *   *

The day was on the downhill side when they saw the smoke from the trading post chimney.

"Oh, Lord," Gwen said, "I hope that doesn't mean Ted's cooking rattlesnake for dinner."

"After three days of *piki* and tea," Stoner said, "even rattlesnake sounds good."

Gwen stopped the burro and slid to the ground. "After three days of Larch Begay's cooking, *I* want the best or nothing." She tested her knees and ankles. "I think I'll walk from here."

"Feeling better?"

"Not much, but we look too much like the Holy Family."

The donkey snorted loudly and wetly.

"Did I offend him?" Gwen asked.

"He's not into White theology." And he was leaving. She could feel it. She put her arm around his neck. Thanks, Friend. It

246

was...well, you know.

Burro nuzzled her shoulder.

"We could bring him with us," Gwen suggested. "I'm sure Stell's cousin would care for him." She gestured toward the desert. "It's a hard life out there."

Stoner shook her head. "He wouldn't be happy. He's chosen the Short Blue Corn Way."

Gwen rubbed the animal's nose. "Well, if you change your mind..."

The burro turned and trotted back to his canyons.

The Chevy Luv was parked by the back door. And the Jeep and Laura Yazzie's beat up Toyota. "Looks as if we're expected," Stoner said. "I wonder if Stell's home from the hospital?"

"Wouldn't surprise me," Gwen said as she tested her ankles. "She has a stubborn streak, not unlike other people I know."

Stoner grinned. "How are you doing?"

Gwen walked around a little. "I'll live. If this is what it feels like to return from the dead, I surely do hope there's no Resurrection."

Now that the terror was over, now that Gwen was here, and safe, she found herself reluctant to go back to everyday life with its stresses and strains and Grandmother problems. She wished now she had told Mrs. Burton that Gwen was missing. *Then we'd see where she stood on the subject of love.*

Gwen put a hand on Stoner's shoulder. "I'm not going to worry about her. I'm going to get an apartment, and get on with my life, and find out what it's like to think for myself. If she wants to reconcile, I'll think it over. But I'm not going to cry for the past any more."

Stoner looked at her. "Did you read my mind?"

"It wasn't hard," Gwen said. "When you grind your teeth, it can only mean one thing."

The back door of the trading post opened. Someone came out and stood looking down the road.

Stell. She shielded her eyes from the sun and looked their way.

"Stell!" Stoner called.

Gwen gave her a little push. "Go on."

She hesitated. "You need help..."

"I'll be all right, Stoner. Go."

She stumbled down the hill, sliding, setting off tiny avalanches as her feet dug into the ground. She reached the hard packed road surface and broke into a run.

Stell caught her in her arms. "You damn fool," she said in a choked voice. "You'll make me old before my time."

"Deal with it," Stoner said with a laugh, and hugged her tight.

Stell wouldn't let her go. Her grip was like iron. Her body was steamy, and she breathed in hiccuppy gasps.

Stoner realized Stell was crying. "It's all right, Stell. Everything's okay."

"I love you, Little Bear," Stell mumbled, trying to get control. "We've got to stop doing things like this to each other." She laughed and dug in her pocket for a tissue, holding Stoner around the shoulders with her other arm.

"I know I gave you a hard time," Stoner said, "but is that any reason to try and choke me?"

Stell loosened her grip a little. "Listen kid, I've got some bad news. Siyamtiwa's dead."

She pressed her head against Stell's shoulder. "I thought so."

Somewhere inside she had known, the moment she had sealed the cave, the moment it was over, it was over for Siyamtiwa, too.

"I'm real sorry," Stell said.

Stoner shook her head, not knowing how to explain. "She was tired. She says she'll be back, one way or another."

Stell rested her hand along Stoner's face. "Then I suspect she will." She brushed Stoner's hair to one side. "Rose Lomahongva went to do whatever needs to be done. We're keeping the Anglos out of this, but you'd probably be welcome."

"No." Whatever was going on there in the Village-That-Has-Forgotten-Its-Name, it had to do with duty, and the passing on of secrets. Her own part was over.

She looked over at Stell, at her firm-muscled body and earnest blue eyes, the streaks of gray in her hair and eyebrows, the smile lines around her mouth and eyes...and felt such a ballooning of love for her, for real, down-to-earth, big-as-life, ordinary, everyday Stell she thought she'd explode.

She embraced Stell again. "I hope you live forever."

"Long enough to be a burden on you, kiddo," Stell said, patting her back.

Gwen finally hobbled up. "Is this something I should worry about?"

"Hell no," Stell said and held out an arm to her. "Plenty to go around. You sure had us frantic, pal."

"I'd have called, but I was tied up."

Stoner groaned.

"By the way," Gwen went on, "Larch Begay's dead."

"Jesus, you didn't kill *another* one, did you?"

Gwen laughed. "Not this time. It was...I'm not sure what it was."

"Well," said Stell. "There's gonna be a lot of dumb tourists running out of gas around here, and that's as far as *my* grieving goes." She pulled Gwen's arm across her shoulder and began walking back toward the trading post.

Stoner took her other side. "Looks like you have a full house."

"Just Ted, and Laura Yazzie. Jimmy Goodnight was here, but he left. Brought back that doll the old woman gave you. Told me some cock-and-bull story about Begay wanting it for voodoo." She shrugged. "Way over my head. Anyway, he got to feeling guilty about taking it, and didn't give it to him."

Stoner fell silent. If Begay had had the doll, she wondered, would it have all come out differently? Would that have shifted the power in his direction? Would she be trapped, deep within the midnight tunnels of Pikyachvi Mesa, waiting to die? Or had Jimmy Goodnight, taking the doll but changing his mind, been playing his part, too?

"What's for dinner?" Gwen was asking.

"Turkey."

Gwen sighed ecstatically.

"Turkey?" Stoner asked. "In August?"

"Yes, turkey in August, you old stick-in-the-mud."

"But how did you know we'd be here today?"

"Didn't," Stell said. "Turkey keeps. "

Stoner grinned, and realized how glad she was to be back in the world of mundane things and practical solutions, where people only know what comes in through their senses, and cook turkey because it keeps.

*　　*　　*

She woke in the night, and for a moment thought she was back in her room at Siyamtiwa's village. Could have sworn, in fact, that it was the sound of drums and rattles that had awakened her. But the night was quiet.

And cold. She fumbled for a flannel shirt, slipped her boots on, and eased out the bunkhouse door.

The desert lay still and empty. No eagle soared overhead, or stirred restlessly on Big Tewa Peak. No coyote prowled the shadows of Long Mesa. The Sacred Mountains slept. Only the stars kept guard.

She sat down on the steps. It's really over, she thought. There was a deep sadness in her, a longing for that stubborn, difficult old woman she had barely known. We didn't even get along, she thought, and smiled, sensing that, for Siyamtiwa, getting along was the last thing that mattered.

Well, Grandmother, you've left me with a nice mess here. Everything I thought was true is upside down.

Magic, *Pahana.* Only magic.

She looked up sharply, then realized she hadn't heard the words at all, but felt them. Felt them deep inside in some soft, uncharted place, a place without boundaries or rules, a place where clocks never ticked and there was no New Year's Eve, a place where she could soar with the eagle and burrow with the mole, a place where there was light and safety…

…and Magic.

Sensing movement, she looked down at the ground. A small gray spider, so pale it seemed to glow, crept toward her across the sand. It reached her boot and climbed it, swung out in space to catch the cuff of her pajamas. It scurried to her knee and sat looking up at her.

She held out her hand.

The spider crawled into her palm.

She lifted it level with her eyes.

We did all right, Grandmother.

Yes, Stoner, we did all right.

She lowered her hand to the ground. The spider disappeared down a tiny crack in the earth.

Magic.

Talavai, Dawn Spirit, spilled mercury across the desert.

THE END

In addition to writing the Stoner McTavish series of novels, Sarah Dreher is a clinical psychologist and prizewinning playwright. She lives in Amherst, Massachusetts, with her family of choice and assorted wild and domesticated beasts.

Other Titles Available

Order from New Victoria Publishers, P.O. Box 27, Norwich, Vt. 05055

Mysteries by Sarah Dreher

OtherWorld—Marylou is kidnapped and held hostage underground at Disney World. On the surface child's play. But underneath? All your favorite characters—eccentric Aunt Hermione, business partner Marylou, psychiatrist Edith Kesselbaum and, of course, devoted lover Gwen…in an adventure that crosses realities. $10.95

A Captive In Time—Stoner is inexplicably transported to a small town in Colorado, time 1871. There she encounters Dot, the saloon keeper, Blue Mary, a local witch/healer, and an enigmatic teenage runaway named Billy. Mysterious fires have the townspeople on edge, a group of suffragists campaigning for women's right to vote is being threatened, and Stoner can't find a phone to call home. $9.95

Something Shady—Travel Agent/Detective Stoner McTavish travels to the coast of Maine with her lover Gwen and risks becoming an inmate in a suspicious rest home to rescue a missing nurse. $8.95

Stoner McTavish—The original Stoner McTavish mystery introduces psychic Aunt Hermione, practical partner Marylou, and Stoner herself, off to the Grand Tetons to rescue dream lover Gwen. $7.95

More Mysteries

Death by the Riverside—J.M.Redmann—Micky Knight uncovers some very personal secrets. Detective Michele Knight (Micky to her friends), hired to take a few pictures, finds herself slugging through thugs and slogging through swamps in an attempt to expose a dangerous drug ring. The investigation turns personal when her own well-hidden past is exposed. $9.95

Deaths of Jocasta—Redmann—The specter of an ugly murder haunts New Orleans.What in hell was the body of a young woman doing in the basement of the Cort Clinic? Could Dr. Cordelia James really have performed the incompetent abortion that killed her? Micky Knight has to answer these questions before the police and the news media find their own convenient solution. $9.95

Hers Was The Sky—Béguin—Hazel and lover, Jo, are rivals in the first women's flying contest. While investigating possible sabotage Hazel falls for Vera, a charming ex-wingwalker and photographer who may be involved in a betting scheme that threatens the integrity of the race. $8.95

She Died Twice—Lauren—Emma looks for the murderer of her childhood sweetheart. Twenty years ago, Emma's friend and first lover, Natalie, mysteriously disappeared. Now the remains of a child are unearthed and Emma is forced to relive the weeks leading up to Natalie's death as she searches for the murderer. $8.95

Woman with Red Hair—Brunel—The mystery of her mother's disappearance brings Magalie to the swamps of the Camargue, the slums of Marseille, and to a shady gypsy woman. With the help of Danielle, her French lover, she learns of her mother's tortured life, and her mother's lover, Celine, the woman with red hair. $8.95